MIKHAIL BULGAKOV'S
THE MASTER AND MARGARITA
A GRAPHIC NOVEL
ANDRZEJ KLIMOWSKI DANUSIA SCHEJBAL

SELF MADE HERO

FIRST PUBLISHED
BY SELFMADEHERO
A DIVISION OF METRO MEDIA LTD
139-141 PANCRAS ROAD
LONDON NW1 1UN
WWW.SELFMADEHERO.COM

A CIP RECORD FOR THIS BOOK IS AVAILABLE FROM THE BRITISH LIBRARY.

ORIGINAL STORY BY MIKHAIL BULGAKOV
ADAPTATION AND ART BY ANDRZEJ KLIMOWSKI AND DANUSIA SCHEJBAL
COVER AND JACKET ILLUSTRATION BY ANDRZEJ KLIMOWSKI
COVER DESIGNER: JEFF WILLIS
DESIGNER AND SPEECH BUBBLES: DOMINIK KLIMOWSKI
FONT DESIGNER: ANDRZEJ KLIMOWSKI
LAYOUT DESIGN ASSISTANCE: KURT YOUNG, ANDY HUCKLE
MANAGING EDITOR AND PUBLISHER: EMMA HAYLEY
EDITOR: DAN LOCKWOOD
EDITORIAL ASSISTANCE: LIZZIE SPRATT
WITH THANKS TO RICHARD DOUST, JANE GOODSIR, NATALIA KLIMOWSKA,
JEREMY TANKARD AND DOUG WALLACE

ISBN: 978-0-9558169-2-5

10 9 8 7 6 5 4 3 2

PRINTED AND BOUND IN SLOVENIA

INTRODUCTION

'THE MASTER AND MARGARITA' IS OFTEN REGARDED AS MIKHAIL BULGAKOV'S MASTERPIECE. IT IS — AMONG OTHER THINGS — A SATIRICAL SWIPE AT THE LITERARY ESTABLISHMENT, A MEDITATION ON THE NATURE OF GOOD AND EVIL, AND A LOVE STORY. THE DEPICTION OF SATAN'S ACOLYTES RUNNING WILD IN MOSCOW IS SIMULTANEOUSLY GRUESOME AND SLAPSTICK, A CHALLENGE TO THE GOVERNING BUREAUCRACY AND A MIRROR HELD UP TO THE UNTHINKING GREED OF THE NOUVEAUX RICHES. THERE ARE CLEAR PARALLELS BETWEEN BULGAKOV'S AUTHORITARIAN TARGETS AND THE RUSSIA OF TODAY; STATE CONTROL, OLIGARCHS AND CORRUPTION REMAIN POTENT ISSUES. THE MESSAGE OF THE NOVEL IS AS TRUE NOW AS IT WAS WHEN IT WAS WRITTEN: THOSE IN AUTHORITY HAVE LESS CONTROL THAN THEY MIGHT REALISE — THERE IS NO BUREAUCRACY WHICH CAN TRULY CRUSH THE HUMAN SPIRIT, AND THEY HAVE NO POWER OVER DEATH.

RECOGNISED AS ONE OF THE ORIGINAL WORKS OF MAGIC REALISM, THE NOVEL'S CHARACTERS AND PLOT ARE FANTASTICAL, LENDING THEMSELVES PERFECTLY TO THE GRAPHIC NOVEL FORMAT. THIS ADAPTATION, PAINTED BY KLIMOWSKI AND SCHEJBAL (IN BLACK AND WHITE AND IN COLOUR RESPECTIVELY), BRINGS BULGAKOV'S DESCRIPTIONS OF MAYHEM IN MOSCOW TO VIVID, RIOTOUS LIFE, WHILE THE SEGMENTS ILLUSTRATING THE KEY MOMENTS OF PONTIUS PILATE'S LIFE UNDERPIN THE ETHICAL AND PHILOSOPHICAL STANCE OF THE NOVEL. IT IS A TESTAMENT TO THE FORM OF THE GRAPHIC NOVEL — AS WELL AS THE GENIUS OF BULGAKOV'S ORIGINAL WORK — THAT THE DIFFERENT LAYERS OF THE STORY CONTRAST WITH AND YET COMPLEMENT ONE ANOTHER, FORMING AN IRIDESCENT, SENSUAL, ANARCHIC WHOLE.

FOLLOW US, READER, ON A STORMY ADVENTURE. FLY ABOVE MOSCOW AND BEYOND. BUT BEFORE LANDING IN THE PARK OF PATRIARCH'S POND ON THAT FATEFUL SPRING DAY, LET US TURN BACK TO THE PREVIOUS SUMMER...

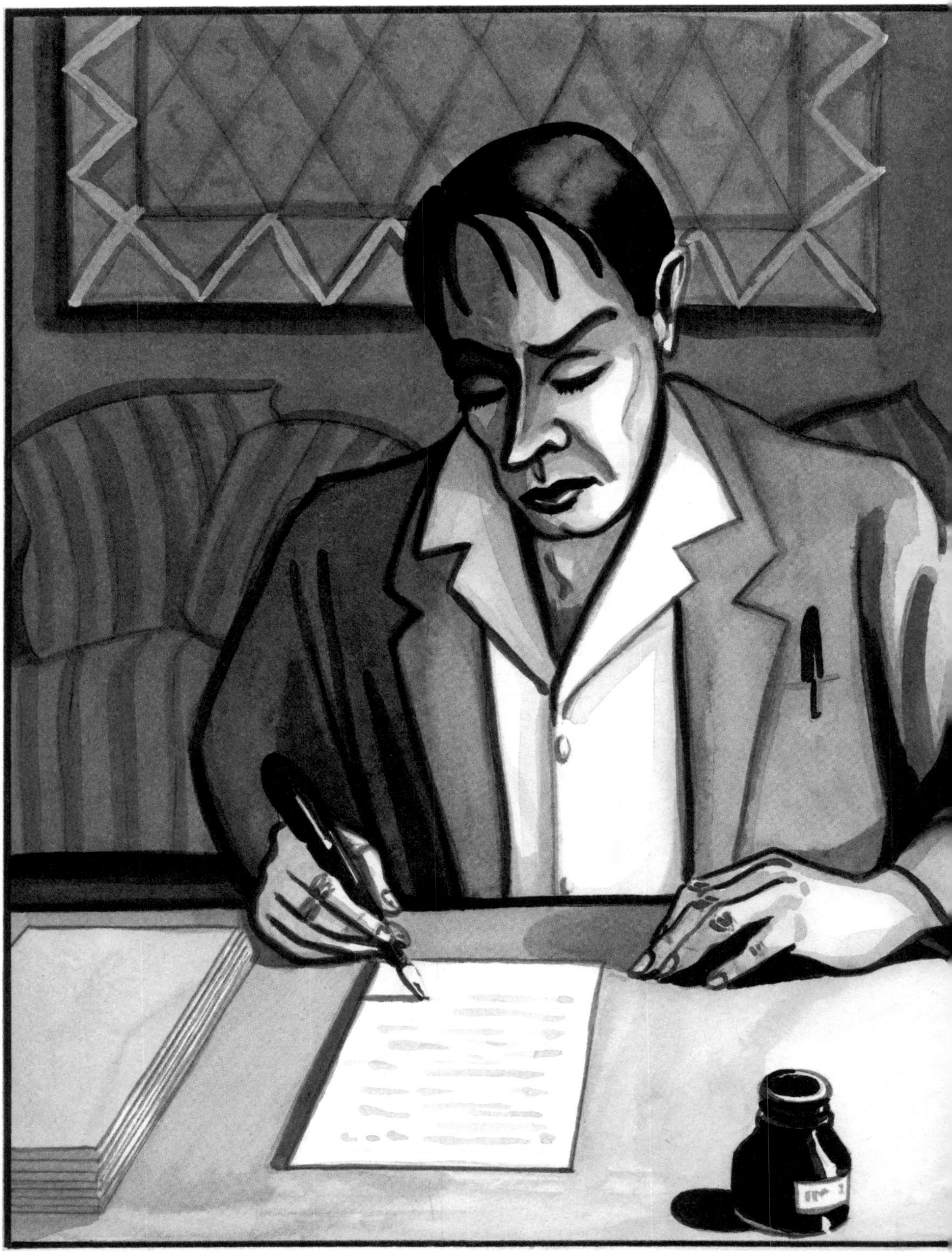

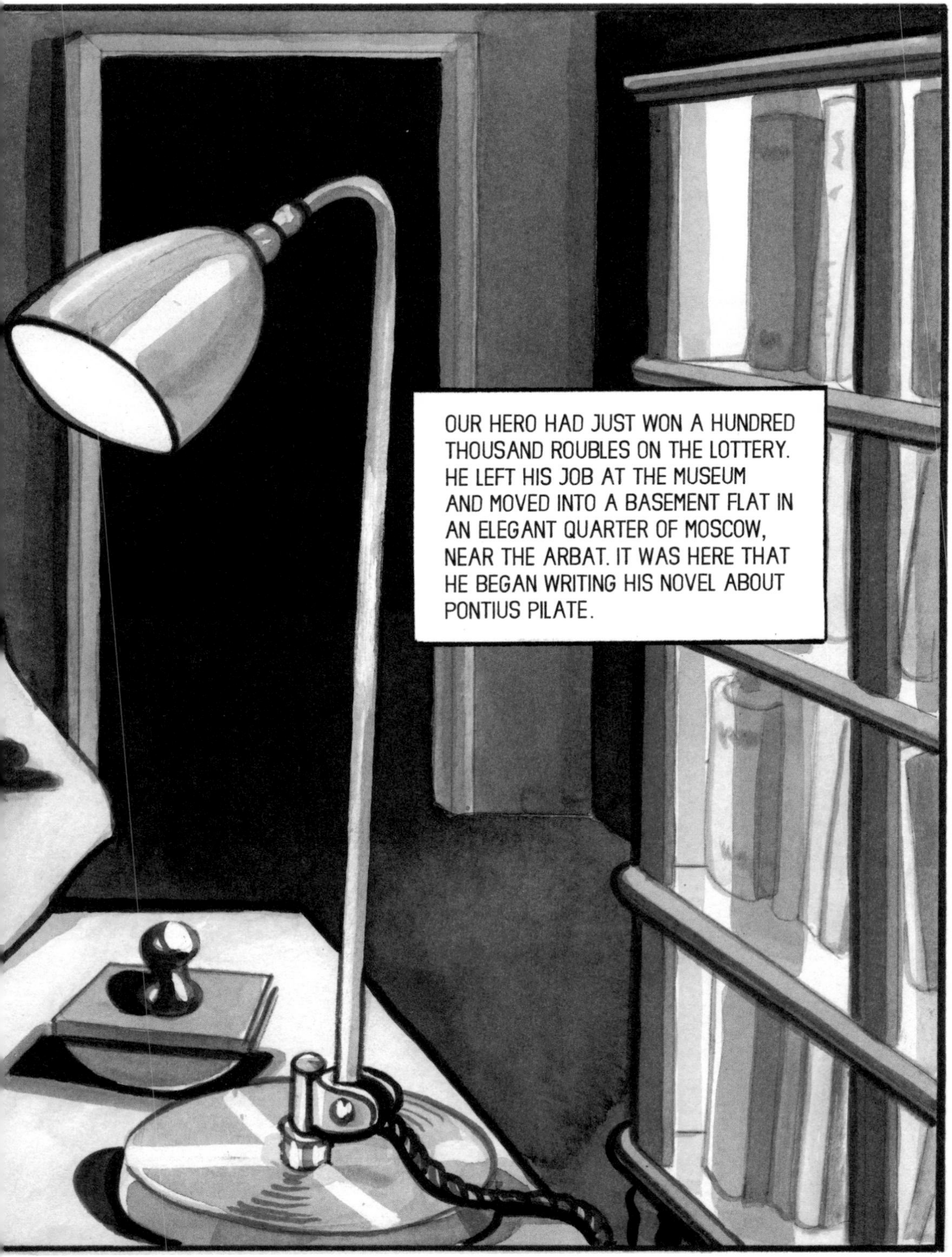
OUR HERO HAD JUST WON A HUNDRED THOUSAND ROUBLES ON THE LOTTERY. HE LEFT HIS JOB AT THE MUSEUM AND MOVED INTO A BASEMENT FLAT IN AN ELEGANT QUARTER OF MOSCOW, NEAR THE ARBAT. IT WAS HERE THAT HE BEGAN WRITING HIS NOVEL ABOUT PONTIUS PILATE.

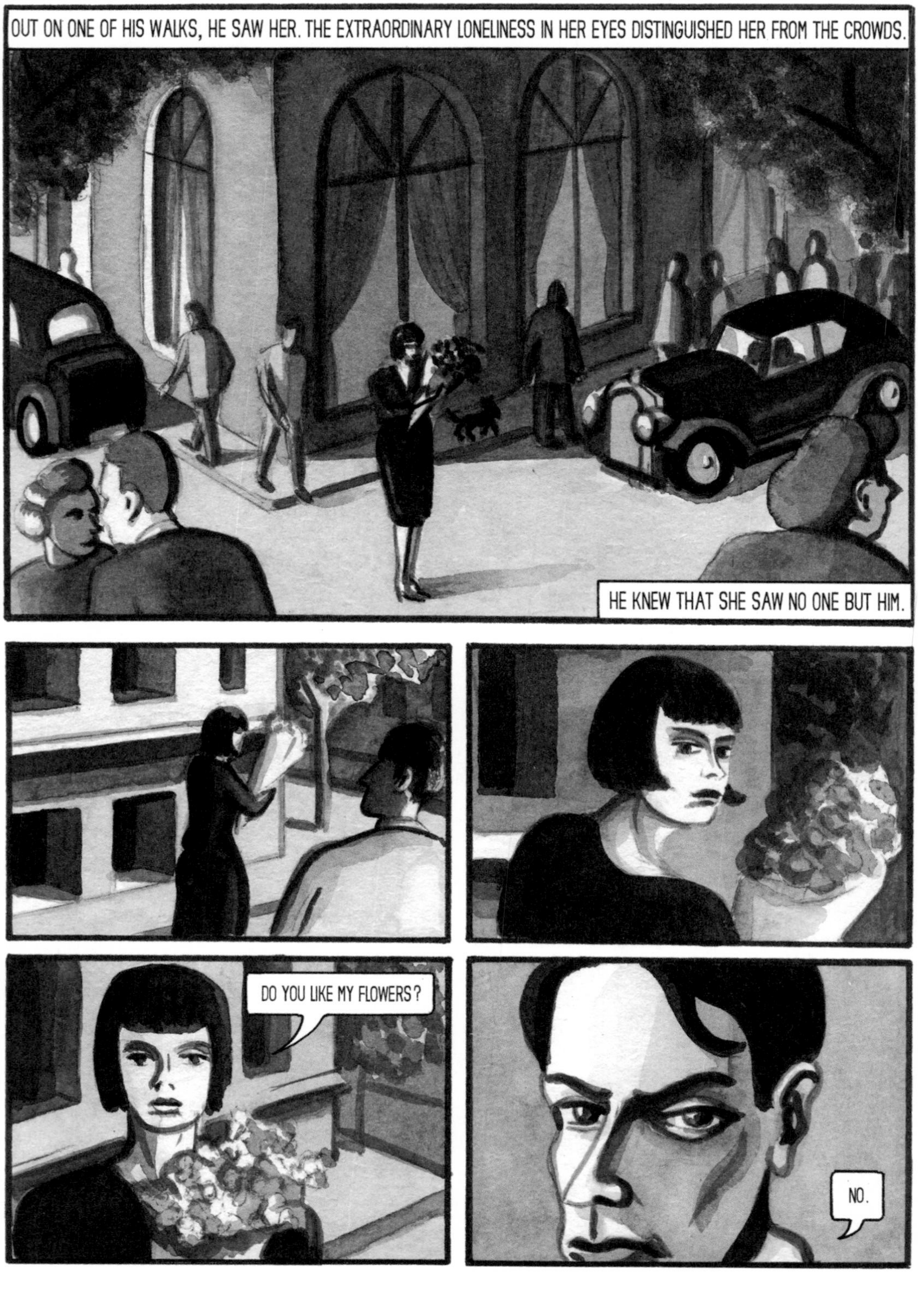
OUT ON ONE OF HIS WALKS, HE SAW HER. THE EXTRAORDINARY LONELINESS IN HER EYES DISTINGUISHED HER FROM THE CROWDS.
HE KNEW THAT SHE SAW NO ONE BUT HIM.
DO YOU LIKE MY FLOWERS?
NO.

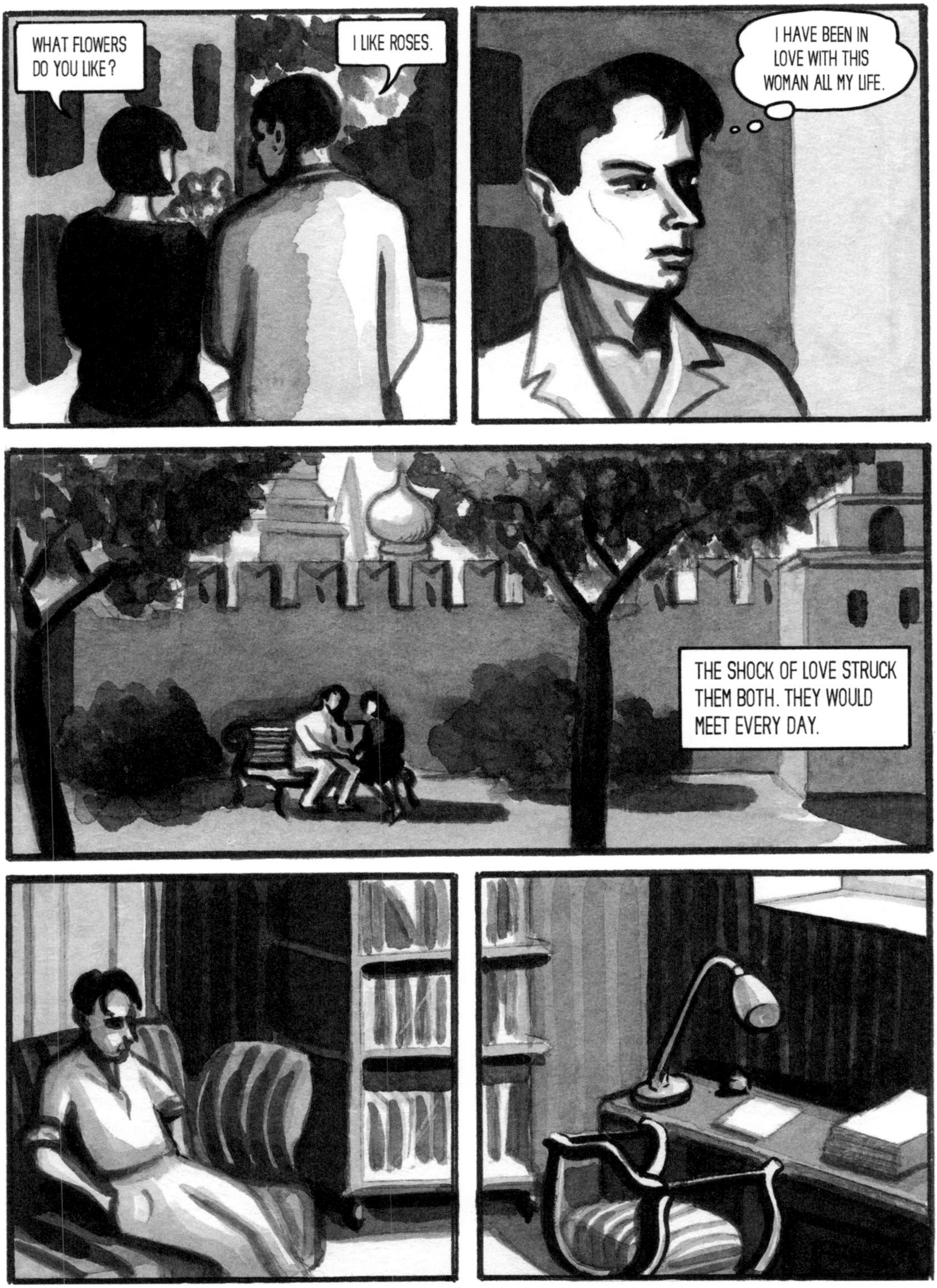
WHAT FLOWERS DO YOU LIKE?
I LIKE ROSES.
I HAVE BEEN IN LOVE WITH THIS WOMAN ALL MY LIFE.
THE SHOCK OF LOVE STRUCK THEM BOTH. THEY WOULD MEET EVERY DAY.

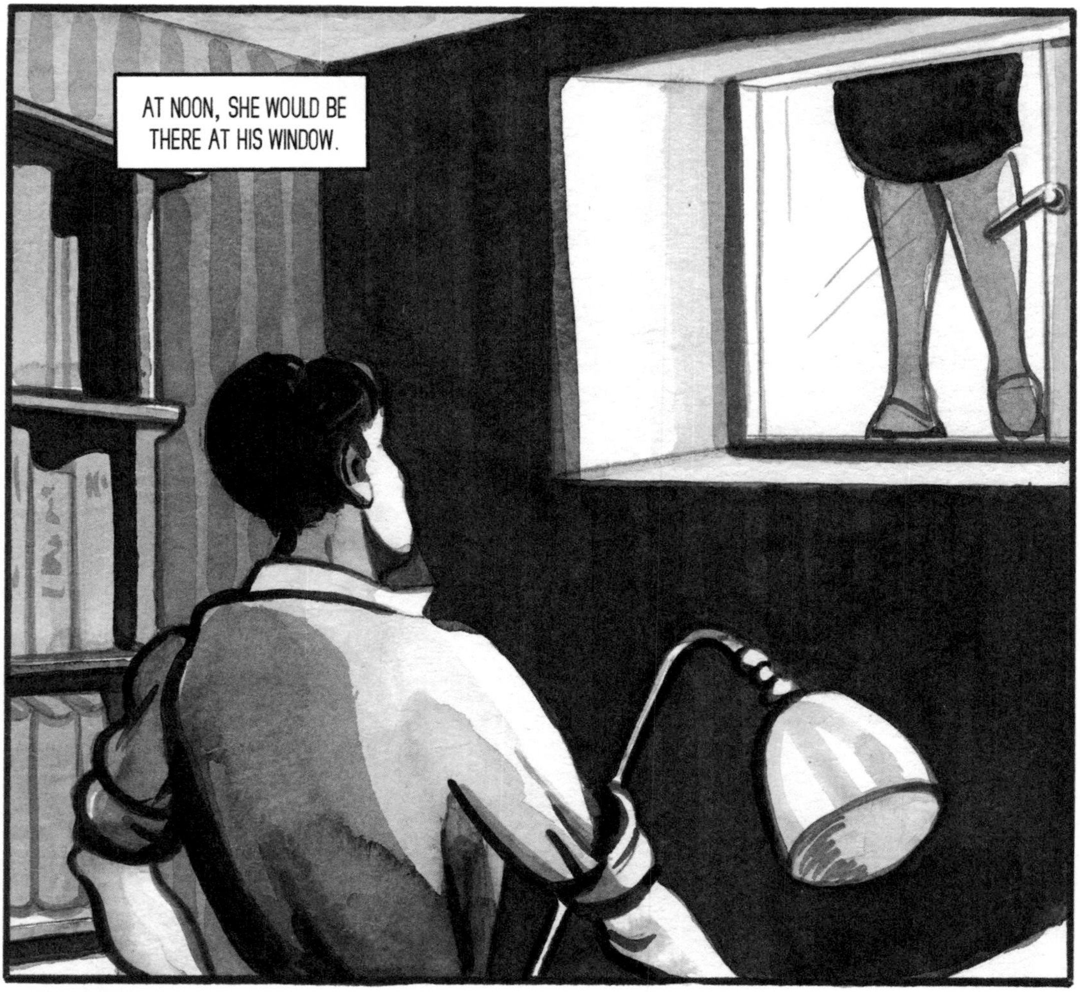
AT NOON, SHE WOULD BE THERE AT HIS WINDOW.

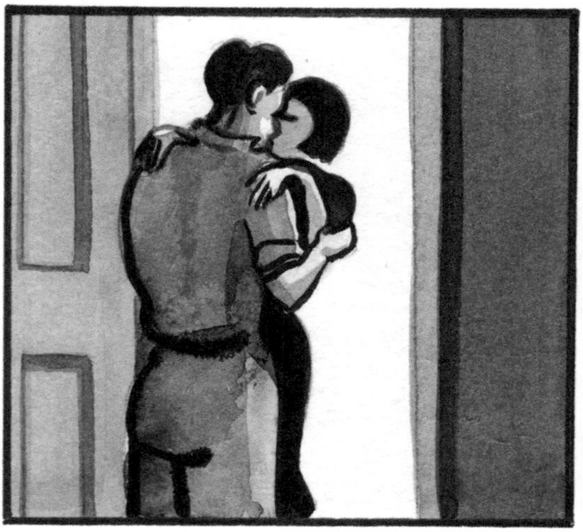

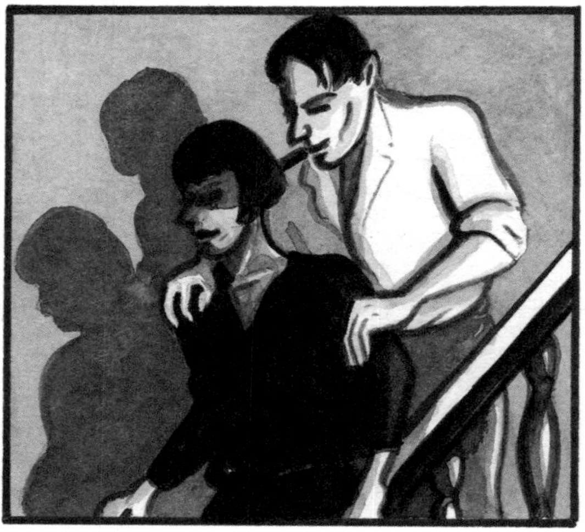

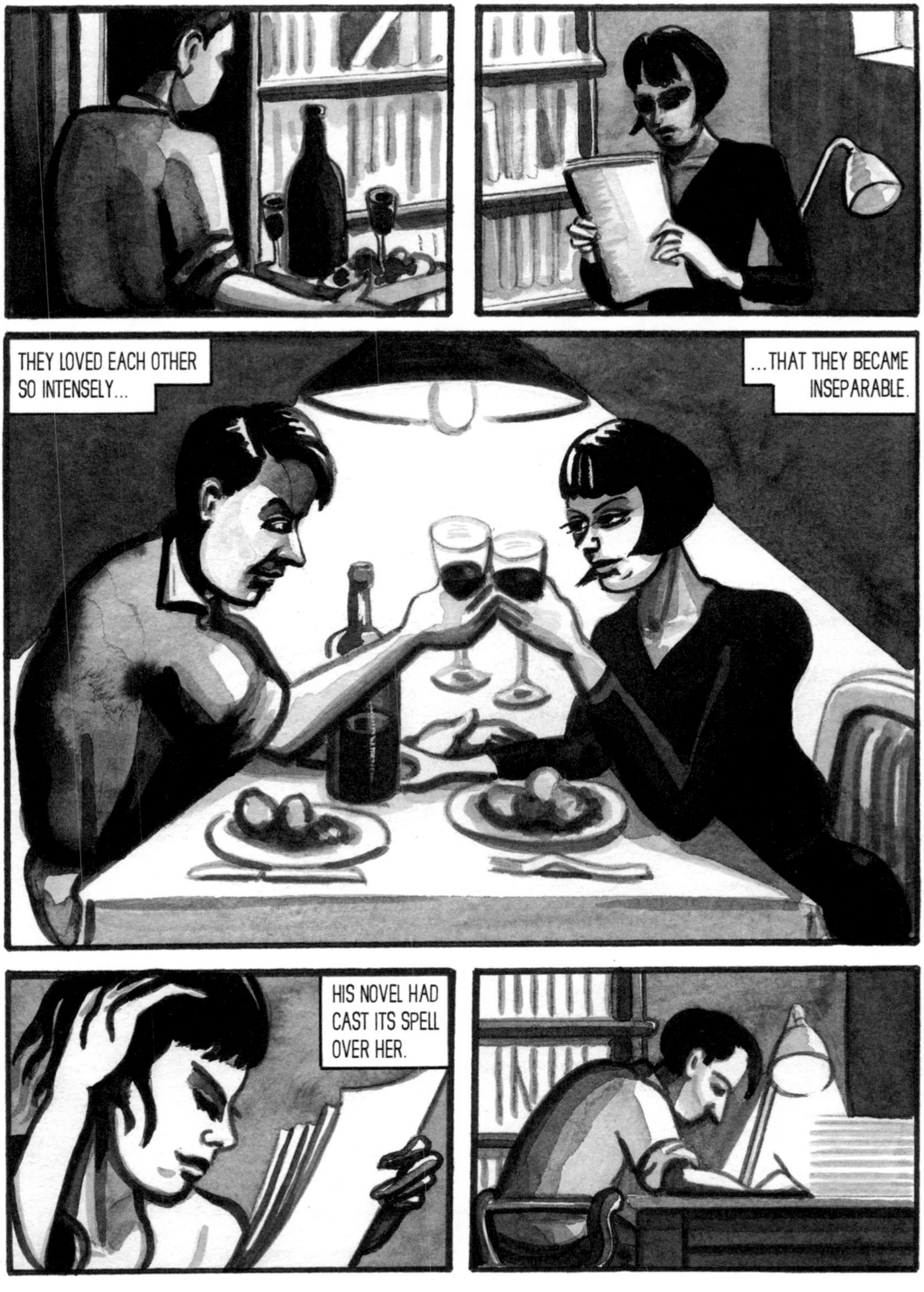
THEY LOVED EACH OTHER SO INTENSELY...
...THAT THEY BECAME INSEPARABLE.
HIS NOVEL HAD CAST ITS SPELL OVER HER.

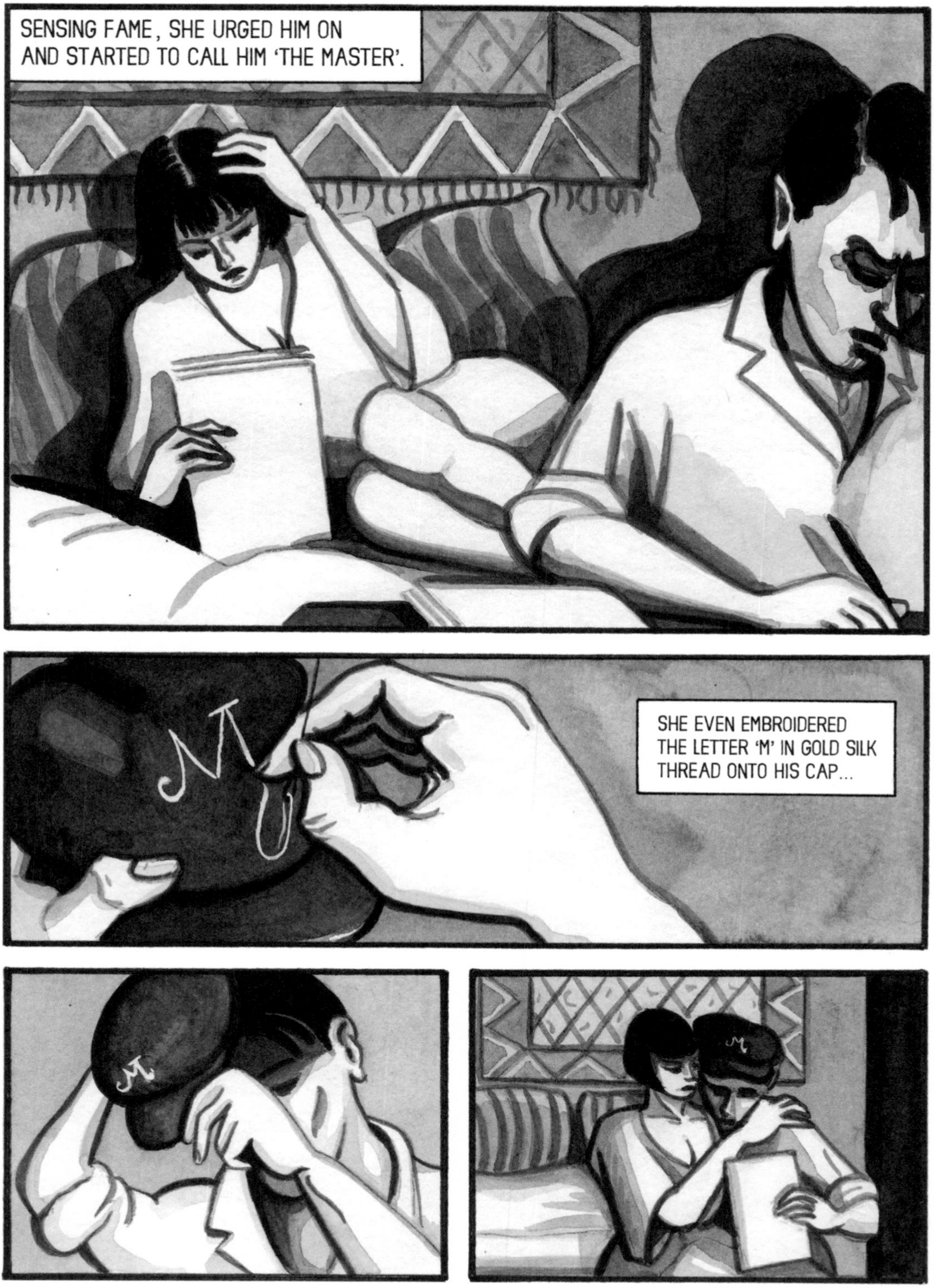
SENSING FAME, SHE URGED HIM ON
AND STARTED TO CALL HIM 'THE MASTER'.
SHE EVEN EMBROIDERED
THE LETTER 'M' IN GOLD SILK
THREAD ONTO HIS CAP...

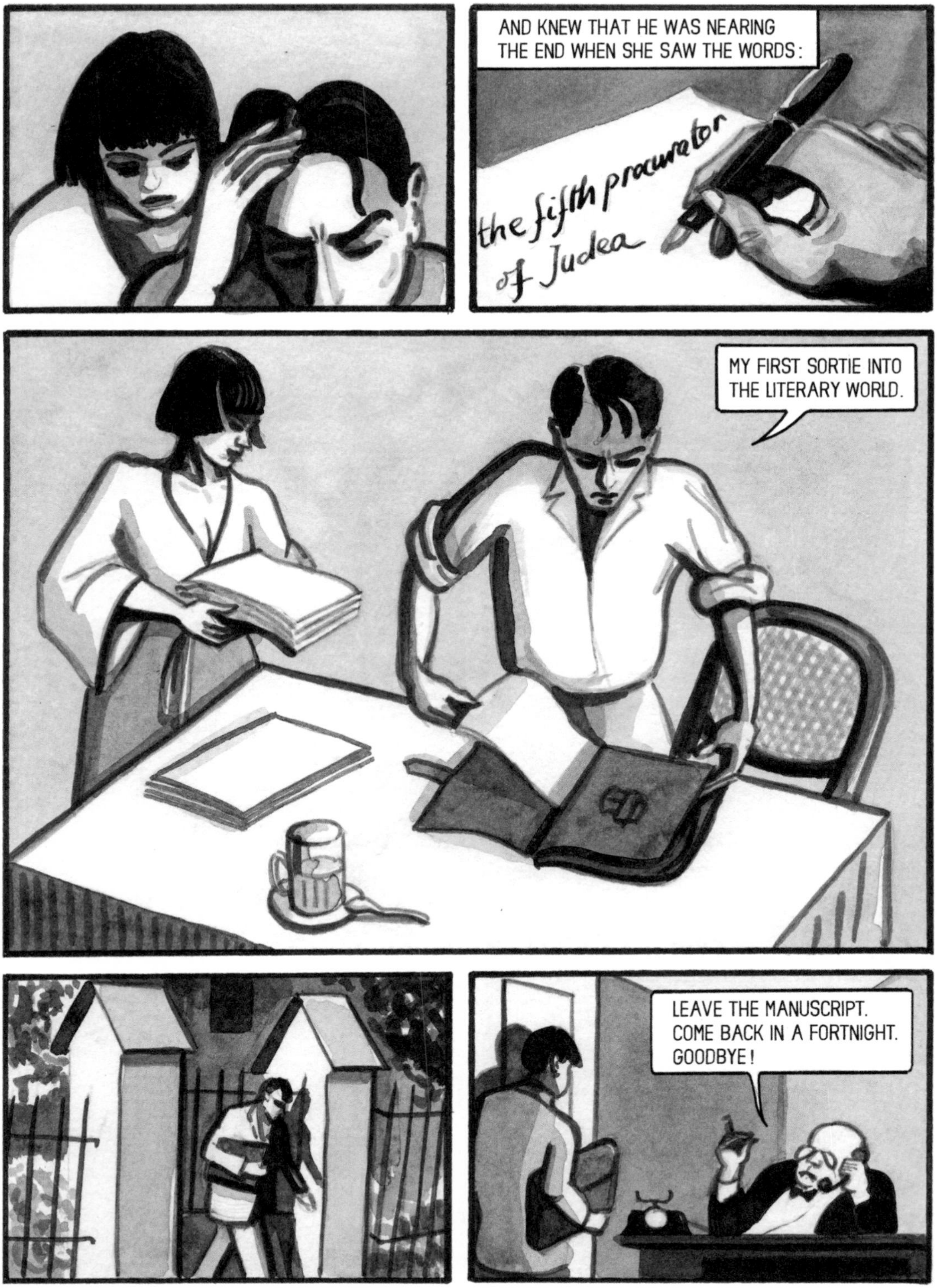
AND KNEW THAT HE WAS NEARING THE END WHEN SHE SAW THE WORDS:
the fifth procurator of Judea
MY FIRST SORTIE INTO THE LITERARY WORLD.
LEAVE THE MANUSCRIPT. COME BACK IN A FORTNIGHT. GOODBYE!

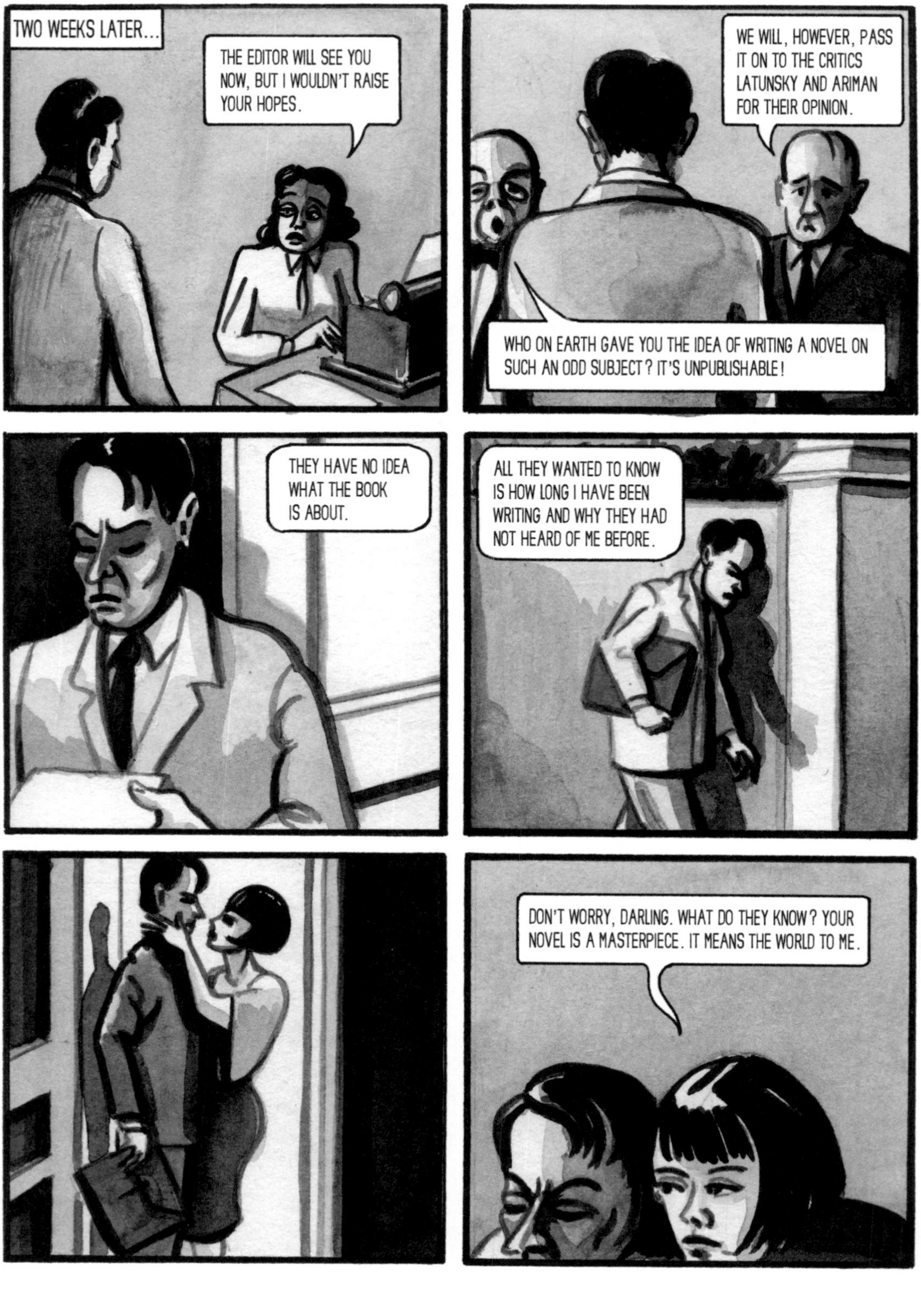
TWO WEEKS LATER...
THE EDITOR WILL SEE YOU NOW, BUT I WOULDN'T RAISE YOUR HOPES.
WE WILL, HOWEVER, PASS IT ON TO THE CRITICS LATUNSKY AND ARIMAN FOR THEIR OPINION.
WHO ON EARTH GAVE YOU THE IDEA OF WRITING A NOVEL ON SUCH AN ODD SUBJECT? IT'S UNPUBLISHABLE!
THEY HAVE NO IDEA WHAT THE BOOK IS ABOUT.
ALL THEY WANTED TO KNOW IS HOW LONG I HAVE BEEN WRITING AND WHY THEY HAD NOT HEARD OF ME BEFORE.
DON'T WORRY, DARLING. WHAT DO THEY KNOW? YOUR NOVEL IS A MASTERPIECE. IT MEANS THE WORLD TO ME.

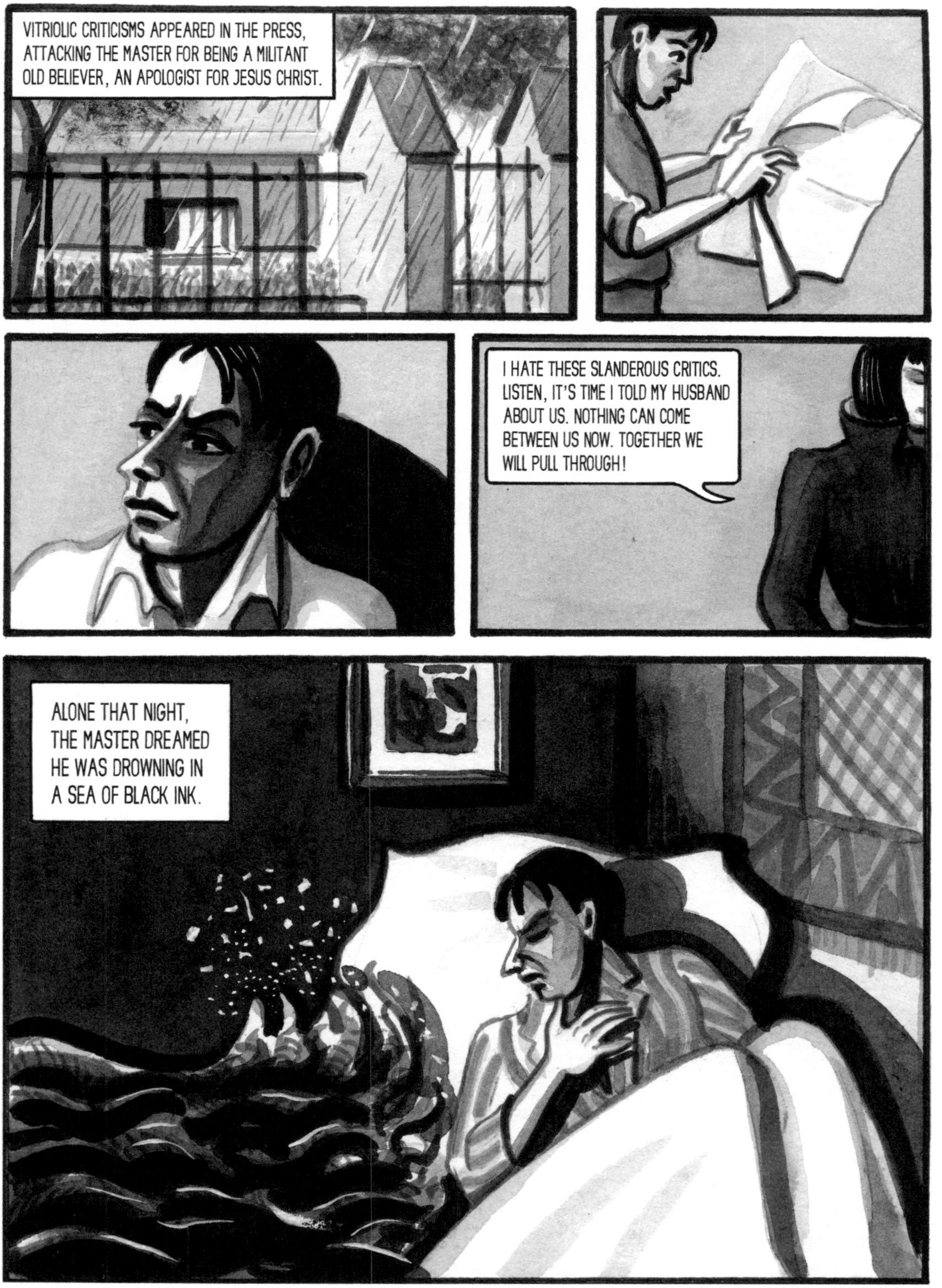
VITRIOLIC CRITICISMS APPEARED IN THE PRESS, ATTACKING THE MASTER FOR BEING A MILITANT OLD BELIEVER, AN APOLOGIST FOR JESUS CHRIST.
I HATE THESE SLANDEROUS CRITICS. LISTEN, IT'S TIME I TOLD MY HUSBAND ABOUT US. NOTHING CAN COME BETWEEN US NOW. TOGETHER WE WILL PULL THROUGH!
ALONE THAT NIGHT, THE MASTER DREAMED HE WAS DROWNING IN A SEA OF BLACK INK.

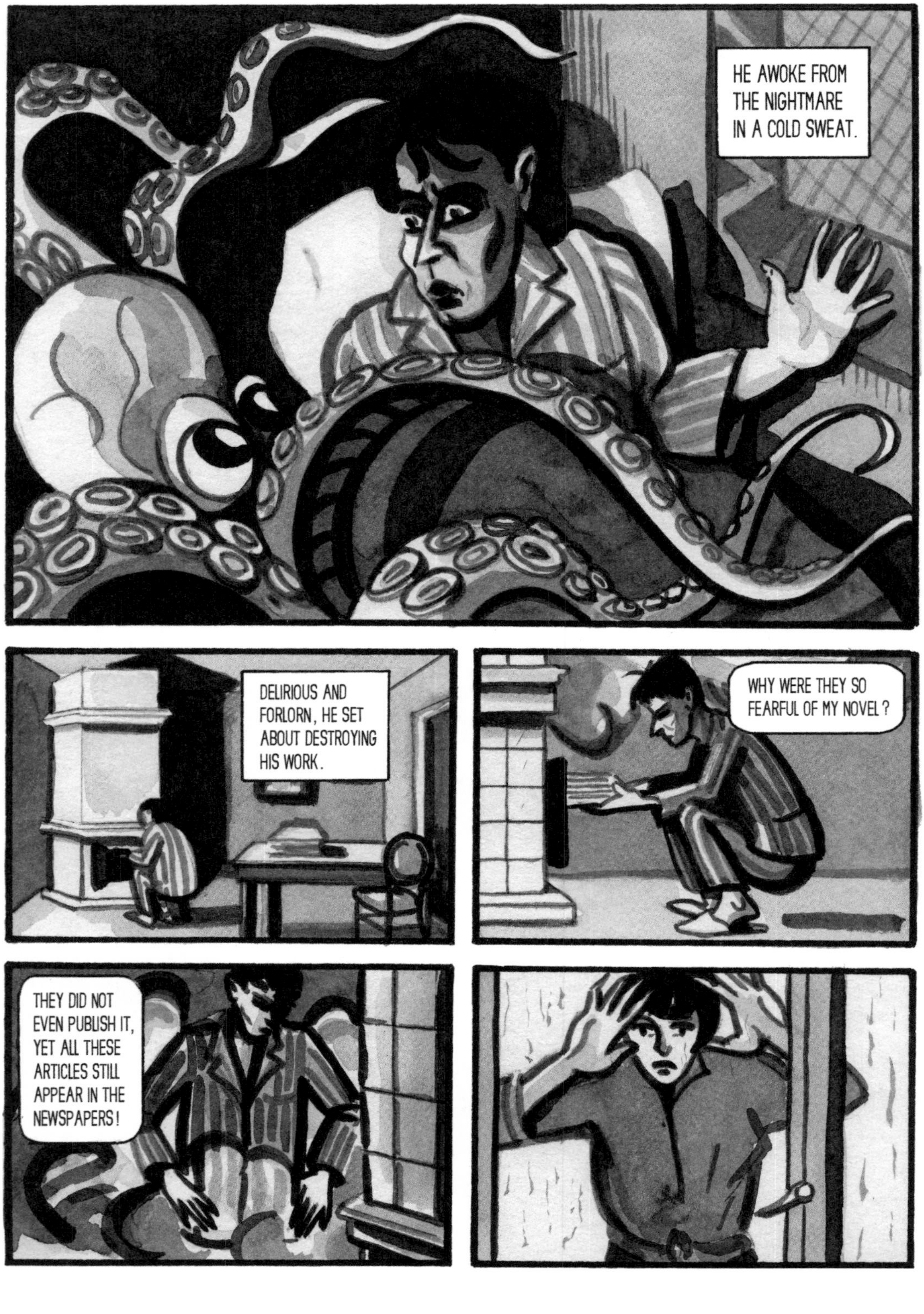
HE AWOKE FROM THE NIGHTMARE IN A COLD SWEAT.
DELIRIOUS AND FORLORN, HE SET ABOUT DESTROYING HIS WORK.
WHY WERE THEY SO FEARFUL OF MY NOVEL?
THEY DID NOT EVEN PUBLISH IT, YET ALL THESE ARTICLES STILL APPEAR IN THE NEWSPAPERS!

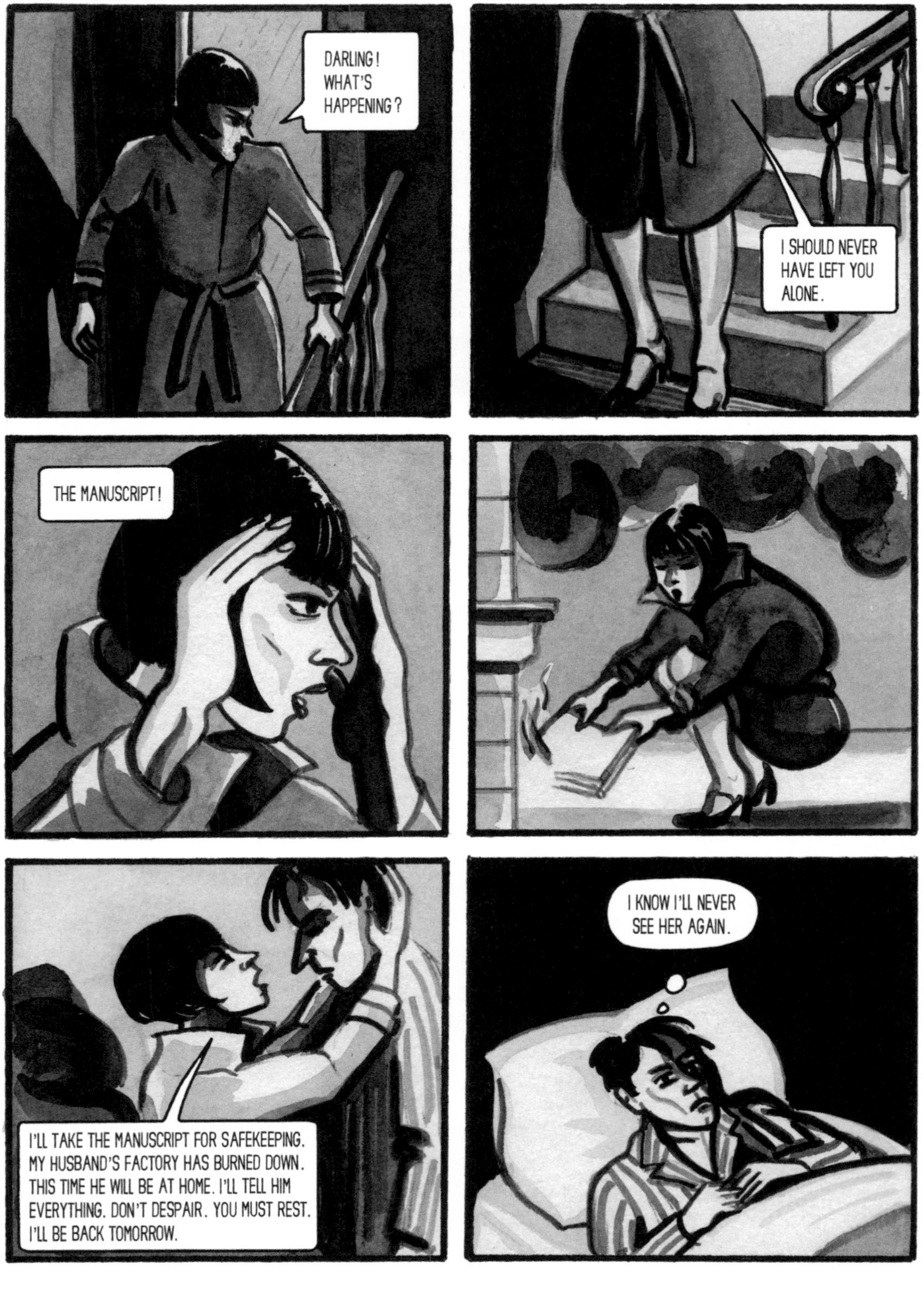
DARLING! WHAT'S HAPPENING?
I SHOULD NEVER HAVE LEFT YOU ALONE.
THE MANUSCRIPT!
I'LL TAKE THE MANUSCRIPT FOR SAFEKEEPING. MY HUSBAND'S FACTORY HAS BURNED DOWN. THIS TIME HE WILL BE AT HOME. I'LL TELL HIM EVERYTHING. DON'T DESPAIR. YOU MUST REST. I'LL BE BACK TOMORROW.
I KNOW I'LL NEVER SEE HER AGAIN.

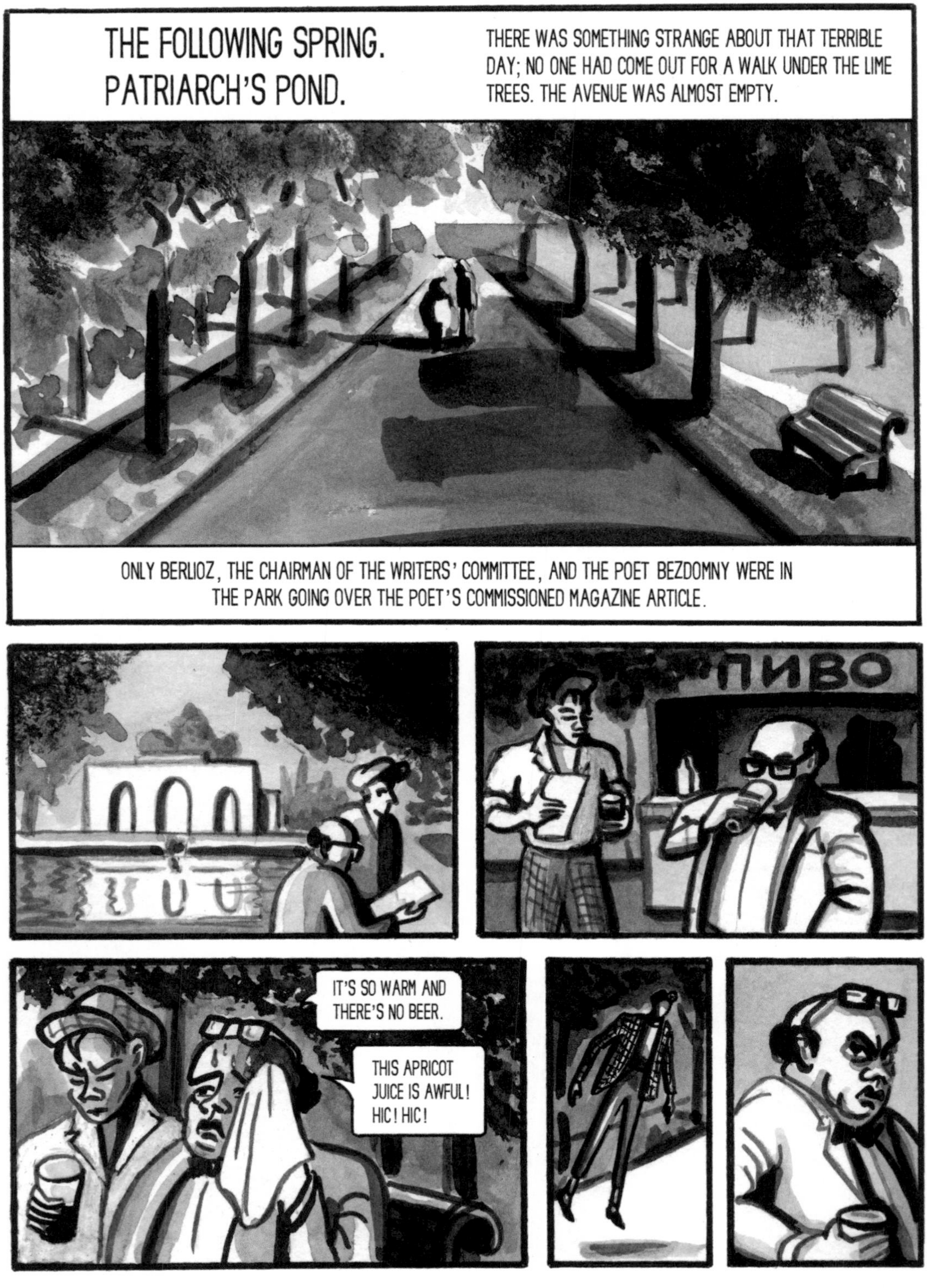
THE FOLLOWING SPRING.
PATRIARCH'S POND.
THERE WAS SOMETHING STRANGE ABOUT THAT TERRIBLE DAY; NO ONE HAD COME OUT FOR A WALK UNDER THE LIME TREES. THE AVENUE WAS ALMOST EMPTY.
ONLY BERLIOZ, THE CHAIRMAN OF THE WRITERS' COMMITTEE, AND THE POET BEZDOMNY WERE IN THE PARK GOING OVER THE POET'S COMMISSIONED MAGAZINE ARTICLE.
ПИВО
IT'S SO WARM AND THERE'S NO BEER.
THIS APRICOT JUICE IS AWFUL! HIC! HIC!

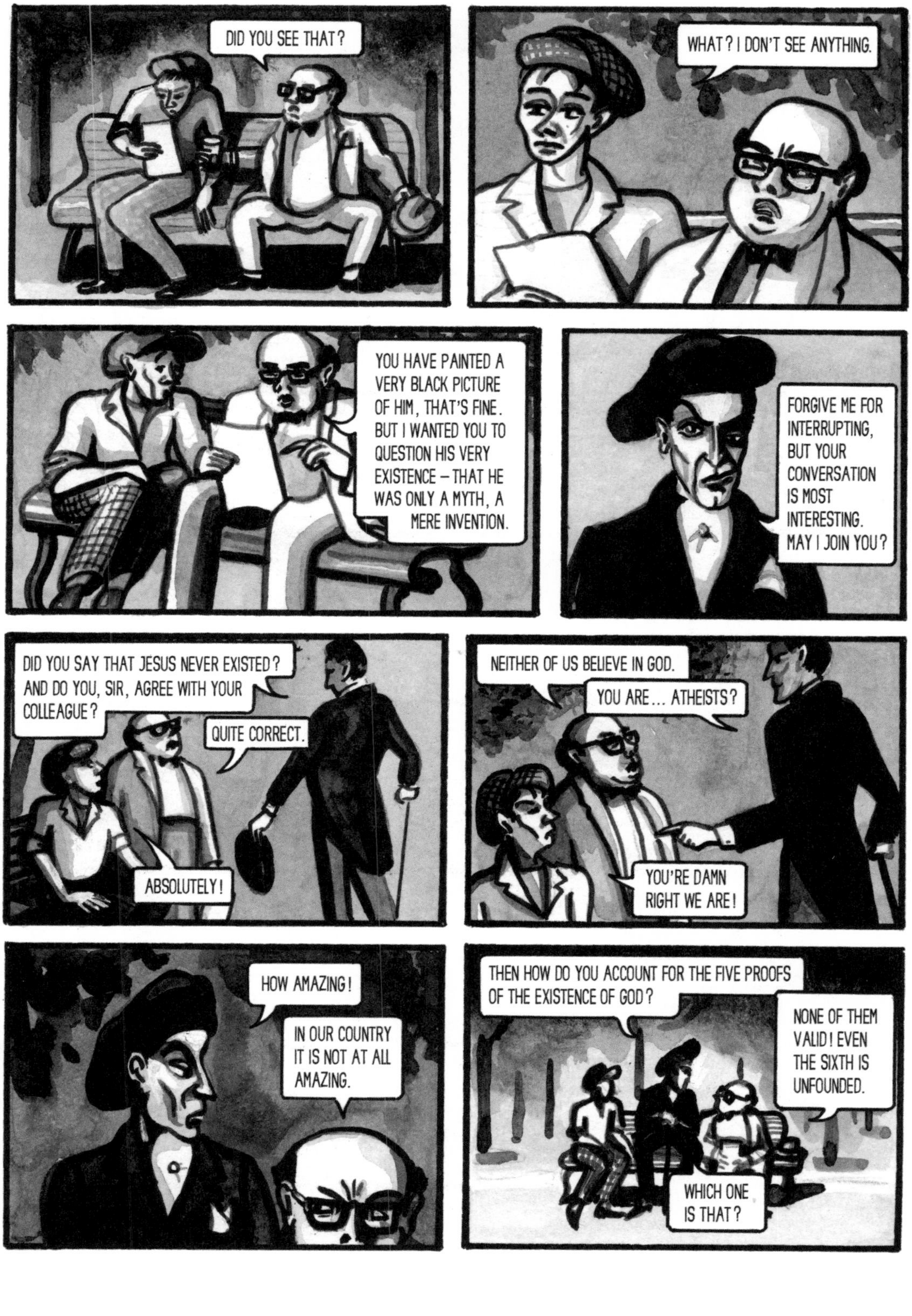
DID YOU SEE THAT?
WHAT? I DON'T SEE ANYTHING.
YOU HAVE PAINTED A VERY BLACK PICTURE OF HIM, THAT'S FINE. BUT I WANTED YOU TO QUESTION HIS VERY EXISTENCE – THAT HE WAS ONLY A MYTH, A MERE INVENTION.
FORGIVE ME FOR INTERRUPTING, BUT YOUR CONVERSATION IS MOST INTERESTING. MAY I JOIN YOU?
DID YOU SAY THAT JESUS NEVER EXISTED? AND DO YOU, SIR, AGREE WITH YOUR COLLEAGUE?
QUITE CORRECT.
ABSOLUTELY!
NEITHER OF US BELIEVE IN GOD.
YOU ARE... ATHEISTS?
YOU'RE DAMN RIGHT WE ARE!
HOW AMAZING!
IN OUR COUNTRY IT IS NOT AT ALL AMAZING.
THEN HOW DO YOU ACCOUNT FOR THE FIVE PROOFS OF THE EXISTENCE OF GOD?
NONE OF THEM VALID! EVEN THE SIXTH IS UNFOUNDED.
WHICH ONE IS THAT?

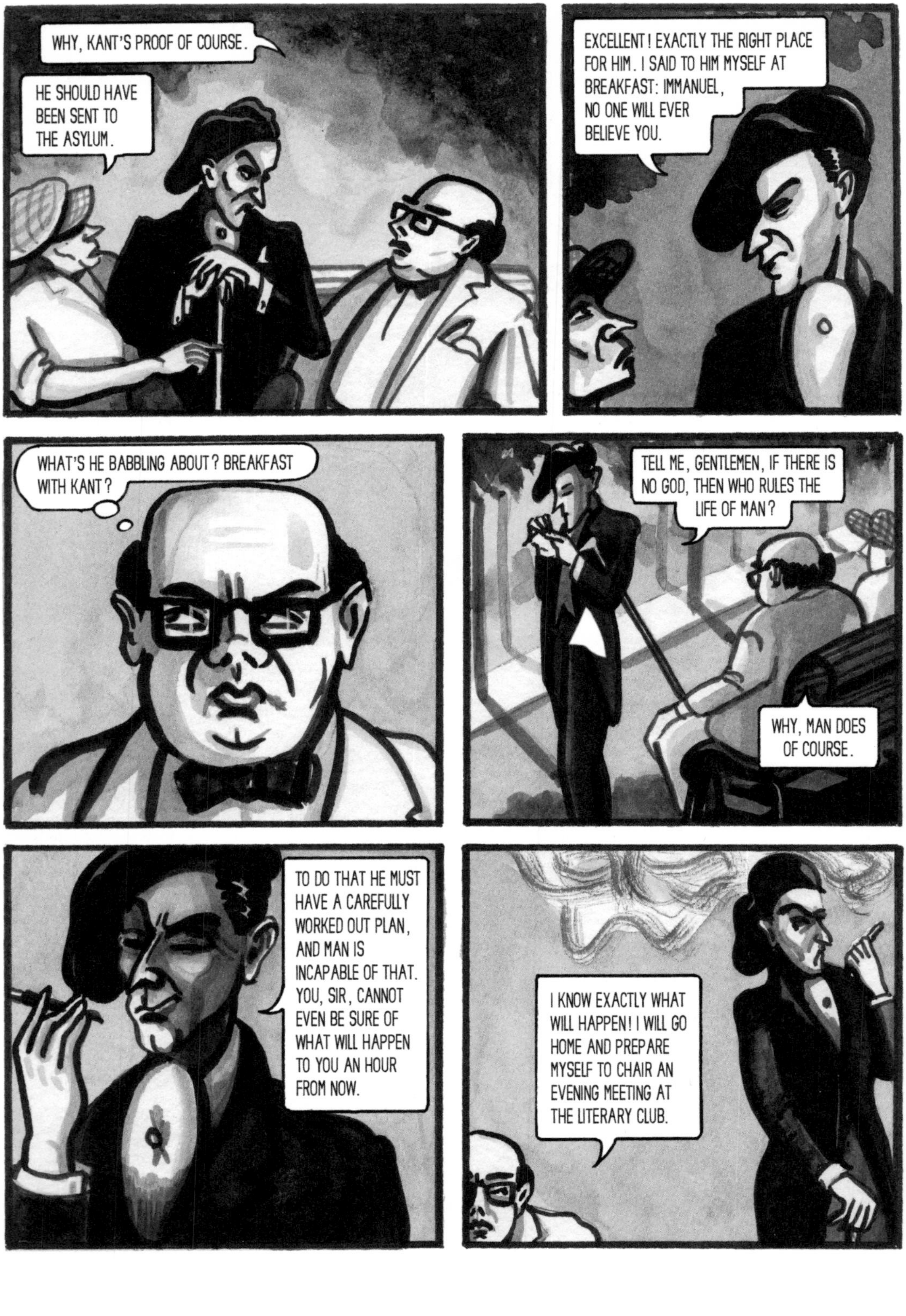
WHY, KANT'S PROOF OF COURSE.
HE SHOULD HAVE BEEN SENT TO THE ASYLUM.
EXCELLENT! EXACTLY THE RIGHT PLACE FOR HIM. I SAID TO HIM MYSELF AT BREAKFAST: IMMANUEL, NO ONE WILL EVER BELIEVE YOU.
WHAT'S HE BABBLING ABOUT? BREAKFAST WITH KANT?
TELL ME, GENTLEMEN, IF THERE IS NO GOD, THEN WHO RULES THE LIFE OF MAN?
WHY, MAN DOES OF COURSE.
TO DO THAT HE MUST HAVE A CAREFULLY WORKED OUT PLAN, AND MAN IS INCAPABLE OF THAT. YOU, SIR, CANNOT EVEN BE SURE OF WHAT WILL HAPPEN TO YOU AN HOUR FROM NOW.
I KNOW EXACTLY WHAT WILL HAPPEN! I WILL GO HOME AND PREPARE MYSELF TO CHAIR AN EVENING MEETING AT THE LITERARY CLUB.

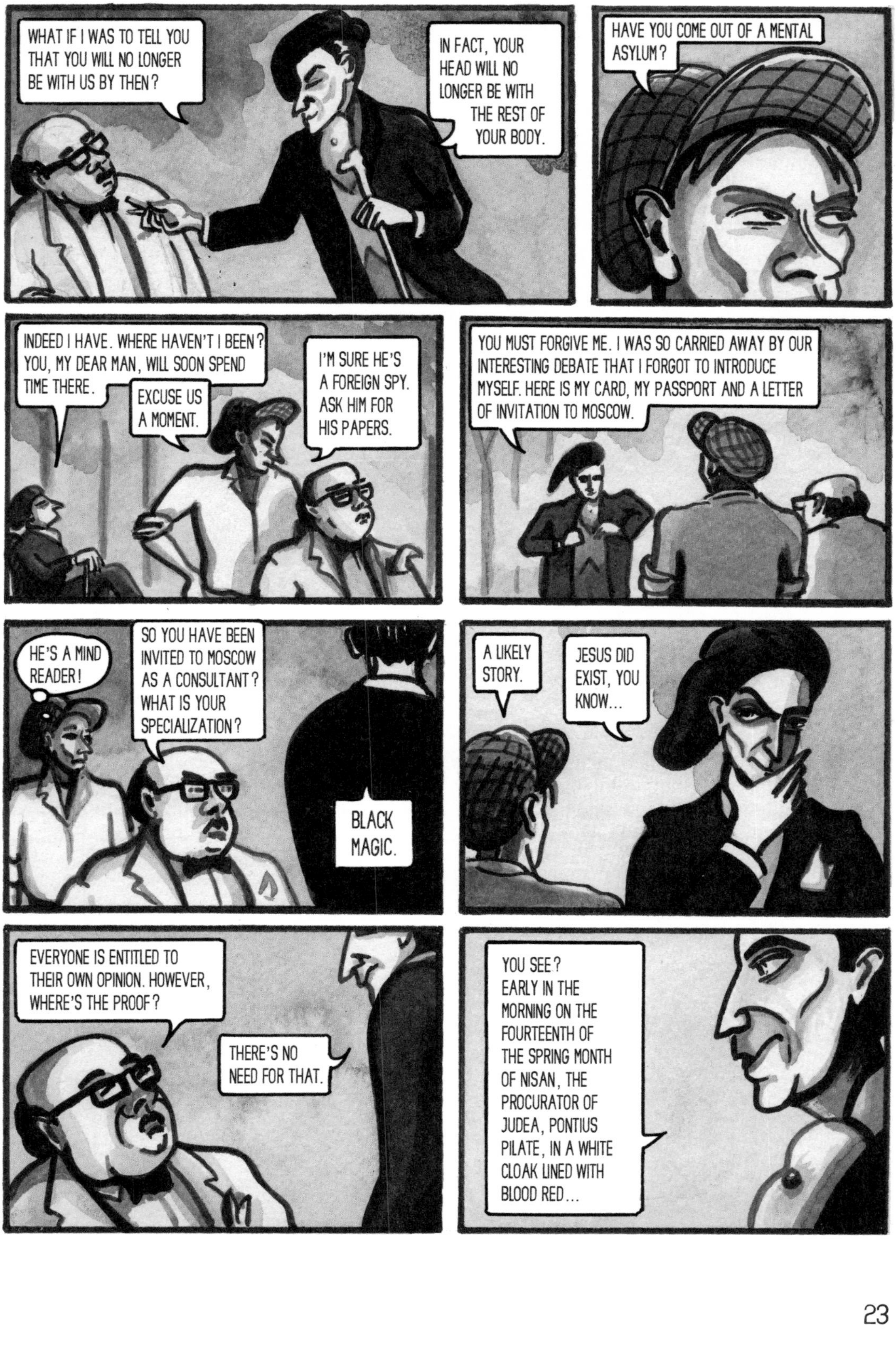

WHAT IF I WAS TO TELL YOU THAT YOU WILL NO LONGER BE WITH US BY THEN?
IN FACT, YOUR HEAD WILL NO LONGER BE WITH THE REST OF YOUR BODY.
HAVE YOU COME OUT OF A MENTAL ASYLUM?
INDEED I HAVE. WHERE HAVEN'T I BEEN? YOU, MY DEAR MAN, WILL SOON SPEND TIME THERE.
EXCUSE US A MOMENT.
I'M SURE HE'S A FOREIGN SPY. ASK HIM FOR HIS PAPERS.
YOU MUST FORGIVE ME. I WAS SO CARRIED AWAY BY OUR INTERESTING DEBATE THAT I FORGOT TO INTRODUCE MYSELF. HERE IS MY CARD, MY PASSPORT AND A LETTER OF INVITATION TO MOSCOW.
HE'S A MIND READER!
SO YOU HAVE BEEN INVITED TO MOSCOW AS A CONSULTANT? WHAT IS YOUR SPECIALIZATION?
BLACK MAGIC.
A LIKELY STORY.
JESUS DID EXIST, YOU KNOW...
EVERYONE IS ENTITLED TO THEIR OWN OPINION. HOWEVER, WHERE'S THE PROOF?
THERE'S NO NEED FOR THAT.
YOU SEE? EARLY IN THE MORNING ON THE FOURTEENTH OF THE SPRING MONTH OF NISAN, THE PROCURATOR OF JUDEA, PONTIUS PILATE, IN A WHITE CLOAK LINED WITH BLOOD RED...

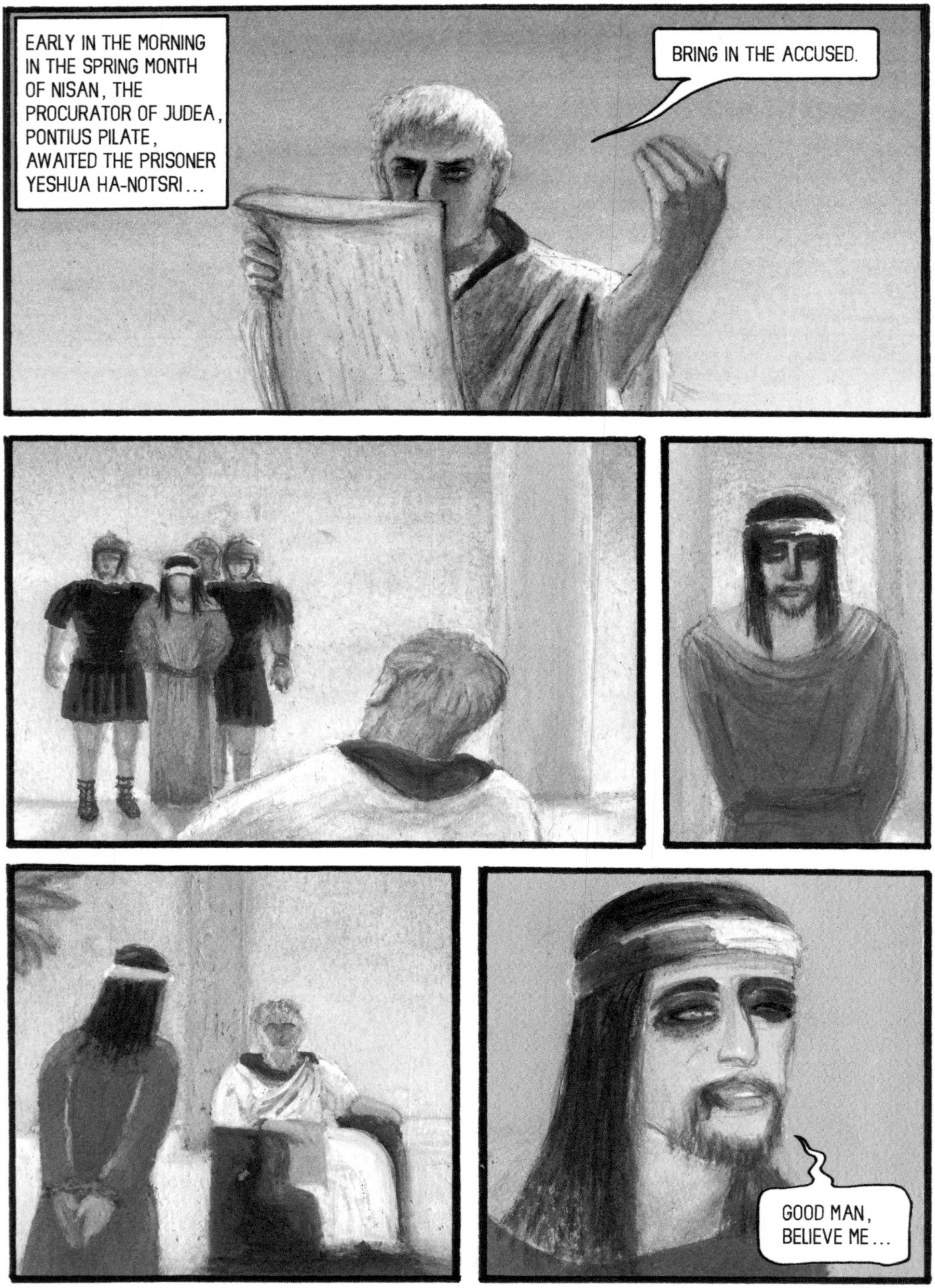
EARLY IN THE MORNING IN THE SPRING MONTH OF NISAN, THE PROCURATOR OF JUDEA, PONTIUS PILATE, AWAITED THE PRISONER YESHUA HA-NOTSRI...
BRING IN THE ACCUSED.
GOOD MAN, BELIEVE ME...

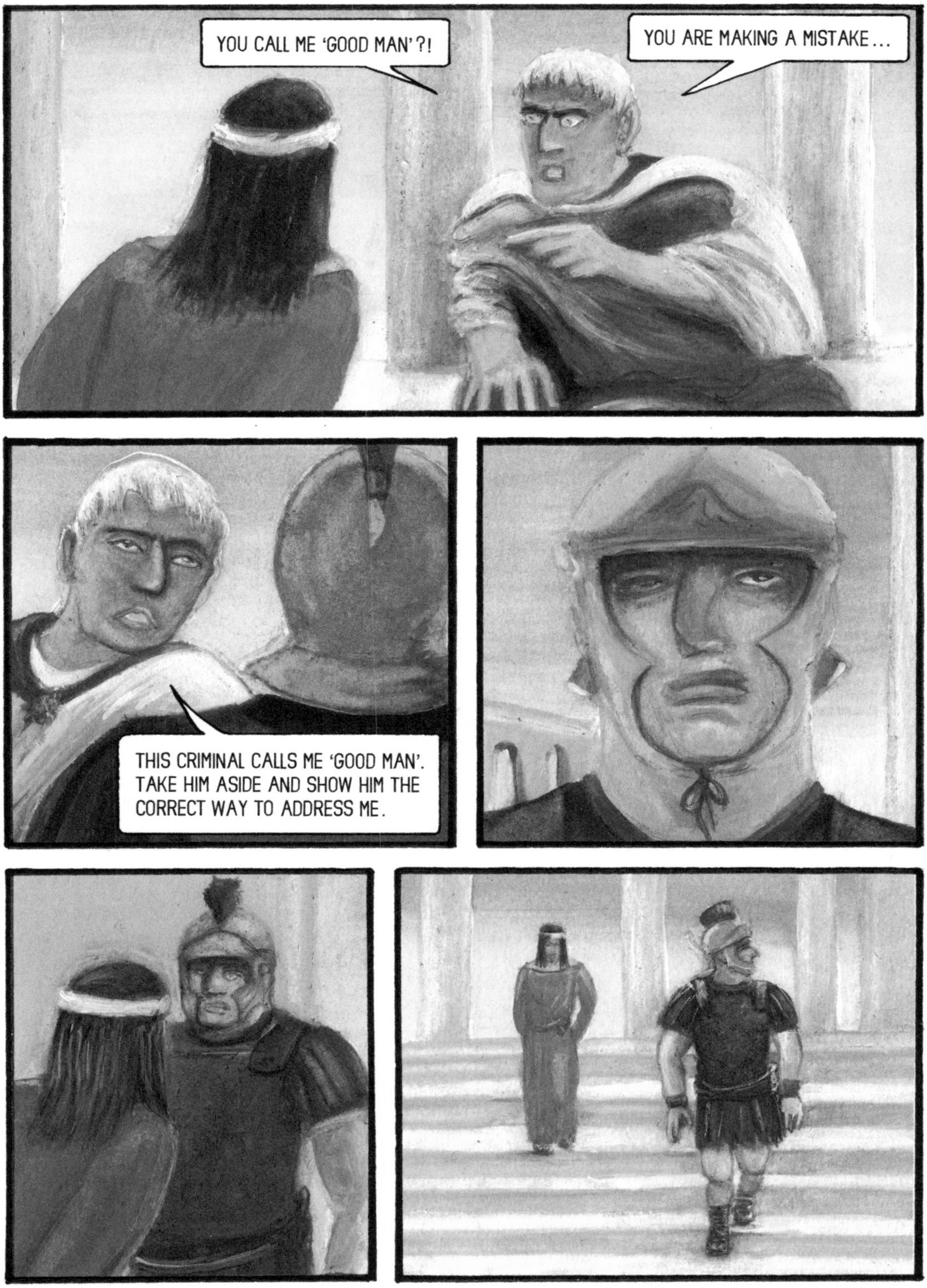
YOU CALL ME 'GOOD MAN'?!
YOU ARE MAKING A MISTAKE...
THIS CRIMINAL CALLS ME 'GOOD MAN'. TAKE HIM ASIDE AND SHOW HIM THE CORRECT WAY TO ADDRESS ME.

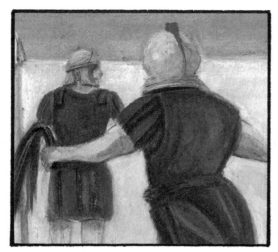

YOU MUST CALL A ROMAN PROCURATOR 'HEGEMON'. DO YOU UNDERSTAND? OR SHALL I HIT YOU AGAIN?

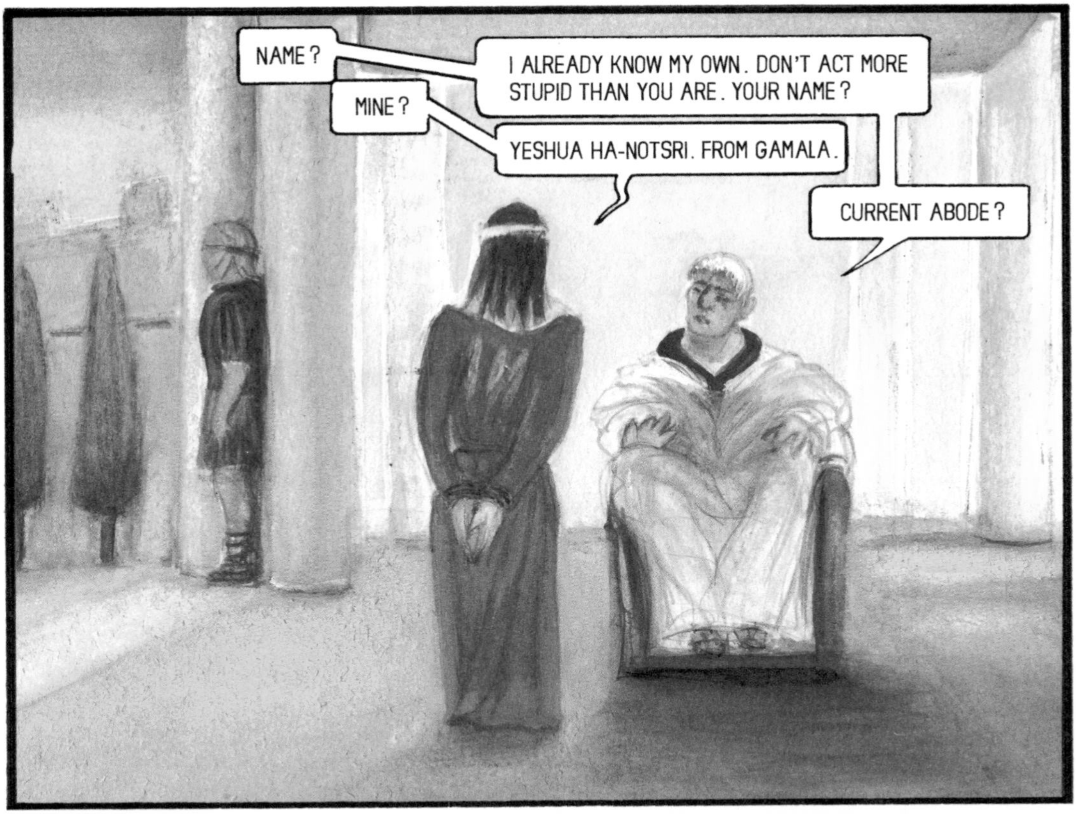
NAME ?
MINE ?
I ALREADY KNOW MY OWN. DON'T ACT MORE STUPID THAN YOU ARE. YOUR NAME ?
YESHUA HA-NOTSRI. FROM GAMALA.
CURRENT ABODE ?

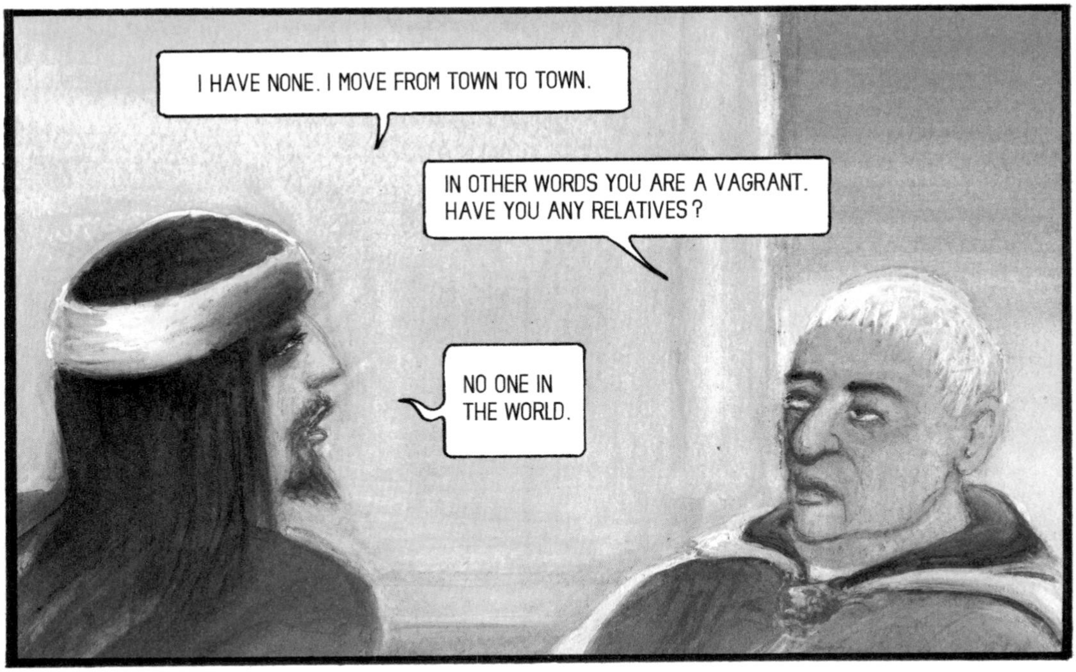
I HAVE NONE. I MOVE FROM TOWN TO TOWN.
IN OTHER WORDS YOU ARE A VAGRANT. HAVE YOU ANY RELATIVES ?
NO ONE IN THE WORLD.

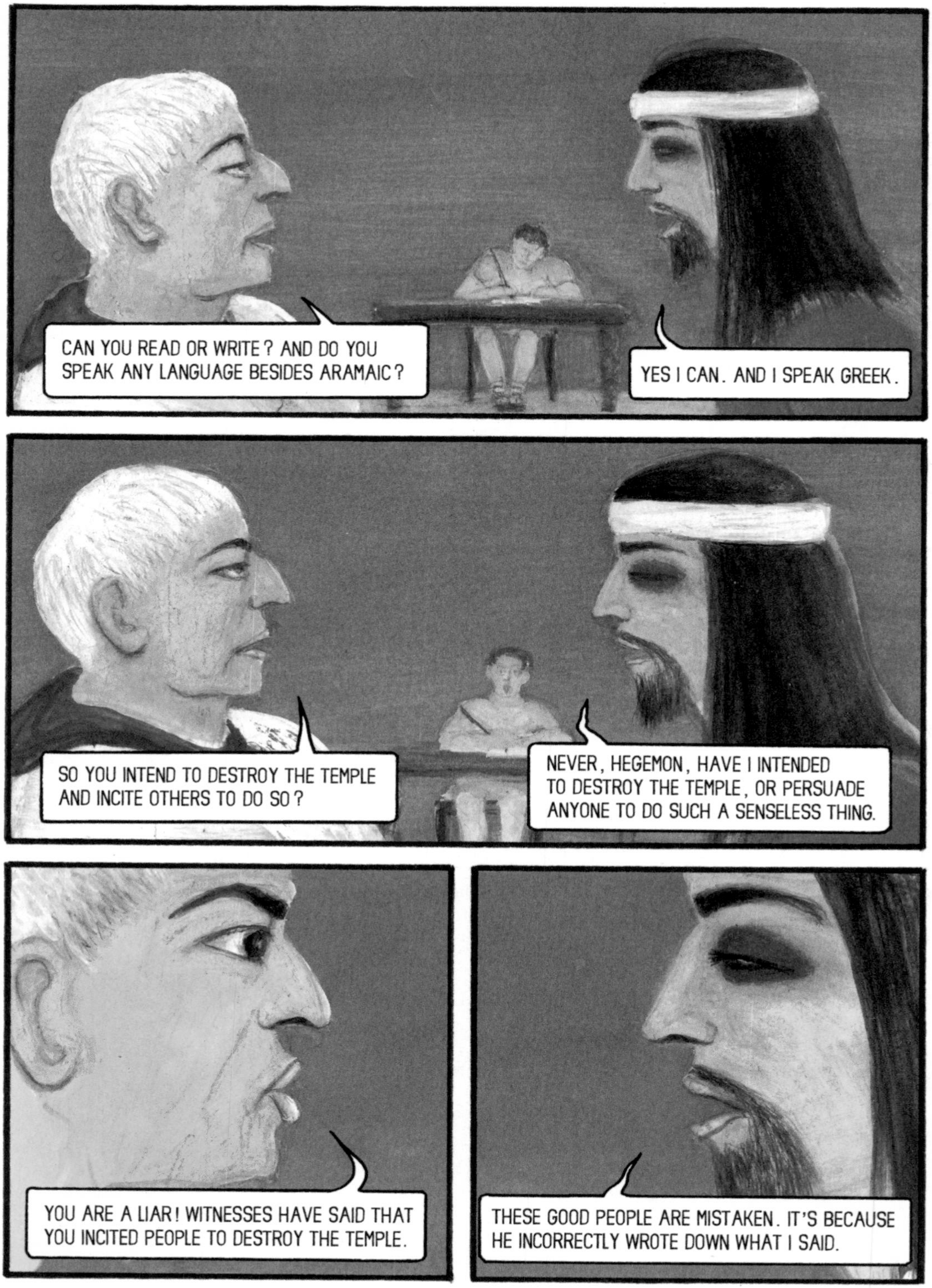
CAN YOU READ OR WRITE? AND DO YOU SPEAK ANY LANGUAGE BESIDES ARAMAIC?
YES I CAN. AND I SPEAK GREEK.
SO YOU INTEND TO DESTROY THE TEMPLE AND INCITE OTHERS TO DO SO?
NEVER, HEGEMON, HAVE I INTENDED TO DESTROY THE TEMPLE, OR PERSUADE ANYONE TO DO SUCH A SENSELESS THING.
YOU ARE A LIAR! WITNESSES HAVE SAID THAT YOU INCITED PEOPLE TO DESTROY THE TEMPLE.
THESE GOOD PEOPLE ARE MISTAKEN. IT'S BECAUSE HE INCORRECTLY WROTE DOWN WHAT I SAID.

WHAT HAS BEEN WRITTEN ABOUT YOU IS ENOUGH TO HANG YOU. WHO IS HE?

MATTHEW THE LEVITE. HE WAS A TAX COLLECTOR. HE LISTENED TO WHAT I HAD TO SAY, THREW HIS MONEY INTO THE ROAD, AND NOW FOLLOWS ME EVERYWHERE, WRITING INCESSANTLY.

A TAX COLLECTOR THROWING AWAY HIS MONEY? WHATEVER NEXT? DID YOU MAKE A SPEECH ABOUT THE TEMPLE TO THE CROWD?

I SAID, HEGEMON, THAT THE TEMPLE OF OLD BELIEFS WOULD FALL DOWN, AND THE NEW TEMPLE OF TRUTH WOULD BE BUILT. METAPHORICALLY SPEAKING.

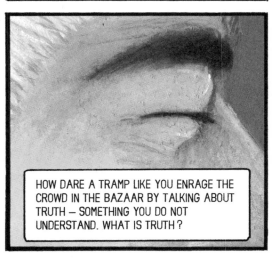

HOW DARE A TRAMP LIKE YOU ENRAGE THE CROWD IN THE BAZAAR BY TALKING ABOUT TRUTH — SOMETHING YOU DO NOT UNDERSTAND. WHAT IS TRUTH?

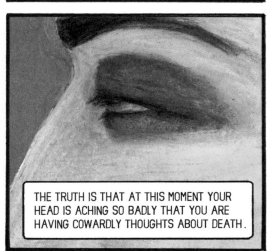

THE TRUTH IS THAT AT THIS MOMENT YOUR HEAD IS ACHING SO BADLY THAT YOU ARE HAVING COWARDLY THOUGHTS ABOUT DEATH.

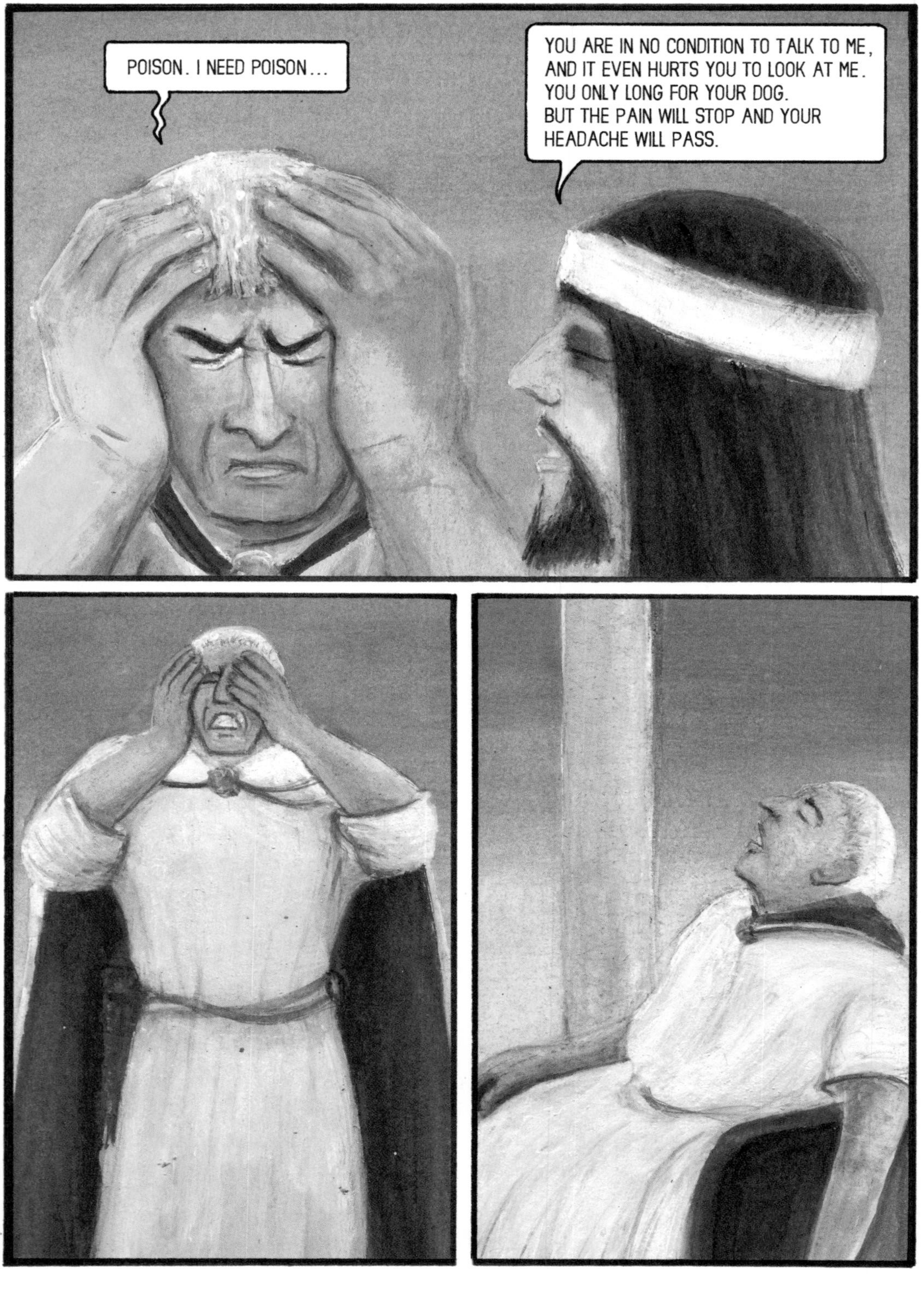
POISON. I NEED POISON...
YOU ARE IN NO CONDITION TO TALK TO ME, AND IT EVEN HURTS YOU TO LOOK AT ME. YOU ONLY LONG FOR YOUR DOG. BUT THE PAIN WILL STOP AND YOUR HEADACHE WILL PASS.

SO, IT HAS GONE. I WOULD ADVISE YOU, HEGEMON, TO LEAVE THIS PALACE AND TAKE A WALK SOMEWHERE.

THERE WILL BE THUNDER LATER. I WOULD BE HAPPY TO GO WITH YOU AND DISCUSS SOME THOUGHTS WHICH YOU MIGHT FIND INTERESTING.

THE TROUBLE IS THAT YOUR MIND IS CLOSED OFF AND YOU HAVE LOST YOUR FAITH IN PEOPLE.

UNTIE HIS HANDS.

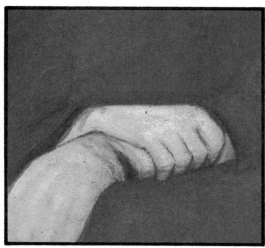

YOU SIMPLY MOVED YOUR HAND THROUGH THE AIR AS IF YOU WERE STROKING SOMETHING.

TELL ME, ARE YOU A GREAT PHYSICIAN? HOW DID YOU KNOW THAT I WANTED TO CALL MY DOG?

31

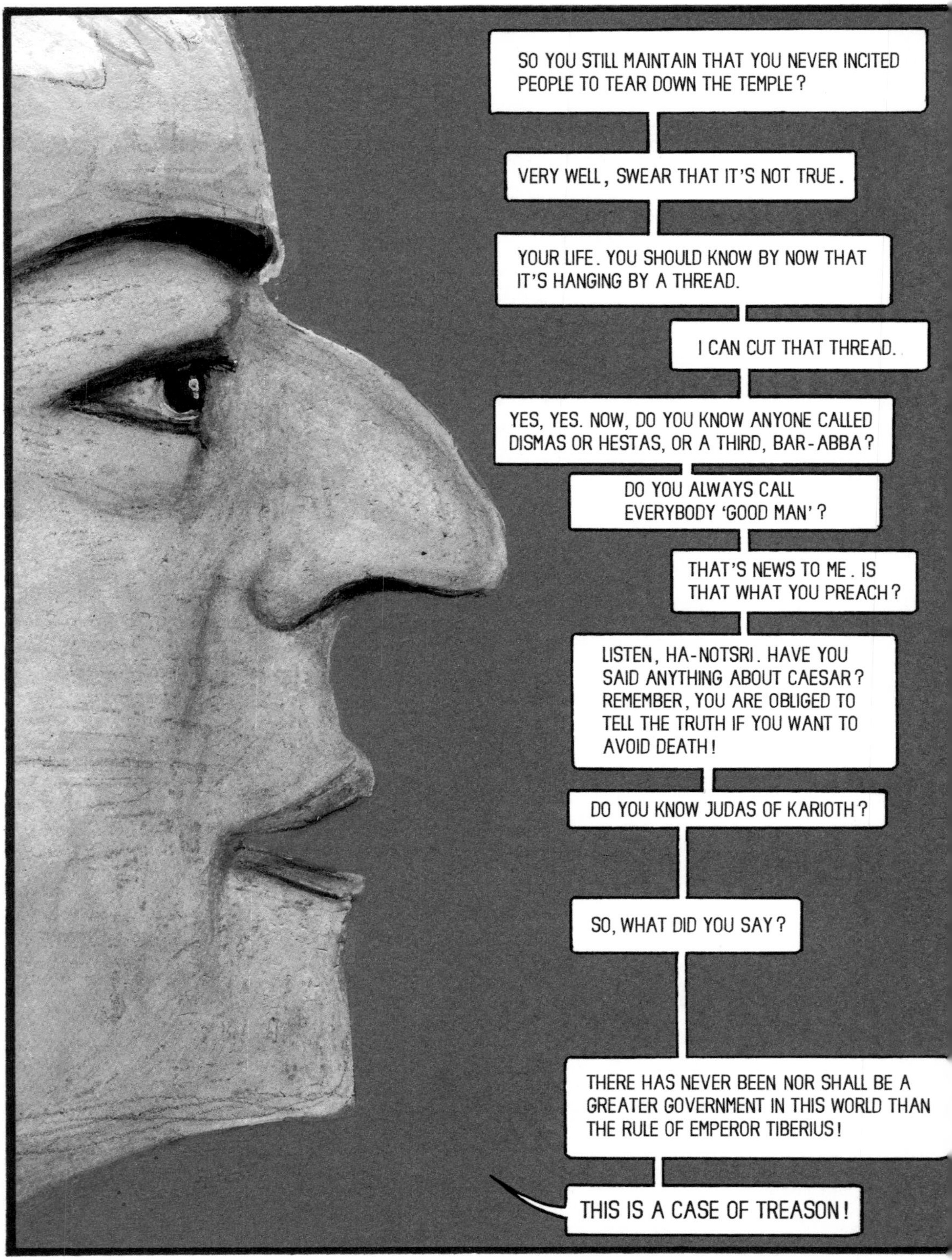
SO YOU STILL MAINTAIN THAT YOU NEVER INCITED PEOPLE TO TEAR DOWN THE TEMPLE?
VERY WELL, SWEAR THAT IT'S NOT TRUE.
YOUR LIFE. YOU SHOULD KNOW BY NOW THAT IT'S HANGING BY A THREAD.
I CAN CUT THAT THREAD.
YES, YES. NOW, DO YOU KNOW ANYONE CALLED DISMAS OR HESTAS, OR A THIRD, BAR-ABBA?
DO YOU ALWAYS CALL EVERYBODY 'GOOD MAN'?
THAT'S NEWS TO ME. IS THAT WHAT YOU PREACH?
LISTEN, HA-NOTSRI. HAVE YOU SAID ANYTHING ABOUT CAESAR? REMEMBER, YOU ARE OBLIGED TO TELL THE TRUTH IF YOU WANT TO AVOID DEATH!
DO YOU KNOW JUDAS OF KARIOTH?
SO, WHAT DID YOU SAY?
THERE HAS NEVER BEEN NOR SHALL BE A GREATER GOVERNMENT IN THIS WORLD THAN THE RULE OF EMPEROR TIBERIUS!
THIS IS A CASE OF TREASON!

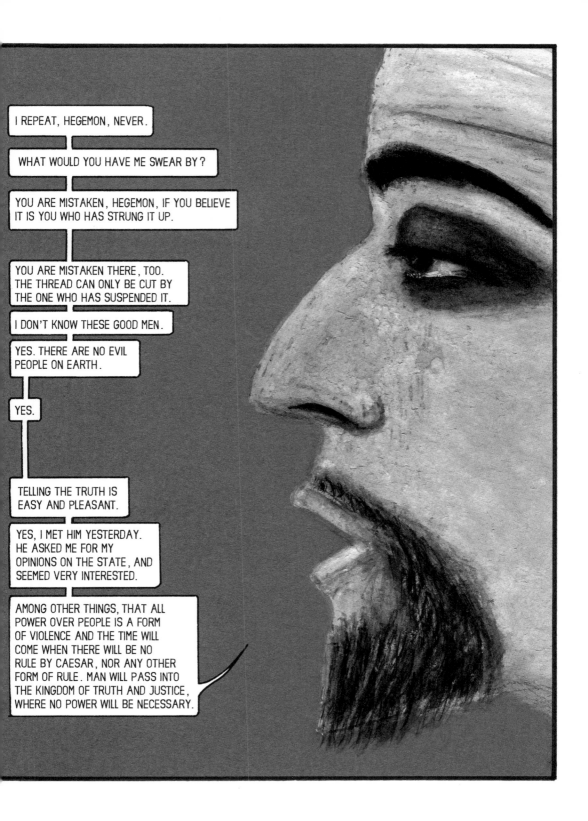

I REPEAT, HEGEMON, NEVER.

WHAT WOULD YOU HAVE ME SWEAR BY?

YOU ARE MISTAKEN, HEGEMON, IF YOU BELIEVE IT IS YOU WHO HAS STRUNG IT UP.

YOU ARE MISTAKEN THERE, TOO. THE THREAD CAN ONLY BE CUT BY THE ONE WHO HAS SUSPENDED IT.

I DON'T KNOW THESE GOOD MEN.

YES. THERE ARE NO EVIL PEOPLE ON EARTH.

YES.

TELLING THE TRUTH IS EASY AND PLEASANT.

YES, I MET HIM YESTERDAY. HE ASKED ME FOR MY OPINIONS ON THE STATE, AND SEEMED VERY INTERESTED.

AMONG OTHER THINGS, THAT ALL POWER OVER PEOPLE IS A FORM OF VIOLENCE AND THE TIME WILL COME WHEN THERE WILL BE NO RULE BY CAESAR, NOR ANY OTHER FORM OF RULE. MAN WILL PASS INTO THE KINGDOM OF TRUTH AND JUSTICE, WHERE NO POWER WILL BE NECESSARY.

33

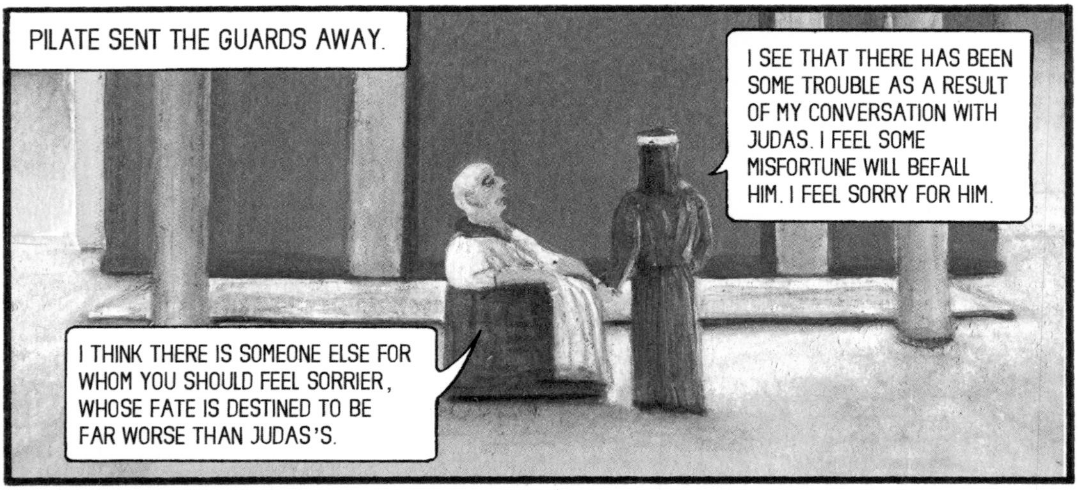
PILATE SENT THE GUARDS AWAY.
I SEE THAT THERE HAS BEEN SOME TROUBLE AS A RESULT OF MY CONVERSATION WITH JUDAS. I FEEL SOME MISFORTUNE WILL BEFALL HIM. I FEEL SORRY FOR HIM.
I THINK THERE IS SOMEONE ELSE FOR WHOM YOU SHOULD FEEL SORRIER, WHOSE FATE IS DESTINED TO BE FAR WORSE THAN JUDAS'S.

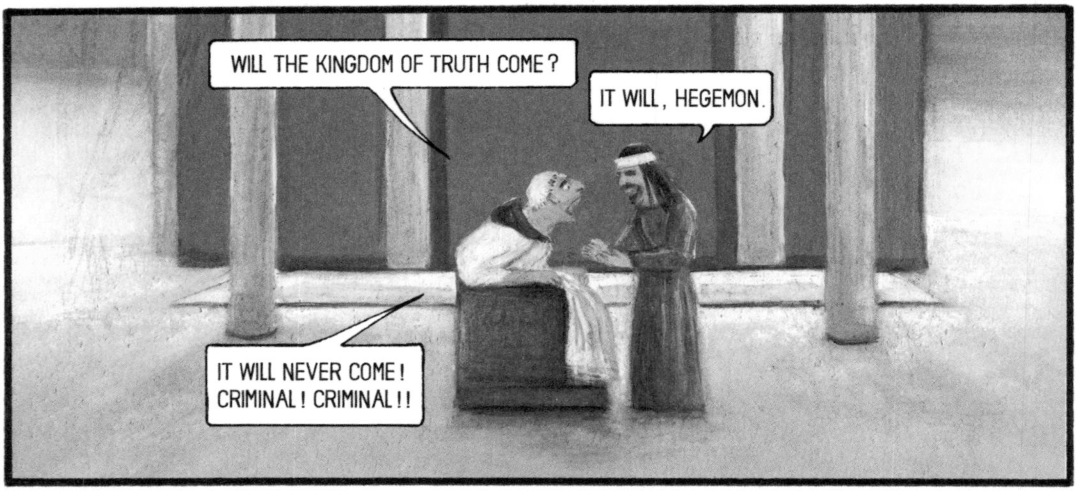
WILL THE KINGDOM OF TRUTH COME?
IT WILL, HEGEMON.
IT WILL NEVER COME! CRIMINAL! CRIMINAL!!

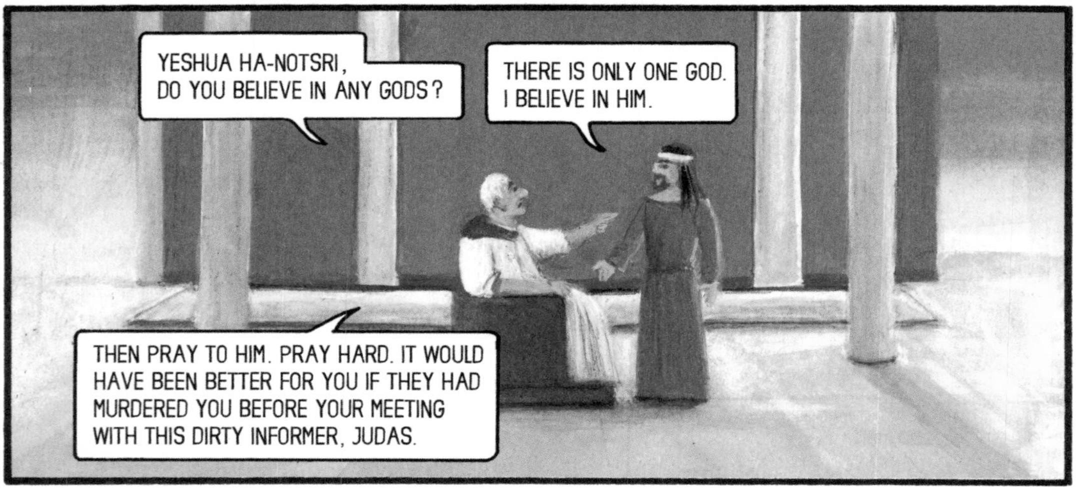
YESHUA HA-NOTSRI, DO YOU BELIEVE IN ANY GODS?
THERE IS ONLY ONE GOD. I BELIEVE IN HIM.
THEN PRAY TO HIM. PRAY HARD. IT WOULD HAVE BEEN BETTER FOR YOU IF THEY HAD MURDERED YOU BEFORE YOUR MEETING WITH THIS DIRTY INFORMER, JUDAS.

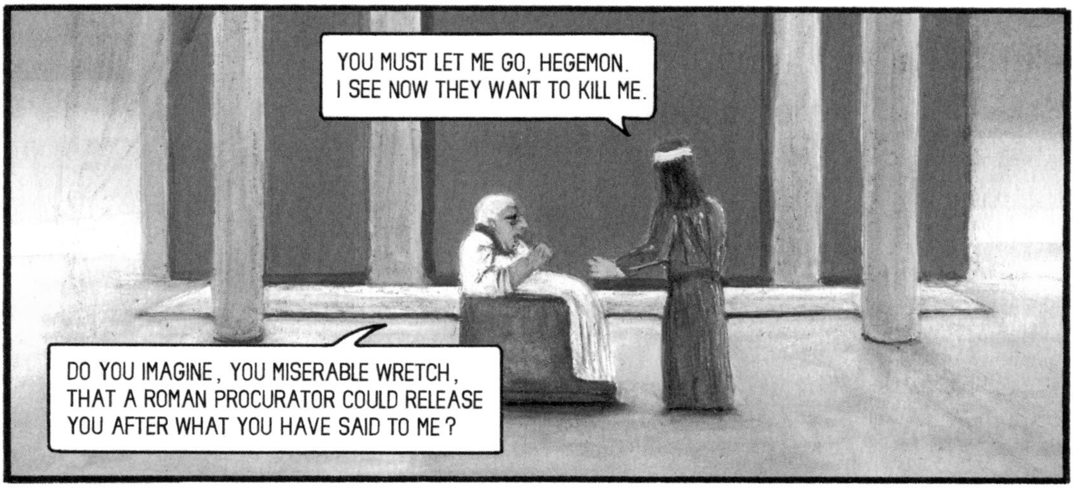
YOU MUST LET ME GO, HEGEMON. I SEE NOW THEY WANT TO KILL ME.
DO YOU IMAGINE, YOU MISERABLE WRETCH, THAT A ROMAN PROCURATOR COULD RELEASE YOU AFTER WHAT YOU HAVE SAID TO ME?

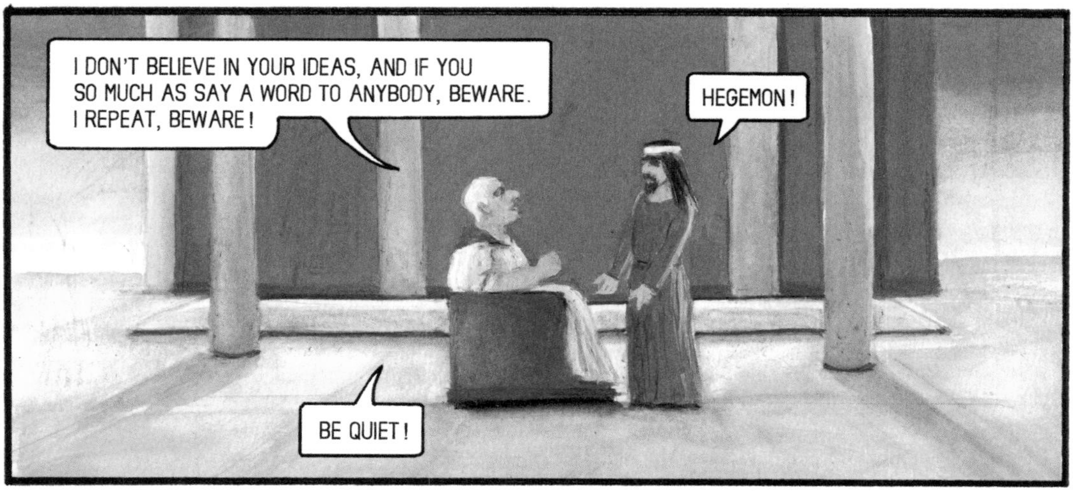
I DON'T BELIEVE IN YOUR IDEAS, AND IF YOU SO MUCH AS SAY A WORD TO ANYBODY, BEWARE. I REPEAT, BEWARE!
HEGEMON!
BE QUIET!

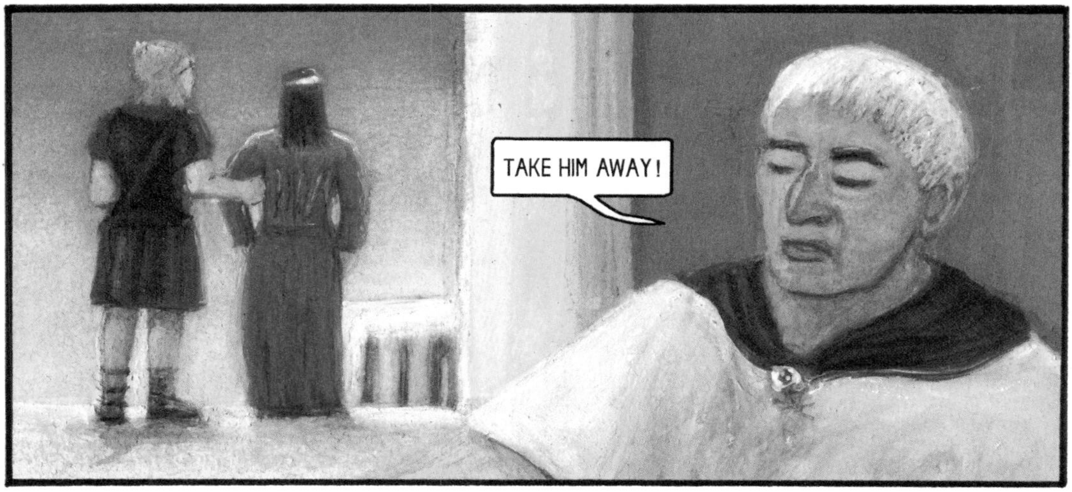
TAKE HIM AWAY!

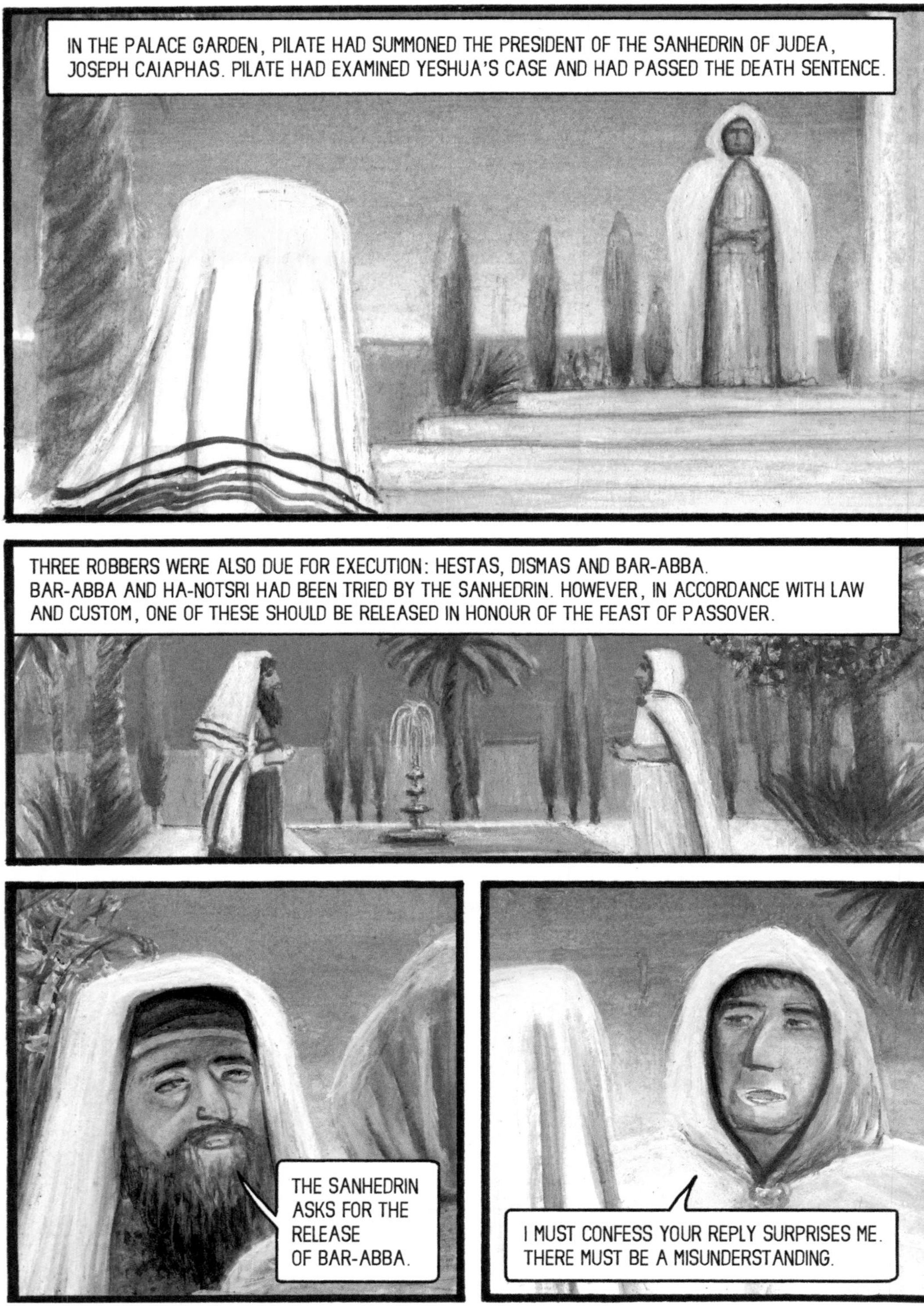
IN THE PALACE GARDEN, PILATE HAD SUMMONED THE PRESIDENT OF THE SANHEDRIN OF JUDEA, JOSEPH CAIAPHAS. PILATE HAD EXAMINED YESHUA'S CASE AND HAD PASSED THE DEATH SENTENCE.
THREE ROBBERS WERE ALSO DUE FOR EXECUTION: HESTAS, DISMAS AND BAR-ABBA. BAR-ABBA AND HA-NOTSRI HAD BEEN TRIED BY THE SANHEDRIN. HOWEVER, IN ACCORDANCE WITH LAW AND CUSTOM, ONE OF THESE SHOULD BE RELEASED IN HONOUR OF THE FEAST OF PASSOVER.
THE SANHEDRIN ASKS FOR THE RELEASE OF BAR-ABBA.
I MUST CONFESS YOUR REPLY SURPRISES ME. THERE MUST BE A MISUNDERSTANDING.

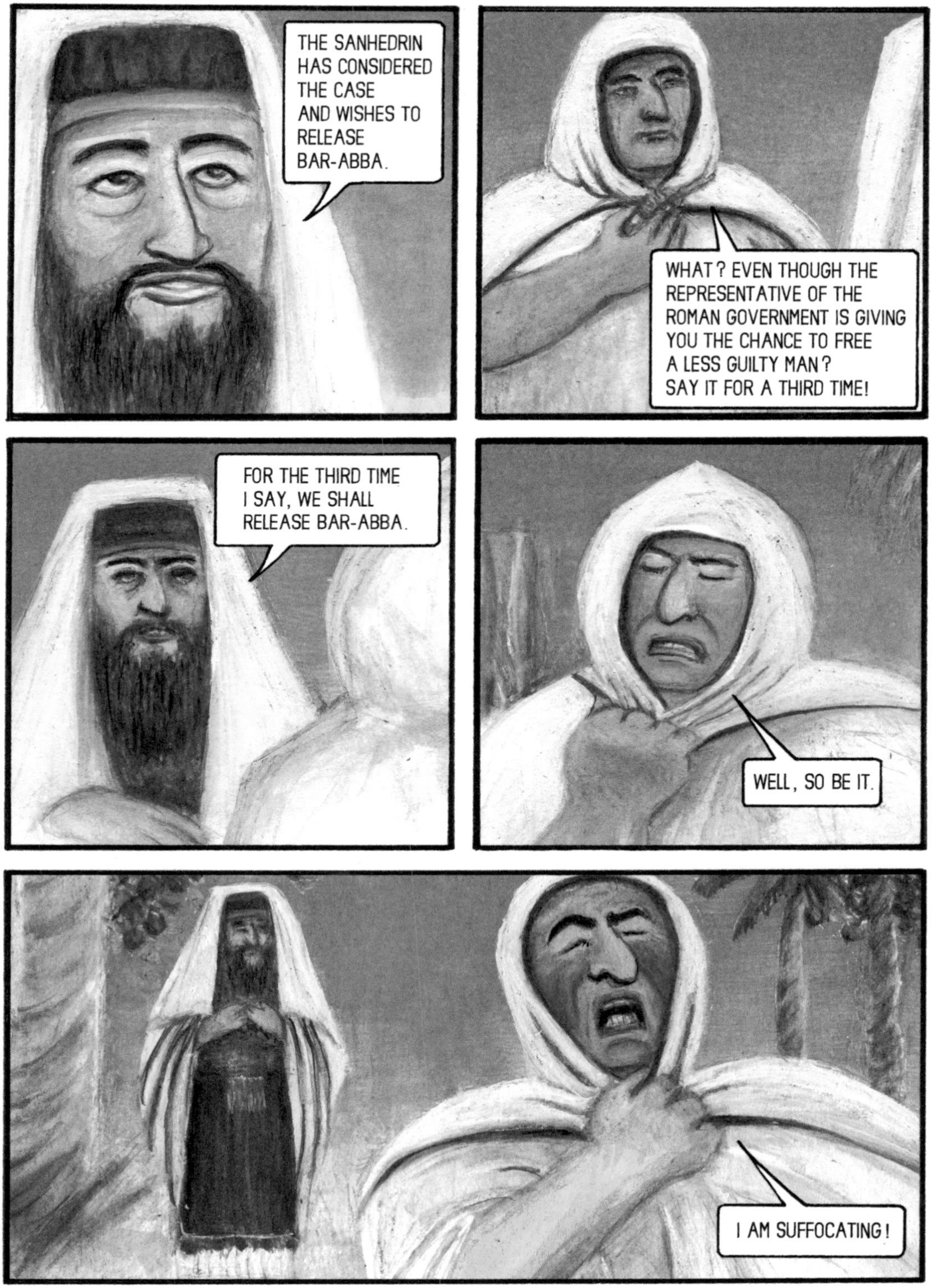
THE SANHEDRIN HAS CONSIDERED THE CASE AND WISHES TO RELEASE BAR-ABBA.
WHAT? EVEN THOUGH THE REPRESENTATIVE OF THE ROMAN GOVERNMENT IS GIVING YOU THE CHANCE TO FREE A LESS GUILTY MAN? SAY IT FOR A THIRD TIME!
FOR THE THIRD TIME I SAY, WE SHALL RELEASE BAR-ABBA.
WELL, SO BE IT.
I AM SUFFOCATING!

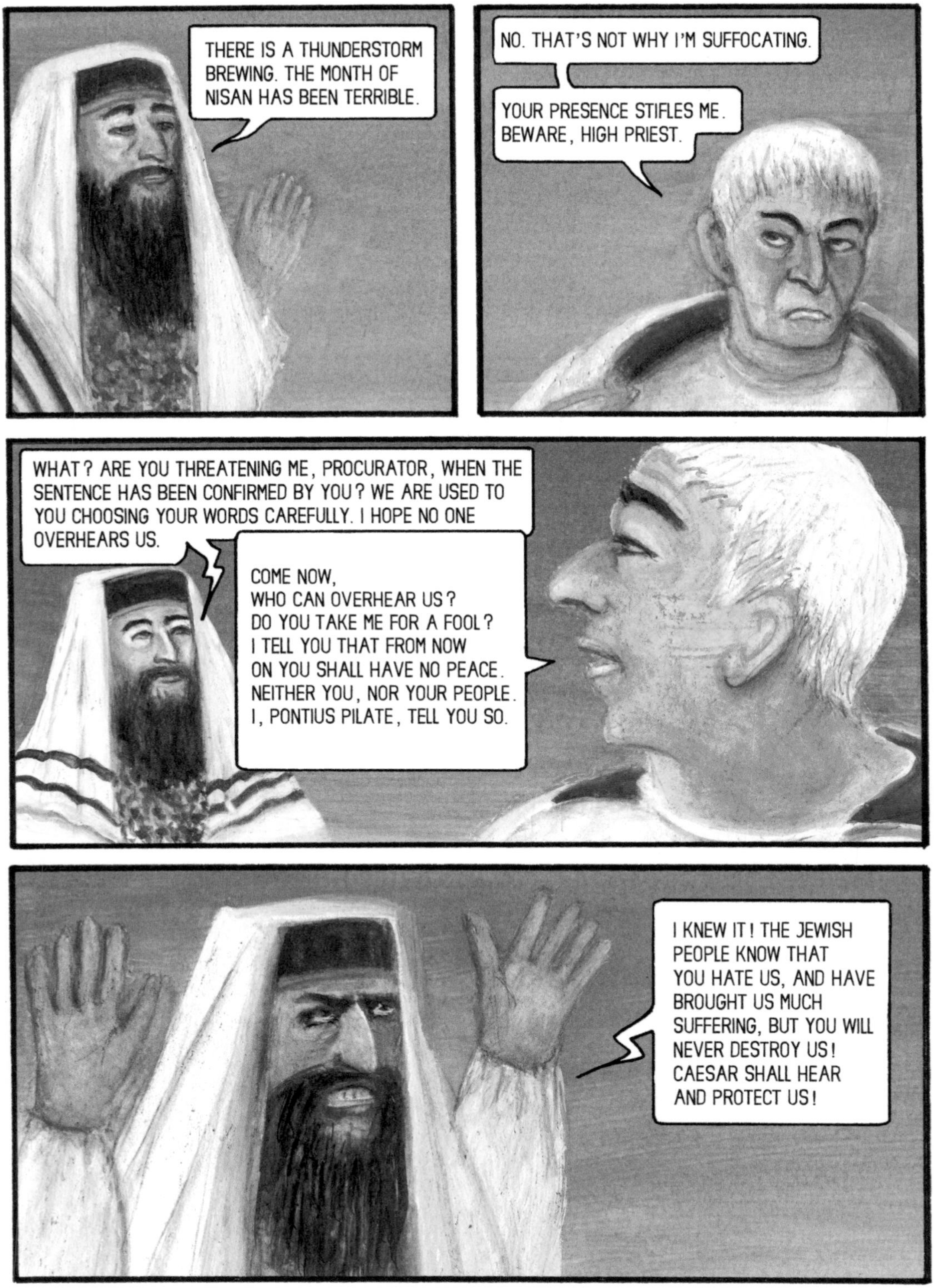
THERE IS A THUNDERSTORM BREWING. THE MONTH OF NISAN HAS BEEN TERRIBLE.
NO. THAT'S NOT WHY I'M SUFFOCATING.
YOUR PRESENCE STIFLES ME. BEWARE, HIGH PRIEST.
WHAT? ARE YOU THREATENING ME, PROCURATOR, WHEN THE SENTENCE HAS BEEN CONFIRMED BY YOU? WE ARE USED TO YOU CHOOSING YOUR WORDS CAREFULLY. I HOPE NO ONE OVERHEARS US.
COME NOW, WHO CAN OVERHEAR US? DO YOU TAKE ME FOR A FOOL? I TELL YOU THAT FROM NOW ON YOU SHALL HAVE NO PEACE. NEITHER YOU, NOR YOUR PEOPLE. I, PONTIUS PILATE, TELL YOU SO.
I KNEW IT! THE JEWISH PEOPLE KNOW THAT YOU HATE US, AND HAVE BROUGHT US MUCH SUFFERING, BUT YOU WILL NEVER DESTROY US! CAESAR SHALL HEAR AND PROTECT US!

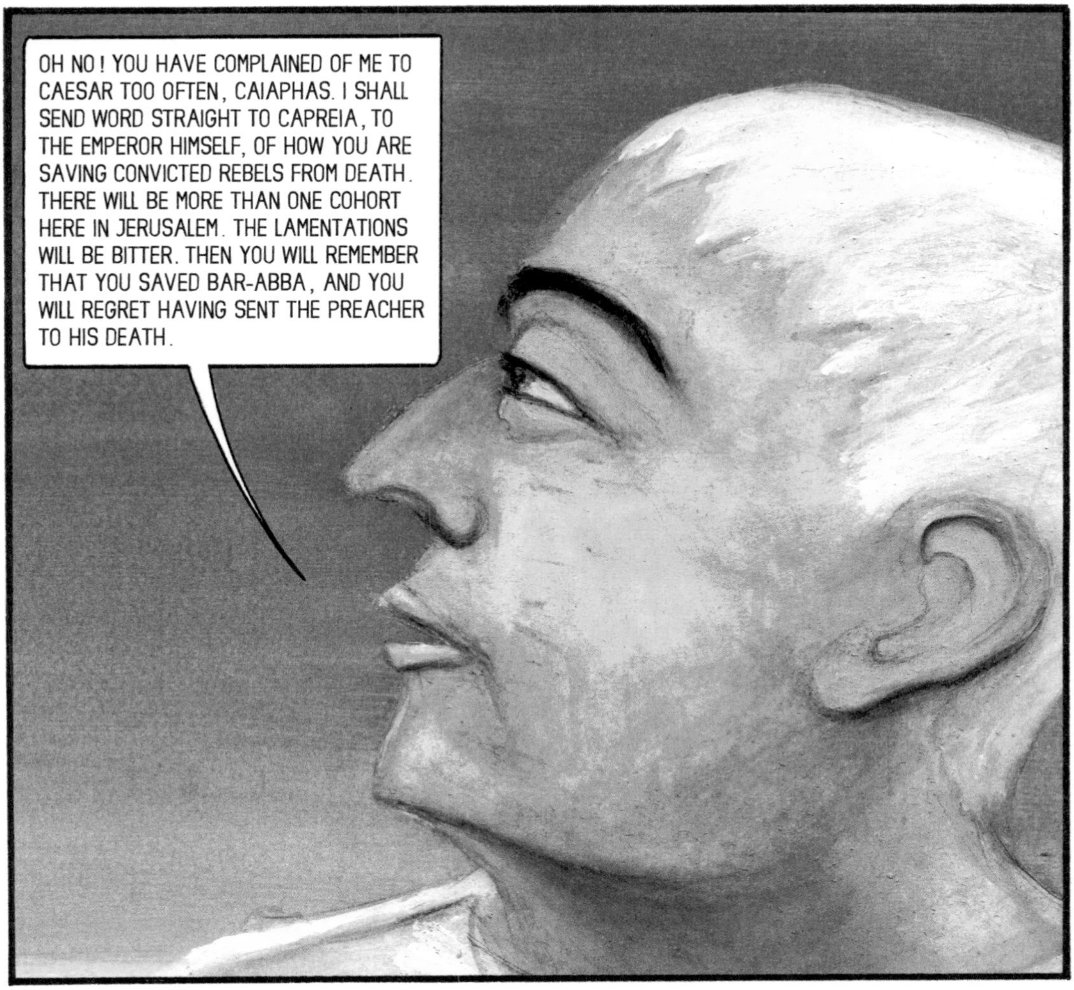
OH NO! YOU HAVE COMPLAINED OF ME TO CAESAR TOO OFTEN, CAIAPHAS. I SHALL SEND WORD STRAIGHT TO CAPREIA, TO THE EMPEROR HIMSELF, OF HOW YOU ARE SAVING CONVICTED REBELS FROM DEATH. THERE WILL BE MORE THAN ONE COHORT HERE IN JERUSALEM. THE LAMENTATIONS WILL BE BITTER. THEN YOU WILL REMEMBER THAT YOU SAVED BAR-ABBA, AND YOU WILL REGRET HAVING SENT THE PREACHER TO HIS DEATH.

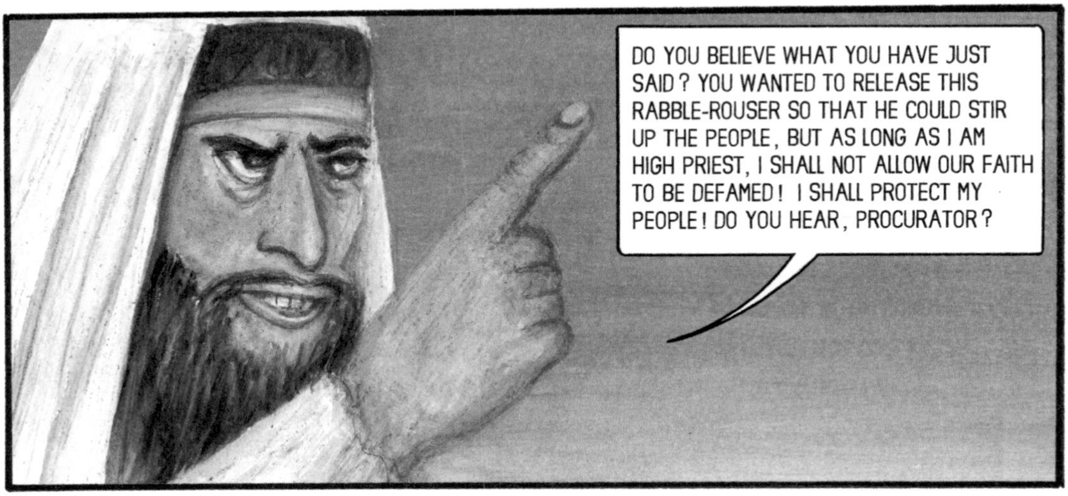
DO YOU BELIEVE WHAT YOU HAVE JUST SAID? YOU WANTED TO RELEASE THIS RABBLE-ROUSER SO THAT HE COULD STIR UP THE PEOPLE, BUT AS LONG AS I AM HIGH PRIEST, I SHALL NOT ALLOW OUR FAITH TO BE DEFAMED! I SHALL PROTECT MY PEOPLE! DO YOU HEAR, PROCURATOR?

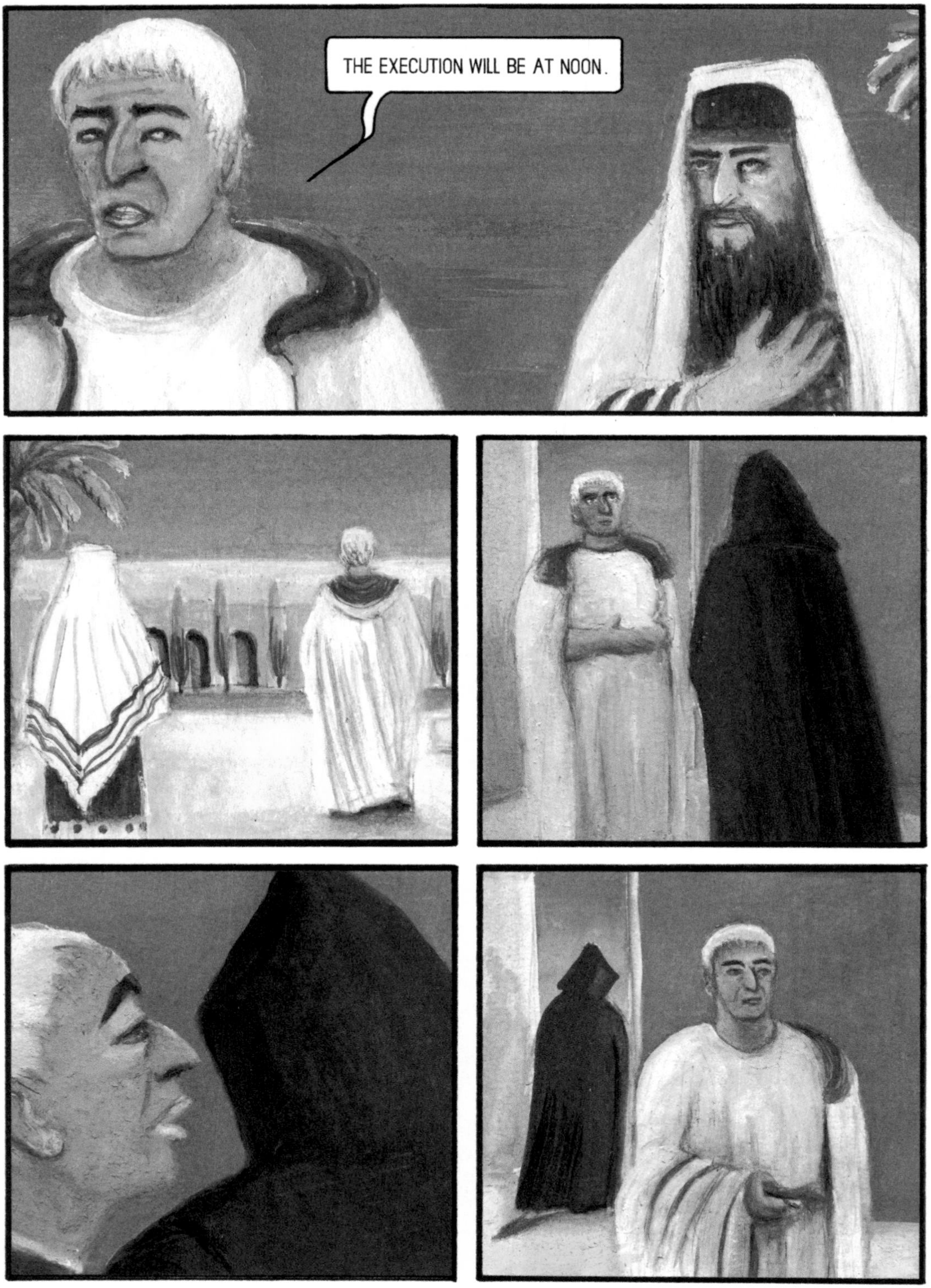
THE EXECUTION WILL BE AT NOON.

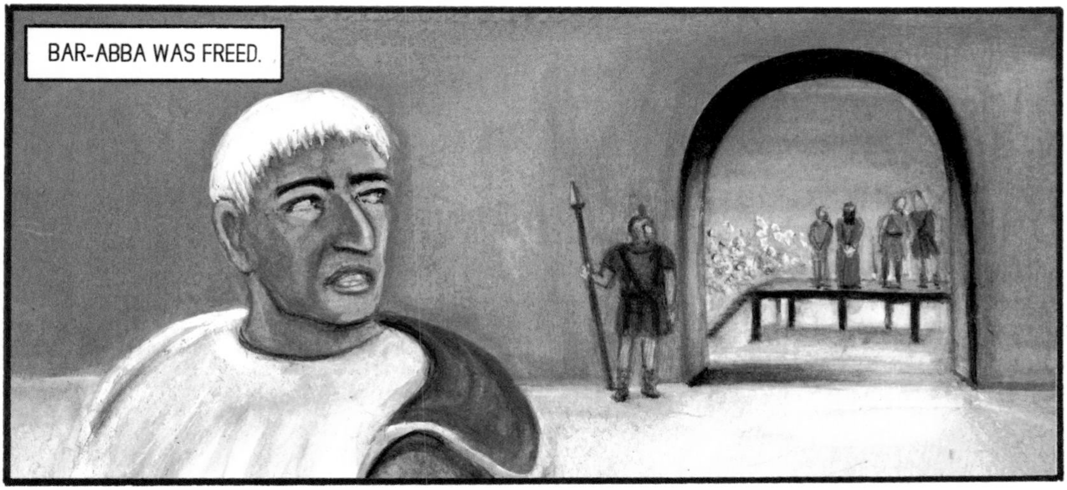
BAR-ABBA WAS FREED.

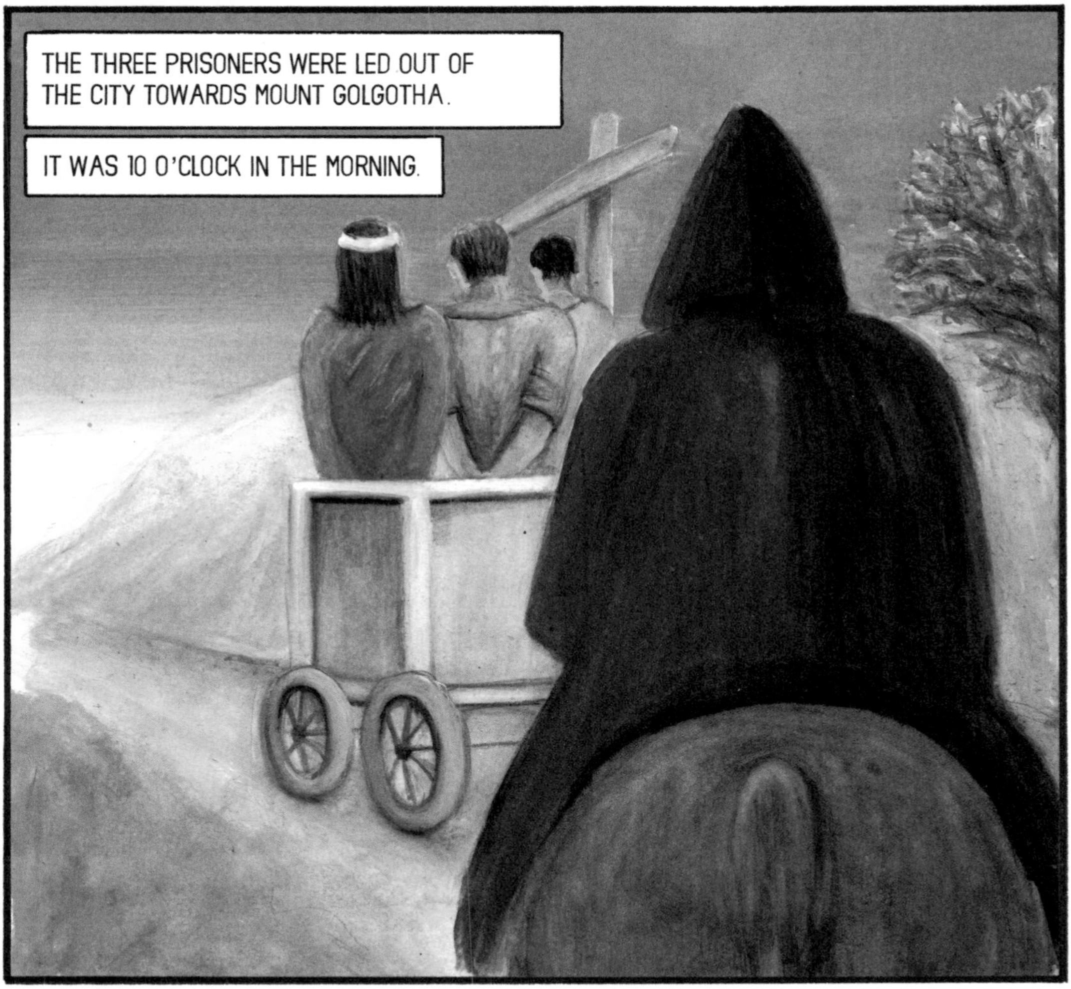
THE THREE PRISONERS WERE LED OUT OF THE CITY TOWARDS MOUNT GOLGOTHA.
IT WAS 10 O'CLOCK IN THE MORNING.

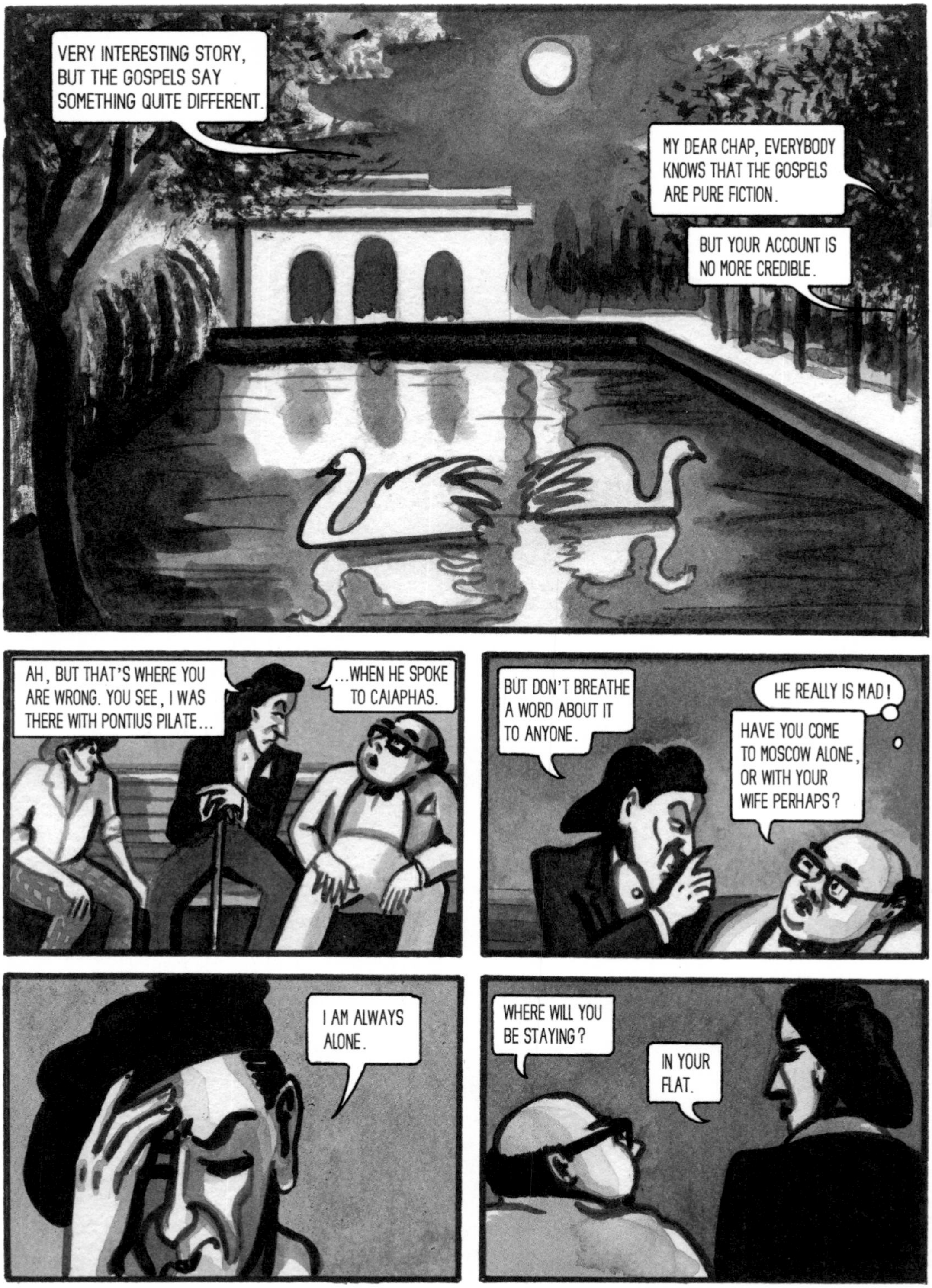
VERY INTERESTING STORY, BUT THE GOSPELS SAY SOMETHING QUITE DIFFERENT.
MY DEAR CHAP, EVERYBODY KNOWS THAT THE GOSPELS ARE PURE FICTION.
BUT YOUR ACCOUNT IS NO MORE CREDIBLE.
AH, BUT THAT'S WHERE YOU ARE WRONG. YOU SEE, I WAS THERE WITH PONTIUS PILATE...
...WHEN HE SPOKE TO CAIAPHAS.
BUT DON'T BREATHE A WORD ABOUT IT TO ANYONE.
HE REALLY IS MAD!
HAVE YOU COME TO MOSCOW ALONE, OR WITH YOUR WIFE PERHAPS?
I AM ALWAYS ALONE.
WHERE WILL YOU BE STAYING?
IN YOUR FLAT.

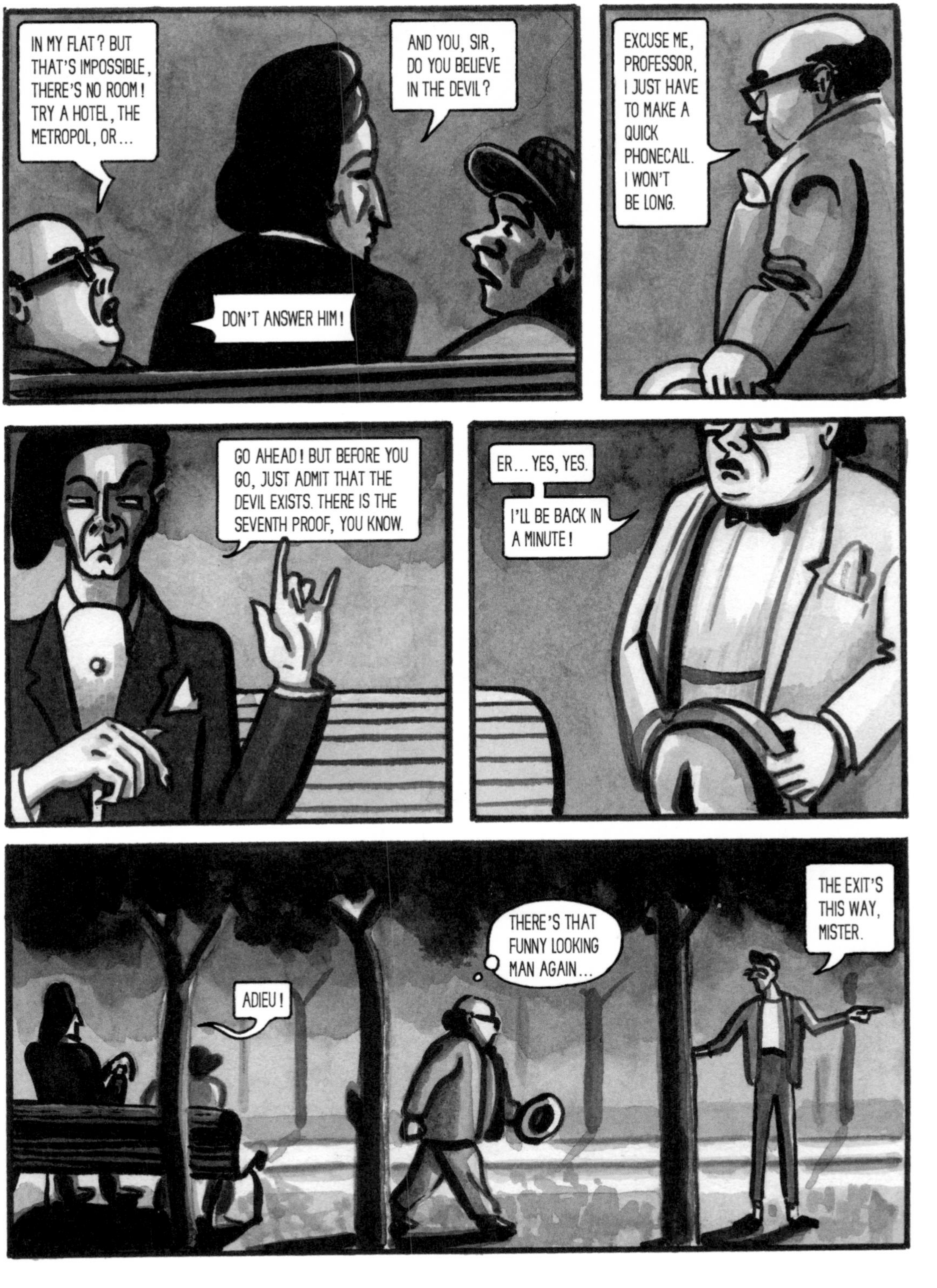
IN MY FLAT? BUT THAT'S IMPOSSIBLE, THERE'S NO ROOM! TRY A HOTEL, THE METROPOL, OR...
AND YOU, SIR, DO YOU BELIEVE IN THE DEVIL?
DON'T ANSWER HIM!
EXCUSE ME, PROFESSOR, I JUST HAVE TO MAKE A QUICK PHONECALL. I WON'T BE LONG.
GO AHEAD! BUT BEFORE YOU GO, JUST ADMIT THAT THE DEVIL EXISTS. THERE IS THE SEVENTH PROOF, YOU KNOW.
ER... YES, YES.
I'LL BE BACK IN A MINUTE!
ADIEU!
THERE'S THAT FUNNY LOOKING MAN AGAIN...
THE EXIT'S THIS WAY, MISTER.

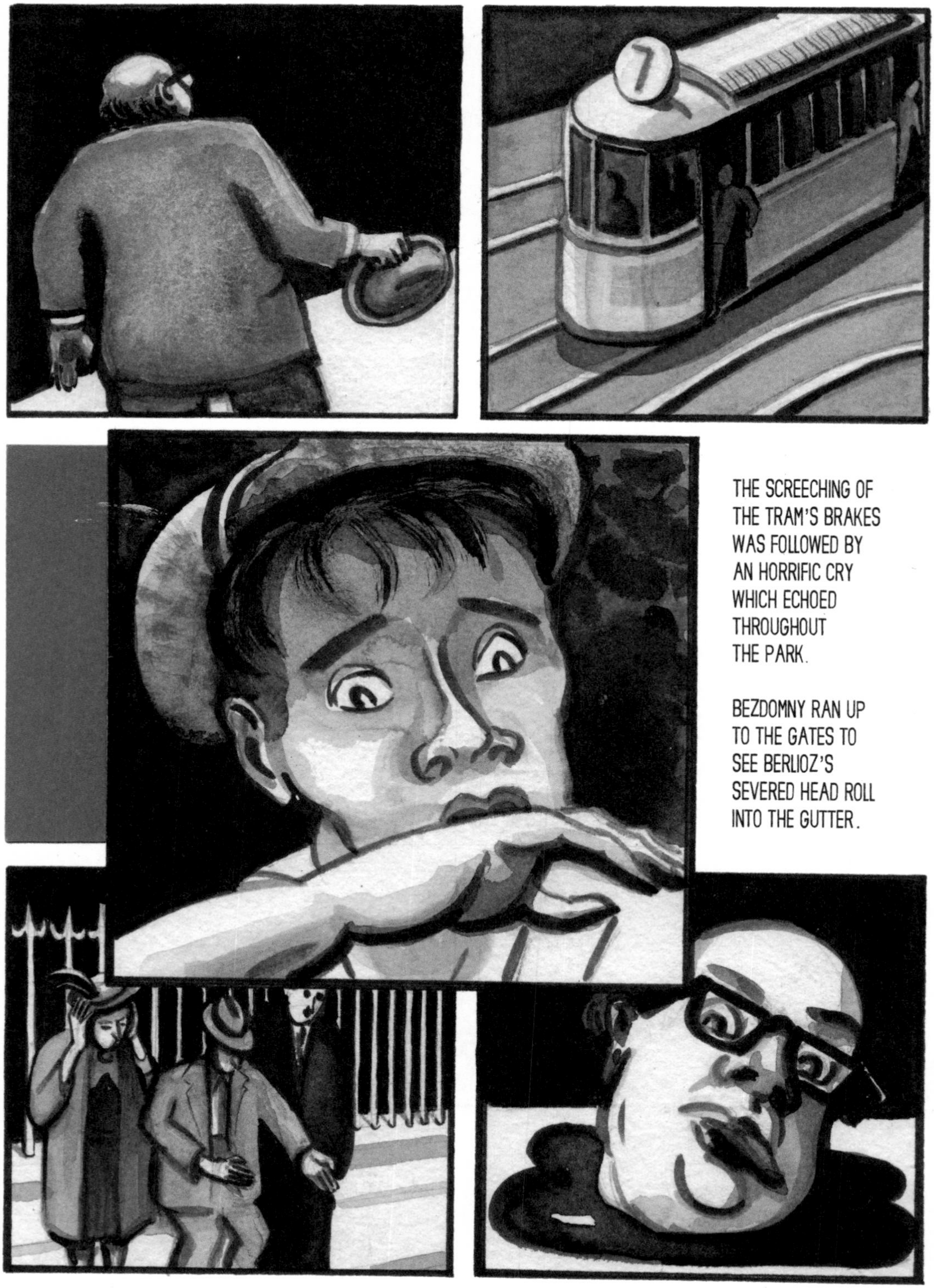
THE SCREECHING OF THE TRAM'S BRAKES WAS FOLLOWED BY AN HORRIFIC CRY WHICH ECHOED THROUGHOUT THE PARK.
BEZDOMNY RAN UP TO THE GATES TO SEE BERLIOZ'S SEVERED HEAD ROLL INTO THE GUTTER.

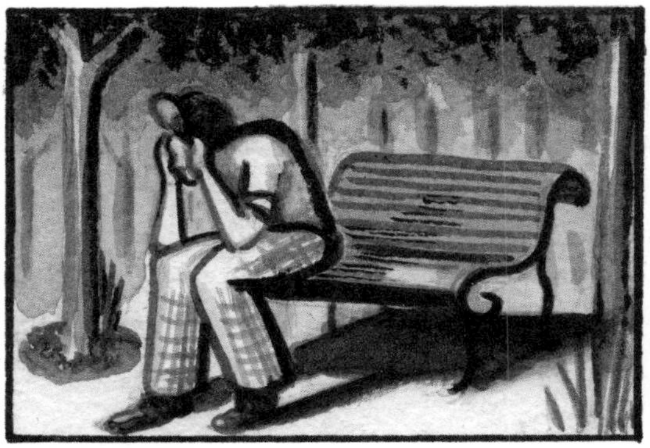

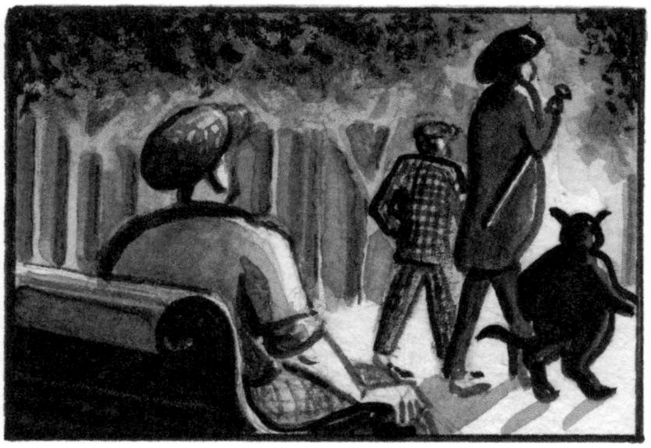

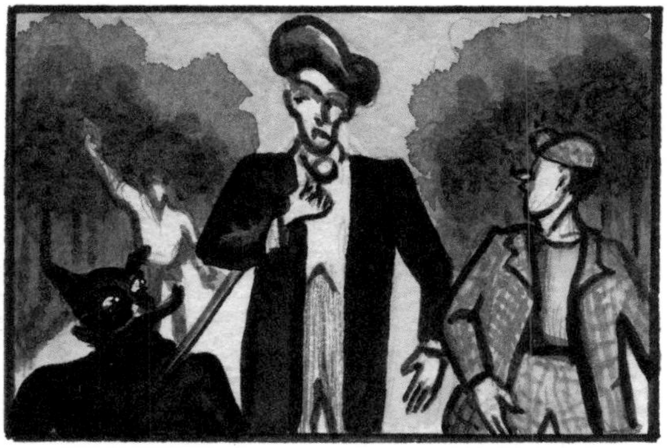

NOW THERE WERE THREE OF THEM; ALONGSIDE THE PROFESSOR AND HIS LANKY COMPANION, A CAT THE SIZE OF A PIG WAS STROKING HIS OFFICER'S MOUSTACHE.

THE POET GAVE CHASE AS THEY WALKED BRISKLY TOWARDS PATRIARCH'S STREET.

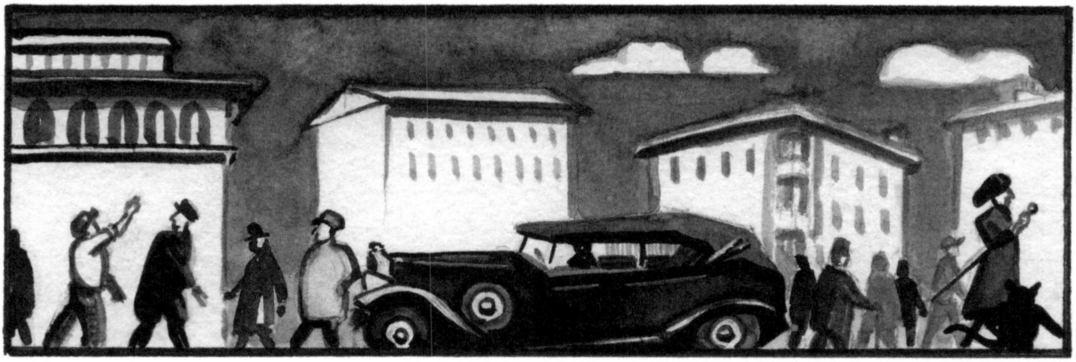

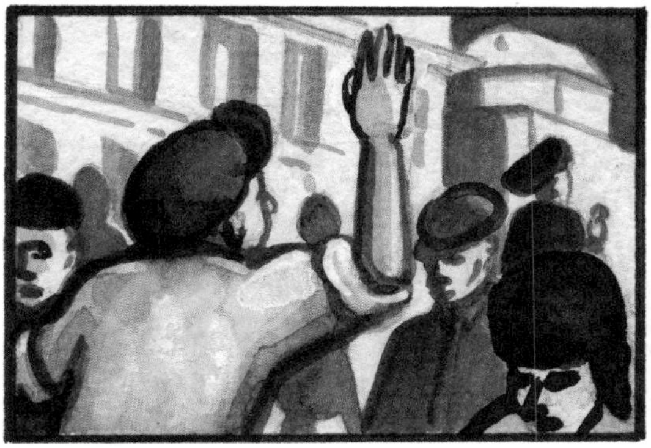

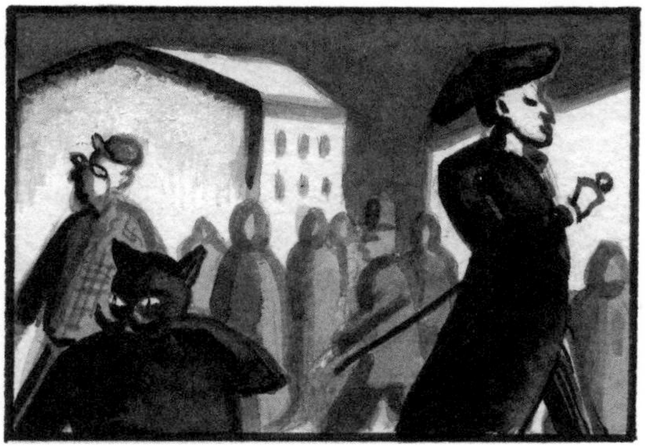

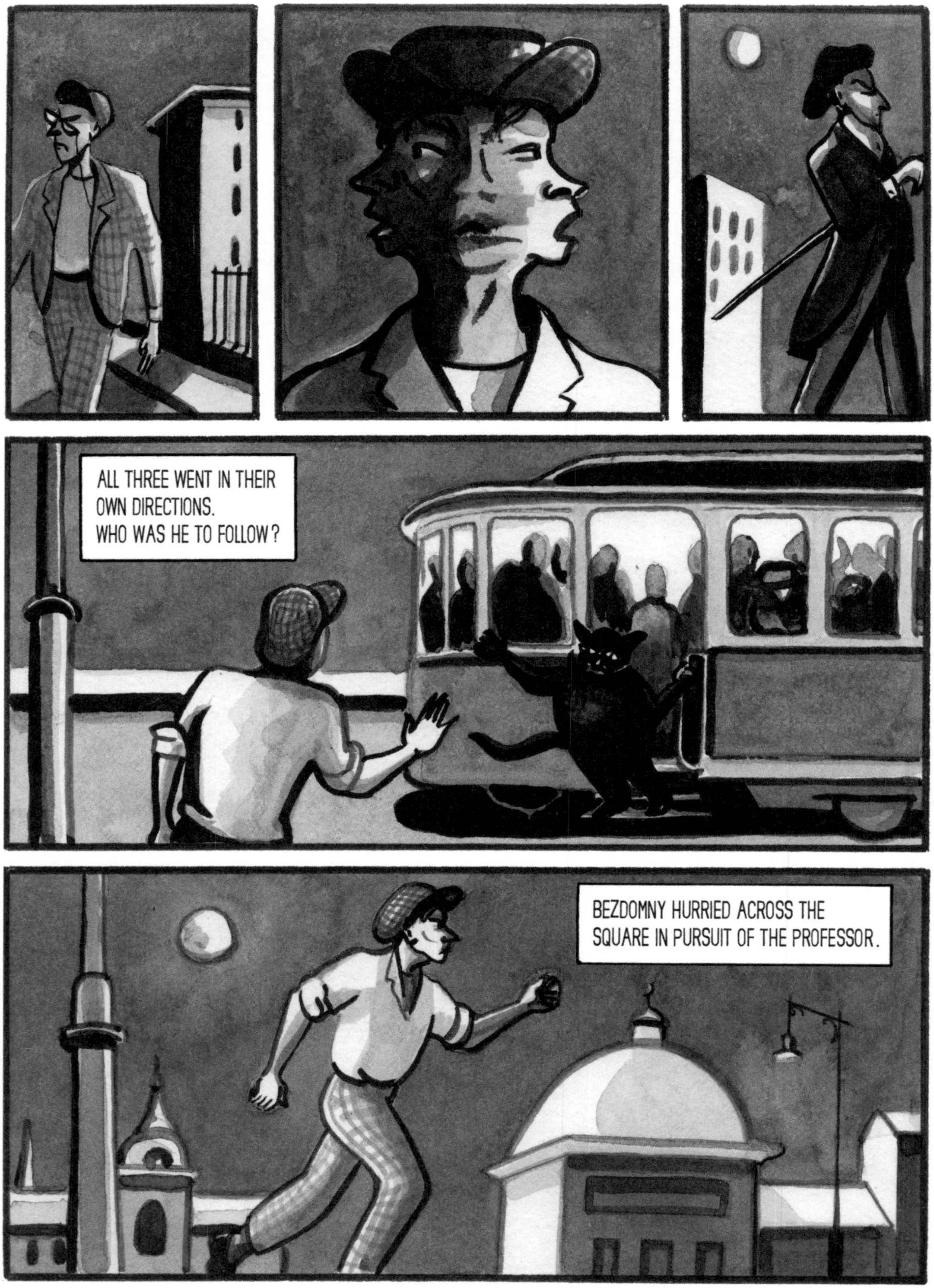
ALL THREE WENT IN THEIR OWN DIRECTIONS. WHO WAS HE TO FOLLOW?
BEZDOMNY HURRIED ACROSS THE SQUARE IN PURSUIT OF THE PROFESSOR.

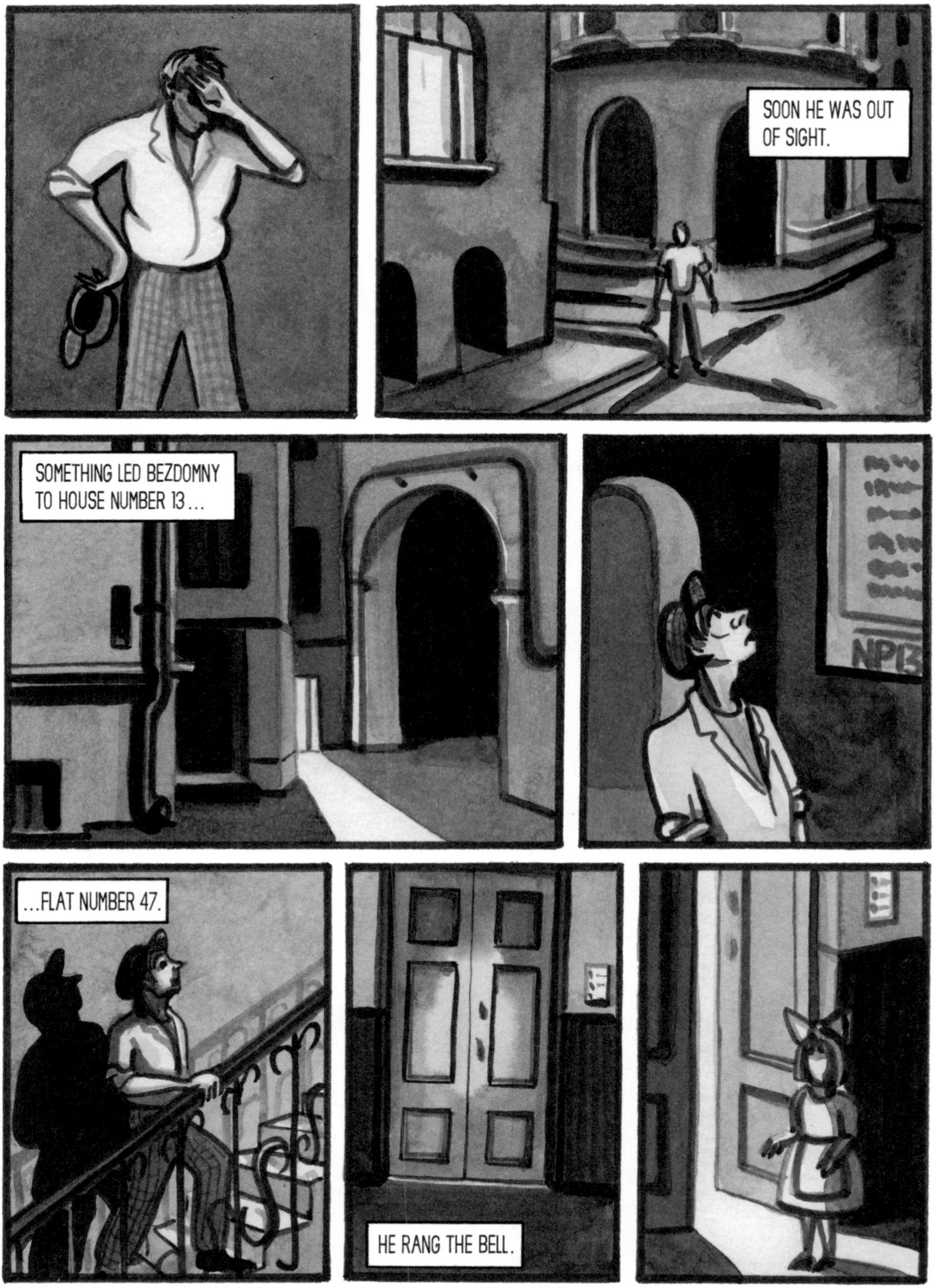
SOON HE WAS OUT OF SIGHT.
SOMETHING LED BEZDOMNY TO HOUSE NUMBER 13...
NP13
...FLAT NUMBER 47.
HE RANG THE BELL.

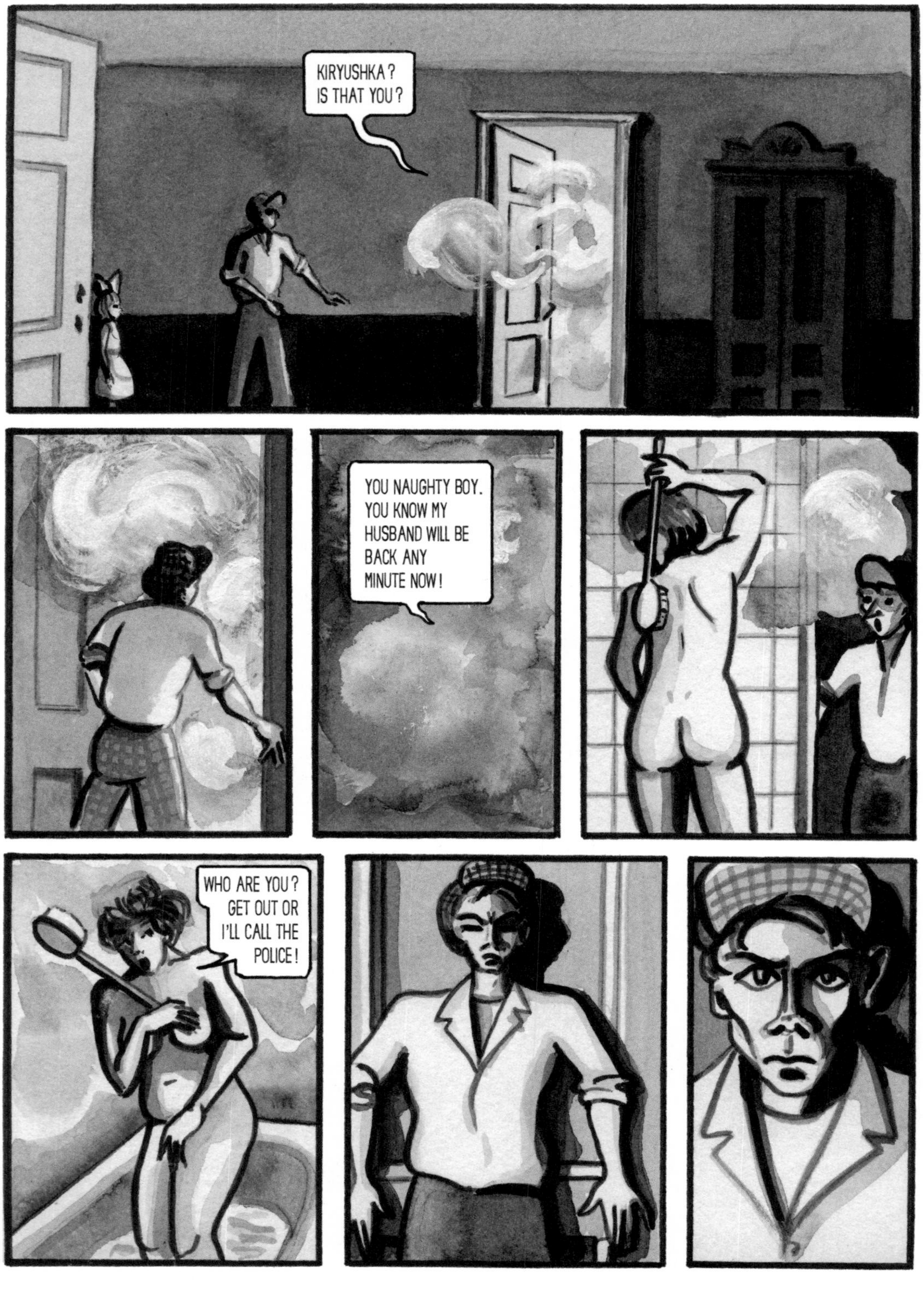
KIRYUSHKA? IS THAT YOU?
YOU NAUGHTY BOY. YOU KNOW MY HUSBAND WILL BE BACK ANY MINUTE NOW!
WHO ARE YOU? GET OUT OR I'LL CALL THE POLICE!

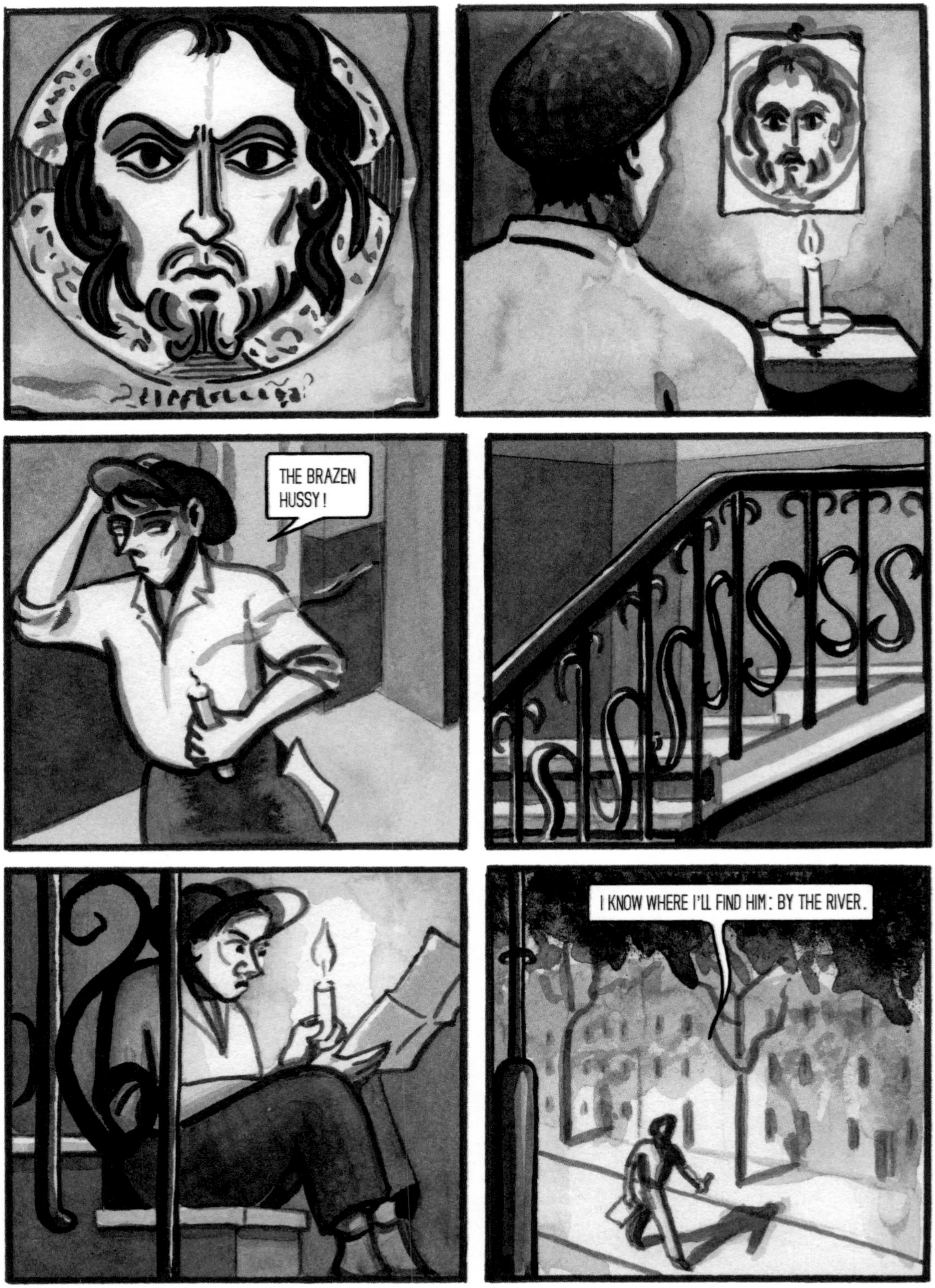
THE BRAZEN HUSSY!
I KNOW WHERE I'LL FIND HIM: BY THE RIVER.

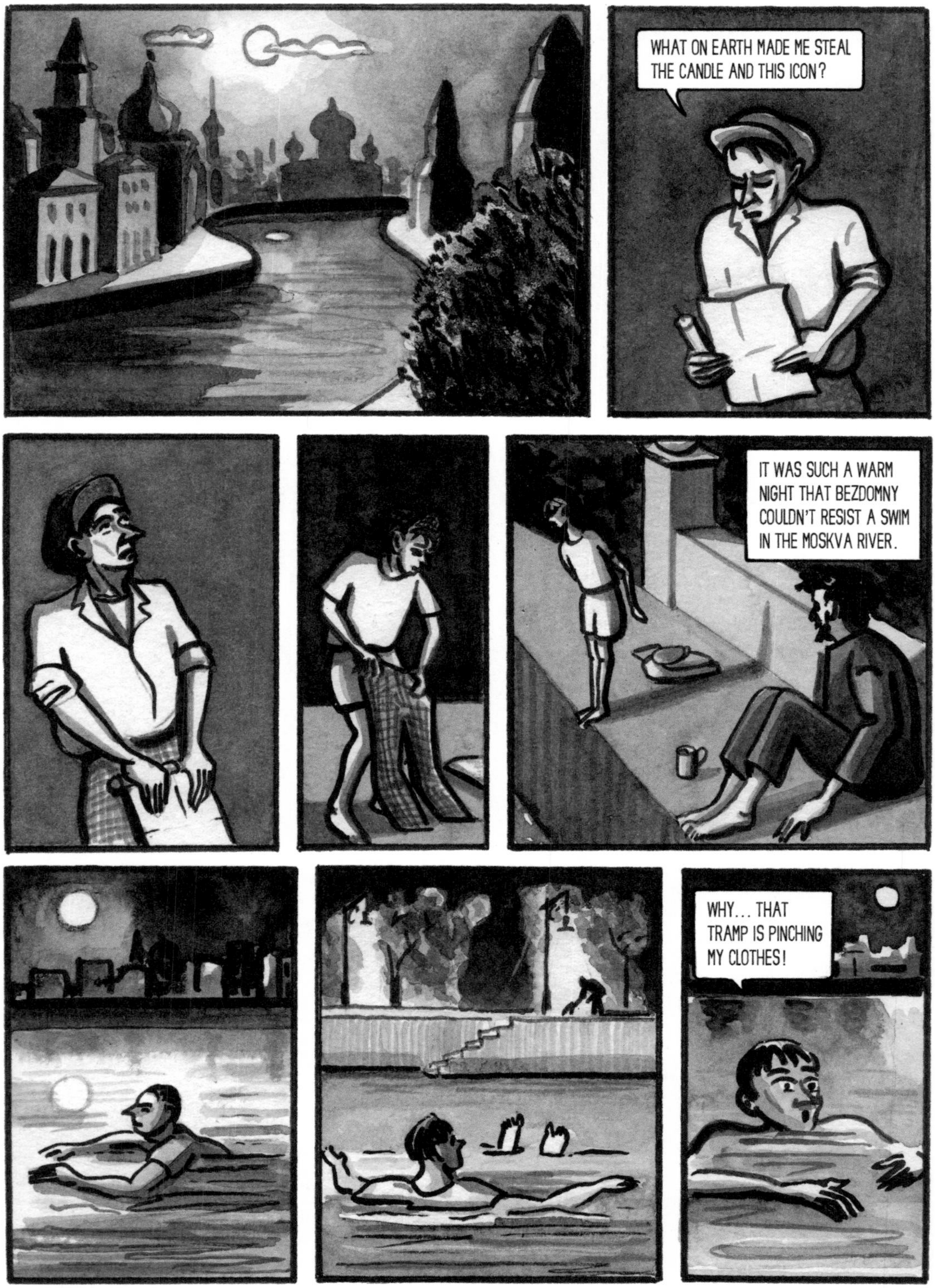
WHAT ON EARTH MADE ME STEAL THE CANDLE AND THIS ICON?
IT WAS SUCH A WARM NIGHT THAT BEZDOMNY COULDN'T RESIST A SWIM IN THE MOSKVA RIVER.
WHY... THAT TRAMP IS PINCHING MY CLOTHES!

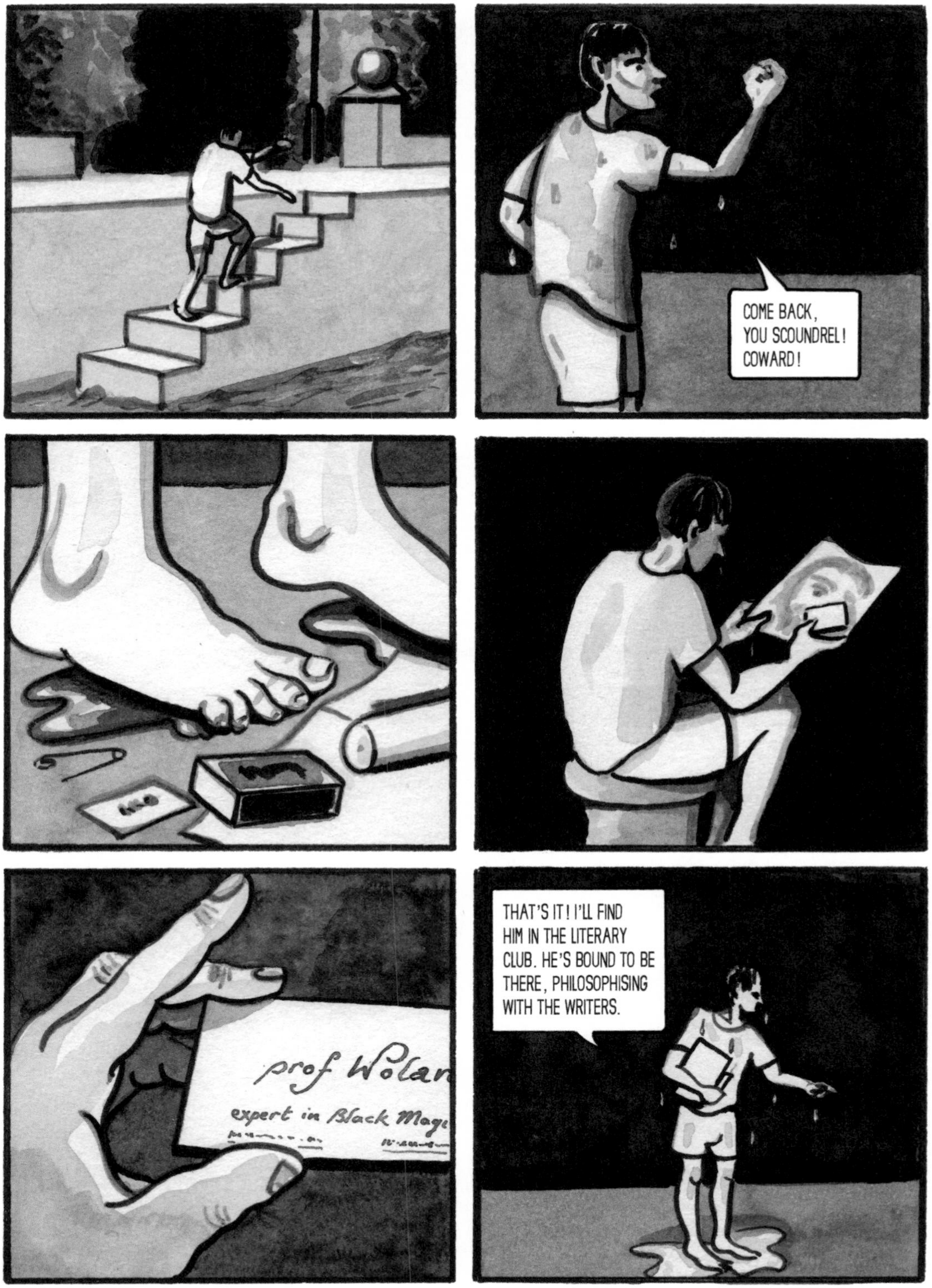
COME BACK,
YOU SCOUNDREL!
COWARD!
prof Wolan
expert in Black Mag
THAT'S IT! I'LL FIND HIM IN THE LITERARY CLUB. HE'S BOUND TO BE THERE, PHILOSOPHISING WITH THE WRITERS.

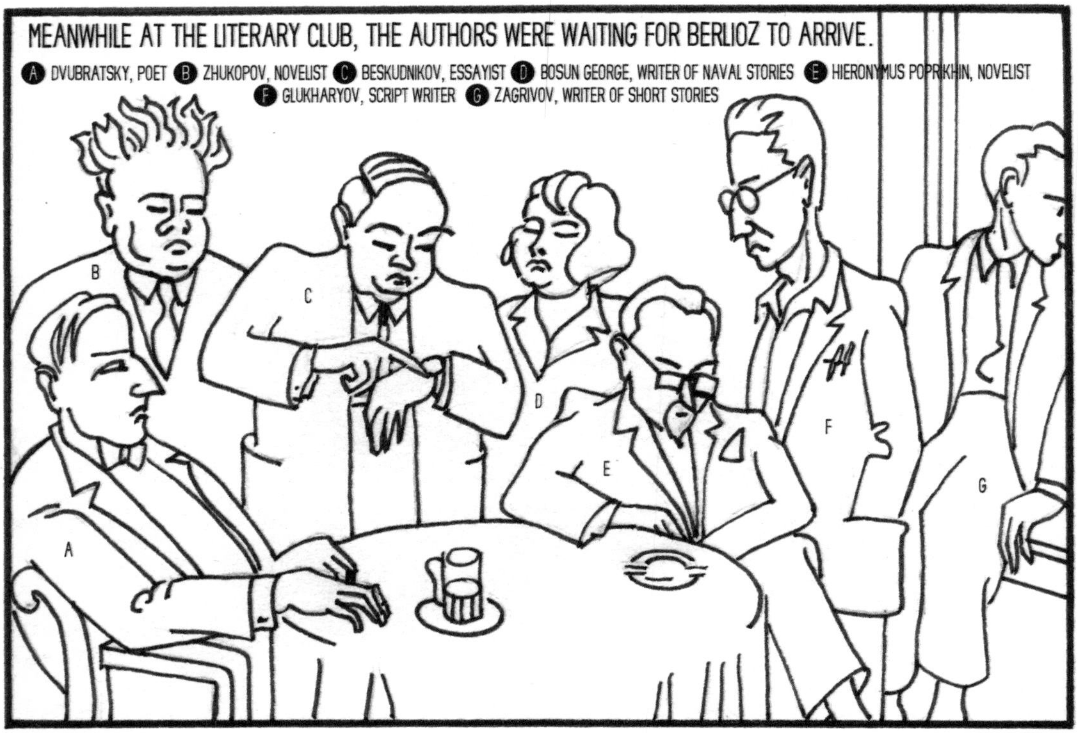
MEANWHILE AT THE LITERARY CLUB, THE AUTHORS WERE WAITING FOR BERLIOZ TO ARRIVE.
A DVUBRATSKY, POET B ZHUKOPOV, NOVELIST C BESKUDNIKOV, ESSAYIST D BOSUN GEORGE, WRITER OF NAVAL STORIES E HIERONYMUS POPRIKHIN, NOVELIST
F GLUKHARYOV, SCRIPT WRITER G ZAGRIVOV, WRITER OF SHORT STORIES
B
C
D
F
E
A
G

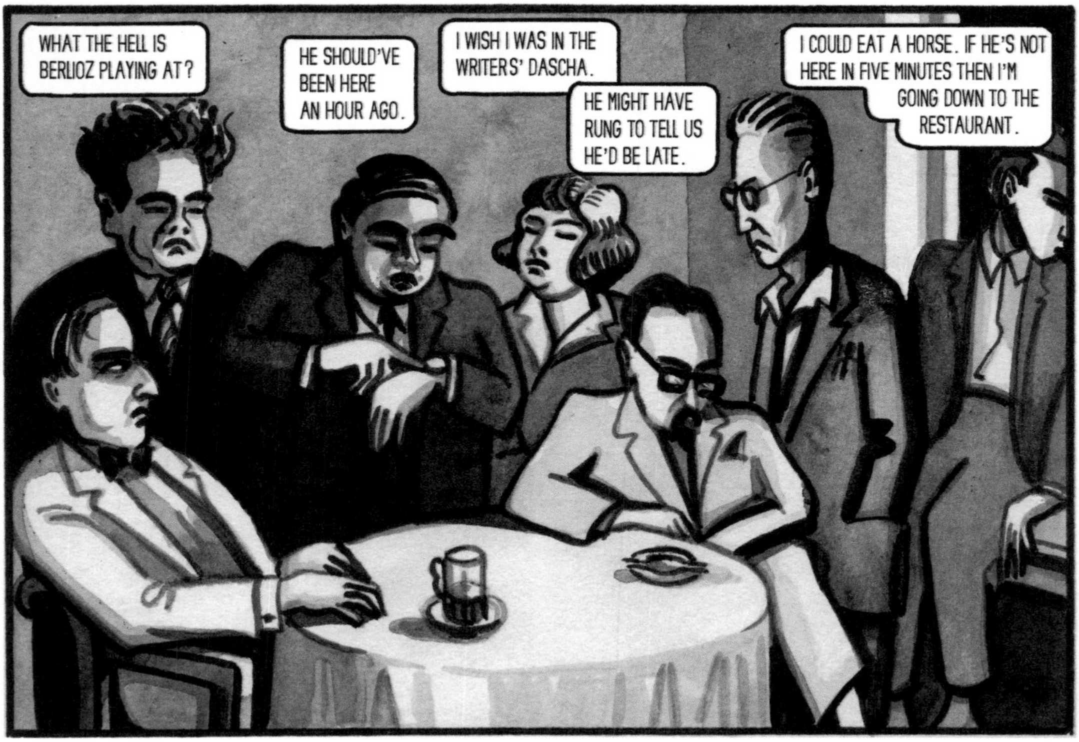
WHAT THE HELL IS BERLIOZ PLAYING AT?
HE SHOULD'VE BEEN HERE AN HOUR AGO.
I WISH I WAS IN THE WRITERS' DASCHA.
HE MIGHT HAVE RUNG TO TELL US HE'D BE LATE.
I COULD EAT A HORSE. IF HE'S NOT HERE IN FIVE MINUTES THEN I'M GOING DOWN TO THE RESTAURANT.

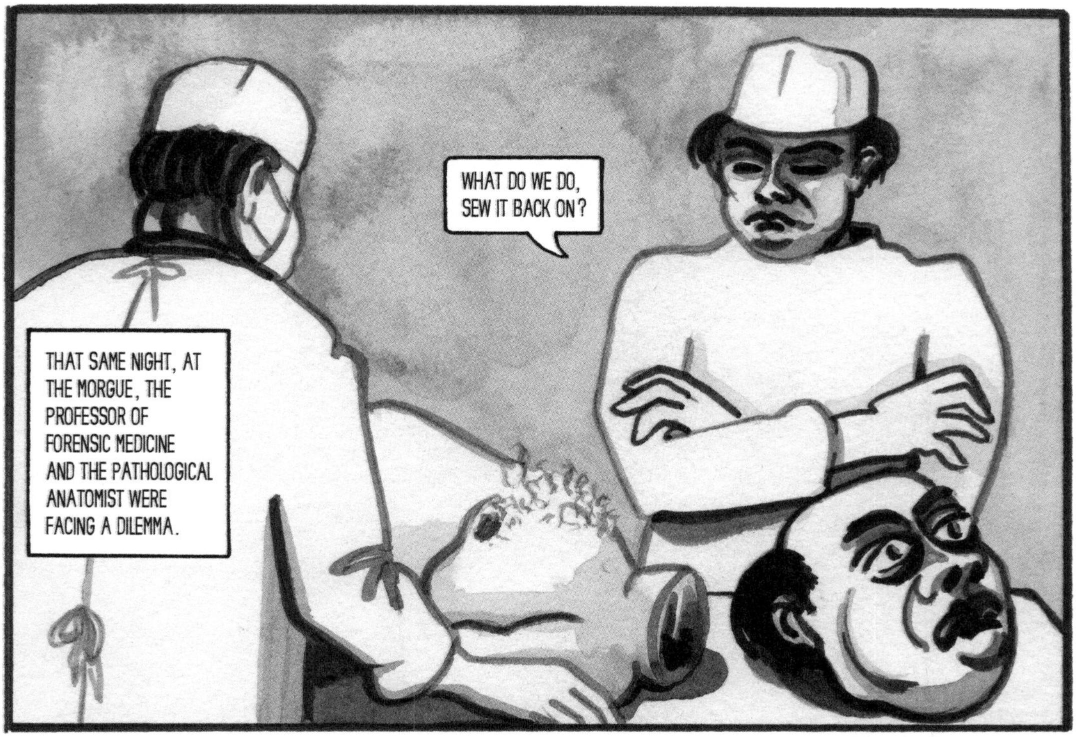
WHAT DO WE DO, SEW IT BACK ON?
THAT SAME NIGHT, AT THE MORGUE, THE PROFESSOR OF FORENSIC MEDICINE AND THE PATHOLOGICAL ANATOMIST WERE FACING A DILEMMA.

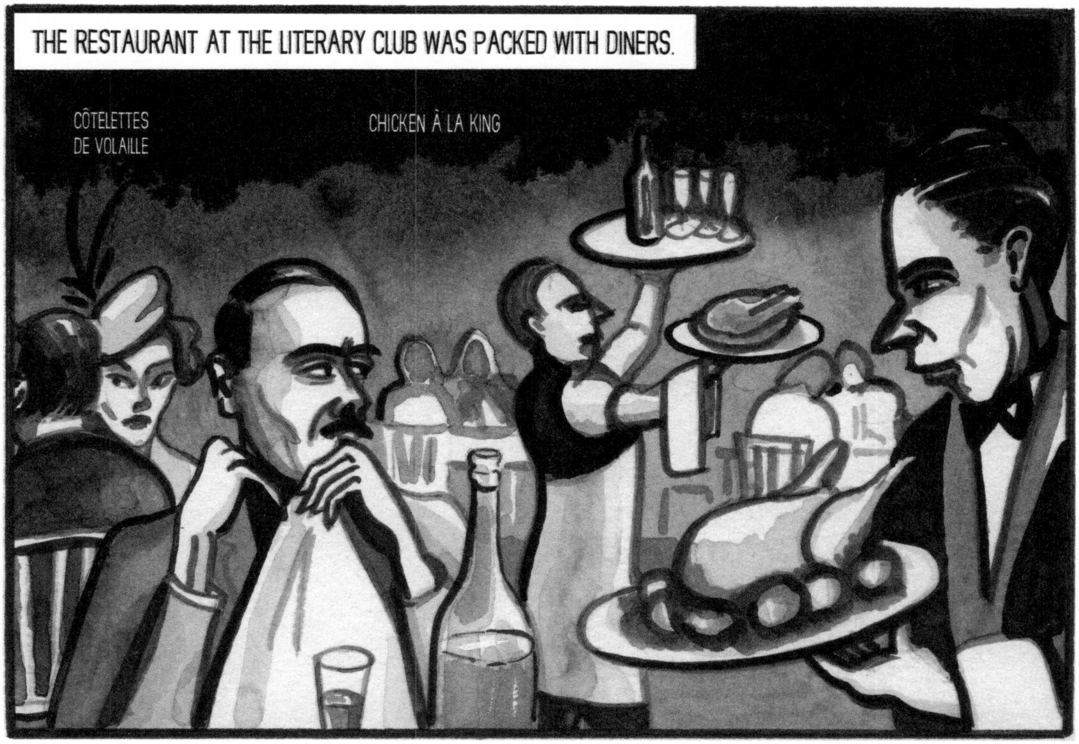
THE RESTAURANT AT THE LITERARY CLUB WAS PACKED WITH DINERS.
CÔTELETTES DE VOLAILLE
CHICKEN À LA KING

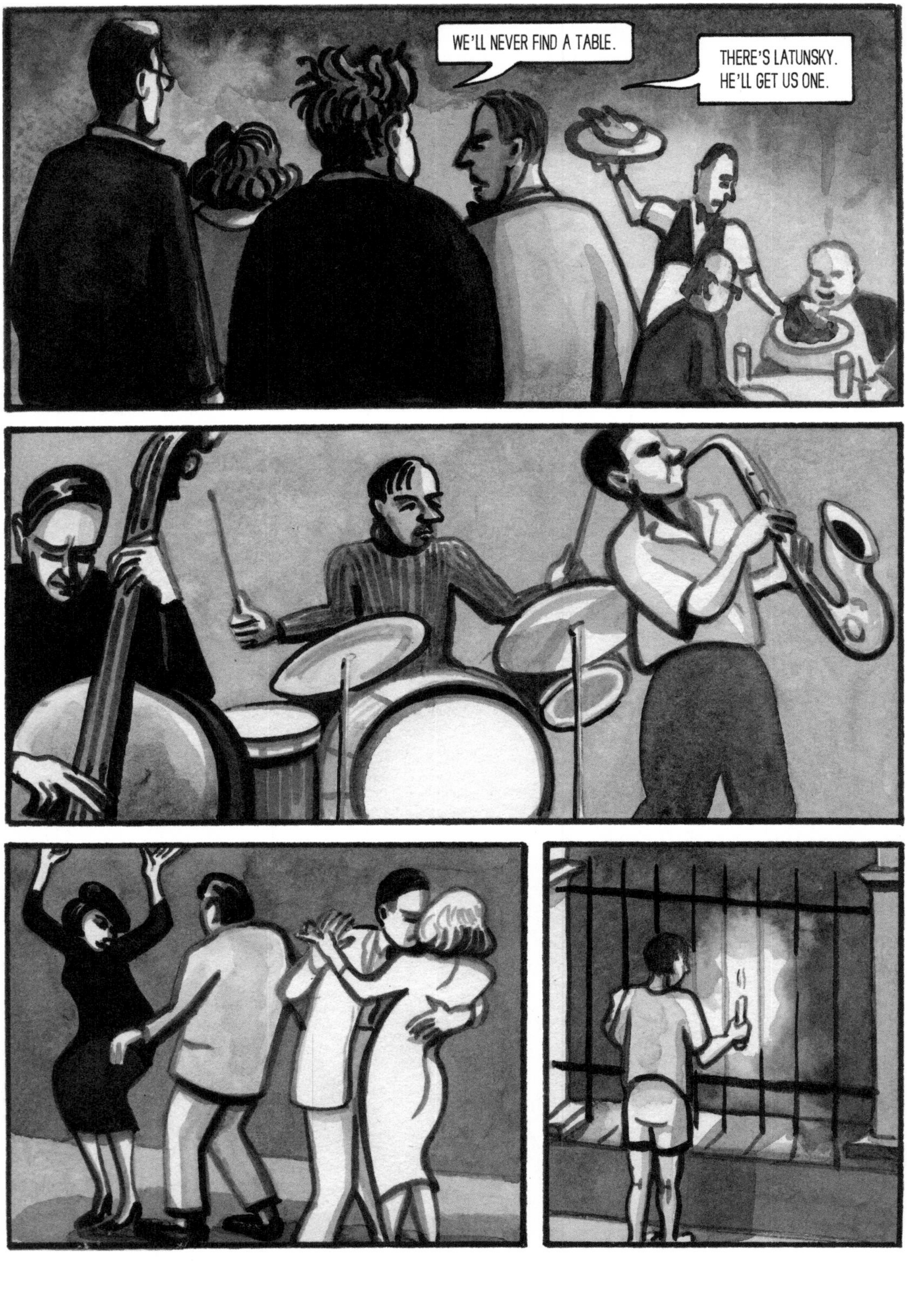
WE'LL NEVER FIND A TABLE.
THERE'S LATUNSKY. HE'LL GET US ONE.

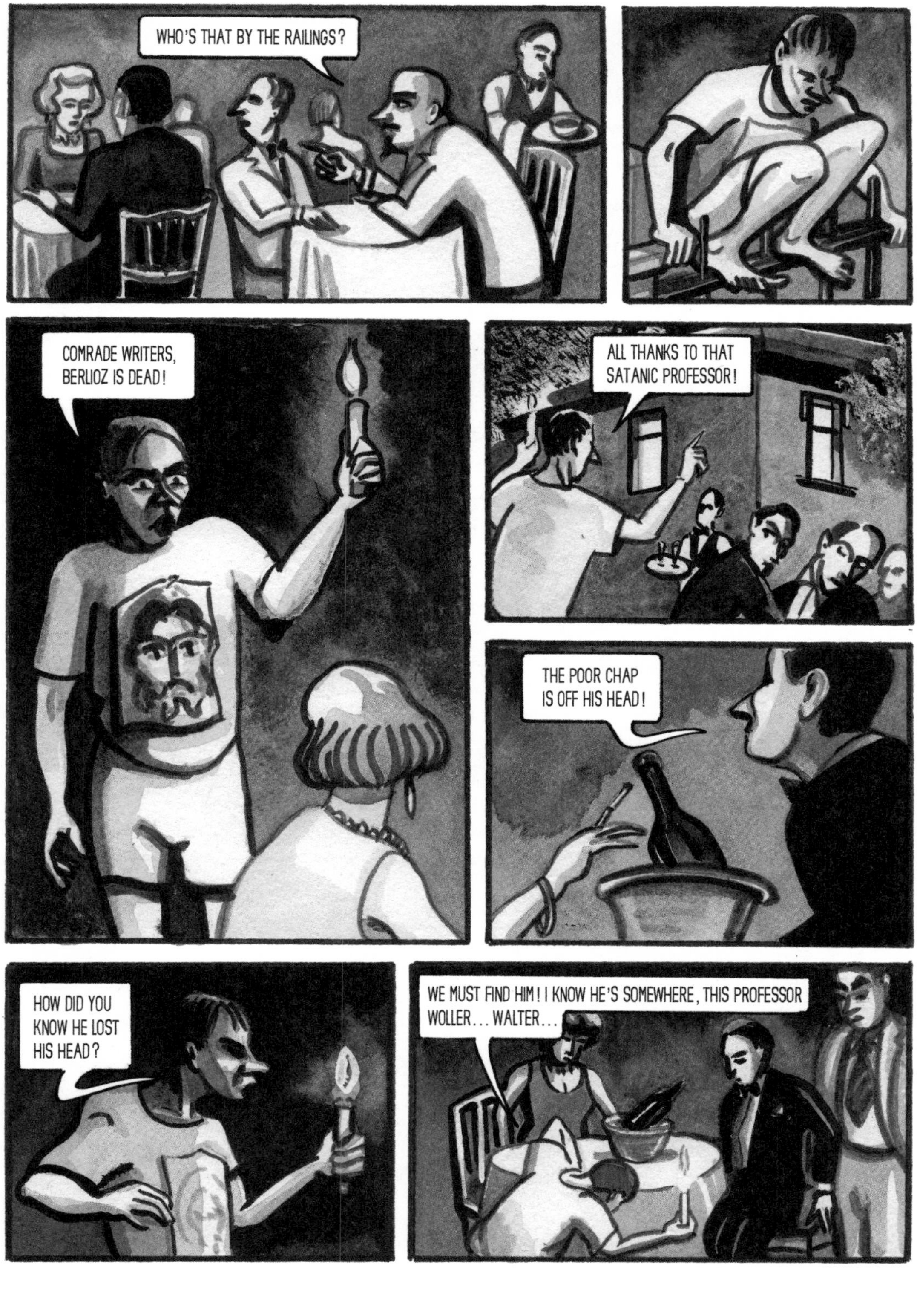
WHO'S THAT BY THE RAILINGS?
COMRADE WRITERS, BERLIOZ IS DEAD!
ALL THANKS TO THAT SATANIC PROFESSOR!
THE POOR CHAP IS OFF HIS HEAD!
HOW DID YOU KNOW HE LOST HIS HEAD?
WE MUST FIND HIM! I KNOW HE'S SOMEWHERE, THIS PROFESSOR WOLLER... WALTER...

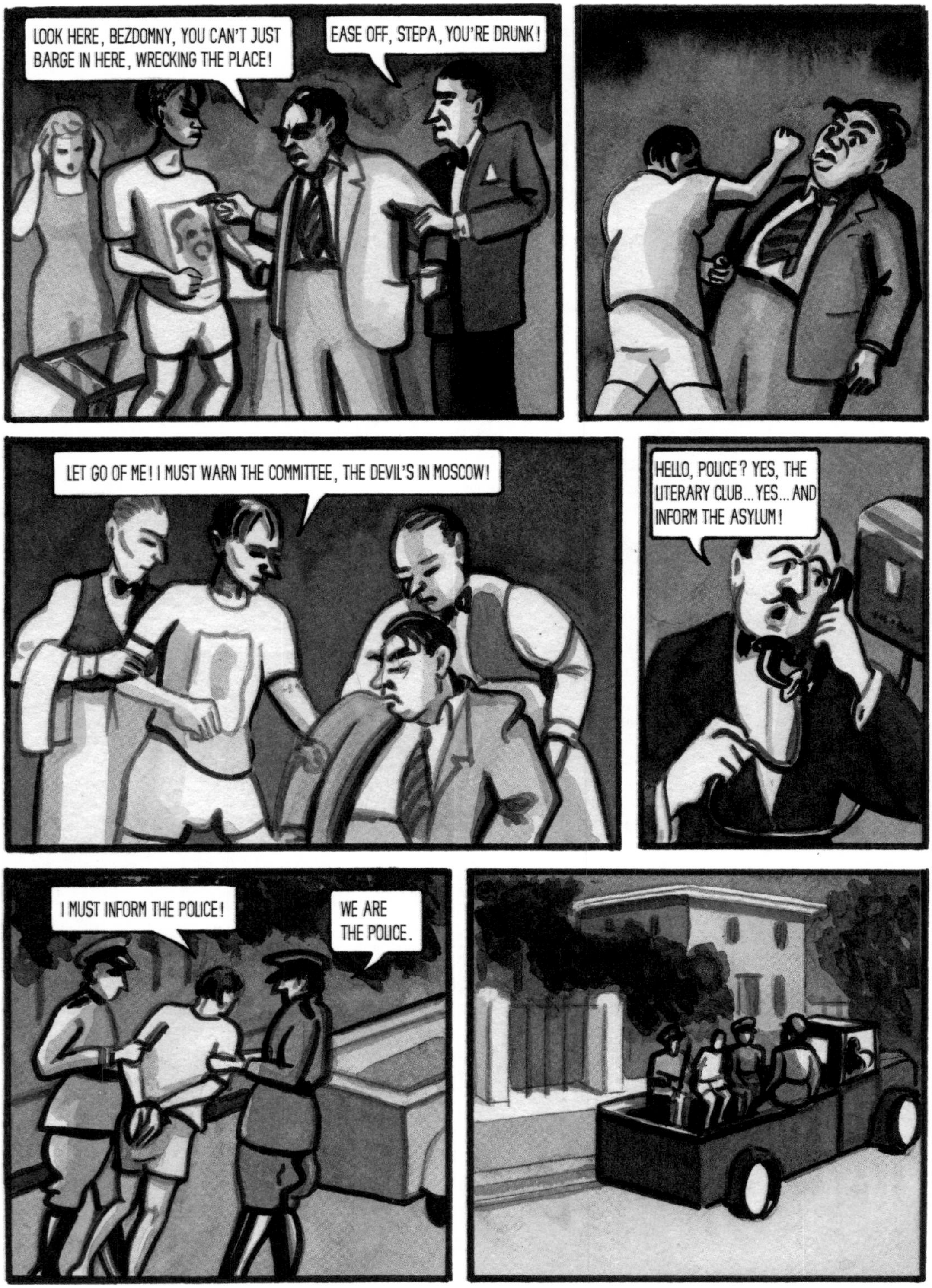
LOOK HERE, BEZDOMNY, YOU CAN'T JUST BARGE IN HERE, WRECKING THE PLACE!
EASE OFF, STEPA, YOU'RE DRUNK!
LET GO OF ME! I MUST WARN THE COMMITTEE, THE DEVIL'S IN MOSCOW!
HELLO, POLICE? YES, THE LITERARY CLUB... YES... AND INFORM THE ASYLUM!
I MUST INFORM THE POLICE!
WE ARE THE POLICE.

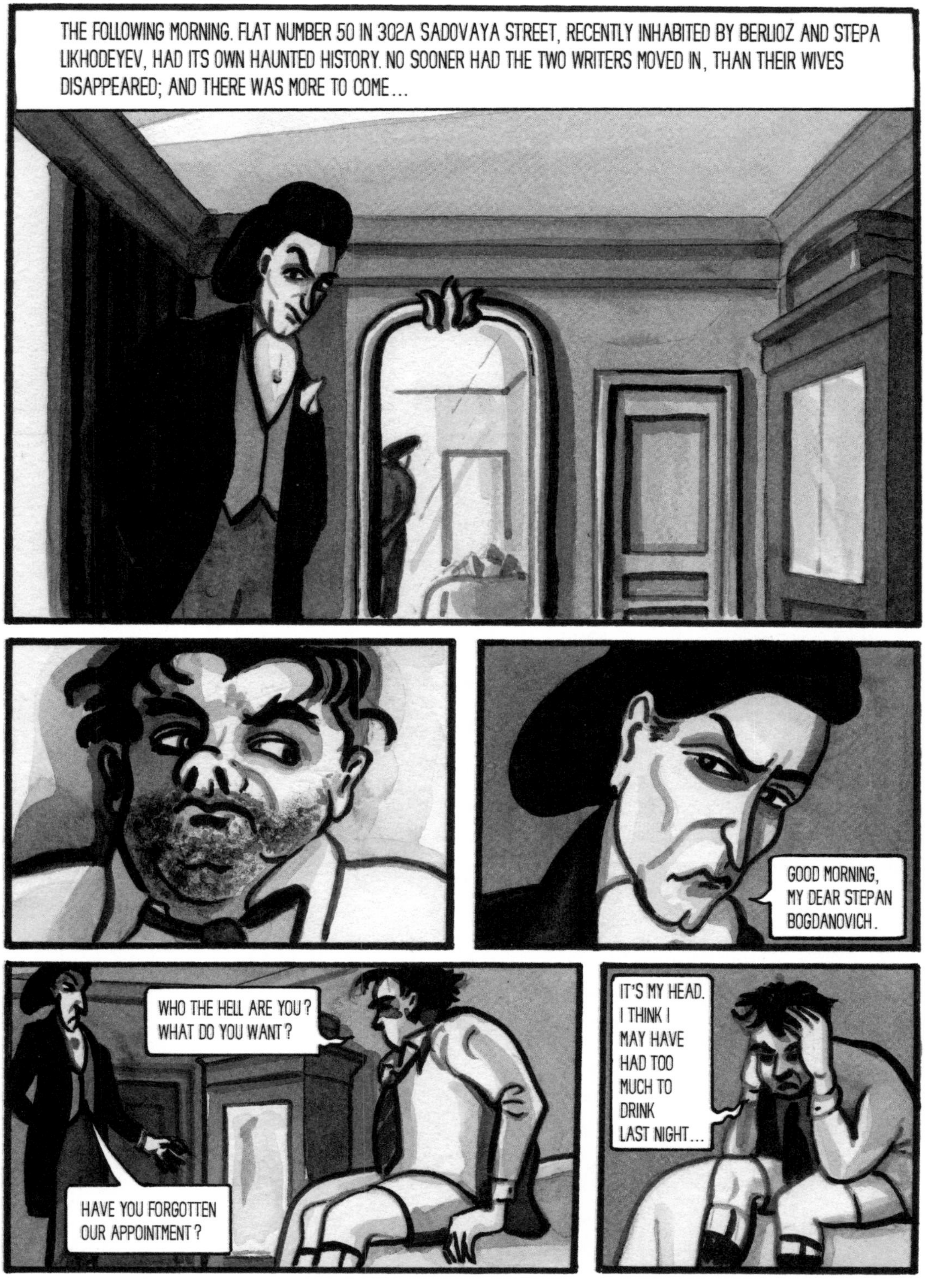
THE FOLLOWING MORNING. FLAT NUMBER 50 IN 302A SADOVAYA STREET, RECENTLY INHABITED BY BERLIOZ AND STEPA LIKHODEYEV, HAD ITS OWN HAUNTED HISTORY. NO SOONER HAD THE TWO WRITERS MOVED IN, THAN THEIR WIVES DISAPPEARED; AND THERE WAS MORE TO COME...
GOOD MORNING, MY DEAR STEPAN BOGDANOVICH.
WHO THE HELL ARE YOU? WHAT DO YOU WANT?
HAVE YOU FORGOTTEN OUR APPOINTMENT?
IT'S MY HEAD. I THINK I MAY HAVE HAD TOO MUCH TO DRINK LAST NIGHT...

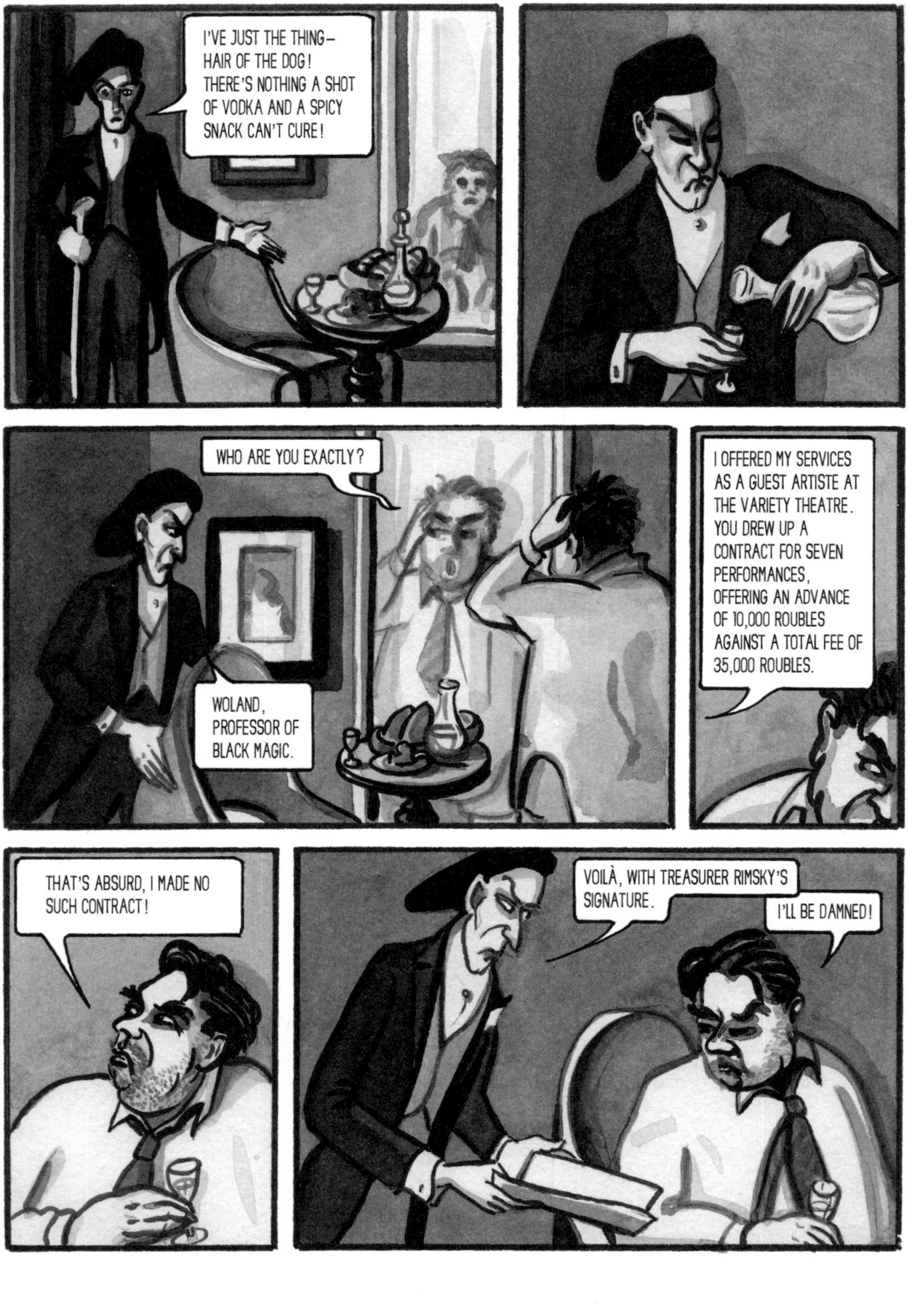
I'VE JUST THE THING—
HAIR OF THE DOG! THERE'S NOTHING A SHOT OF VODKA AND A SPICY SNACK CAN'T CURE!
WHO ARE YOU EXACTLY?
WOLAND, PROFESSOR OF BLACK MAGIC.
I OFFERED MY SERVICES AS A GUEST ARTISTE AT THE VARIETY THEATRE. YOU DREW UP A CONTRACT FOR SEVEN PERFORMANCES, OFFERING AN ADVANCE OF 10,000 ROUBLES AGAINST A TOTAL FEE OF 35,000 ROUBLES.
THAT'S ABSURD, I MADE NO SUCH CONTRACT!
VOILÀ, WITH TREASURER RIMSKY'S SIGNATURE.
I'LL BE DAMNED!

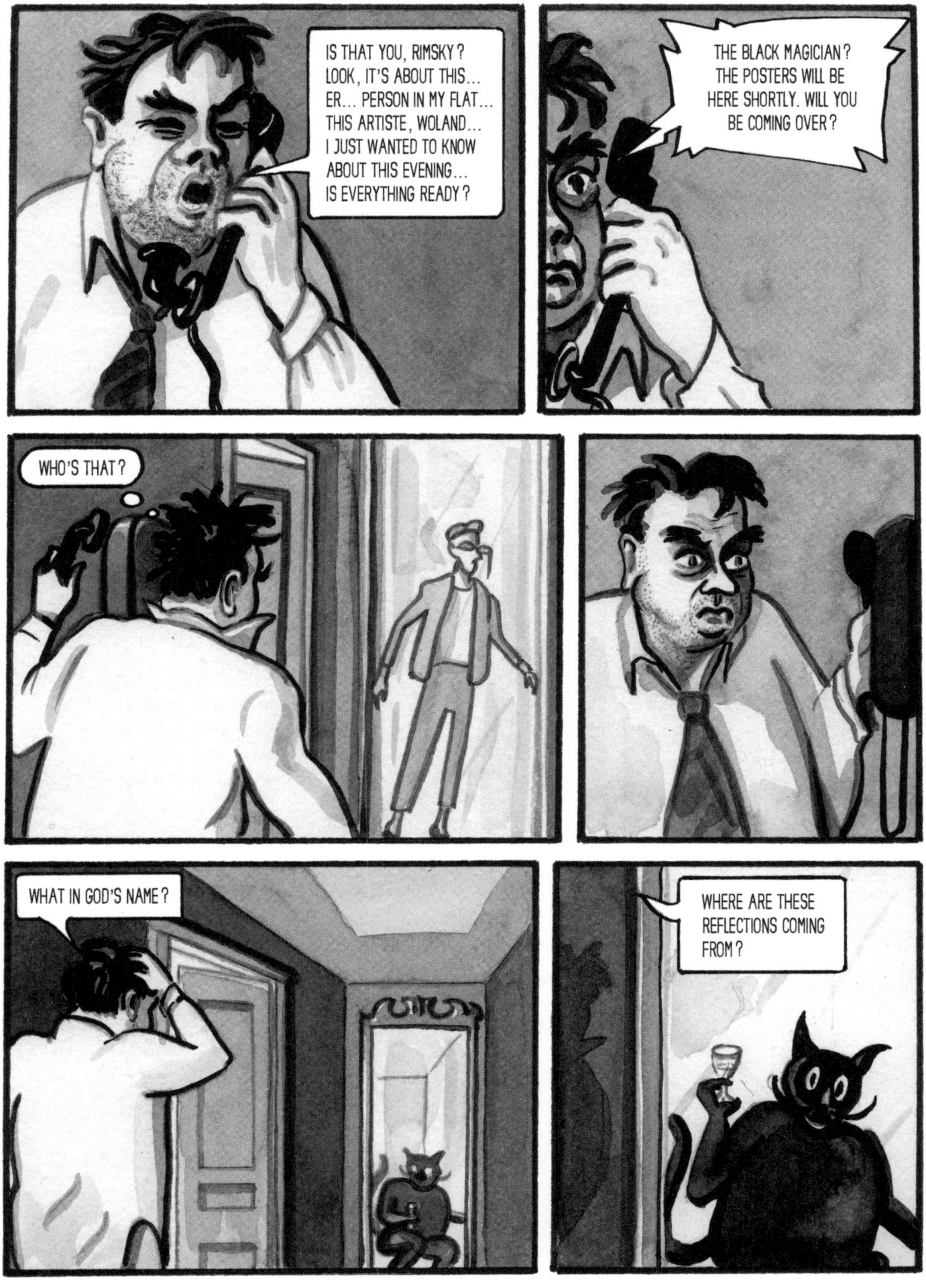
IS THAT YOU, RIMSKY? LOOK, IT'S ABOUT THIS... ER... PERSON IN MY FLAT... THIS ARTISTE, WOLAND... I JUST WANTED TO KNOW ABOUT THIS EVENING... IS EVERYTHING READY?
THE BLACK MAGICIAN? THE POSTERS WILL BE HERE SHORTLY. WILL YOU BE COMING OVER?
WHO'S THAT?
WHAT IN GOD'S NAME?
WHERE ARE THESE REFLECTIONS COMING FROM?

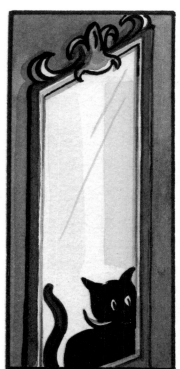

DON'T BE NERVOUS, THE CAT IS MINE.

REST ASSURED, THEY ARE MY ASSISTANTS.

AND MY ASSISTANTS NEED A PLACE TO STAY, SO IT SEEMS THAT ONE PERSON IN THIS FLAT IS SUPERFLUOUS.

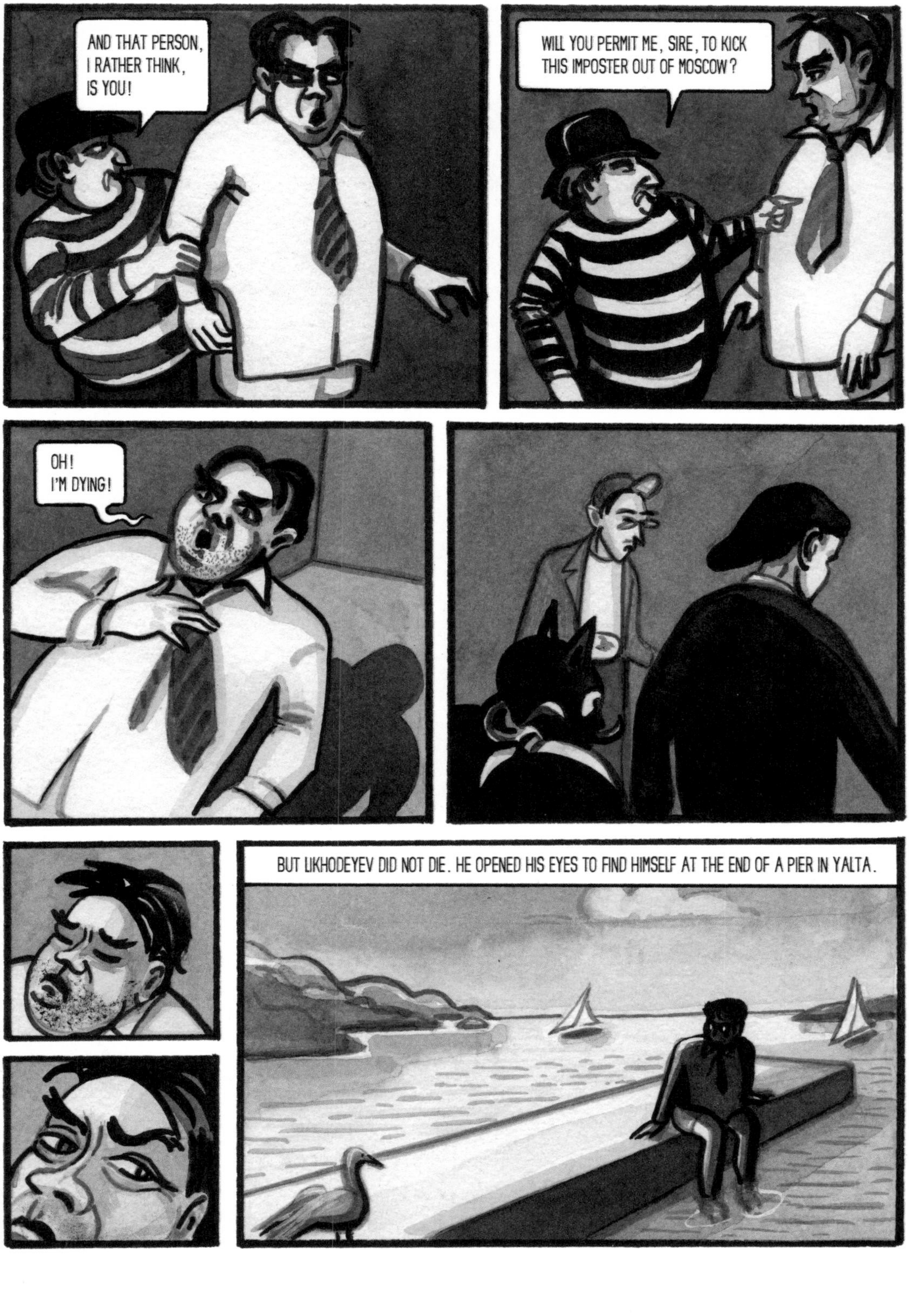
AND THAT PERSON, I RATHER THINK, IS YOU!
WILL YOU PERMIT ME, SIRE, TO KICK THIS IMPOSTER OUT OF MOSCOW?
OH! I'M DYING!
BUT LIKHODEYEV DID NOT DIE. HE OPENED HIS EYES TO FIND HIMSELF AT THE END OF A PIER IN YALTA.

THE LUNATIC ASYLUM
ON THE OUTSKIRTS OF MOSCOW.

SO, WHERE IS THE NEWCOMER?

THIS WAY, DOCTOR.

HOW DO YOU DO?
MY NAME IS
DOCTOR
STRAVINSKY.

HE'S SO
DIGNIFIED.
JUST LIKE
PONTIUS
PILATE.

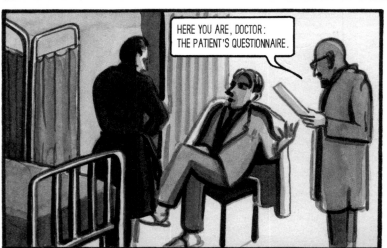

HERE YOU ARE, DOCTOR:
THE PATIENT'S QUESTIONNAIRE.

DELIRIUM TREMENS,
SCHIZOPHRENIA.

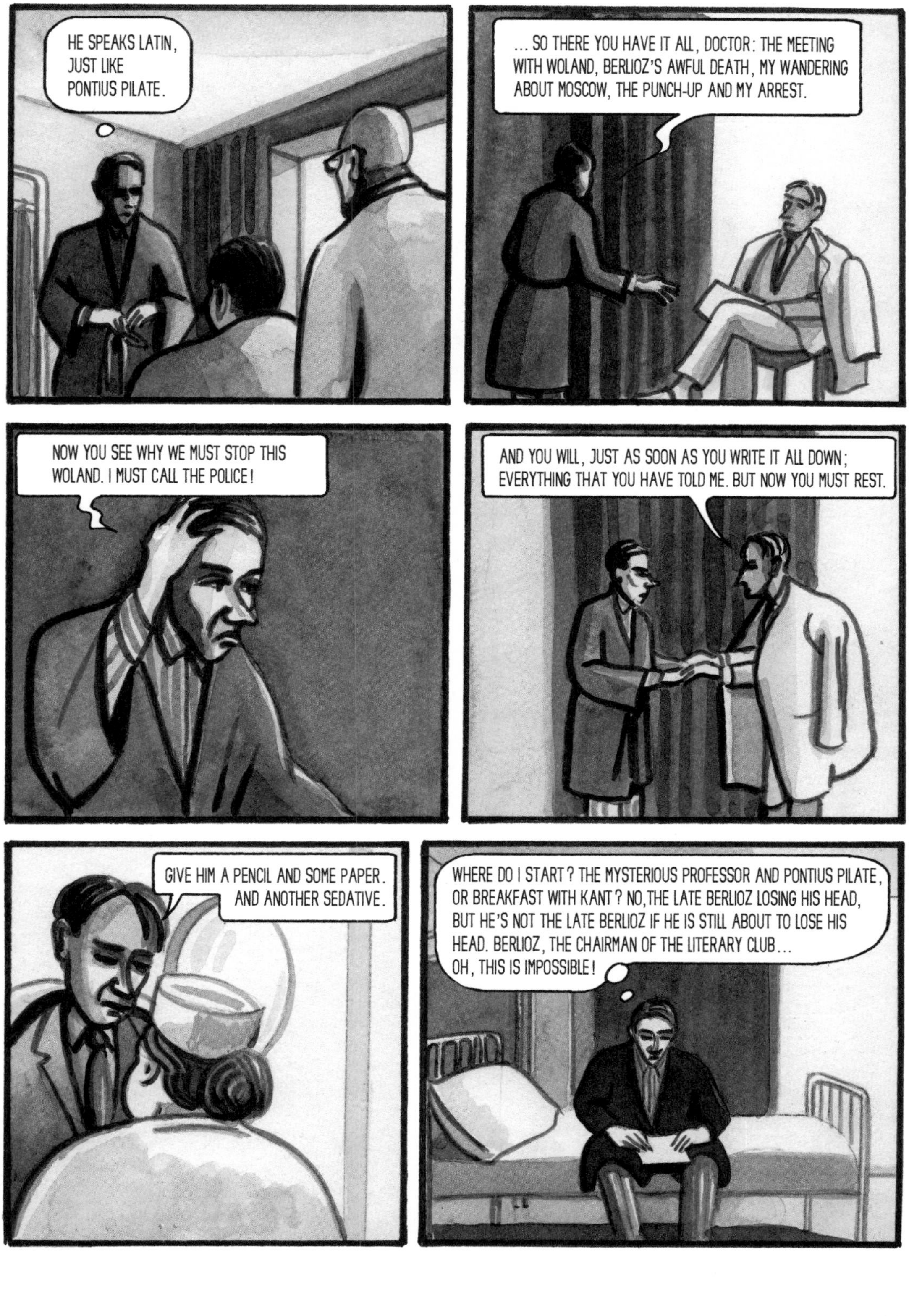
HE SPEAKS LATIN, JUST LIKE PONTIUS PILATE.
... SO THERE YOU HAVE IT ALL, DOCTOR: THE MEETING WITH WOLAND, BERLIOZ'S AWFUL DEATH, MY WANDERING ABOUT MOSCOW, THE PUNCH-UP AND MY ARREST.
NOW YOU SEE WHY WE MUST STOP THIS WOLAND. I MUST CALL THE POLICE!
AND YOU WILL, JUST AS SOON AS YOU WRITE IT ALL DOWN; EVERYTHING THAT YOU HAVE TOLD ME. BUT NOW YOU MUST REST.
GIVE HIM A PENCIL AND SOME PAPER. AND ANOTHER SEDATIVE.
WHERE DO I START? THE MYSTERIOUS PROFESSOR AND PONTIUS PILATE, OR BREAKFAST WITH KANT? NO, THE LATE BERLIOZ LOSING HIS HEAD, BUT HE'S NOT THE LATE BERLIOZ IF HE IS STILL ABOUT TO LOSE HIS HEAD. BERLIOZ, THE CHAIRMAN OF THE LITERARY CLUB... OH, THIS IS IMPOSSIBLE!

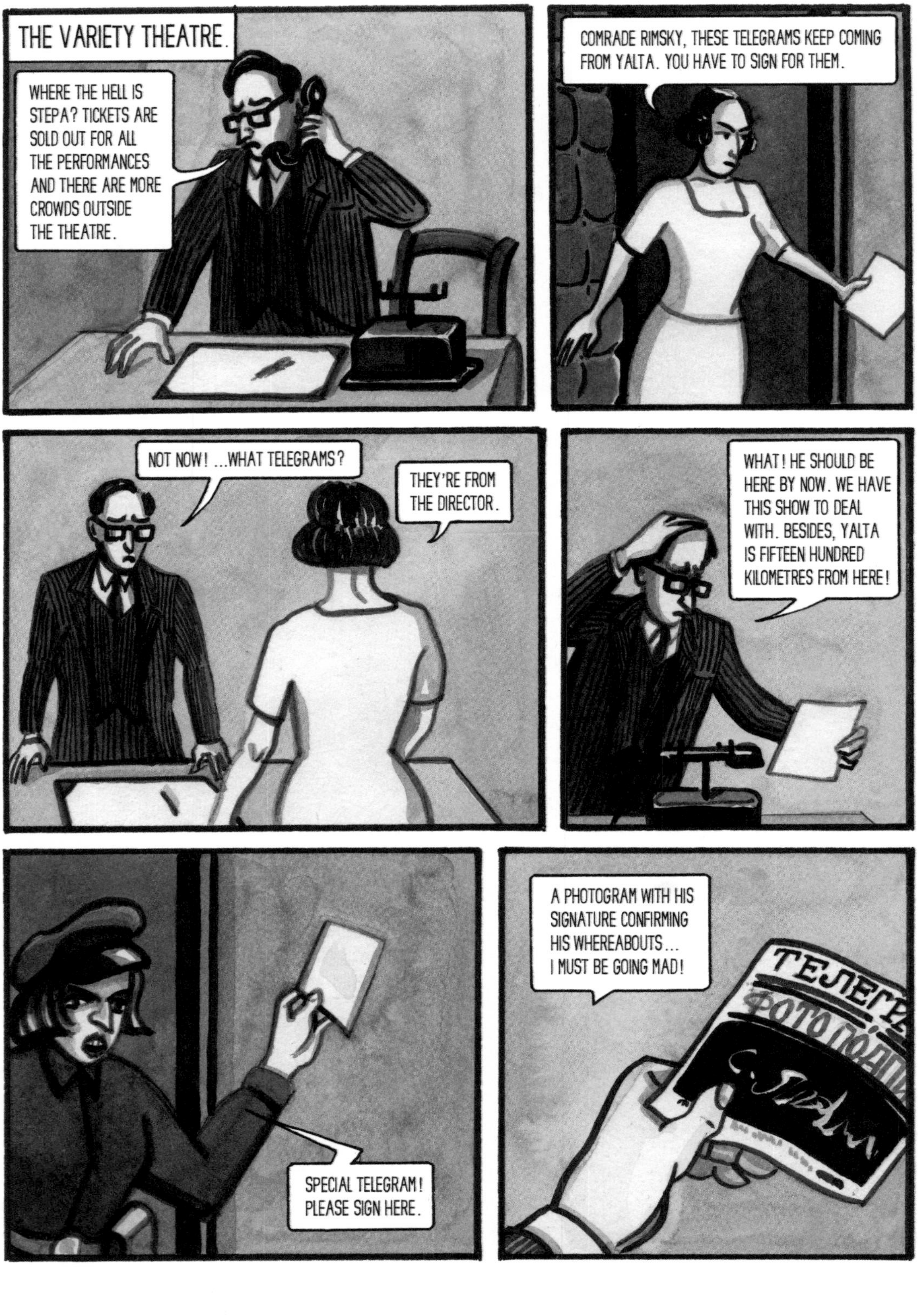
THE VARIETY THEATRE.
WHERE THE HELL IS STEPA? TICKETS ARE SOLD OUT FOR ALL THE PERFORMANCES AND THERE ARE MORE CROWDS OUTSIDE THE THEATRE.
COMRADE RIMSKY, THESE TELEGRAMS KEEP COMING FROM YALTA. YOU HAVE TO SIGN FOR THEM.
NOT NOW! ...WHAT TELEGRAMS?
THEY'RE FROM THE DIRECTOR.
WHAT! HE SHOULD BE HERE BY NOW. WE HAVE THIS SHOW TO DEAL WITH. BESIDES, YALTA IS FIFTEEN HUNDRED KILOMETRES FROM HERE!
SPECIAL TELEGRAM! PLEASE SIGN HERE.
A PHOTOGRAM WITH HIS SIGNATURE CONFIRMING HIS WHEREABOUTS... I MUST BE GOING MAD!
ТЕЛЕГР
ФОТО ПОДП

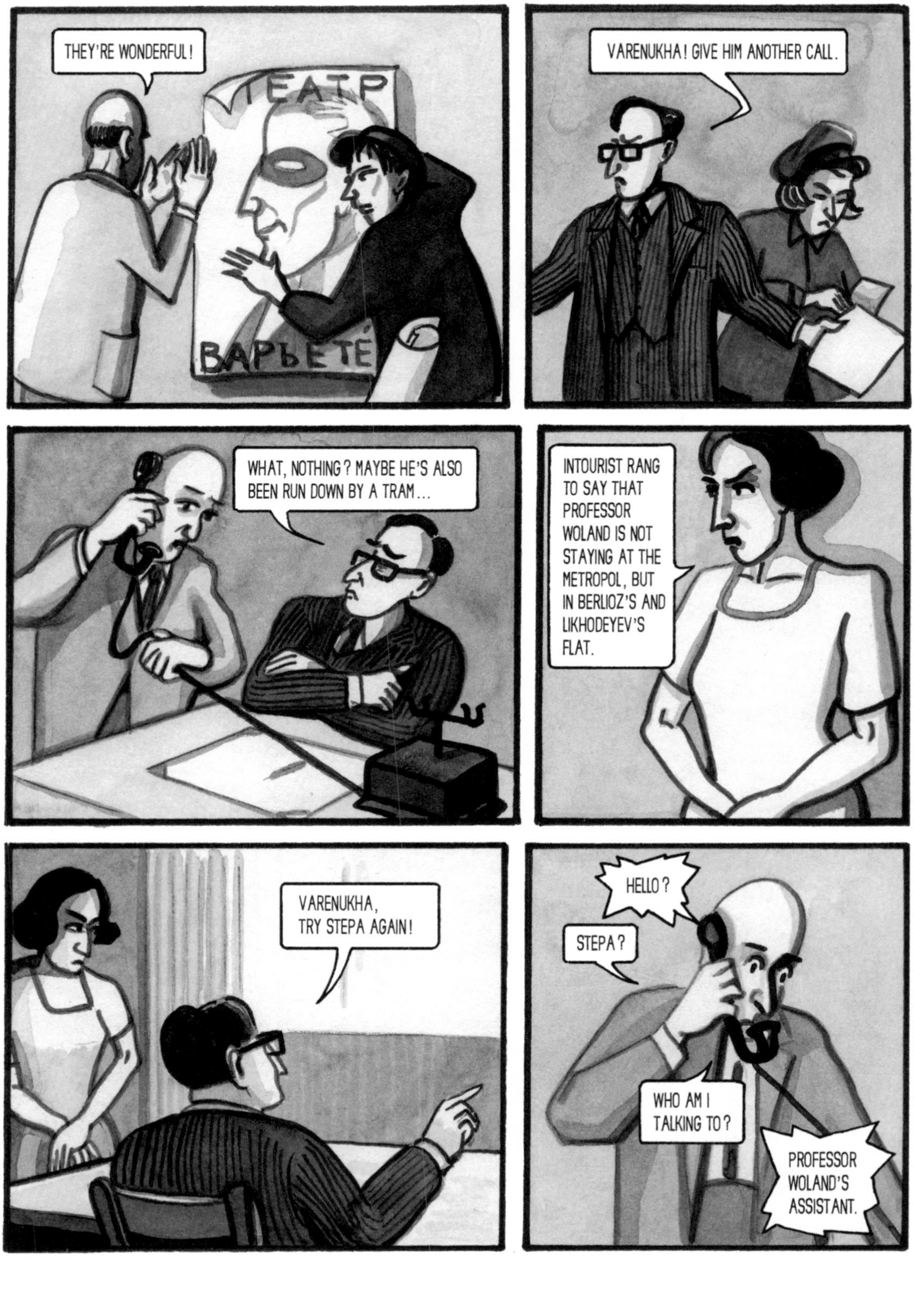
THEY'RE WONDERFUL!
ТЕАТР
ВАРЬЕТЕ
VARENUKHA! GIVE HIM ANOTHER CALL.
WHAT, NOTHING? MAYBE HE'S ALSO BEEN RUN DOWN BY A TRAM...
INTOURIST RANG TO SAY THAT PROFESSOR WOLAND IS NOT STAYING AT THE METROPOL, BUT IN BERLIOZ'S AND LIKHODEYEV'S FLAT.
VARENUKHA, TRY STEPA AGAIN!
HELLO?
STEPA?
WHO AM I TALKING TO?
PROFESSOR WOLAND'S ASSISTANT.

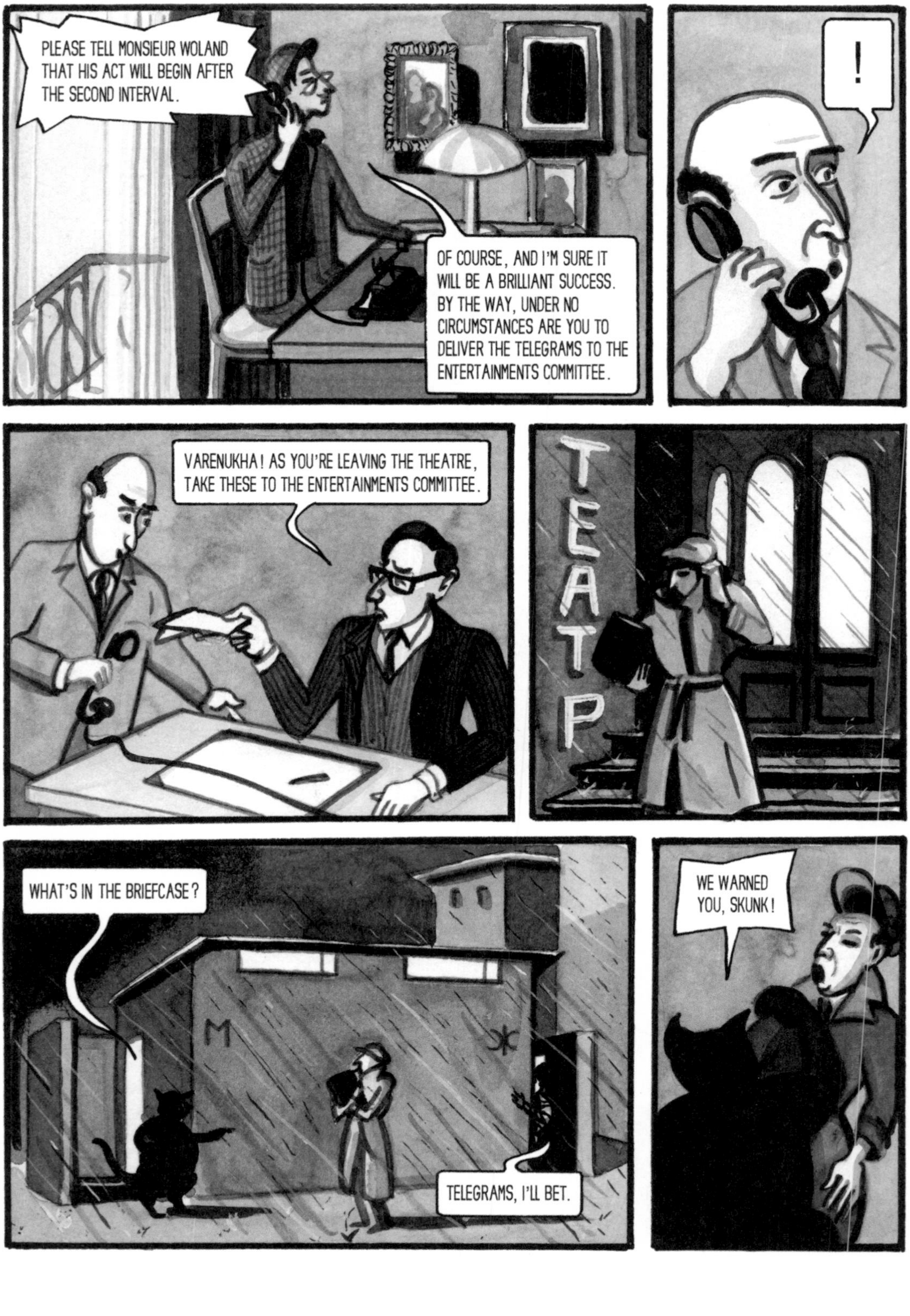
PLEASE TELL MONSIEUR WOLAND THAT HIS ACT WILL BEGIN AFTER THE SECOND INTERVAL.
OF COURSE, AND I'M SURE IT WILL BE A BRILLIANT SUCCESS. BY THE WAY, UNDER NO CIRCUMSTANCES ARE YOU TO DELIVER THE TELEGRAMS TO THE ENTERTAINMENTS COMMITTEE.
!
VARENUKHA! AS YOU'RE LEAVING THE THEATRE, TAKE THESE TO THE ENTERTAINMENTS COMMITTEE.
TEATP
WHAT'S IN THE BRIEFCASE?
M
TELEGRAMS, I'LL BET.
WE WARNED YOU, SKUNK!

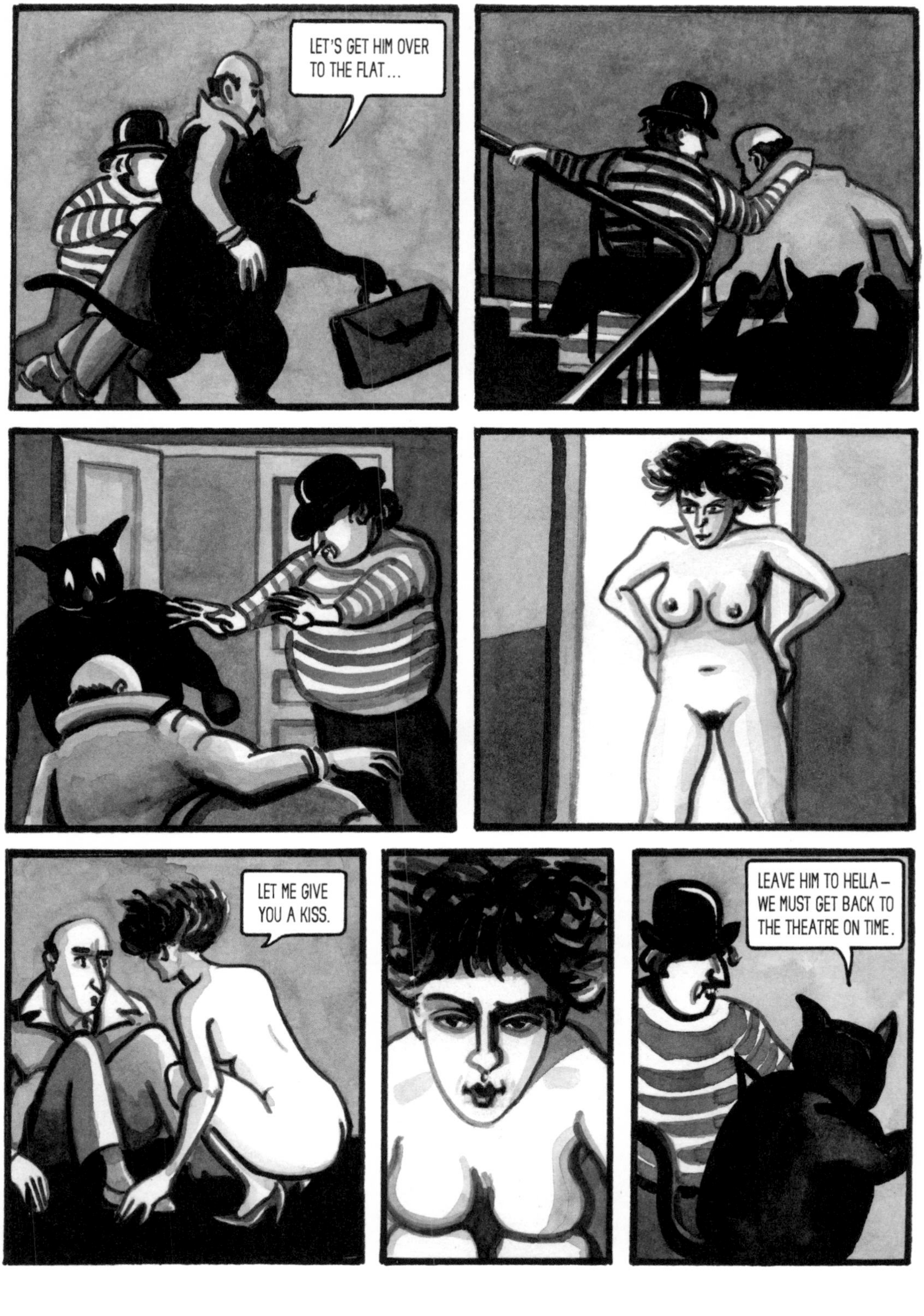
LET'S GET HIM OVER TO THE FLAT...
LET ME GIVE YOU A KISS.
LEAVE HIM TO HELLA – WE MUST GET BACK TO THE THEATRE ON TIME.

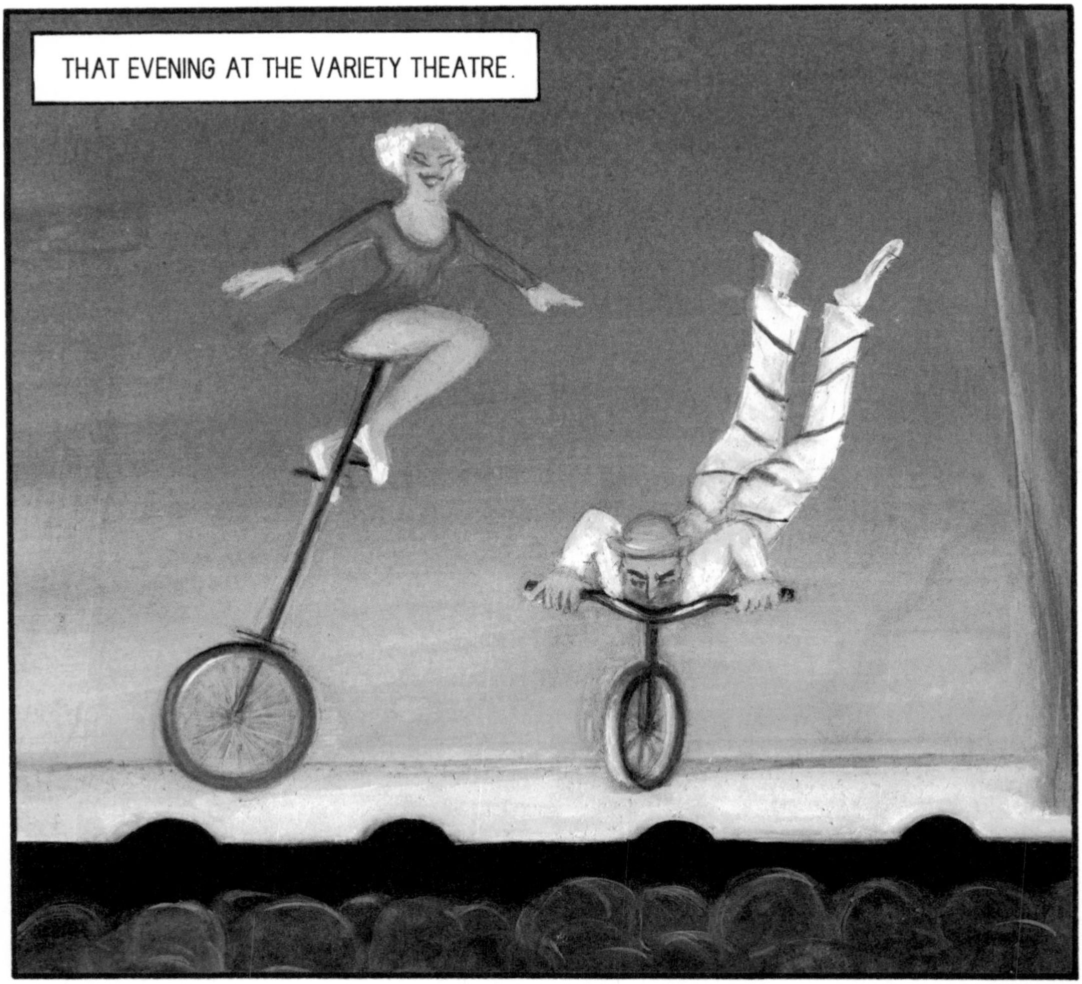
THAT EVENING AT THE VARIETY THEATRE.

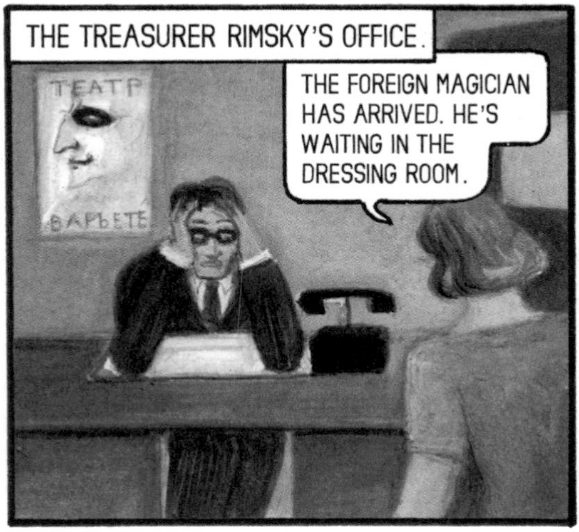
THE TREASURER RIMSKY'S OFFICE.
ТЕАТР
ВАРЬЕТЕ
THE FOREIGN MAGICIAN HAS ARRIVED. HE'S WAITING IN THE DRESSING ROOM.

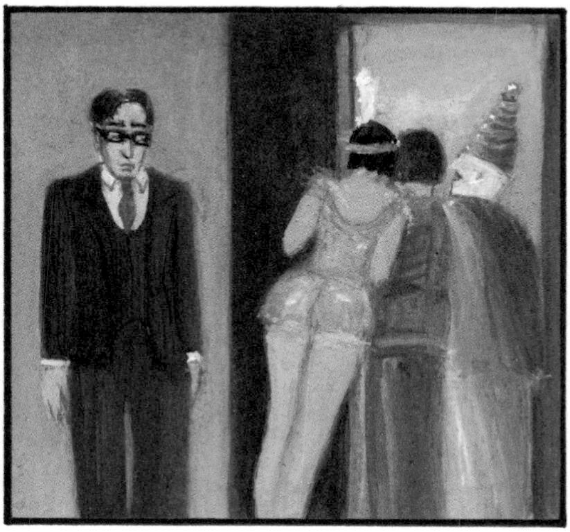

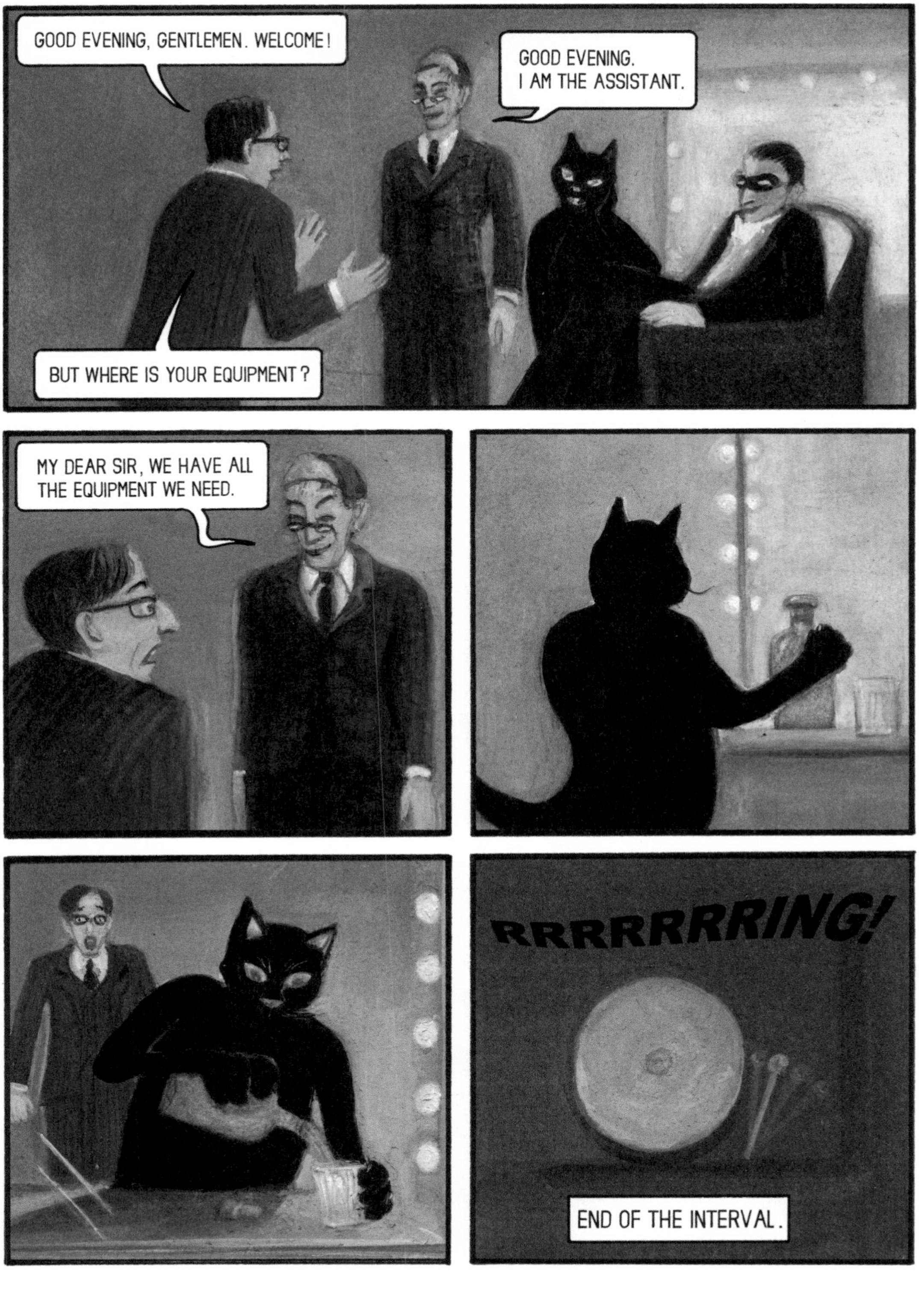
GOOD EVENING, GENTLEMEN. WELCOME!
GOOD EVENING. I AM THE ASSISTANT.
BUT WHERE IS YOUR EQUIPMENT?
MY DEAR SIR, WE HAVE ALL THE EQUIPMENT WE NEED.
RRRRRRRRING!
END OF THE INTERVAL.

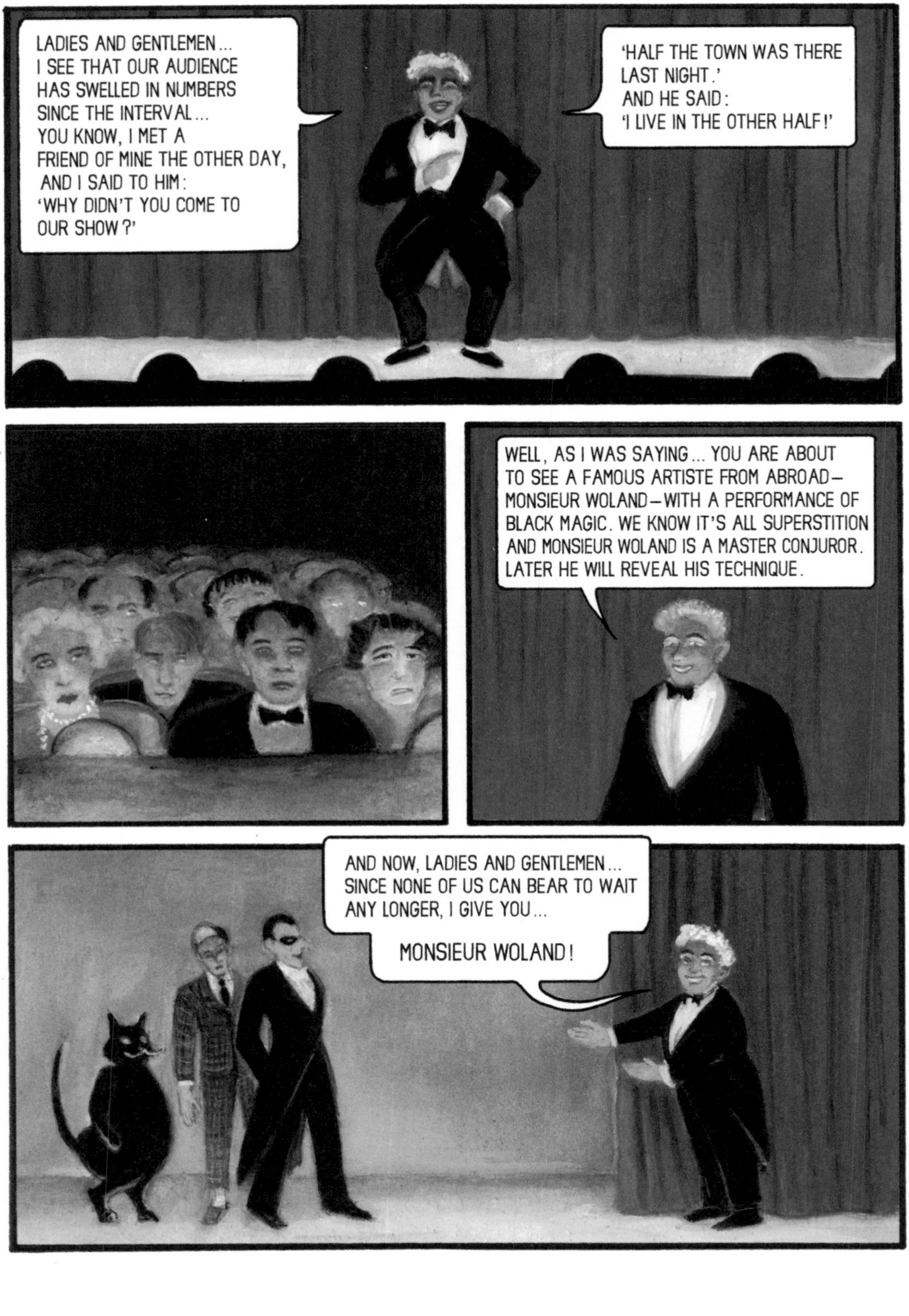
LADIES AND GENTLEMEN... I SEE THAT OUR AUDIENCE HAS SWELLED IN NUMBERS SINCE THE INTERVAL... YOU KNOW, I MET A FRIEND OF MINE THE OTHER DAY, AND I SAID TO HIM: 'WHY DIDN'T YOU COME TO OUR SHOW?'
'HALF THE TOWN WAS THERE LAST NIGHT.' AND HE SAID: 'I LIVE IN THE OTHER HALF!'
WELL, AS I WAS SAYING... YOU ARE ABOUT TO SEE A FAMOUS ARTISTE FROM ABROAD– MONSIEUR WOLAND–WITH A PERFORMANCE OF BLACK MAGIC. WE KNOW IT'S ALL SUPERSTITION AND MONSIEUR WOLAND IS A MASTER CONJUROR. LATER HE WILL REVEAL HIS TECHNIQUE.
AND NOW, LADIES AND GENTLEMEN... SINCE NONE OF US CAN BEAR TO WAIT ANY LONGER, I GIVE YOU...
MONSIEUR WOLAND!

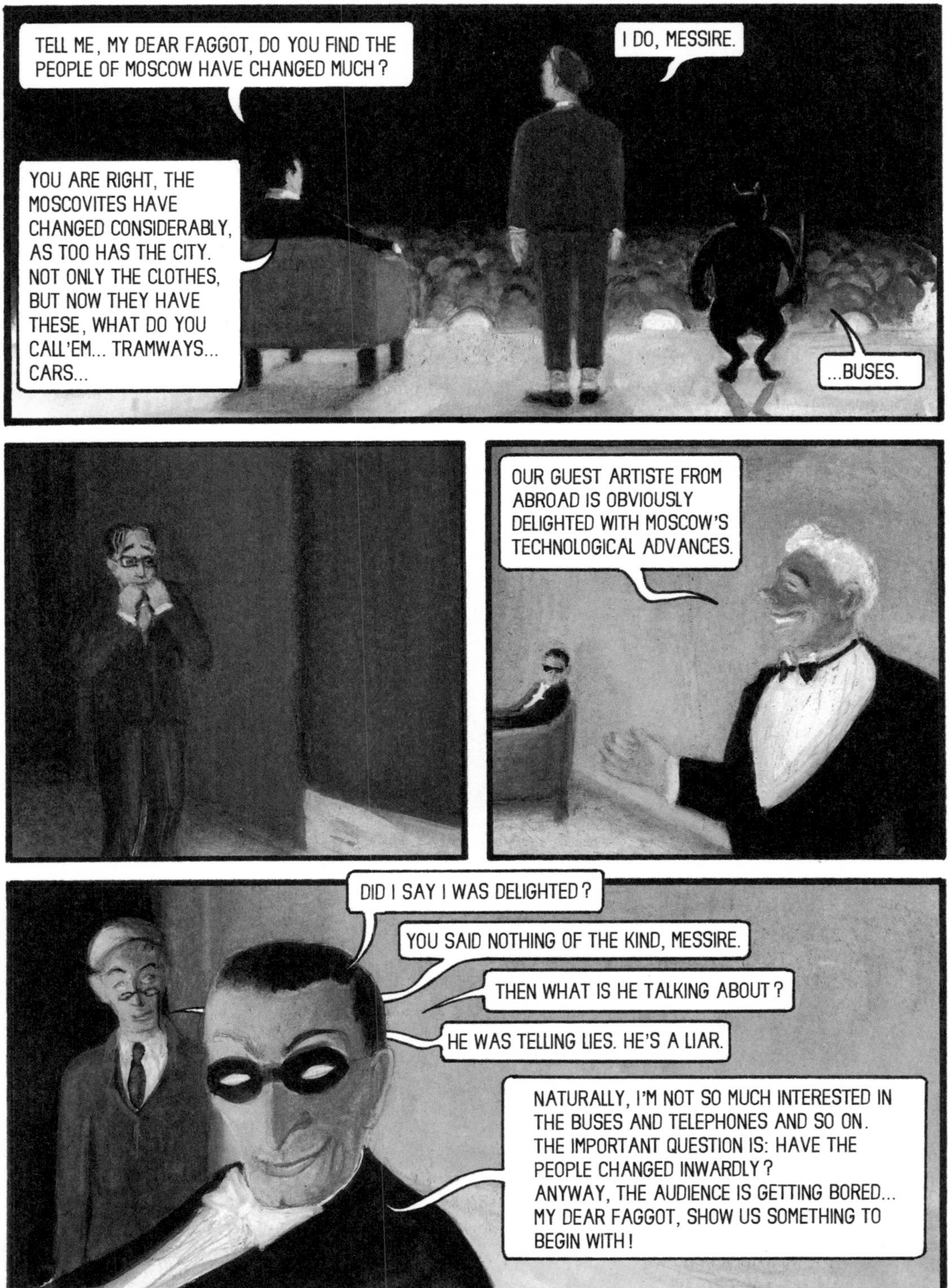

TELL ME, MY DEAR FAGGOT, DO YOU FIND THE PEOPLE OF MOSCOW HAVE CHANGED MUCH?
I DO, MESSIRE.
YOU ARE RIGHT, THE MOSCOVITES HAVE CHANGED CONSIDERABLY, AS TOO HAS THE CITY. NOT ONLY THE CLOTHES, BUT NOW THEY HAVE THESE, WHAT DO YOU CALL'EM... TRAMWAYS... CARS...
...BUSES.
OUR GUEST ARTISTE FROM ABROAD IS OBVIOUSLY DELIGHTED WITH MOSCOW'S TECHNOLOGICAL ADVANCES.
DID I SAY I WAS DELIGHTED?
YOU SAID NOTHING OF THE KIND, MESSIRE.
THEN WHAT IS HE TALKING ABOUT?
HE WAS TELLING LIES. HE'S A LIAR.
NATURALLY, I'M NOT SO MUCH INTERESTED IN THE BUSES AND TELEPHONES AND SO ON. THE IMPORTANT QUESTION IS: HAVE THE PEOPLE CHANGED INWARDLY? ANYWAY, THE AUDIENCE IS GETTING BORED... MY DEAR FAGGOT, SHOW US SOMETHING TO BEGIN WITH!

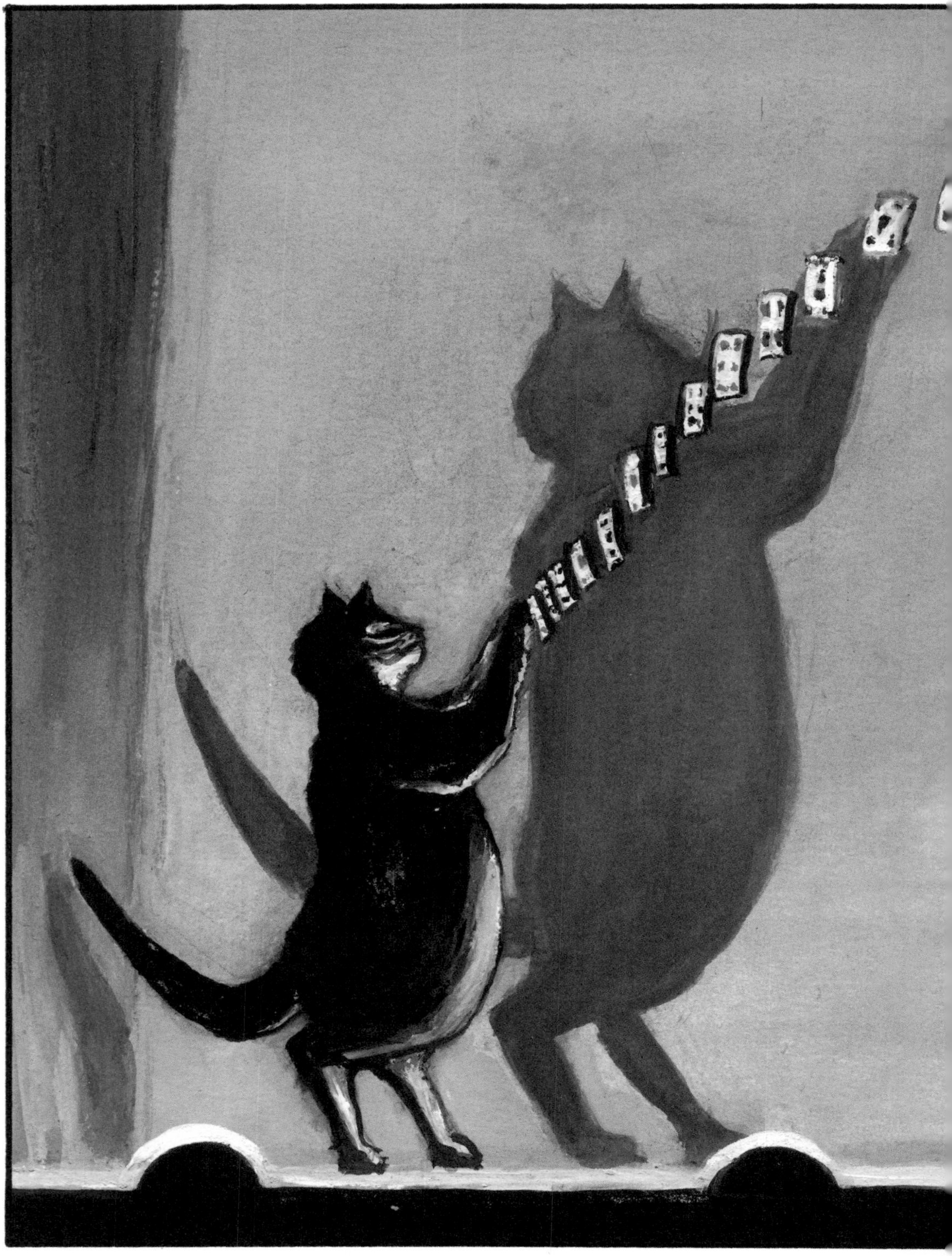

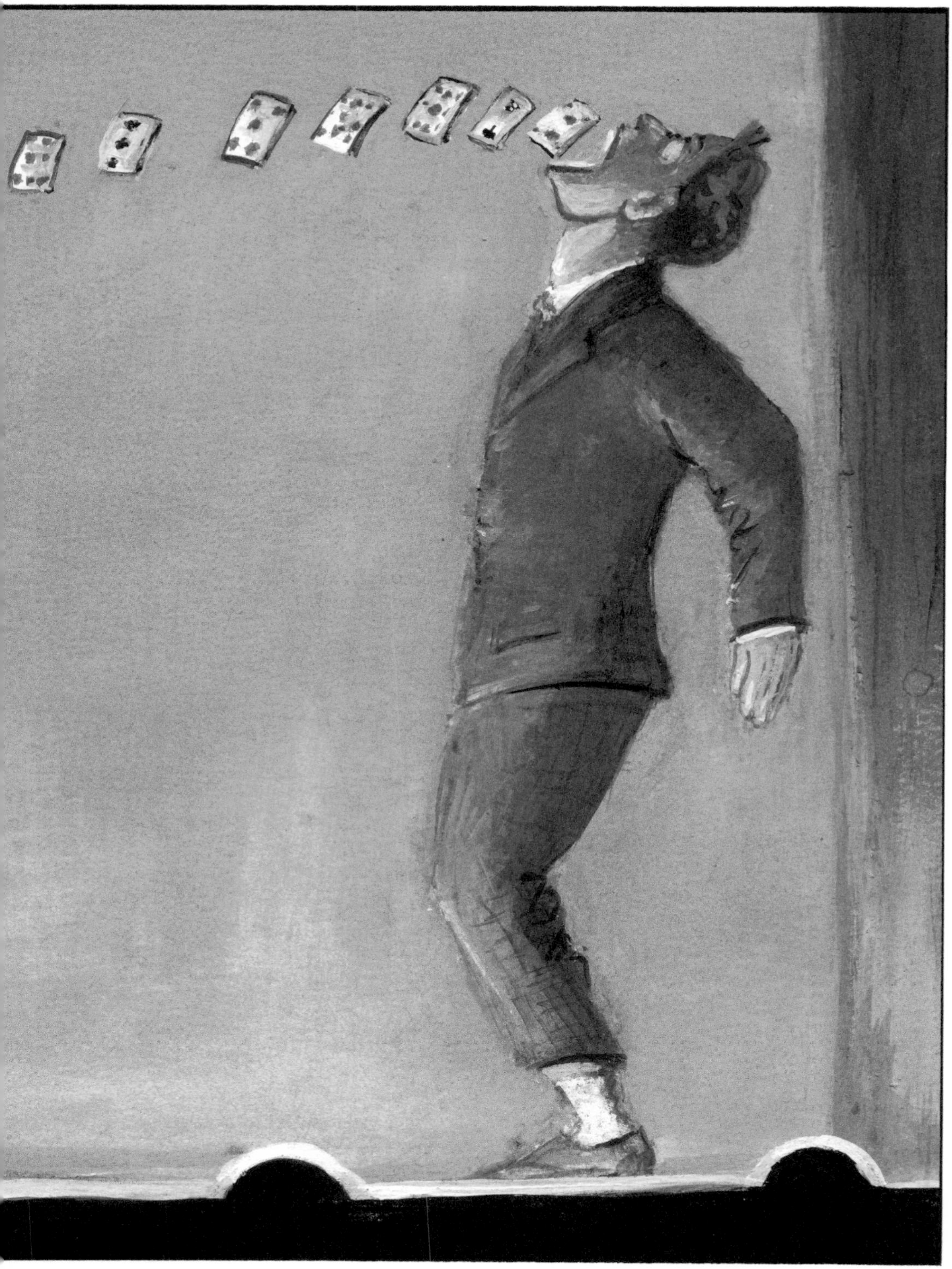

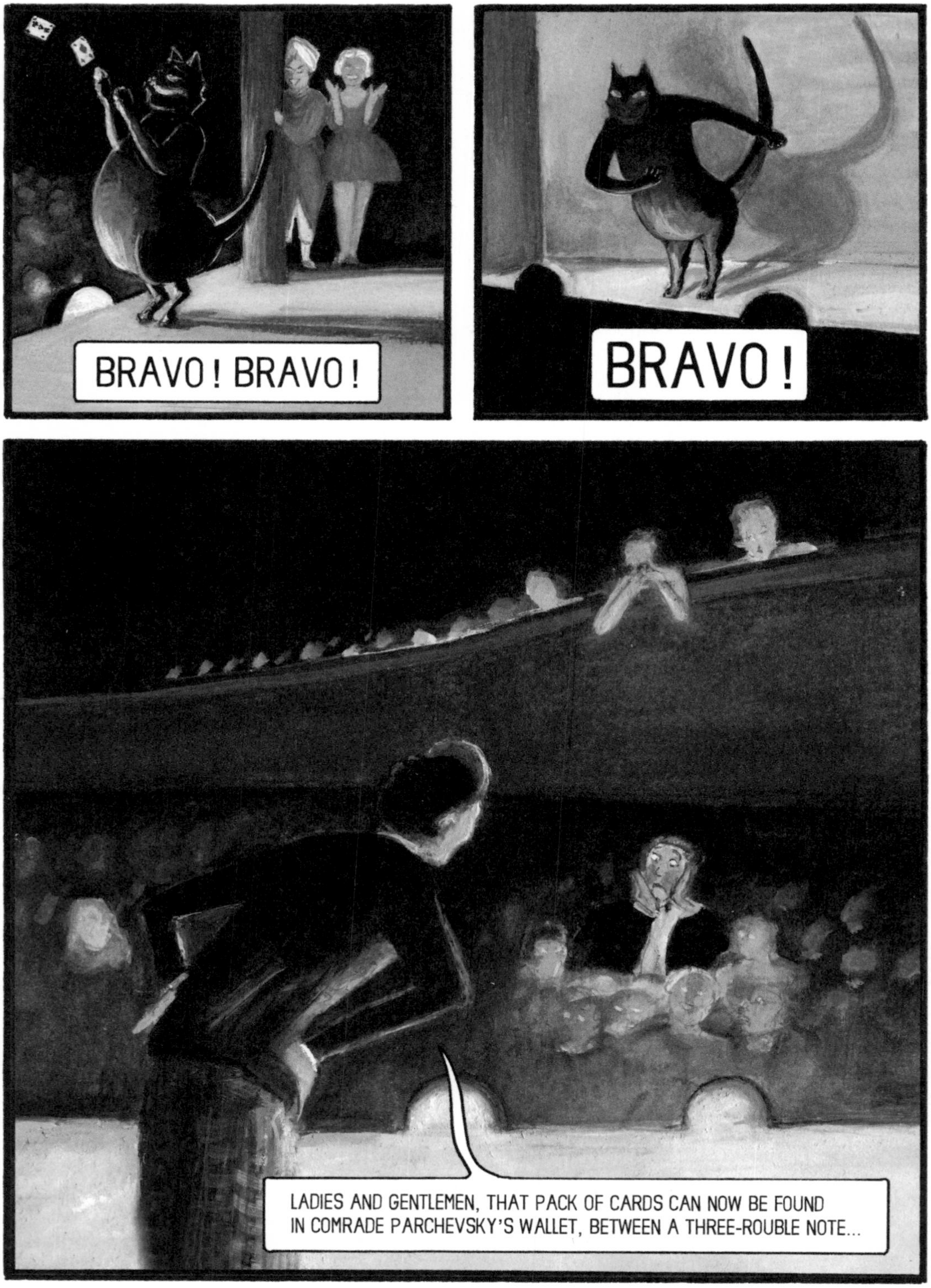
BRAVO! BRAVO!
BRAVO!
LADIES AND GENTLEMEN, THAT PACK OF CARDS CAN NOW BE FOUND IN COMRADE PARCHEVSKY'S WALLET, BETWEEN A THREE-ROUBLE NOTE...

AND A SUMMONS TO APPEAR IN COURT FOR NON-PAYMENT OF ALIMONY.

THAT'S AN OLD TRICK! THE MAN IN THE STALLS IS PART OF THE ACT!

THINK SO? IN THAT CASE YOU'RE A PLANT, TOO.

...BECAUSE THERE'S A PACKET OF CARDS IN YOUR POCKET.

HE'S RIGHT! MY GOD — IT'S REAL MONEY!

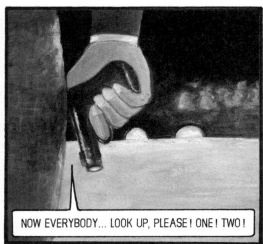

NOW EVERYBODY... LOOK UP, PLEASE! ONE! TWO!

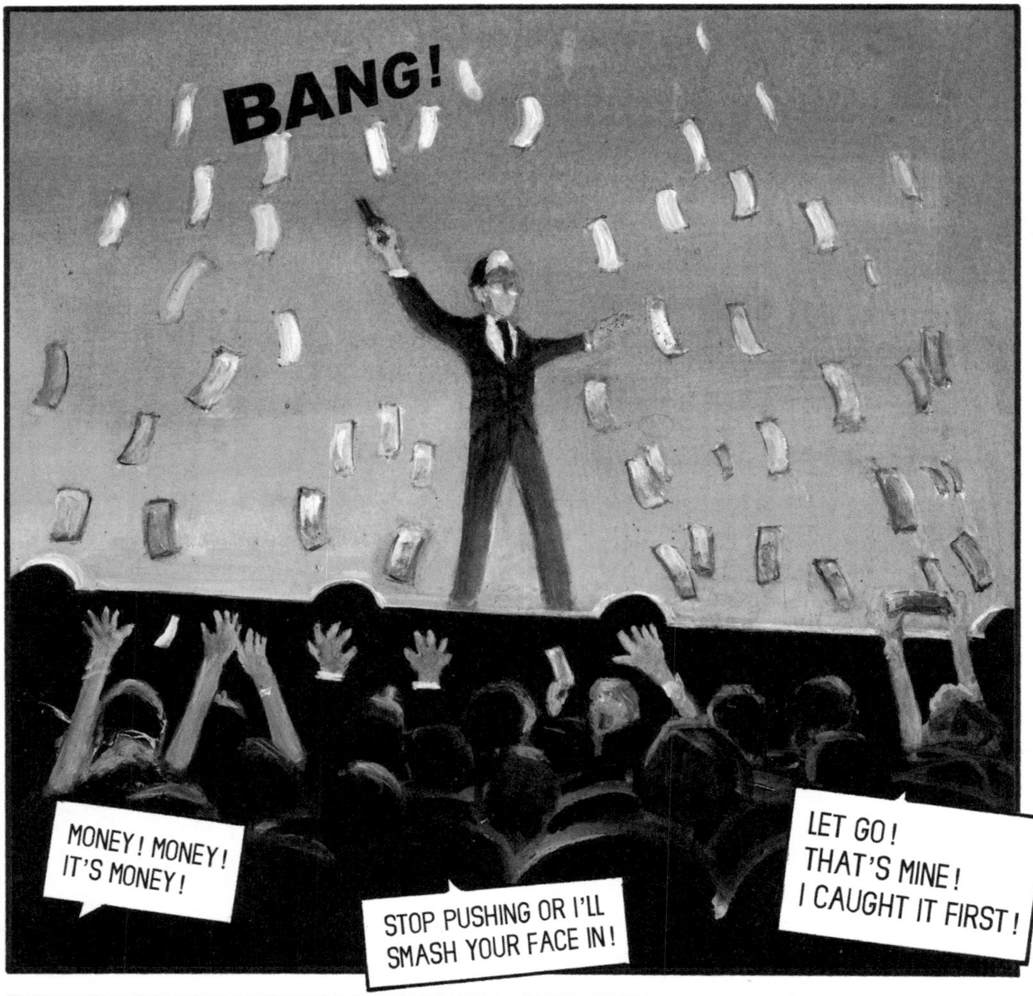
BANG!
MONEY! MONEY! IT'S MONEY!
STOP PUSHING OR I'LL SMASH YOUR FACE IN!
LET GO! THAT'S MINE! I CAUGHT IT FIRST!

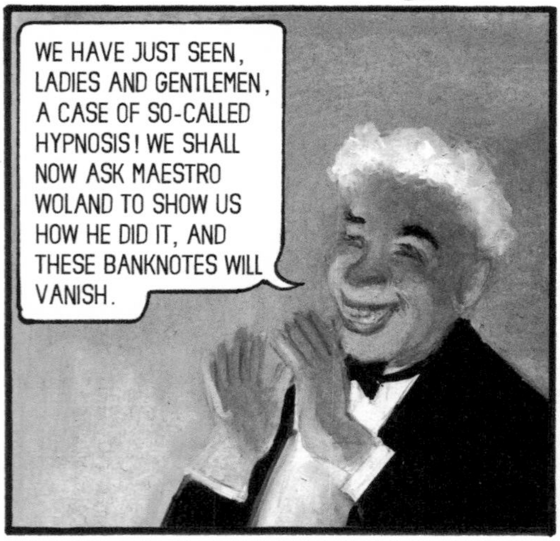
WE HAVE JUST SEEN, LADIES AND GENTLEMEN, A CASE OF SO-CALLED HYPNOSIS! WE SHALL NOW ASK MAESTRO WOLAND TO SHOW US HOW HE DID IT, AND THESE BANKNOTES WILL VANISH.

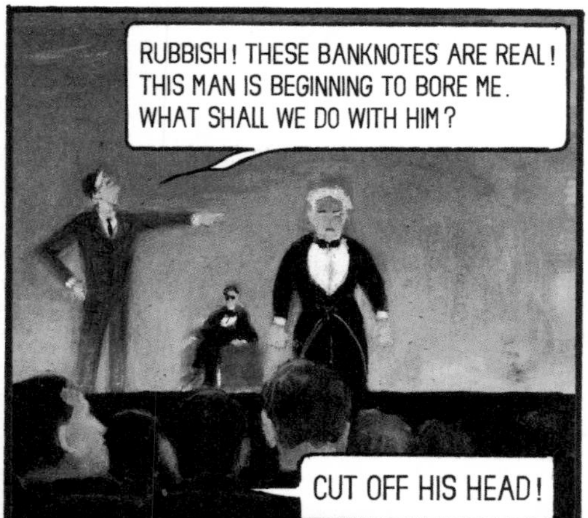
RUBBISH! THESE BANKNOTES ARE REAL! THIS MAN IS BEGINNING TO BORE ME. WHAT SHALL WE DO WITH HIM?
CUT OFF HIS HEAD!

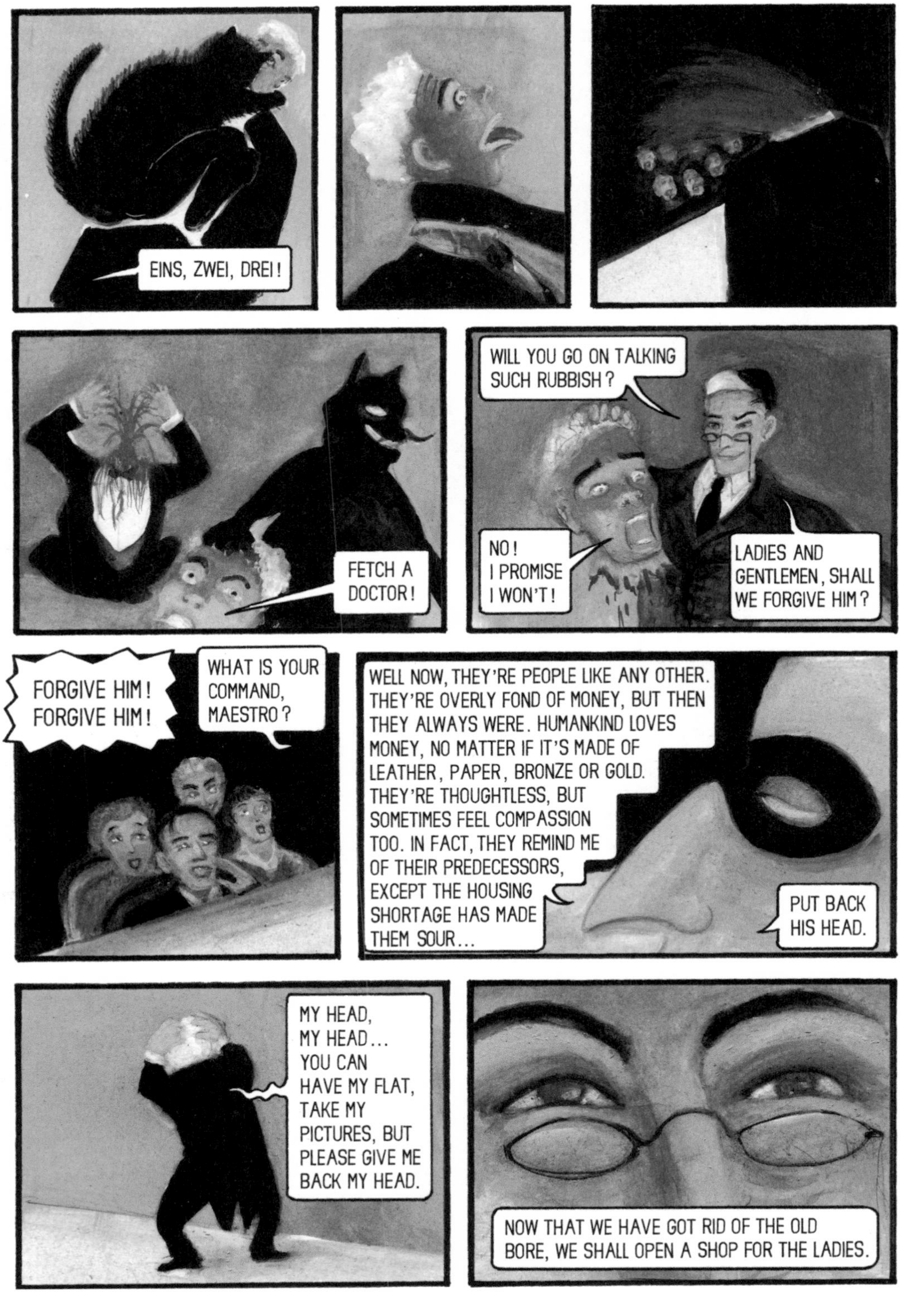
EINS, ZWEI, DREI!
FETCH A DOCTOR!
WILL YOU GO ON TALKING SUCH RUBBISH?
NO! I PROMISE I WON'T!
LADIES AND GENTLEMEN, SHALL WE FORGIVE HIM?
FORGIVE HIM! FORGIVE HIM!
WHAT IS YOUR COMMAND, MAESTRO?
WELL NOW, THEY'RE PEOPLE LIKE ANY OTHER. THEY'RE OVERLY FOND OF MONEY, BUT THEN THEY ALWAYS WERE. HUMANKIND LOVES MONEY, NO MATTER IF IT'S MADE OF LEATHER, PAPER, BRONZE OR GOLD. THEY'RE THOUGHTLESS, BUT SOMETIMES FEEL COMPASSION TOO. IN FACT, THEY REMIND ME OF THEIR PREDECESSORS, EXCEPT THE HOUSING SHORTAGE HAS MADE THEM SOUR...
PUT BACK HIS HEAD.
MY HEAD, MY HEAD... YOU CAN HAVE MY FLAT, TAKE MY PICTURES, BUT PLEASE GIVE ME BACK MY HEAD.
NOW THAT WE HAVE GOT RID OF THE OLD BORE, WE SHALL OPEN A SHOP FOR THE LADIES.

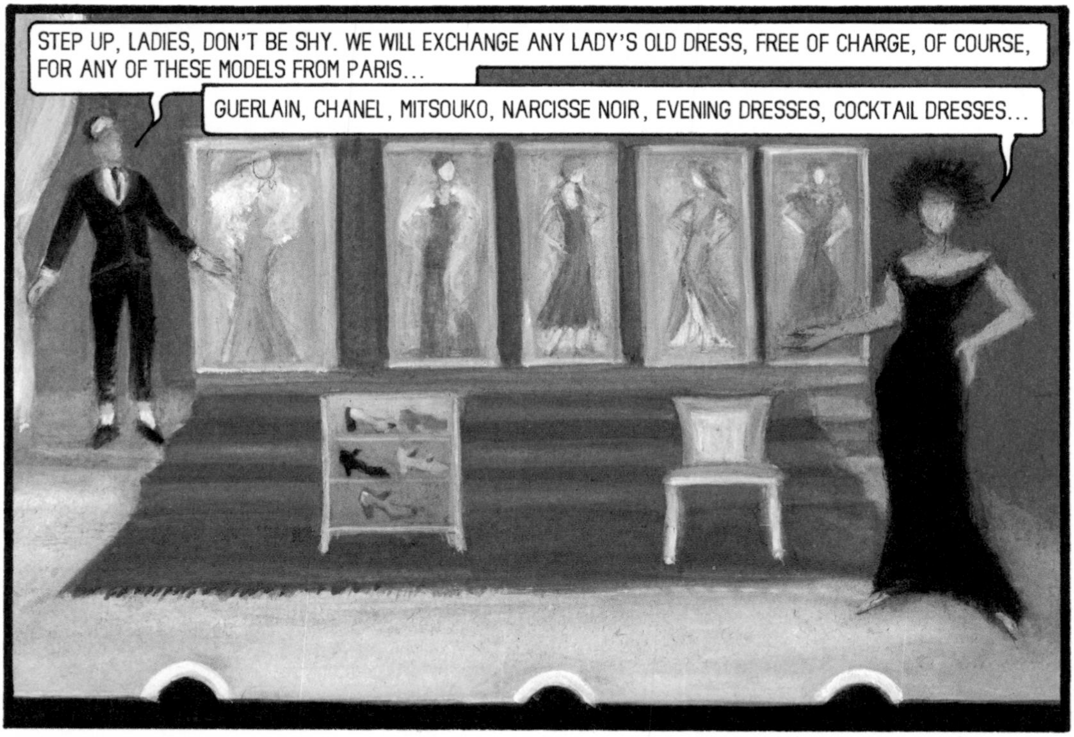
STEP UP, LADIES, DON'T BE SHY. WE WILL EXCHANGE ANY LADY'S OLD DRESS, FREE OF CHARGE, OF COURSE, FOR ANY OF THESE MODELS FROM PARIS...
GUERLAIN, CHANEL, MITSOUKO, NARCISSE NOIR, EVENING DRESSES, COCKTAIL DRESSES...

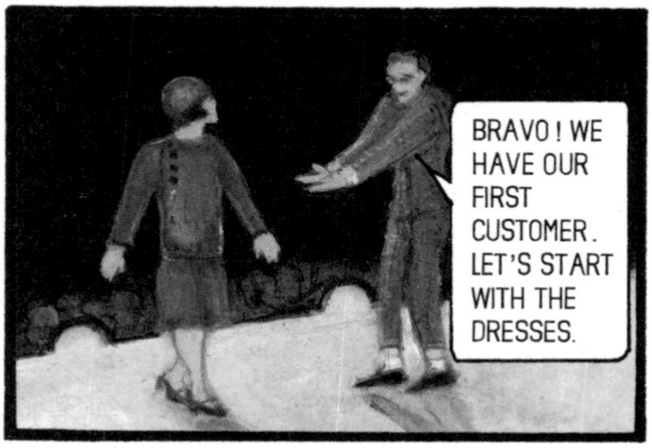
BRAVO! WE HAVE OUR FIRST CUSTOMER. LET'S START WITH THE DRESSES.

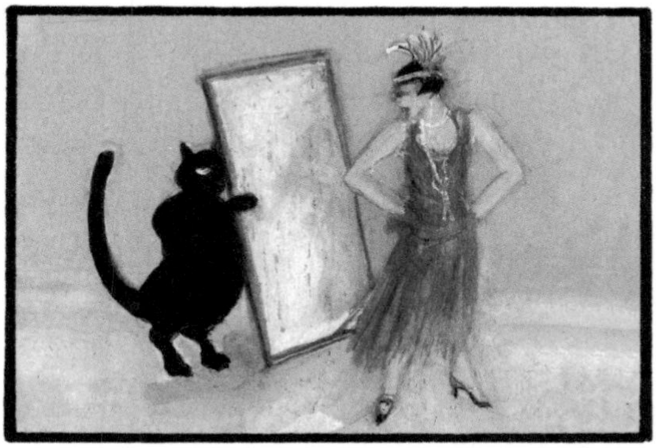

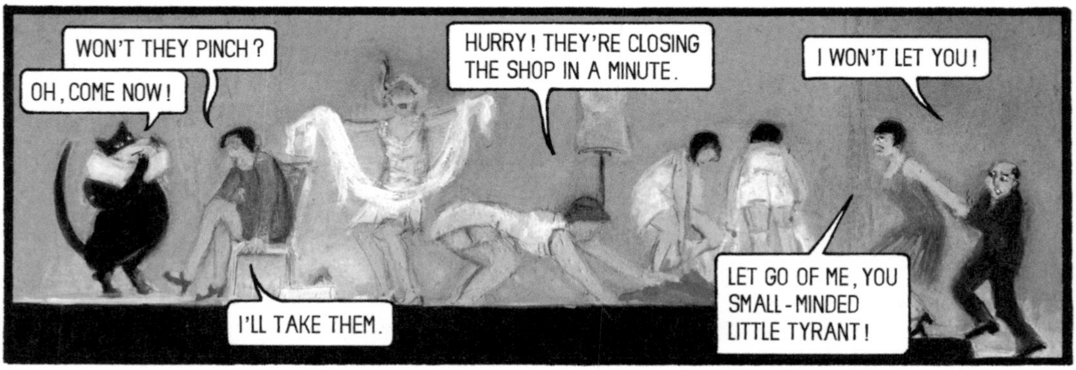
WON'T THEY PINCH?
OH, COME NOW!
I'LL TAKE THEM.
HURRY! THEY'RE CLOSING THE SHOP IN A MINUTE.
I WON'T LET YOU!
LET GO OF ME, YOU SMALL-MINDED LITTLE TYRANT!

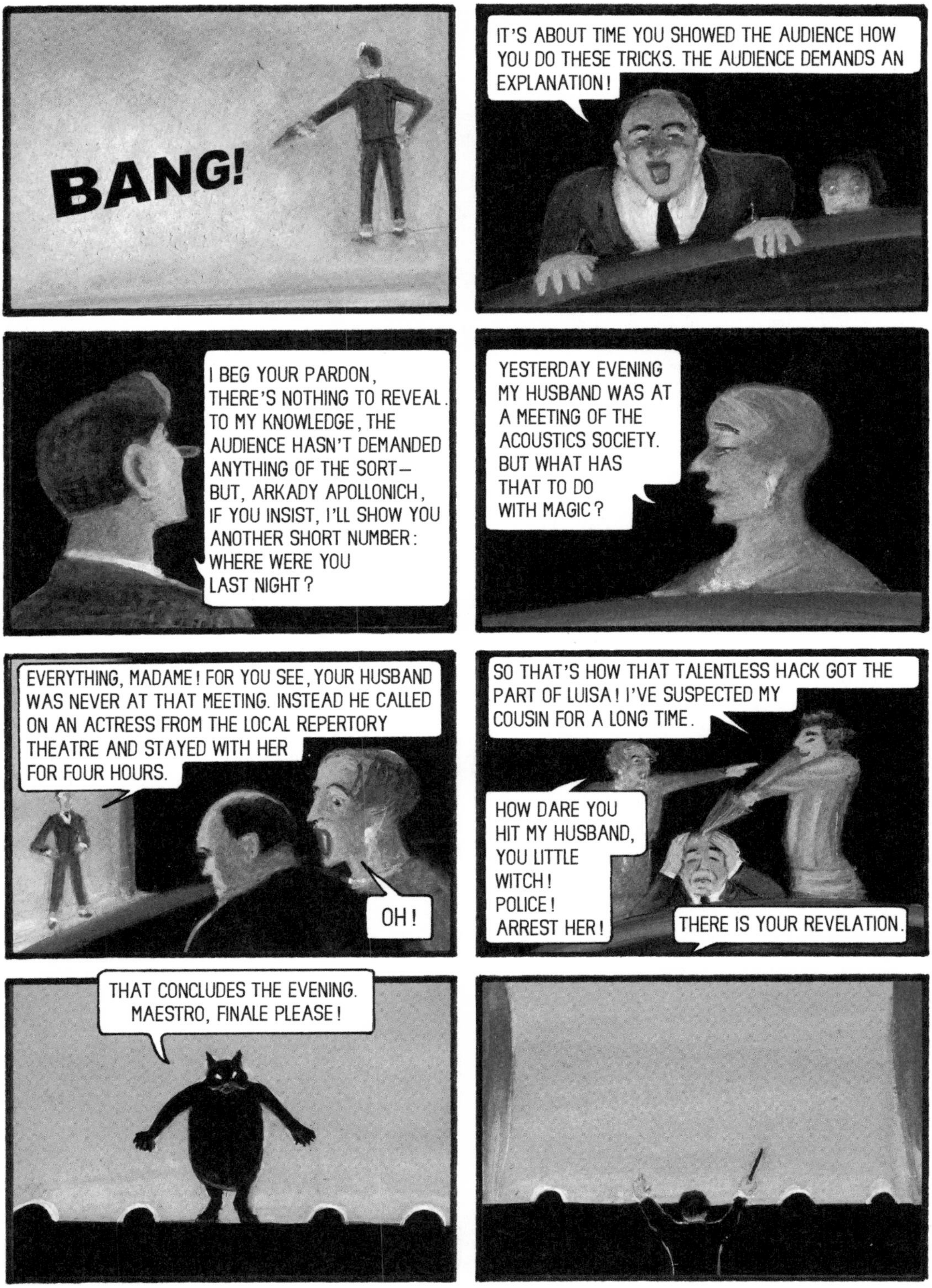
BANG!
IT'S ABOUT TIME YOU SHOWED THE AUDIENCE HOW YOU DO THESE TRICKS. THE AUDIENCE DEMANDS AN EXPLANATION!
I BEG YOUR PARDON, THERE'S NOTHING TO REVEAL. TO MY KNOWLEDGE, THE AUDIENCE HASN'T DEMANDED ANYTHING OF THE SORT— BUT, ARKADY APOLLONICH, IF YOU INSIST, I'LL SHOW YOU ANOTHER SHORT NUMBER: WHERE WERE YOU LAST NIGHT?
YESTERDAY EVENING MY HUSBAND WAS AT A MEETING OF THE ACOUSTICS SOCIETY. BUT WHAT HAS THAT TO DO WITH MAGIC?
EVERYTHING, MADAME! FOR YOU SEE, YOUR HUSBAND WAS NEVER AT THAT MEETING. INSTEAD HE CALLED ON AN ACTRESS FROM THE LOCAL REPERTORY THEATRE AND STAYED WITH HER FOR FOUR HOURS.
OH!
SO THAT'S HOW THAT TALENTLESS HACK GOT THE PART OF LUISA! I'VE SUSPECTED MY COUSIN FOR A LONG TIME.
HOW DARE YOU HIT MY HUSBAND, YOU LITTLE WITCH! POLICE! ARREST HER!
THERE IS YOUR REVELATION.
THAT CONCLUDES THE EVENING. MAESTRO, FINALE PLEASE!

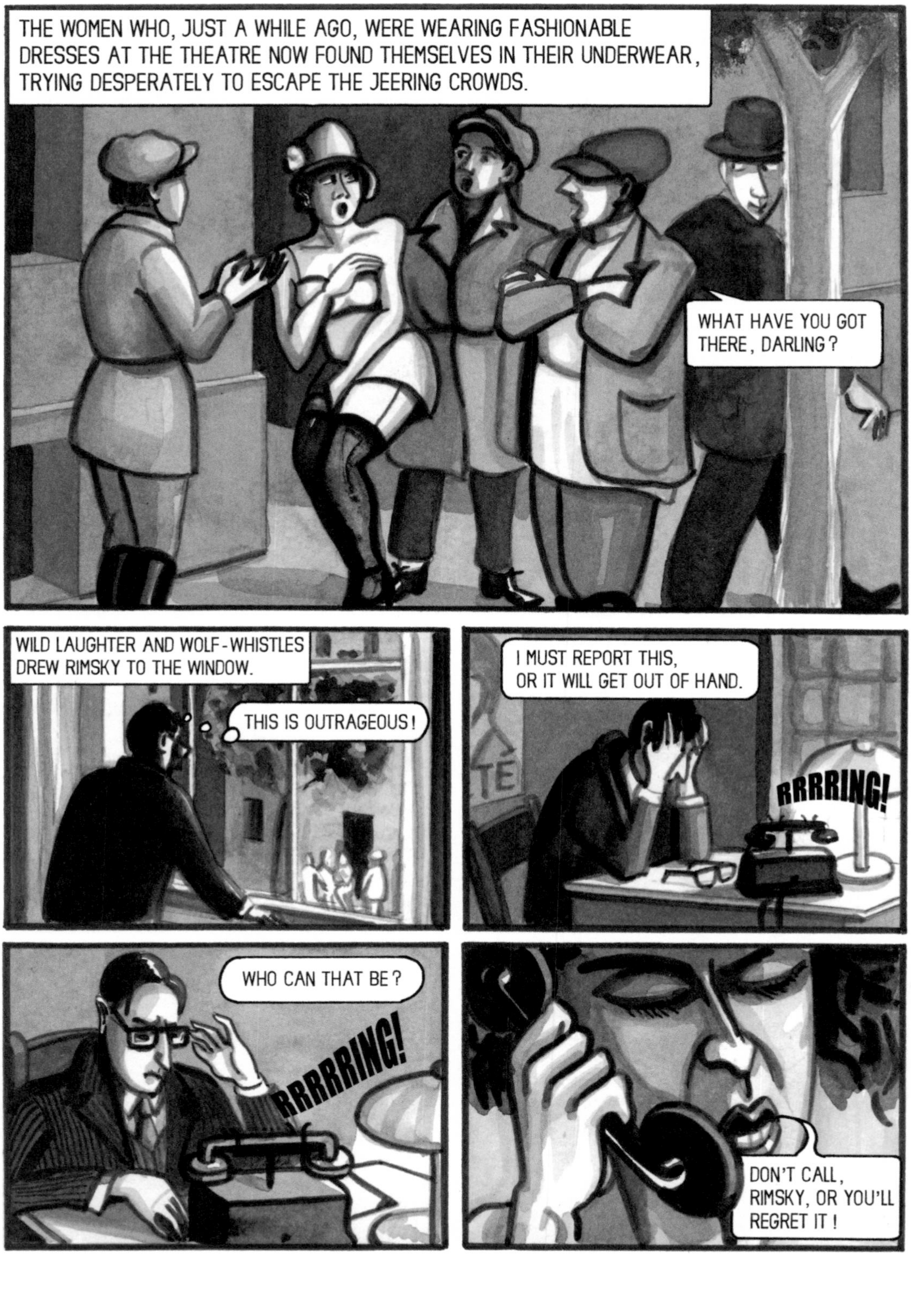
THE WOMEN WHO, JUST A WHILE AGO, WERE WEARING FASHIONABLE DRESSES AT THE THEATRE NOW FOUND THEMSELVES IN THEIR UNDERWEAR, TRYING DESPERATELY TO ESCAPE THE JEERING CROWDS.
WHAT HAVE YOU GOT THERE, DARLING?
WILD LAUGHTER AND WOLF-WHISTLES DREW RIMSKY TO THE WINDOW.
THIS IS OUTRAGEOUS!
I MUST REPORT THIS, OR IT WILL GET OUT OF HAND.
RRRRING!
WHO CAN THAT BE?
RRRRRING!
DON'T CALL, RIMSKY, OR YOU'LL REGRET IT!

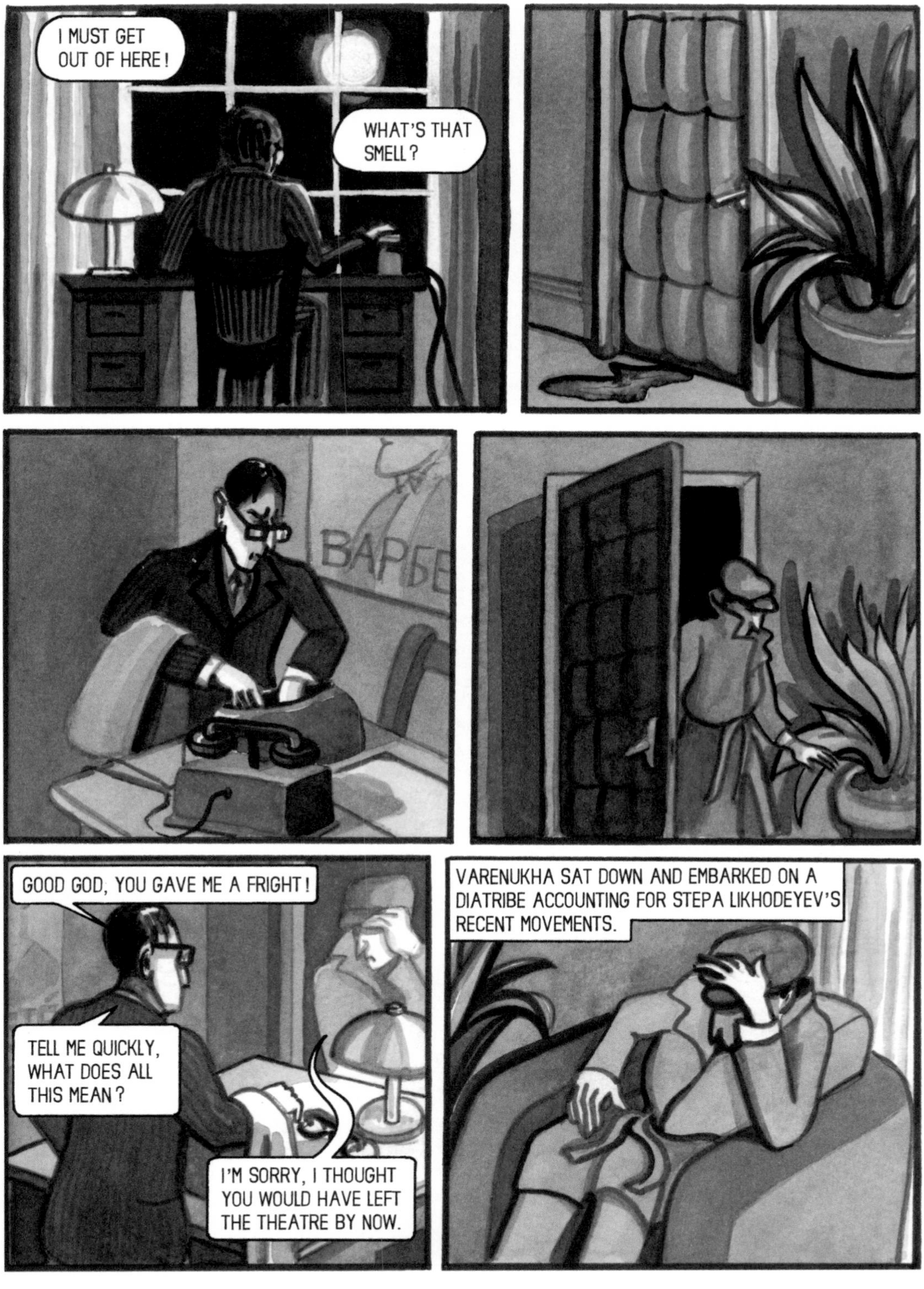
I MUST GET OUT OF HERE!
WHAT'S THAT SMELL?
ВАРБЕ
GOOD GOD, YOU GAVE ME A FRIGHT!
TELL ME QUICKLY, WHAT DOES ALL THIS MEAN?
I'M SORRY, I THOUGHT YOU WOULD HAVE LEFT THE THEATRE BY NOW.
VARENUKHA SAT DOWN AND EMBARKED ON A DIATRIBE ACCOUNTING FOR STEPA LIKHODEYEV'S RECENT MOVEMENTS.

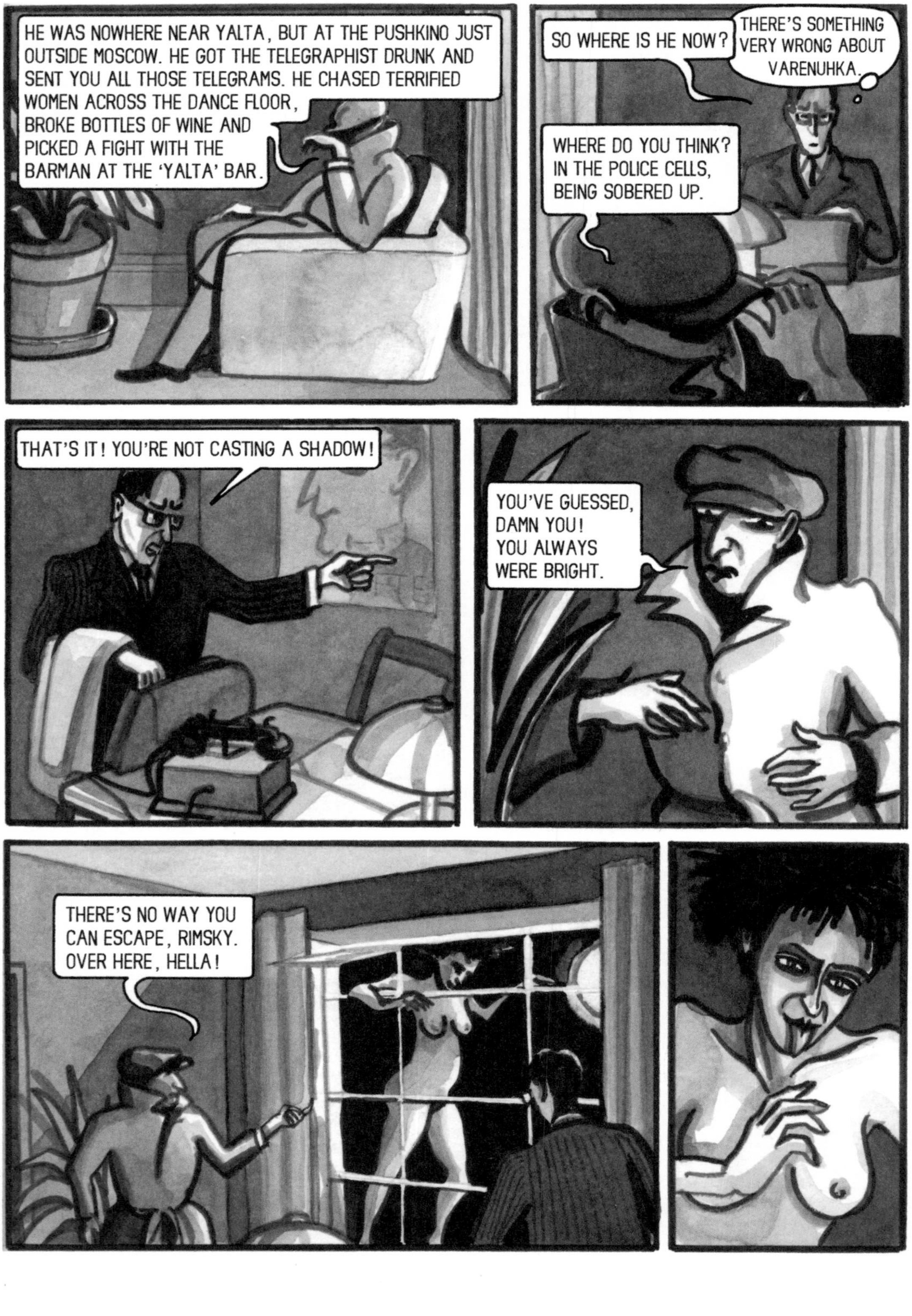
HE WAS NOWHERE NEAR YALTA, BUT AT THE PUSHKINO JUST OUTSIDE MOSCOW. HE GOT THE TELEGRAPHIST DRUNK AND SENT YOU ALL THOSE TELEGRAMS. HE CHASED TERRIFIED WOMEN ACROSS THE DANCE FLOOR, BROKE BOTTLES OF WINE AND PICKED A FIGHT WITH THE BARMAN AT THE 'YALTA' BAR.
SO WHERE IS HE NOW?
THERE'S SOMETHING VERY WRONG ABOUT VARENUHKA.
WHERE DO YOU THINK? IN THE POLICE CELLS, BEING SOBERED UP.
THAT'S IT! YOU'RE NOT CASTING A SHADOW!
YOU'VE GUESSED, DAMN YOU! YOU ALWAYS WERE BRIGHT.
THERE'S NO WAY YOU CAN ESCAPE, RIMSKY. OVER HERE, HELLA!

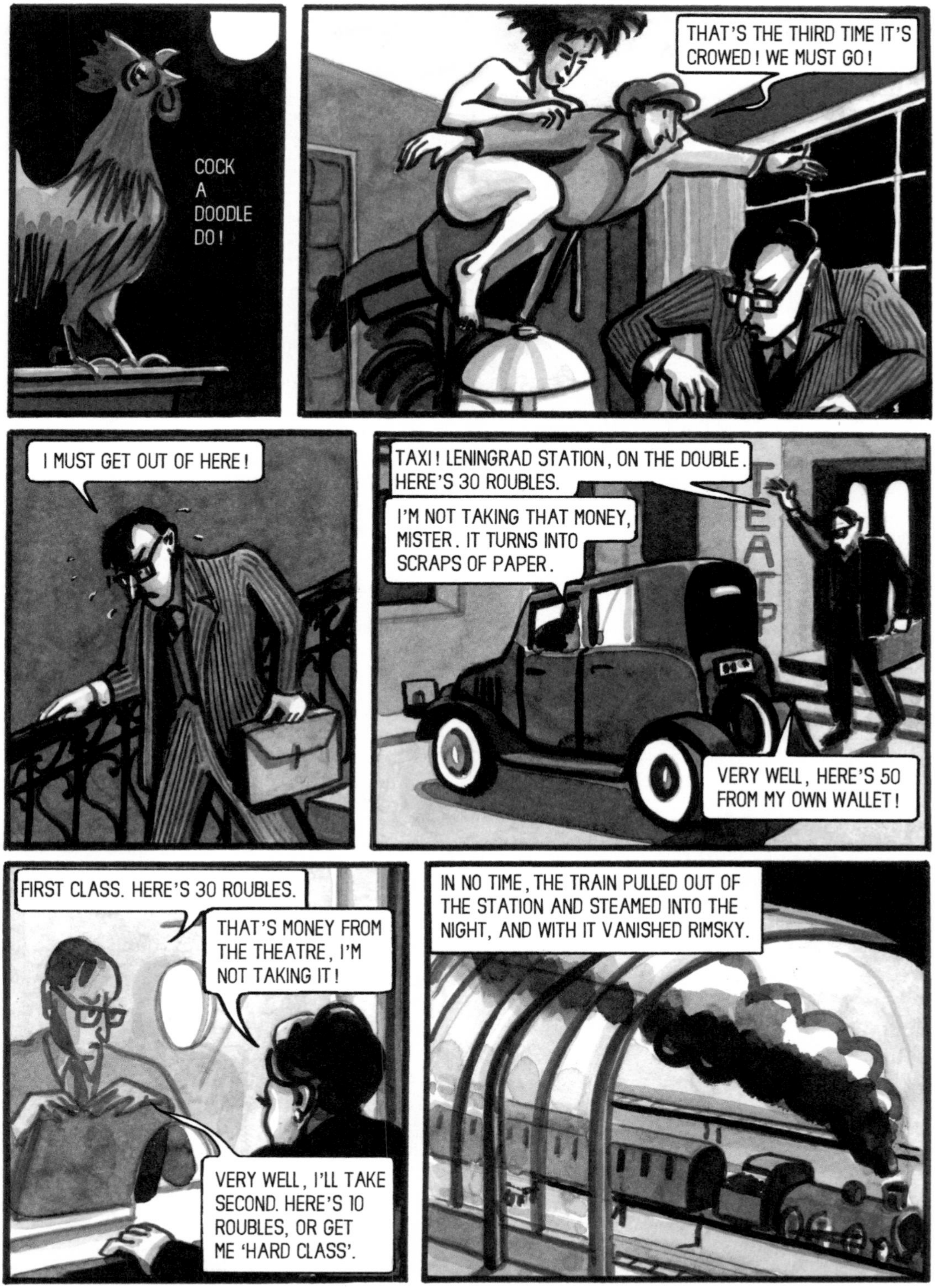
COCK A DOODLE DO!
THAT'S THE THIRD TIME IT'S CROWED! WE MUST GO!
I MUST GET OUT OF HERE!
TAXI! LENINGRAD STATION, ON THE DOUBLE. HERE'S 30 ROUBLES.
I'M NOT TAKING THAT MONEY, MISTER. IT TURNS INTO SCRAPS OF PAPER.
VERY WELL, HERE'S 50 FROM MY OWN WALLET!
FIRST CLASS. HERE'S 30 ROUBLES.
THAT'S MONEY FROM THE THEATRE, I'M NOT TAKING IT!
VERY WELL, I'LL TAKE SECOND. HERE'S 10 ROUBLES, OR GET ME 'HARD CLASS'.
IN NO TIME, THE TRAIN PULLED OUT OF THE STATION AND STEAMED INTO THE NIGHT, AND WITH IT VANISHED RIMSKY.

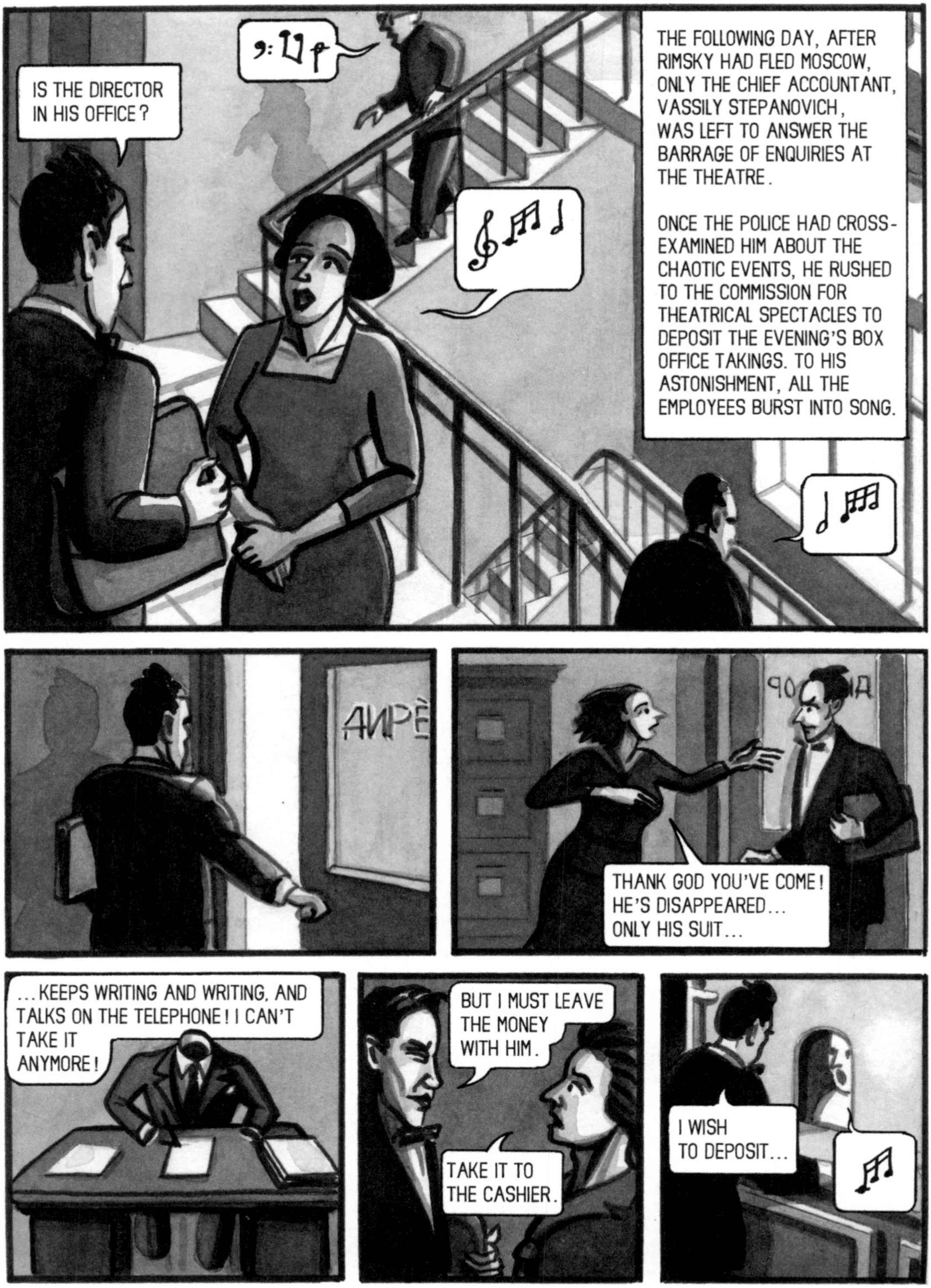
IS THE DIRECTOR IN HIS OFFICE?
THE FOLLOWING DAY, AFTER RIMSKY HAD FLED MOSCOW, ONLY THE CHIEF ACCOUNTANT, VASSILY STEPANOVICH, WAS LEFT TO ANSWER THE BARRAGE OF ENQUIRIES AT THE THEATRE.
ONCE THE POLICE HAD CROSS-EXAMINED HIM ABOUT THE CHAOTIC EVENTS, HE RUSHED TO THE COMMISSION FOR THEATRICAL SPECTACLES TO DEPOSIT THE EVENING'S BOX OFFICE TAKINGS. TO HIS ASTONISHMENT, ALL THE EMPLOYEES BURST INTO SONG.
THANK GOD YOU'VE COME! HE'S DISAPPEARED... ONLY HIS SUIT...
...KEEPS WRITING AND WRITING, AND TALKS ON THE TELEPHONE! I CAN'T TAKE IT ANYMORE!
BUT I MUST LEAVE THE MONEY WITH HIM.
TAKE IT TO THE CASHIER.
I WISH TO DEPOSIT...

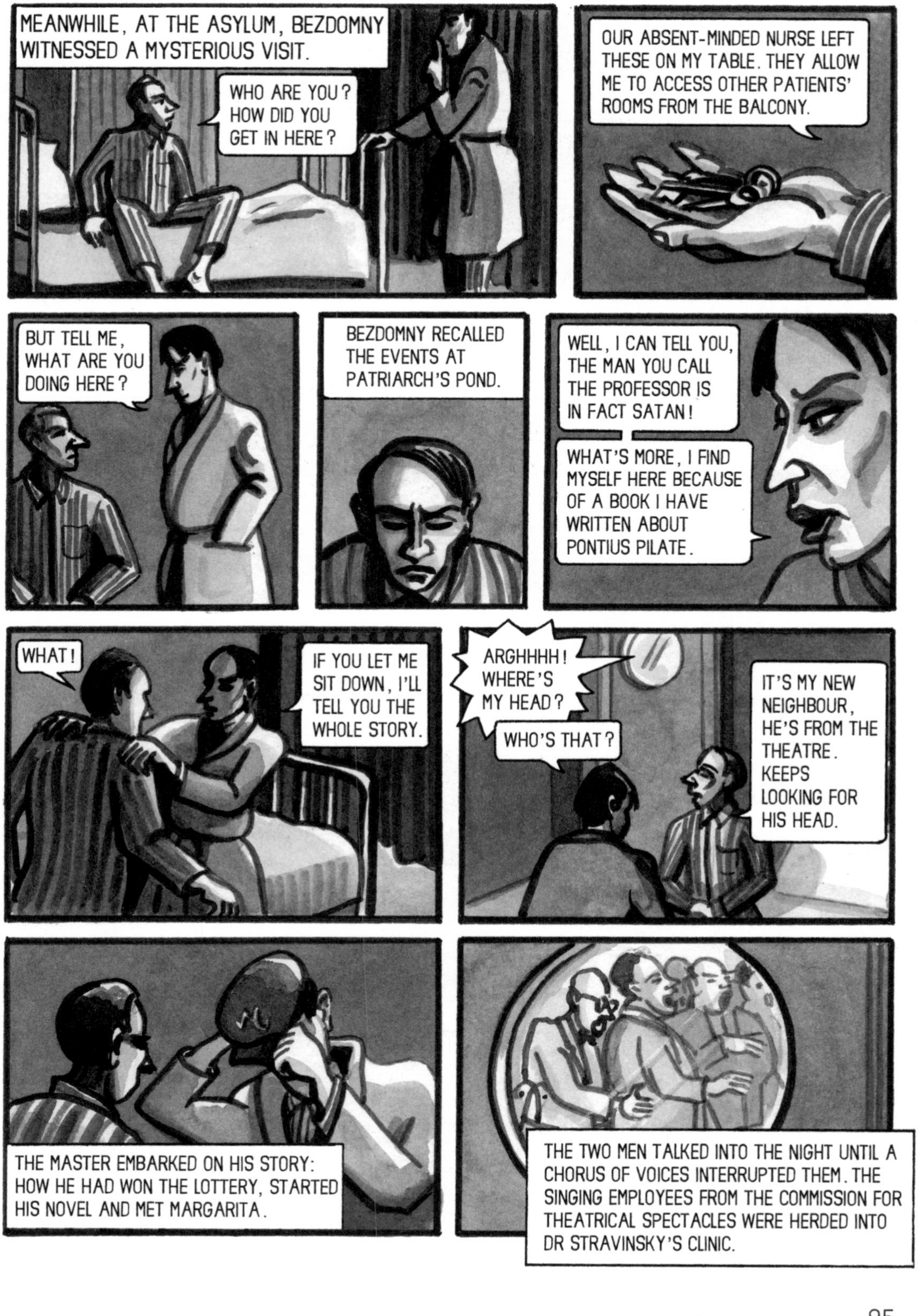
MEANWHILE, AT THE ASYLUM, BEZDOMNY WITNESSED A MYSTERIOUS VISIT.
WHO ARE YOU? HOW DID YOU GET IN HERE?
OUR ABSENT-MINDED NURSE LEFT THESE ON MY TABLE. THEY ALLOW ME TO ACCESS OTHER PATIENTS' ROOMS FROM THE BALCONY.
BUT TELL ME, WHAT ARE YOU DOING HERE?
BEZDOMNY RECALLED THE EVENTS AT PATRIARCH'S POND.
WELL, I CAN TELL YOU, THE MAN YOU CALL THE PROFESSOR IS IN FACT SATAN!
WHAT'S MORE, I FIND MYSELF HERE BECAUSE OF A BOOK I HAVE WRITTEN ABOUT PONTIUS PILATE.
WHAT!
IF YOU LET ME SIT DOWN, I'LL TELL YOU THE WHOLE STORY.
ARGHHHH! WHERE'S MY HEAD?
WHO'S THAT?
IT'S MY NEW NEIGHBOUR, HE'S FROM THE THEATRE. KEEPS LOOKING FOR HIS HEAD.
THE MASTER EMBARKED ON HIS STORY: HOW HE HAD WON THE LOTTERY, STARTED HIS NOVEL AND MET MARGARITA.
THE TWO MEN TALKED INTO THE NIGHT UNTIL A CHORUS OF VOICES INTERRUPTED THEM. THE SINGING EMPLOYEES FROM THE COMMISSION FOR THEATRICAL SPECTACLES WERE HERDED INTO DR STRAVINSKY'S CLINIC.

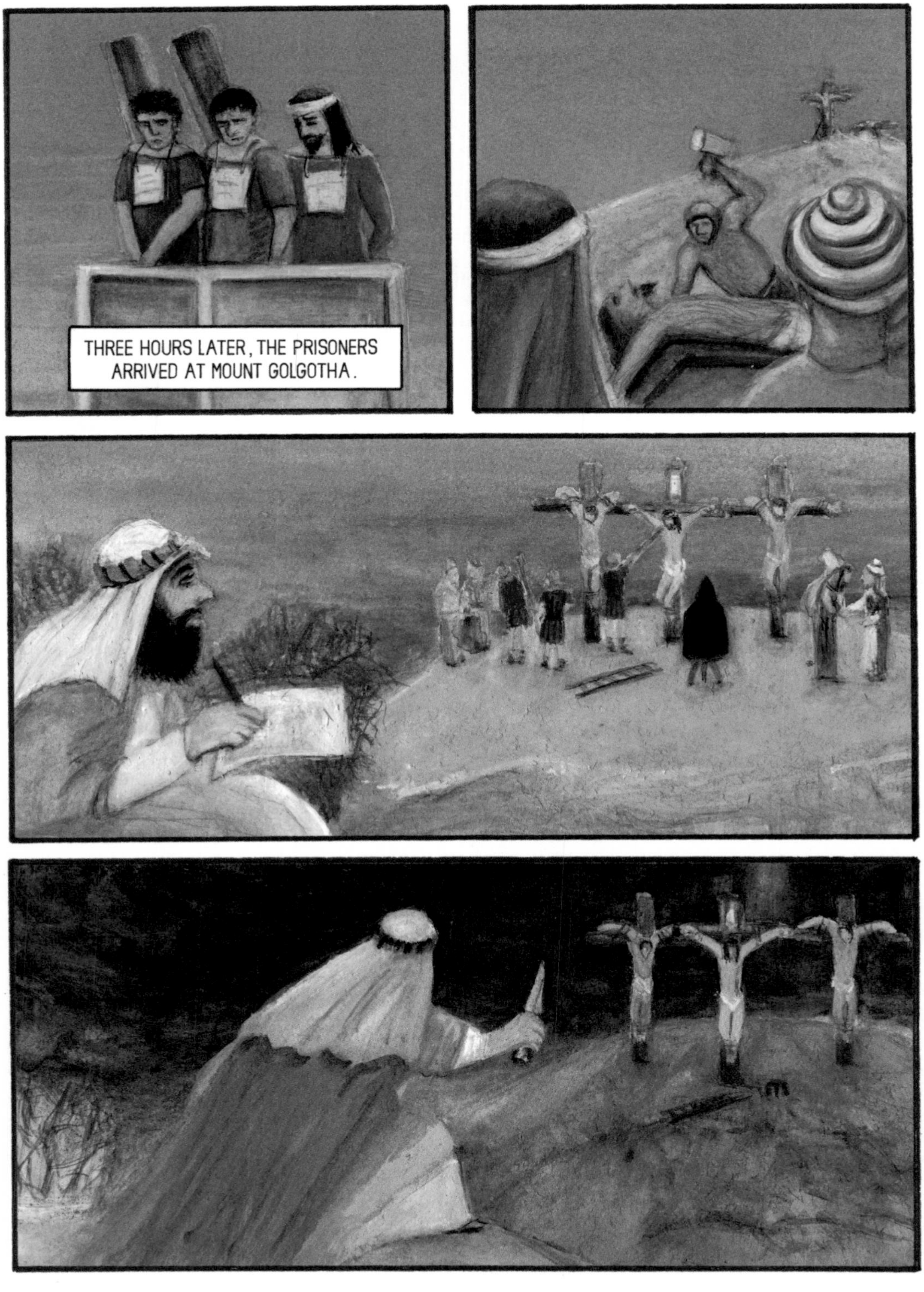
THREE HOURS LATER, THE PRISONERS ARRIVED AT MOUNT GOLGOTHA.

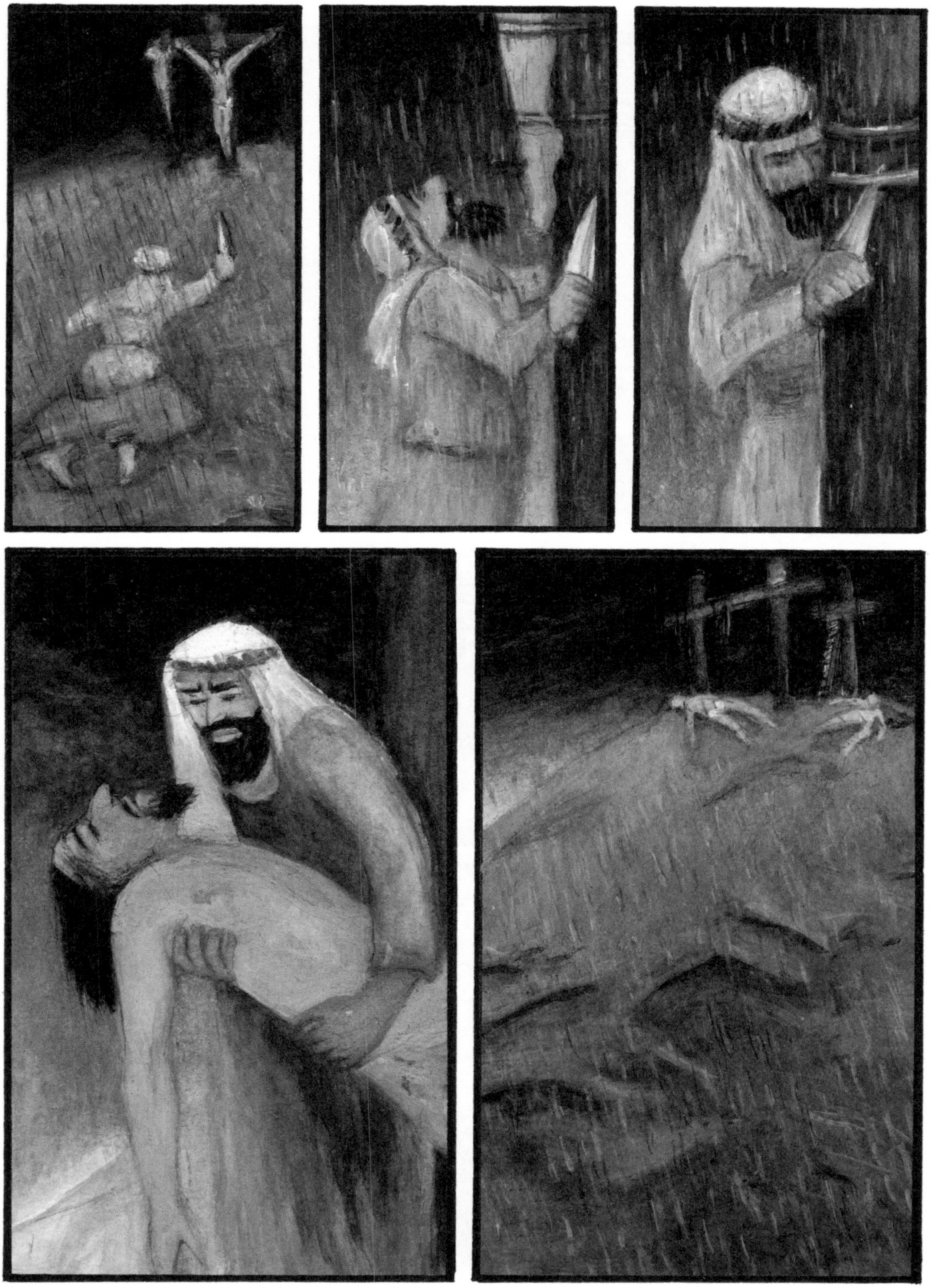

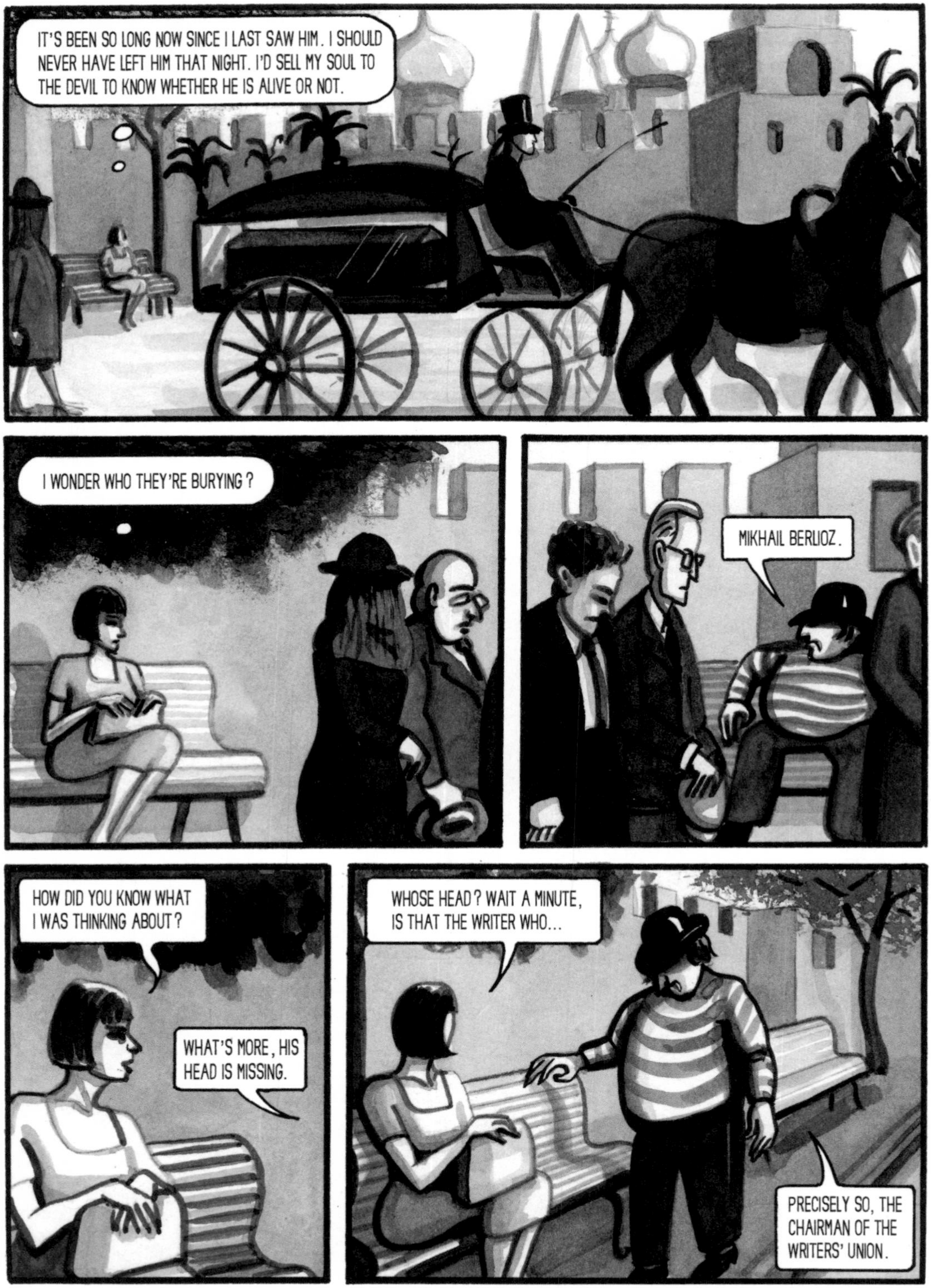
IT'S BEEN SO LONG NOW SINCE I LAST SAW HIM. I SHOULD NEVER HAVE LEFT HIM THAT NIGHT. I'D SELL MY SOUL TO THE DEVIL TO KNOW WHETHER HE IS ALIVE OR NOT.
I WONDER WHO THEY'RE BURYING?
MIKHAIL BERLIOZ.
HOW DID YOU KNOW WHAT I WAS THINKING ABOUT?
WHAT'S MORE, HIS HEAD IS MISSING.
WHOSE HEAD? WAIT A MINUTE, IS THAT THE WRITER WHO...
PRECISELY SO, THE CHAIRMAN OF THE WRITERS' UNION.

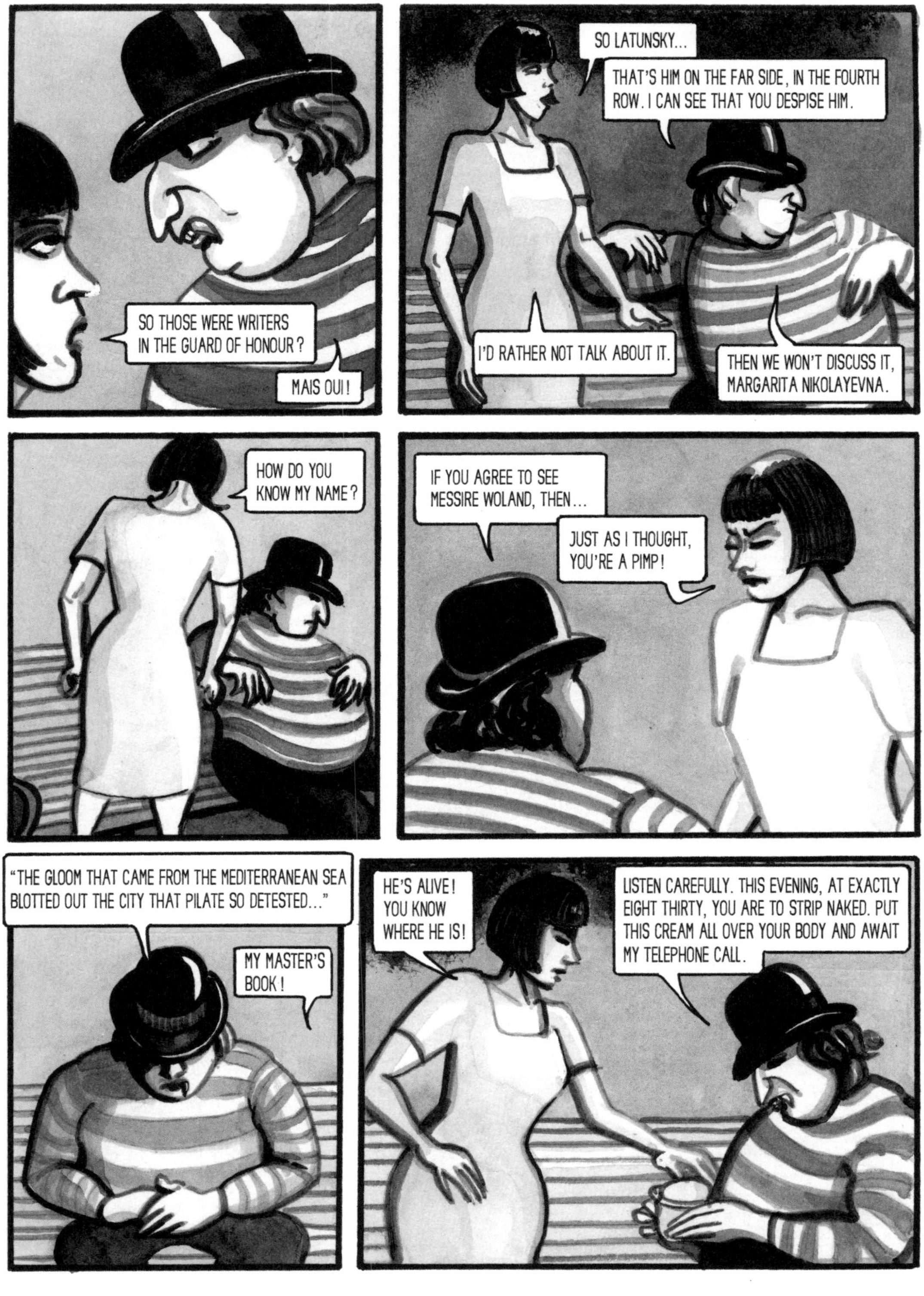
SO THOSE WERE WRITERS IN THE GUARD OF HONOUR?
MAIS OUI!
SO LATUNSKY...
THAT'S HIM ON THE FAR SIDE, IN THE FOURTH ROW. I CAN SEE THAT YOU DESPISE HIM.
I'D RATHER NOT TALK ABOUT IT.
THEN WE WON'T DISCUSS IT, MARGARITA NIKOLAYEVNA.
HOW DO YOU KNOW MY NAME?
IF YOU AGREE TO SEE MESSIRE WOLAND, THEN...
JUST AS I THOUGHT, YOU'RE A PIMP!
"THE GLOOM THAT CAME FROM THE MEDITERRANEAN SEA BLOTTED OUT THE CITY THAT PILATE SO DETESTED..."
MY MASTER'S BOOK!
HE'S ALIVE! YOU KNOW WHERE HE IS!
LISTEN CAREFULLY. THIS EVENING, AT EXACTLY EIGHT THIRTY, YOU ARE TO STRIP NAKED. PUT THIS CREAM ALL OVER YOUR BODY AND AWAIT MY TELEPHONE CALL.

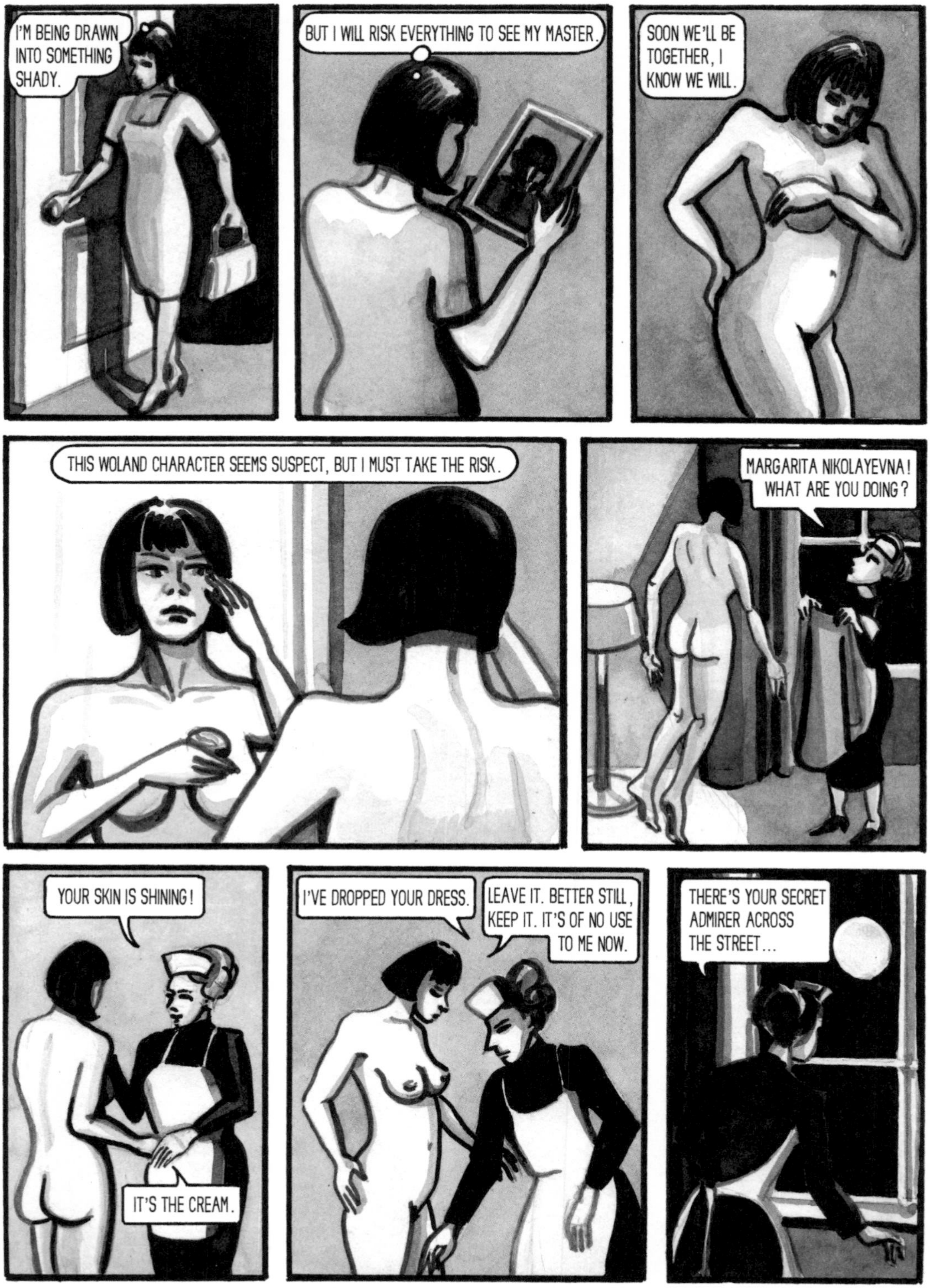
I'M BEING DRAWN INTO SOMETHING SHADY.
BUT I WILL RISK EVERYTHING TO SEE MY MASTER.
SOON WE'LL BE TOGETHER, I KNOW WE WILL.
THIS WOLAND CHARACTER SEEMS SUSPECT, BUT I MUST TAKE THE RISK.
MARGARITA NIKOLAYEVNA! WHAT ARE YOU DOING?
YOUR SKIN IS SHINING!
IT'S THE CREAM.
I'VE DROPPED YOUR DRESS.
LEAVE IT. BETTER STILL, KEEP IT. IT'S OF NO USE TO ME NOW.
THERE'S YOUR SECRET ADMIRER ACROSS THE STREET...

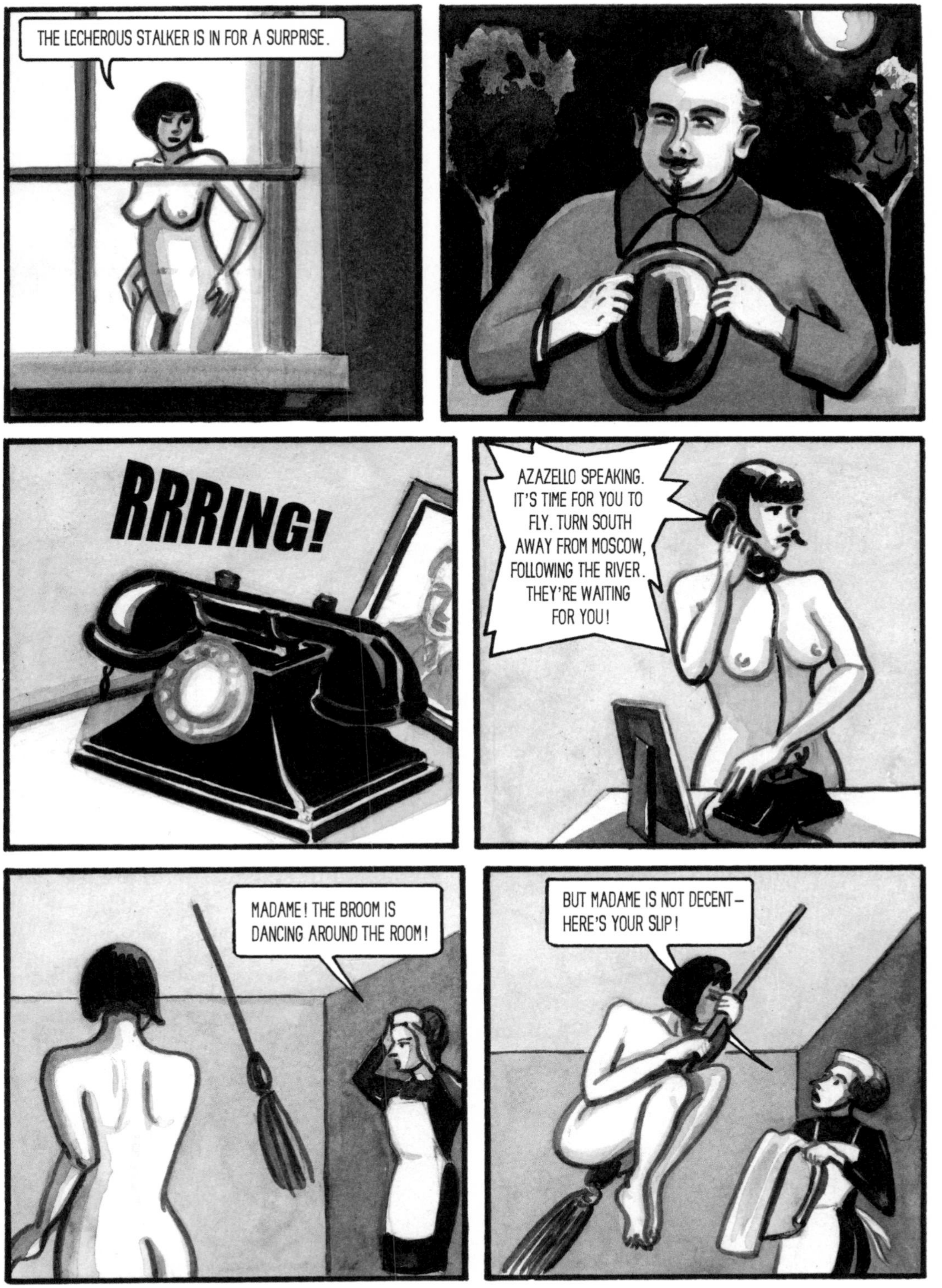
THE LECHEROUS STALKER IS IN FOR A SURPRISE.
RRRING!
AZAZELLO SPEAKING. IT'S TIME FOR YOU TO FLY. TURN SOUTH AWAY FROM MOSCOW, FOLLOWING THE RIVER. THEY'RE WAITING FOR YOU!
MADAME! THE BROOM IS DANCING AROUND THE ROOM!
BUT MADAME IS NOT DECENT– HERE'S YOUR SLIP!

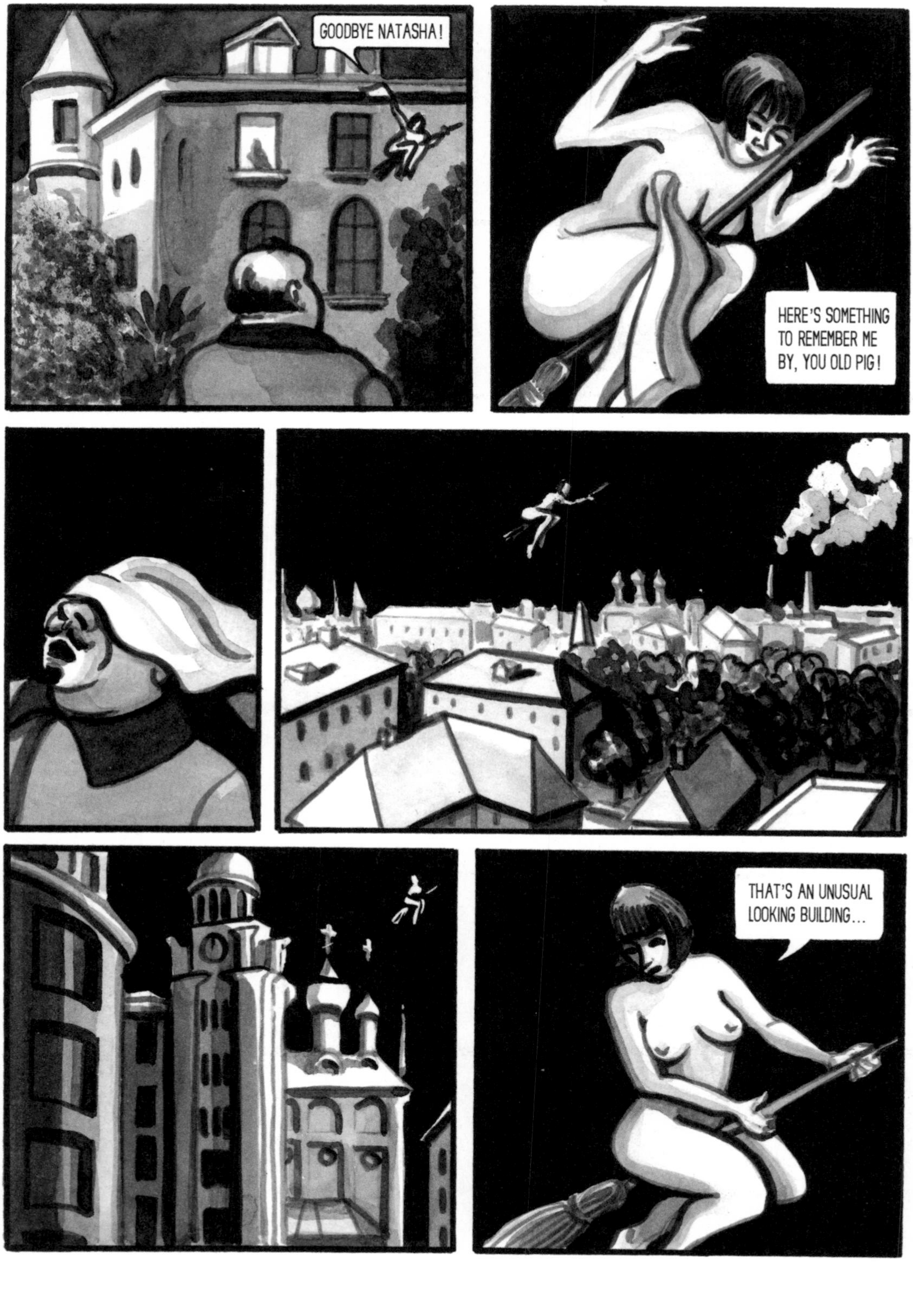
GOODBYE NATASHA!
HERE'S SOMETHING TO REMEMBER ME BY, YOU OLD PIG!
THAT'S AN UNUSUAL LOOKING BUILDING...

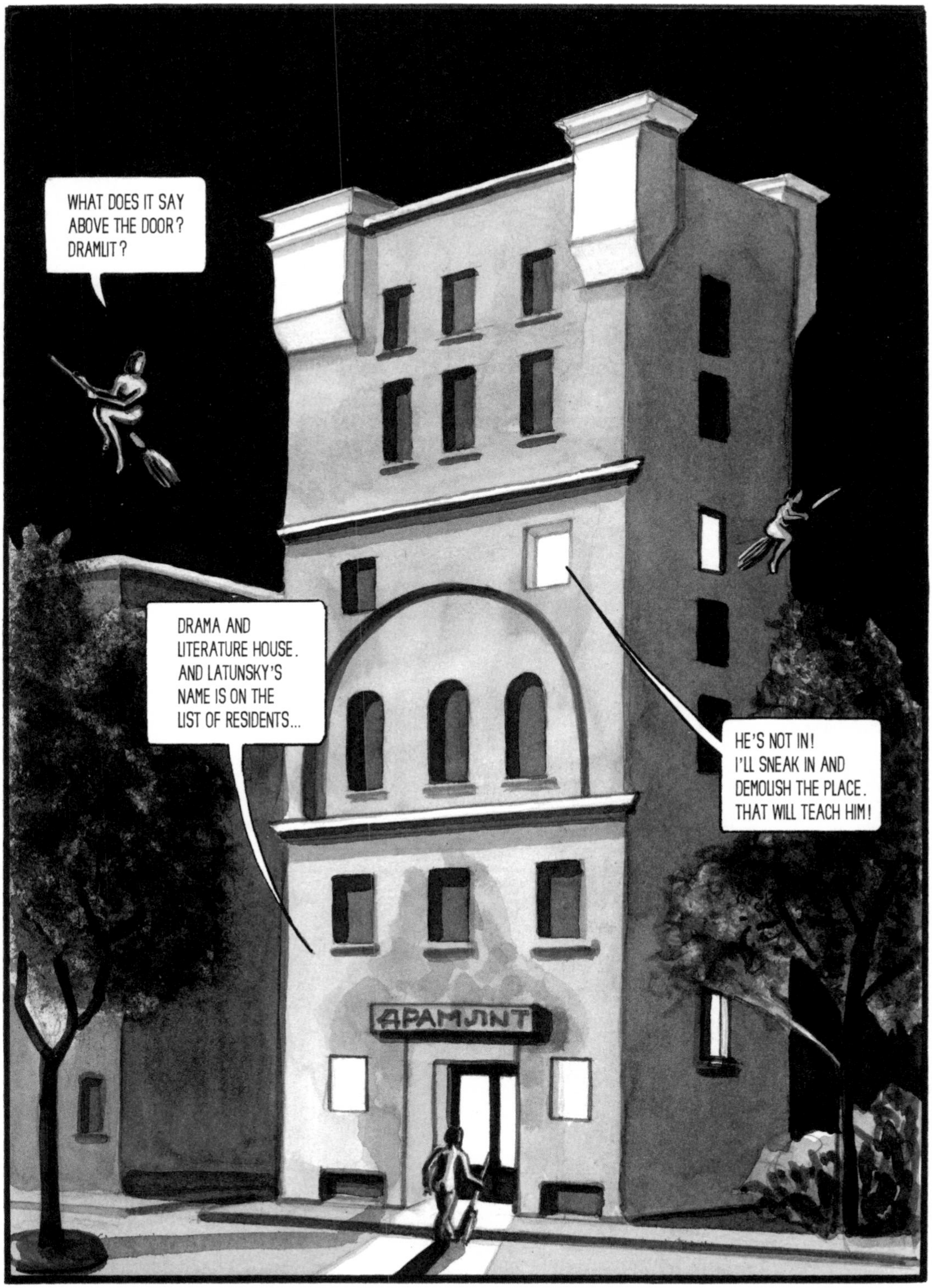
WHAT DOES IT SAY ABOVE THE DOOR? DRAMLIT?
DRAMA AND LITERATURE HOUSE. AND LATUNSKY'S NAME IS ON THE LIST OF RESIDENTS...
HE'S NOT IN! I'LL SNEAK IN AND DEMOLISH THE PLACE. THAT WILL TEACH HIM!
ДРАМЛИТ

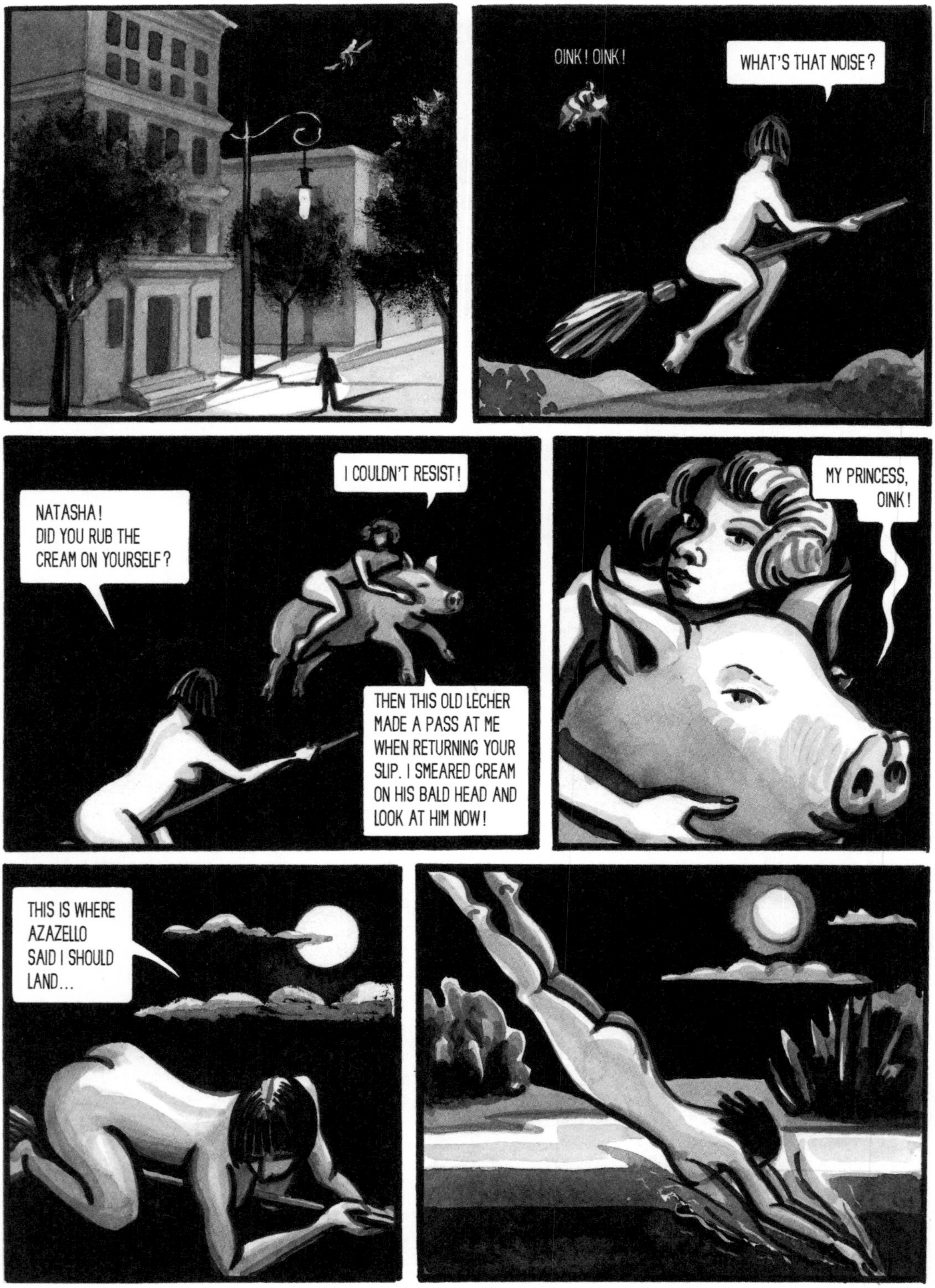
OINK! OINK!
WHAT'S THAT NOISE?
NATASHA! DID YOU RUB THE CREAM ON YOURSELF?
I COULDN'T RESIST!
THEN THIS OLD LECHER MADE A PASS AT ME WHEN RETURNING YOUR SLIP. I SMEARED CREAM ON HIS BALD HEAD AND LOOK AT HIM NOW!
MY PRINCESS, OINK!
THIS IS WHERE AZAZELLO SAID I SHOULD LAND...

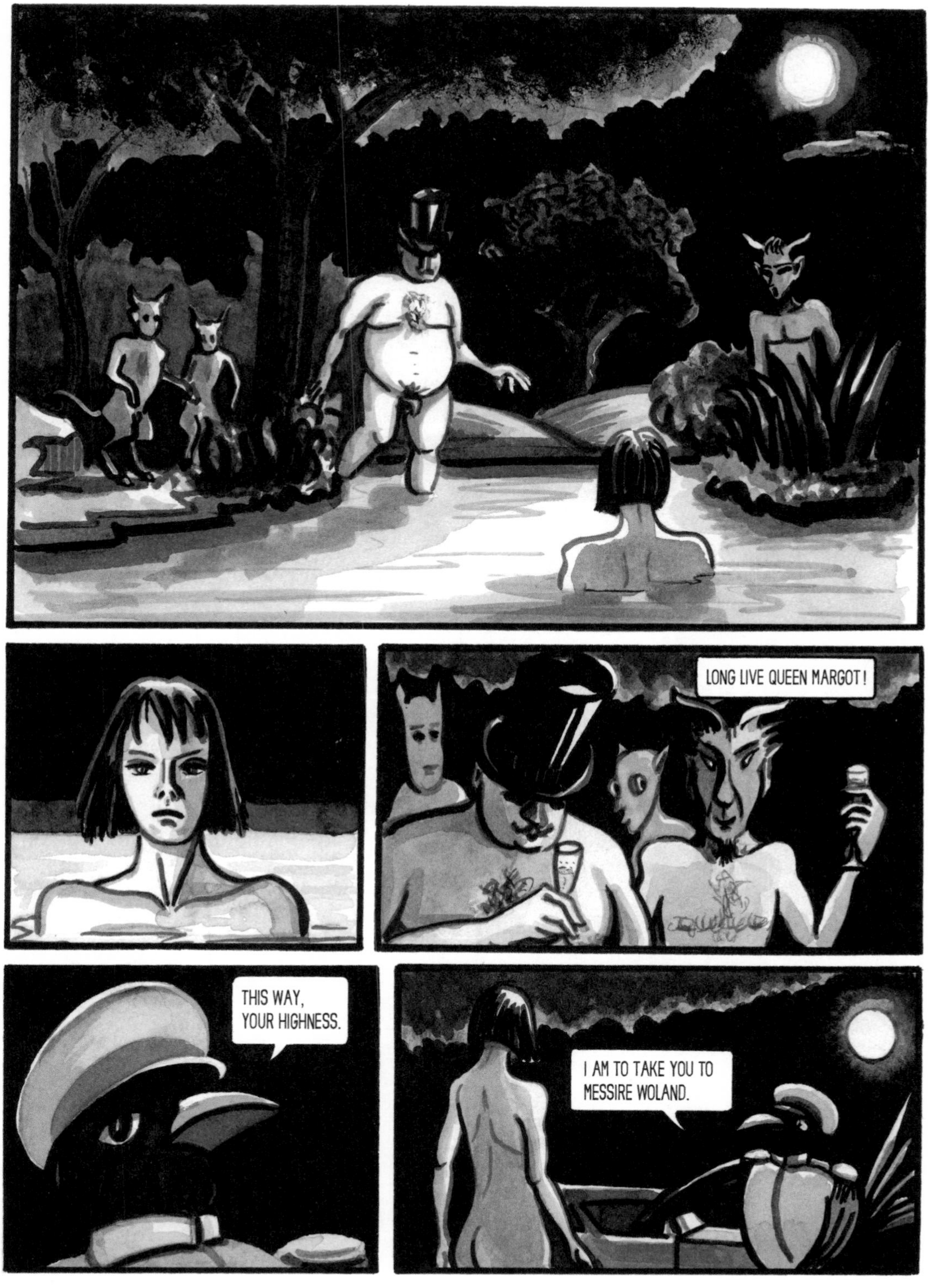
LONG LIVE QUEEN MARGOT!
THIS WAY, YOUR HIGHNESS.
I AM TO TAKE YOU TO MESSIRE WOLAND.

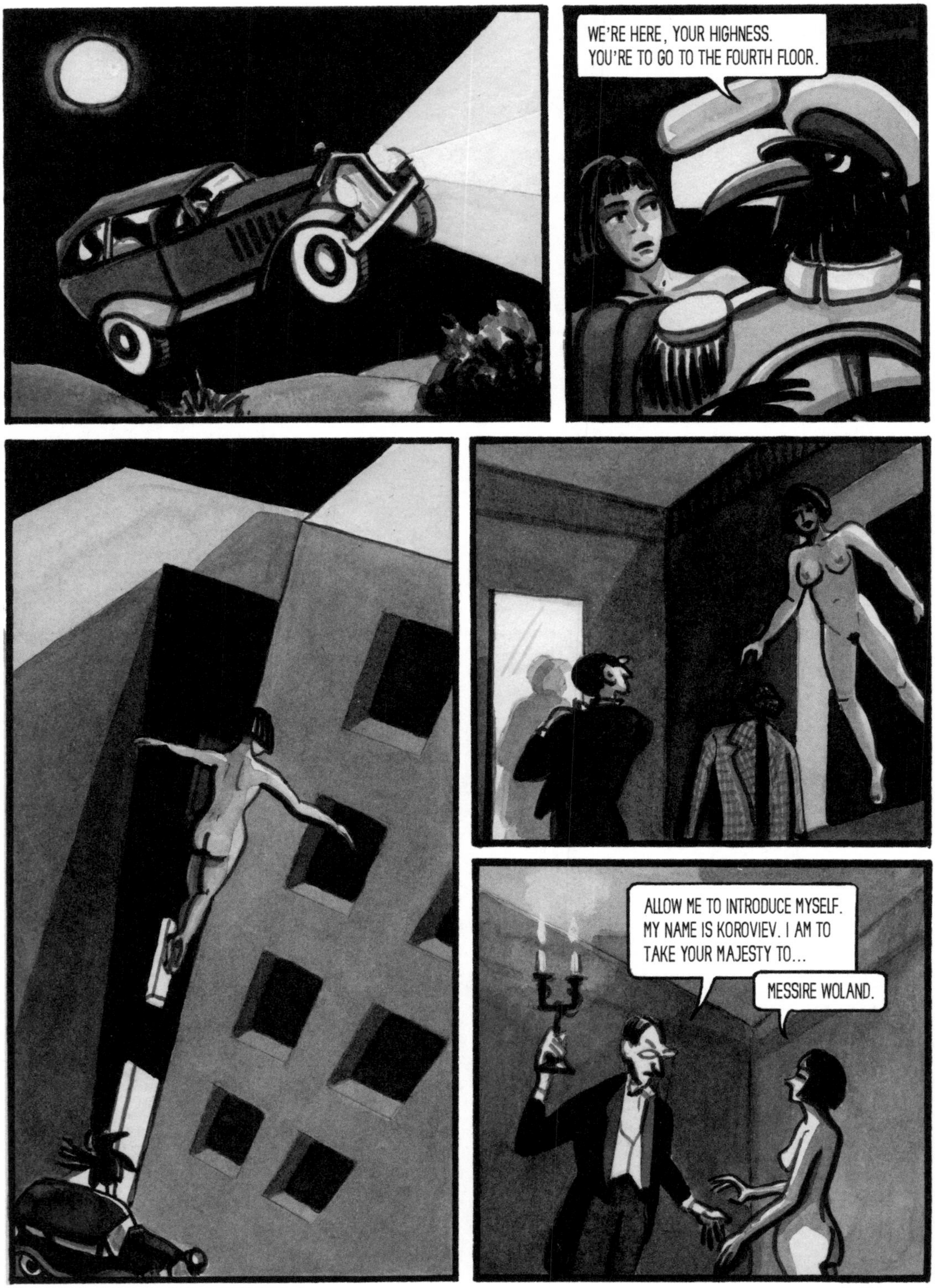
WE'RE HERE, YOUR HIGHNESS.
YOU'RE TO GO TO THE FOURTH FLOOR.
ALLOW ME TO INTRODUCE MYSELF. MY NAME IS KOROVIEV. I AM TO TAKE YOUR MAJESTY TO...
MESSIRE WOLAND.

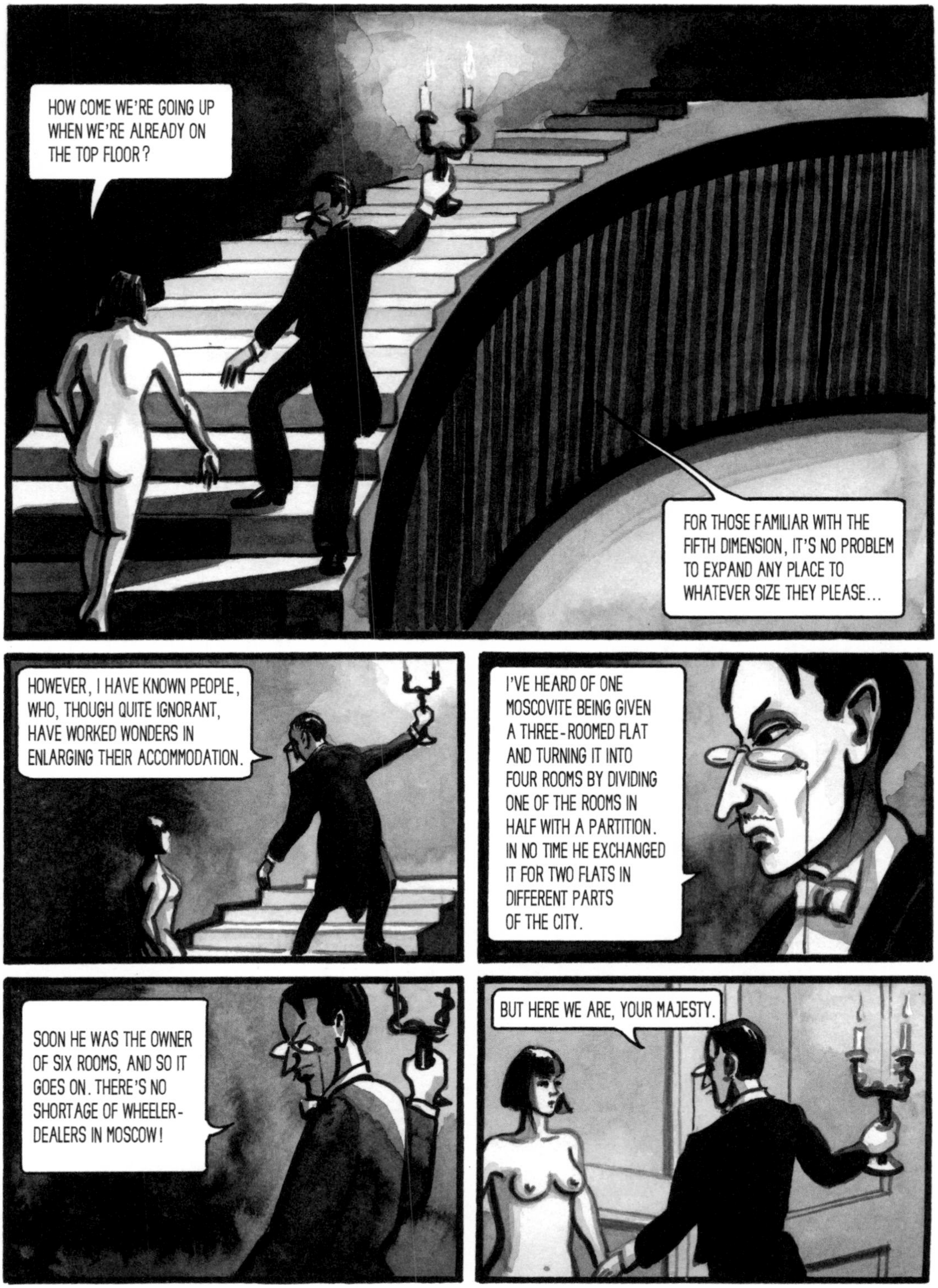
HOW COME WE'RE GOING UP WHEN WE'RE ALREADY ON THE TOP FLOOR?
FOR THOSE FAMILIAR WITH THE FIFTH DIMENSION, IT'S NO PROBLEM TO EXPAND ANY PLACE TO WHATEVER SIZE THEY PLEASE...
HOWEVER, I HAVE KNOWN PEOPLE, WHO, THOUGH QUITE IGNORANT, HAVE WORKED WONDERS IN ENLARGING THEIR ACCOMMODATION.
I'VE HEARD OF ONE MOSCOVITE BEING GIVEN A THREE-ROOMED FLAT AND TURNING IT INTO FOUR ROOMS BY DIVIDING ONE OF THE ROOMS IN HALF WITH A PARTITION. IN NO TIME HE EXCHANGED IT FOR TWO FLATS IN DIFFERENT PARTS OF THE CITY.
SOON HE WAS THE OWNER OF SIX ROOMS, AND SO IT GOES ON. THERE'S NO SHORTAGE OF WHEELER-DEALERS IN MOSCOW!
BUT HERE WE ARE, YOUR MAJESTY.

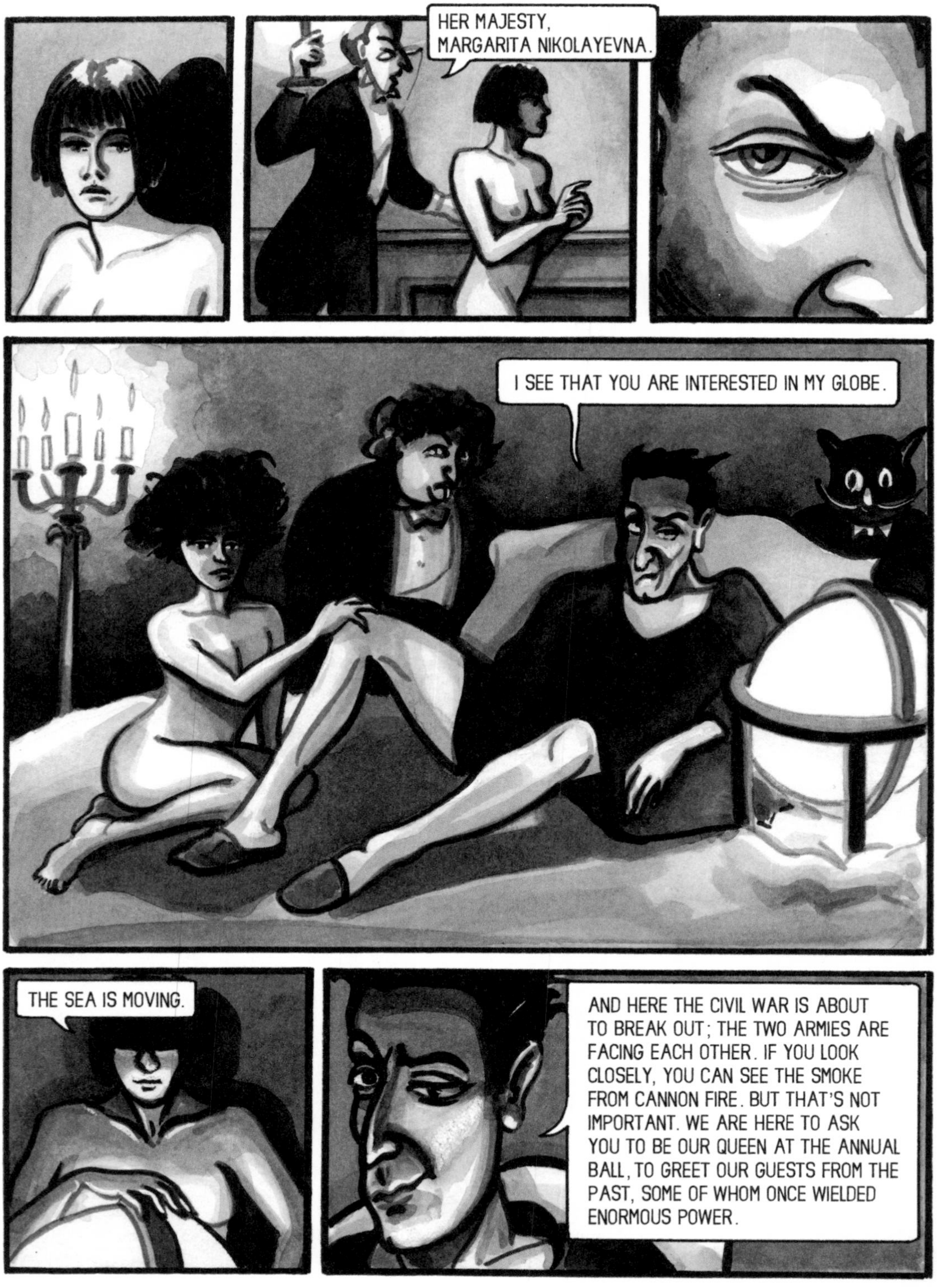
HER MAJESTY, MARGARITA NIKOLAYEVNA.
I SEE THAT YOU ARE INTERESTED IN MY GLOBE.
THE SEA IS MOVING.
AND HERE THE CIVIL WAR IS ABOUT TO BREAK OUT; THE TWO ARMIES ARE FACING EACH OTHER. IF YOU LOOK CLOSELY, YOU CAN SEE THE SMOKE FROM CANNON FIRE. BUT THAT'S NOT IMPORTANT. WE ARE HERE TO ASK YOU TO BE OUR QUEEN AT THE ANNUAL BALL, TO GREET OUR GUESTS FROM THE PAST, SOME OF WHOM ONCE WIELDED ENORMOUS POWER.

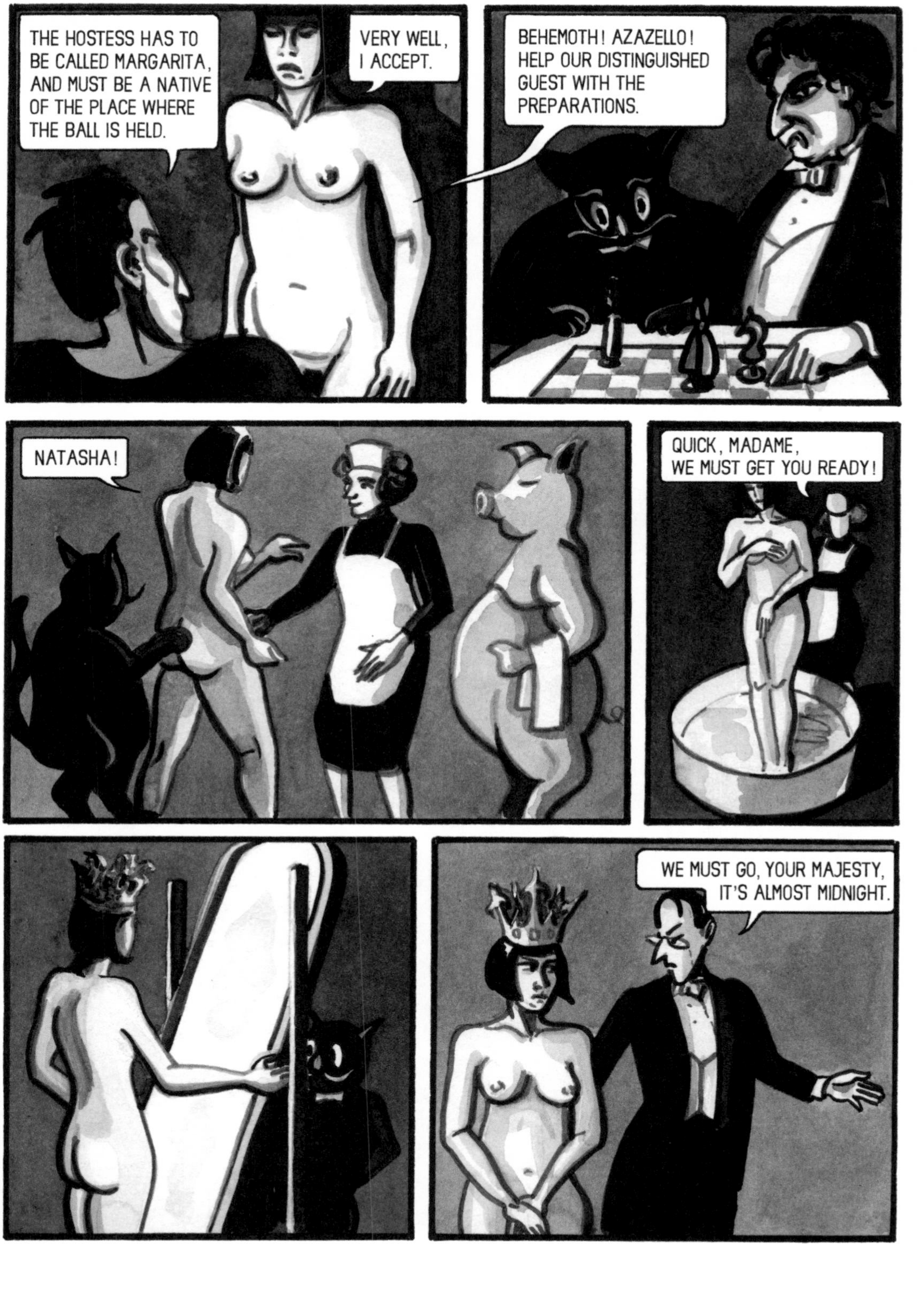
THE HOSTESS HAS TO BE CALLED MARGARITA, AND MUST BE A NATIVE OF THE PLACE WHERE THE BALL IS HELD.
VERY WELL, I ACCEPT.
BEHEMOTH! AZAZELLO! HELP OUR DISTINGUISHED GUEST WITH THE PREPARATIONS.
NATASHA!
QUICK, MADAME, WE MUST GET YOU READY!
WE MUST GO, YOUR MAJESTY, IT'S ALMOST MIDNIGHT.

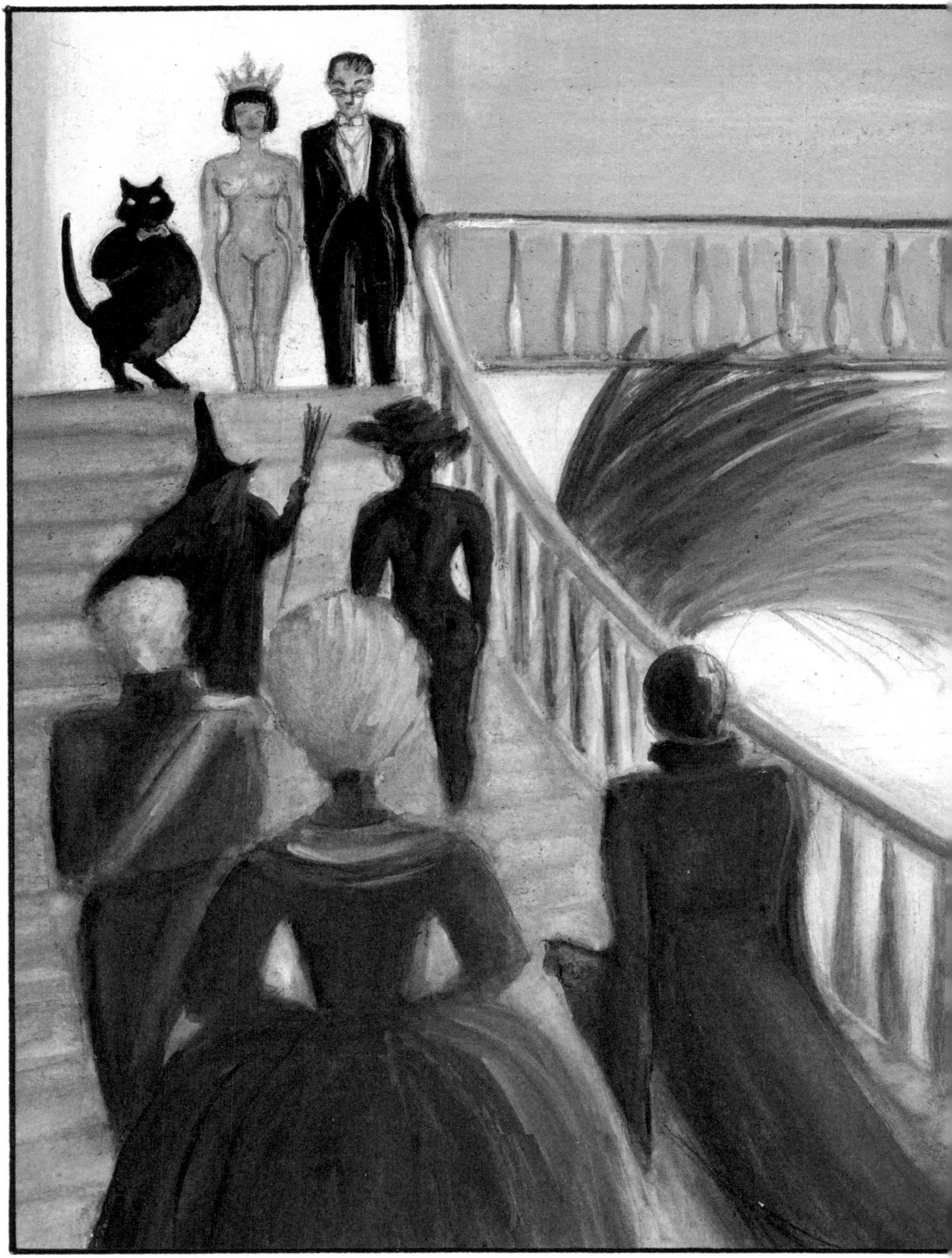

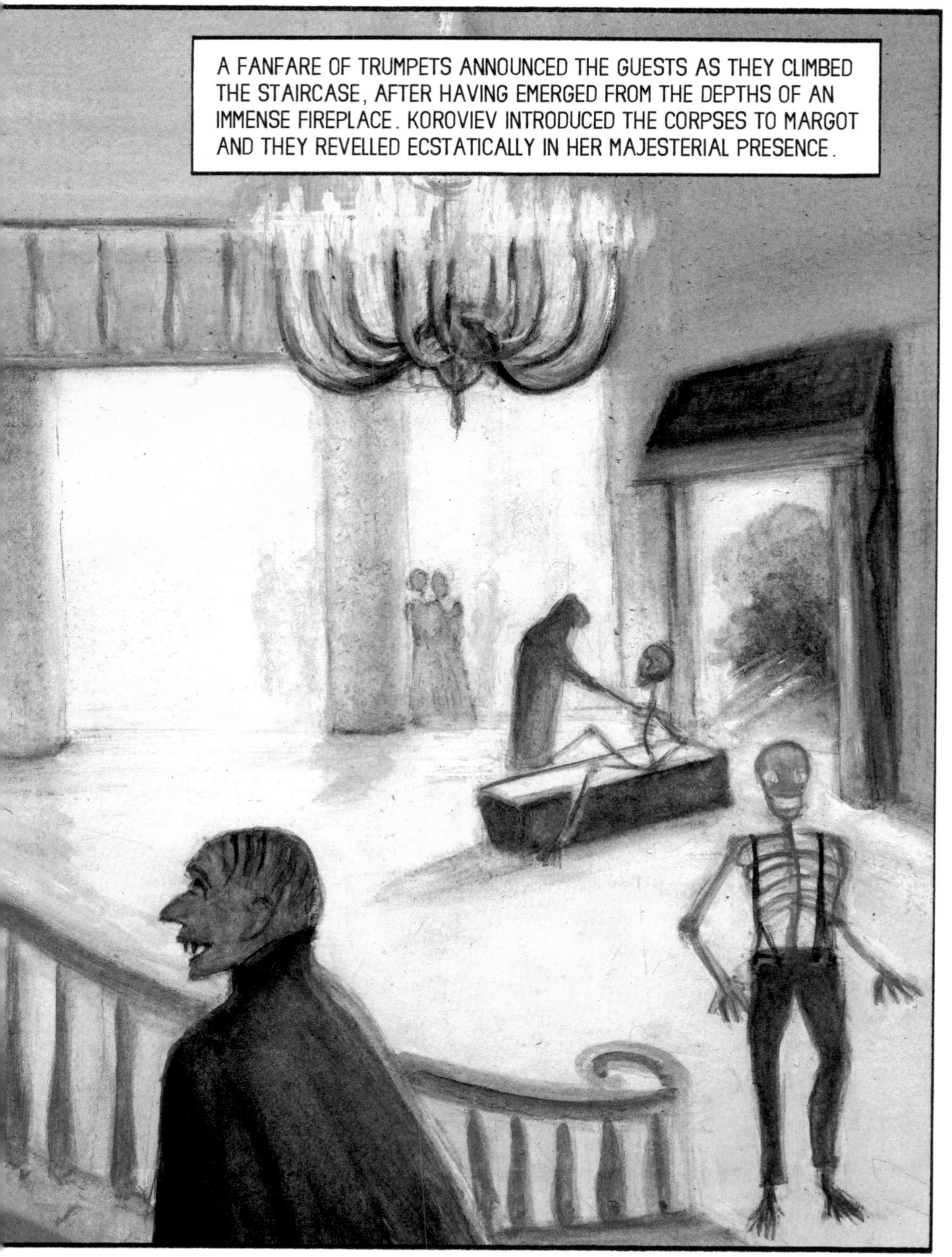
A FANFARE OF TRUMPETS ANNOUNCED THE GUESTS AS THEY CLIMBED THE STAIRCASE, AFTER HAVING EMERGED FROM THE DEPTHS OF AN IMMENSE FIREPLACE. KOROVIEV INTRODUCED THE CORPSES TO MARGOT AND THEY REVELLED ECSTATICALLY IN HER MAJESTERIAL PRESENCE.

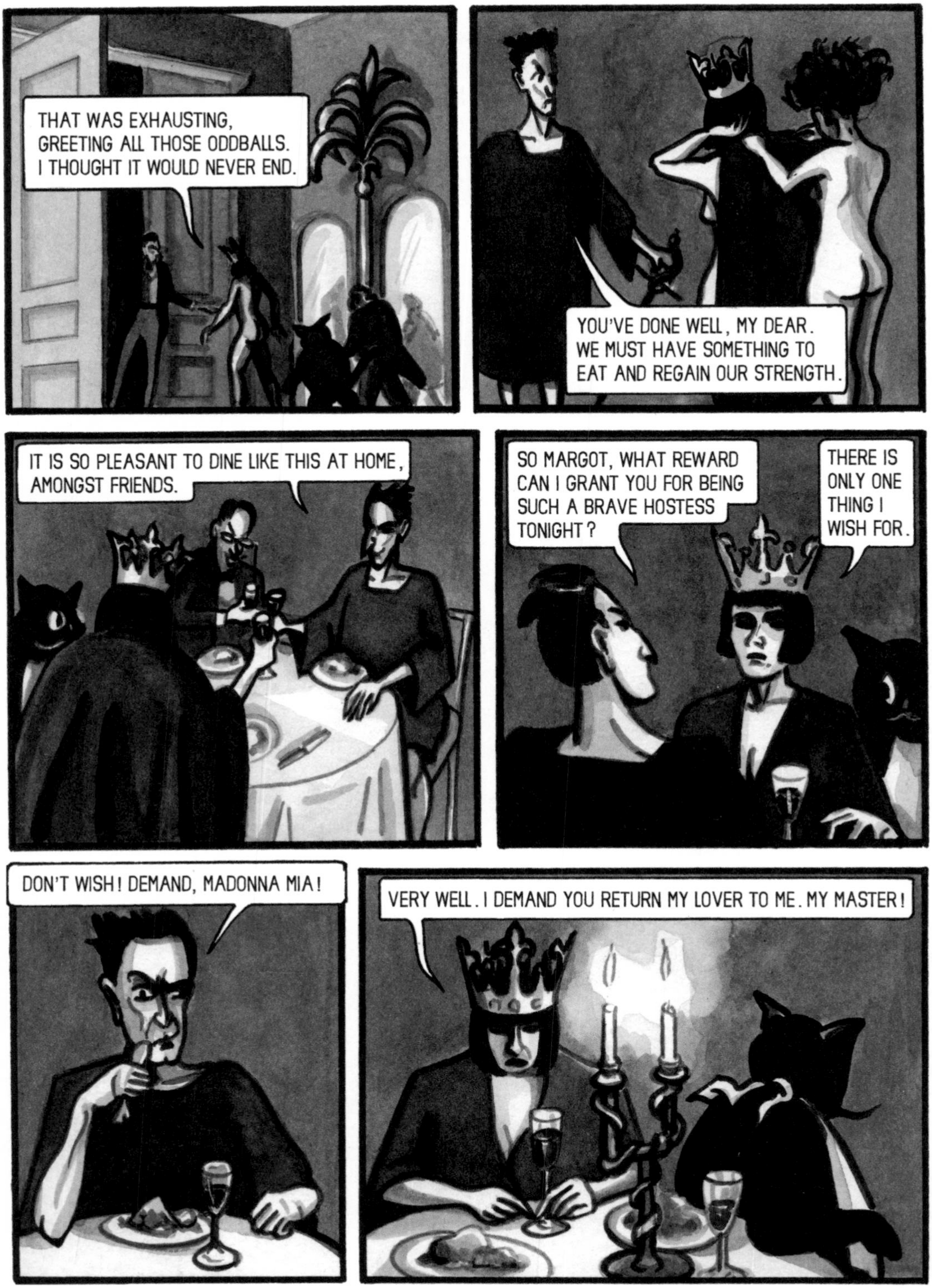
THAT WAS EXHAUSTING, GREETING ALL THOSE ODDBALLS. I THOUGHT IT WOULD NEVER END.
YOU'VE DONE WELL, MY DEAR. WE MUST HAVE SOMETHING TO EAT AND REGAIN OUR STRENGTH.
IT IS SO PLEASANT TO DINE LIKE THIS AT HOME, AMONGST FRIENDS.
SO MARGOT, WHAT REWARD CAN I GRANT YOU FOR BEING SUCH A BRAVE HOSTESS TONIGHT?
THERE IS ONLY ONE THING I WISH FOR.
DON'T WISH! DEMAND, MADONNA MIA!
VERY WELL. I DEMAND YOU RETURN MY LOVER TO ME. MY MASTER!

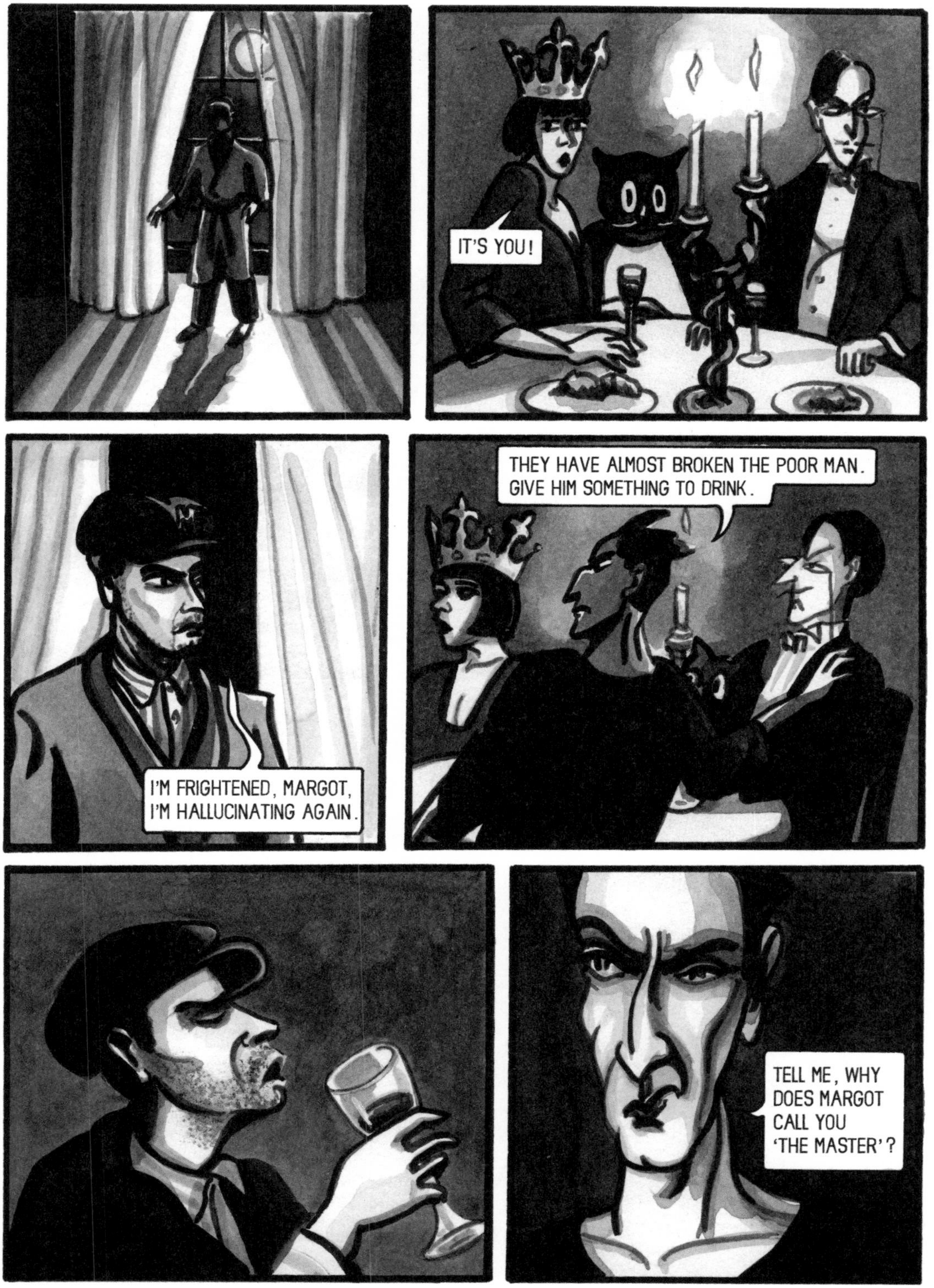
IT'S YOU!
I'M FRIGHTENED, MARGOT, I'M HALLUCINATING AGAIN.
THEY HAVE ALMOST BROKEN THE POOR MAN. GIVE HIM SOMETHING TO DRINK.
TELL ME, WHY DOES MARGOT CALL YOU 'THE MASTER'?

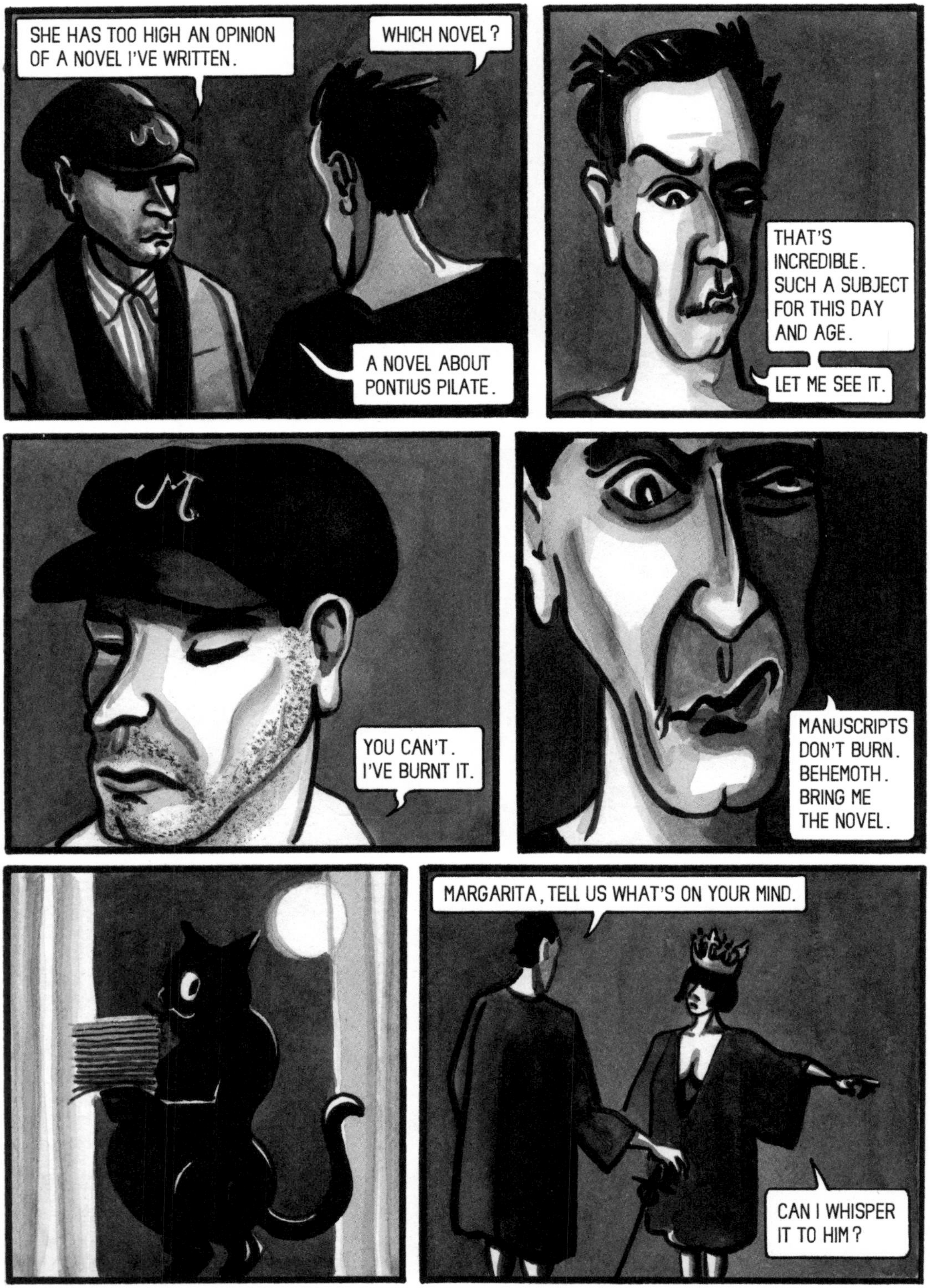
SHE HAS TOO HIGH AN OPINION OF A NOVEL I'VE WRITTEN.
WHICH NOVEL?
A NOVEL ABOUT PONTIUS PILATE.
THAT'S INCREDIBLE. SUCH A SUBJECT FOR THIS DAY AND AGE.
LET ME SEE IT.
YOU CAN'T. I'VE BURNT IT.
MANUSCRIPTS DON'T BURN. BEHEMOTH. BRING ME THE NOVEL.
MARGARITA, TELL US WHAT'S ON YOUR MIND.
CAN I WHISPER IT TO HIM?

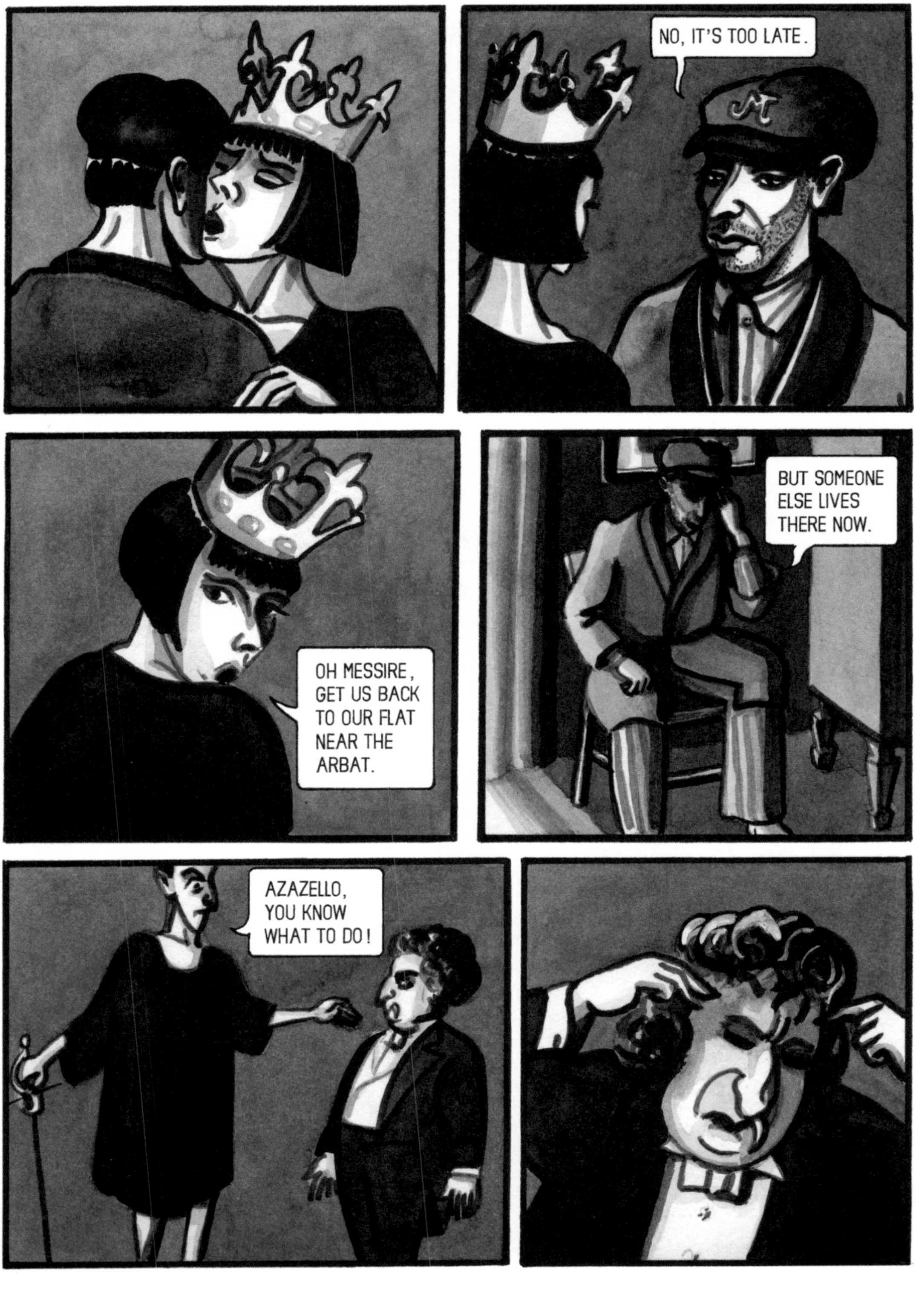
NO, IT'S TOO LATE.
OH MESSIRE, GET US BACK TO OUR FLAT NEAR THE ARBAT.
BUT SOMEONE ELSE LIVES THERE NOW.
AZAZELLO, YOU KNOW WHAT TO DO!

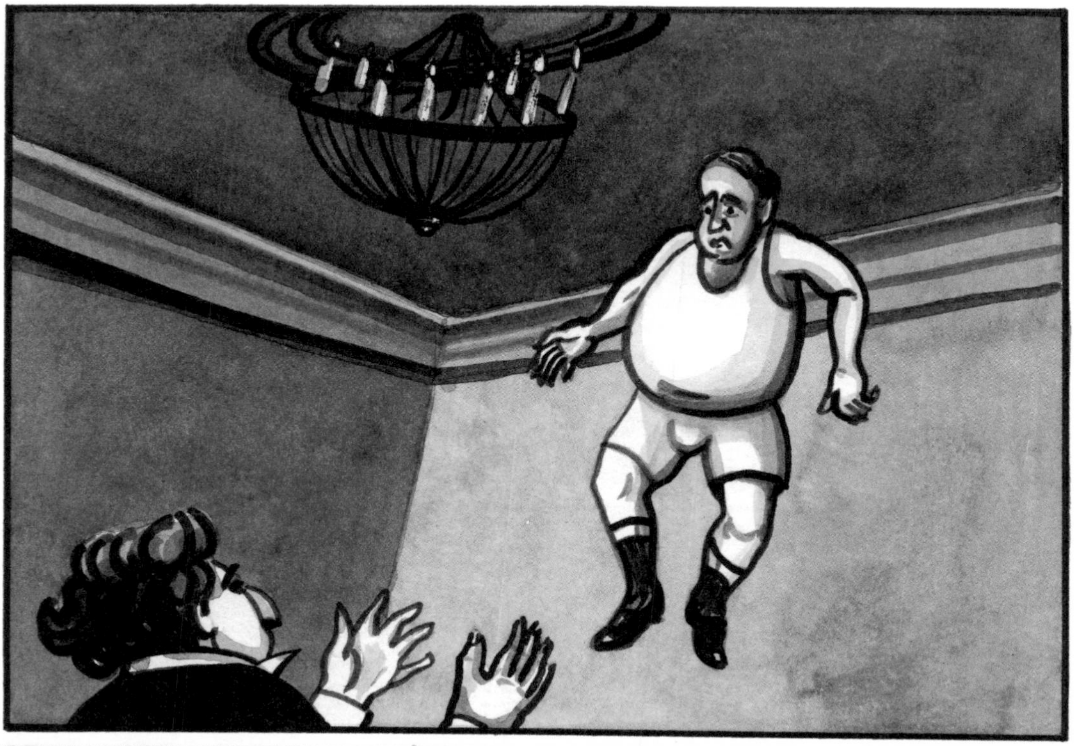

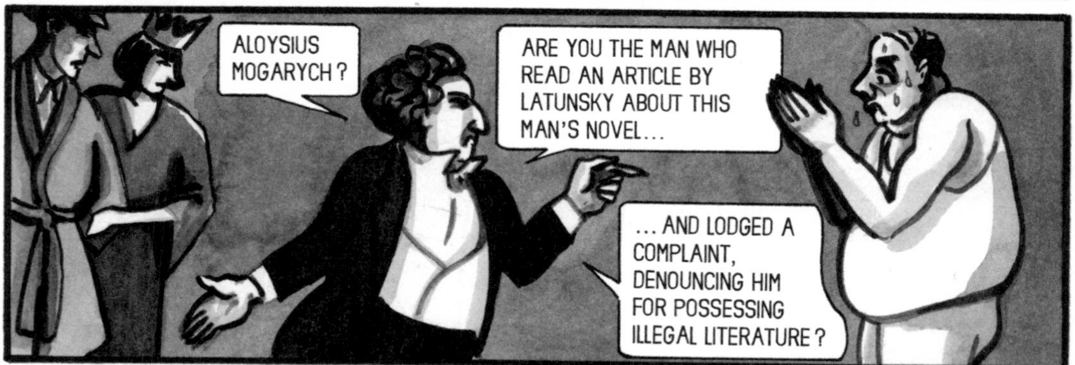

ALOYSIUS MOGARYCH?
ARE YOU THE MAN WHO READ AN ARTICLE BY LATUNSKY ABOUT THIS MAN'S NOVEL...
...AND LODGED A COMPLAINT, DENOUNCING HIM FOR POSSESSING ILLEGAL LITERATURE?

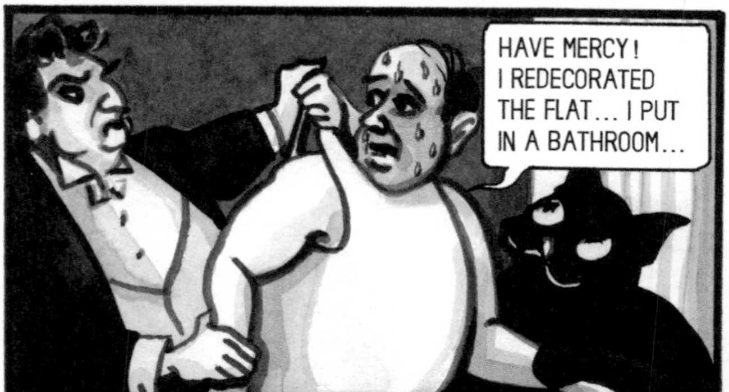

HAVE MERCY! I REDECORATED THE FLAT... I PUT IN A BATHROOM...

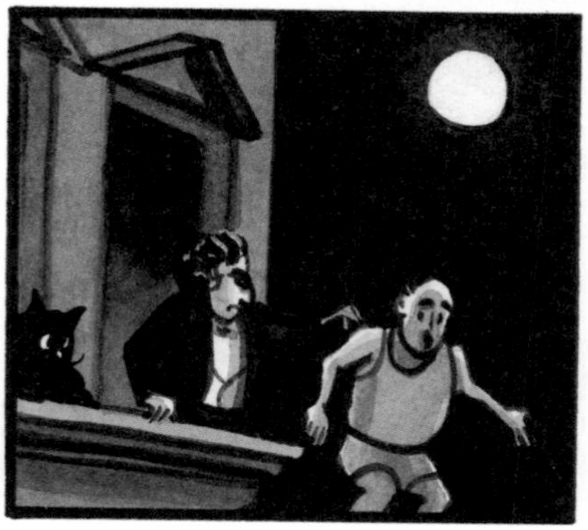

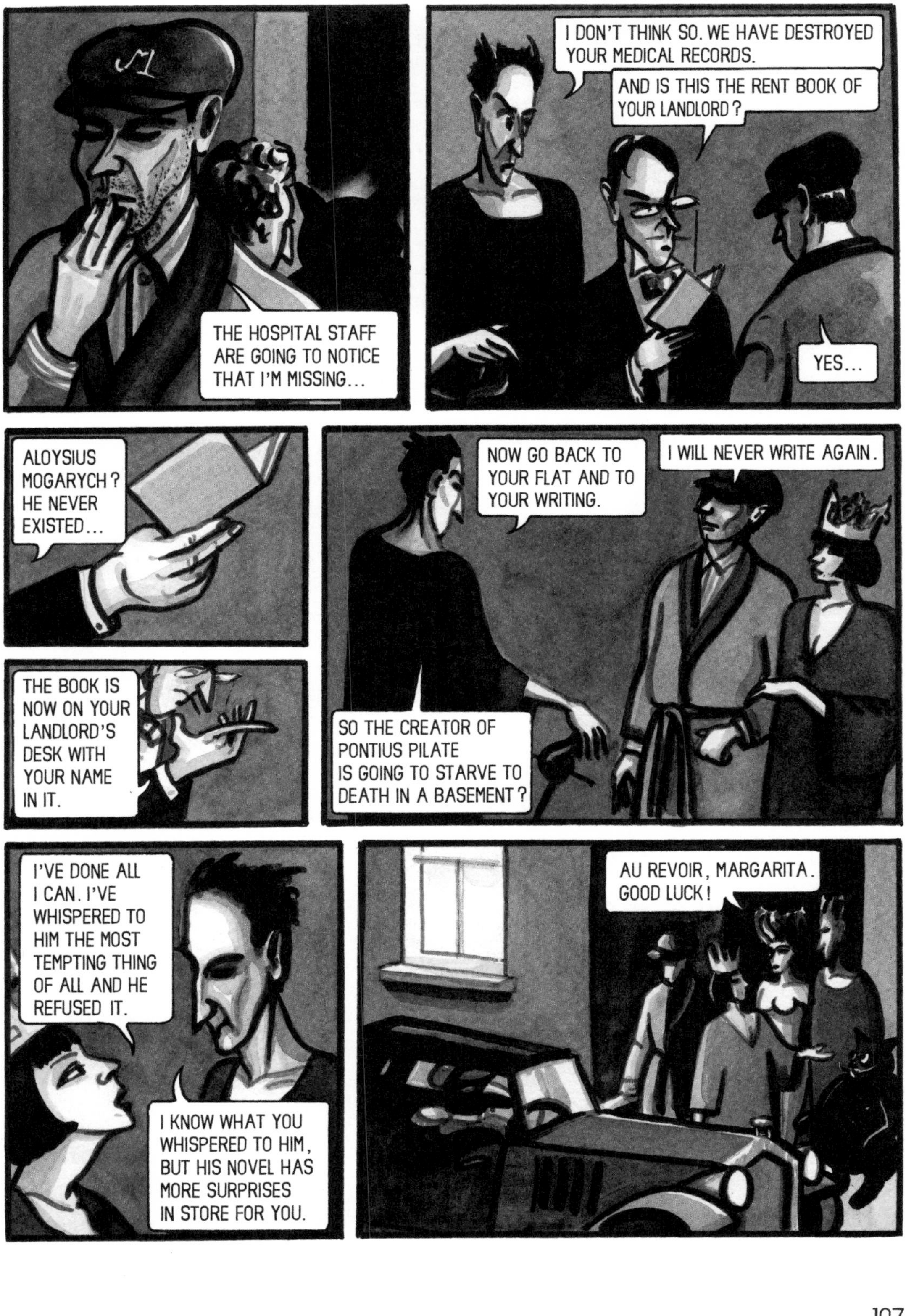
THE HOSPITAL STAFF ARE GOING TO NOTICE THAT I'M MISSING...
I DON'T THINK SO. WE HAVE DESTROYED YOUR MEDICAL RECORDS.
AND IS THIS THE RENT BOOK OF YOUR LANDLORD?
YES...
ALOYSIUS MOGARYCH? HE NEVER EXISTED...
THE BOOK IS NOW ON YOUR LANDLORD'S DESK WITH YOUR NAME IN IT.
NOW GO BACK TO YOUR FLAT AND TO YOUR WRITING.
I WILL NEVER WRITE AGAIN.
SO THE CREATOR OF PONTIUS PILATE IS GOING TO STARVE TO DEATH IN A BASEMENT?
I'VE DONE ALL I CAN. I'VE WHISPERED TO HIM THE MOST TEMPTING THING OF ALL AND HE REFUSED IT.
I KNOW WHAT YOU WHISPERED TO HIM, BUT HIS NOVEL HAS MORE SURPRISES IN STORE FOR YOU.
AU REVOIR, MARGARITA. GOOD LUCK!

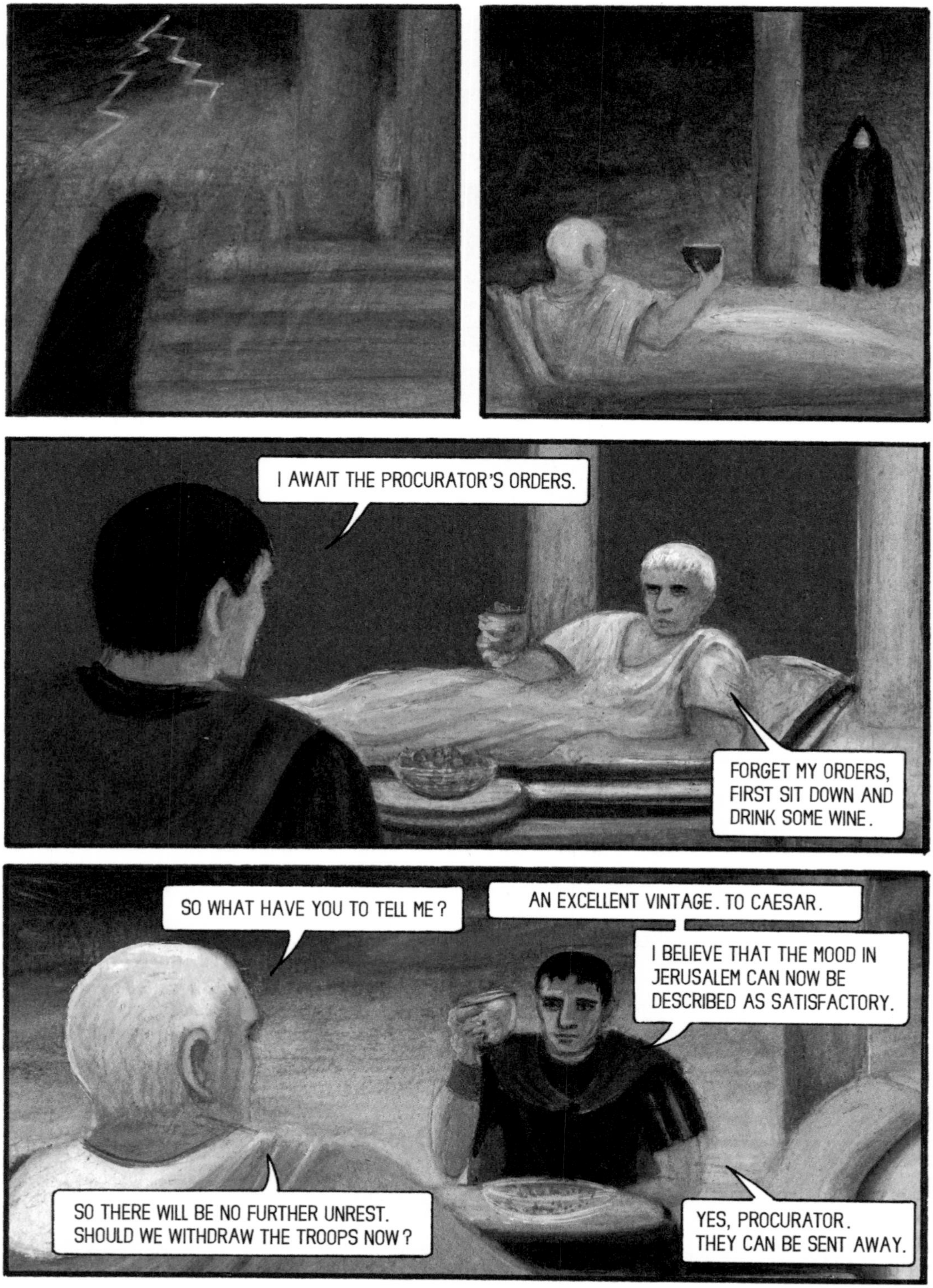
I AWAIT THE PROCURATOR'S ORDERS.
FORGET MY ORDERS, FIRST SIT DOWN AND DRINK SOME WINE.
SO WHAT HAVE YOU TO TELL ME?
AN EXCELLENT VINTAGE. TO CAESAR.
I BELIEVE THAT THE MOOD IN JERUSALEM CAN NOW BE DESCRIBED AS SATISFACTORY.
SO THERE WILL BE NO FURTHER UNREST. SHOULD WE WITHDRAW THE TROOPS NOW?
YES, PROCURATOR. THEY CAN BE SENT AWAY.

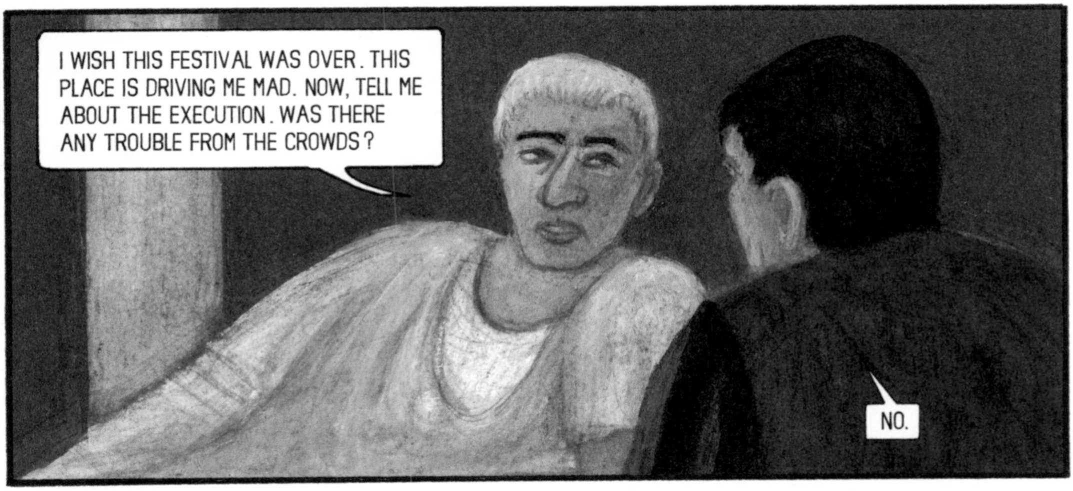
I WISH THIS FESTIVAL WAS OVER. THIS PLACE IS DRIVING ME MAD. NOW, TELL ME ABOUT THE EXECUTION. WAS THERE ANY TROUBLE FROM THE CROWDS?
NO.

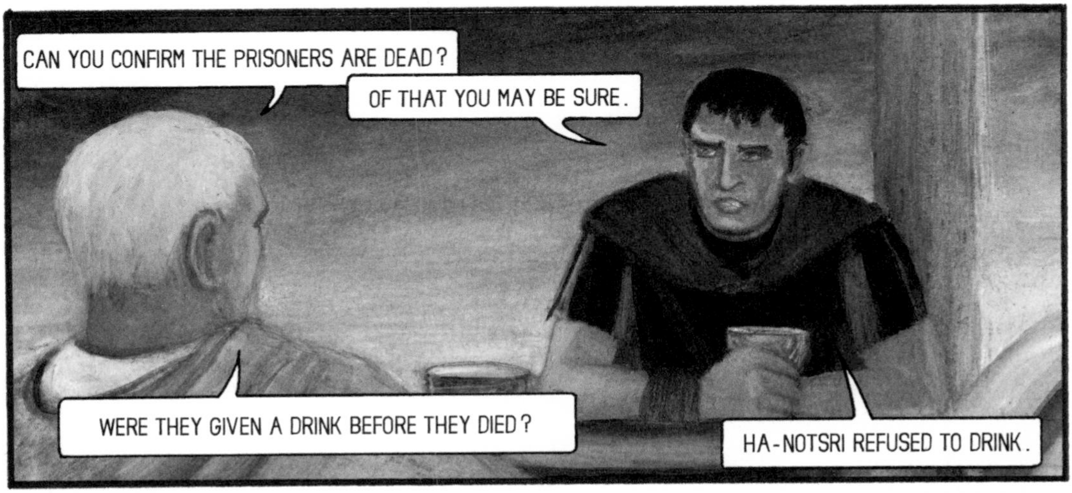
CAN YOU CONFIRM THE PRISONERS ARE DEAD?
OF THAT YOU MAY BE SURE.
WERE THEY GIVEN A DRINK BEFORE THEY DIED?
HA-NOTSRI REFUSED TO DRINK.

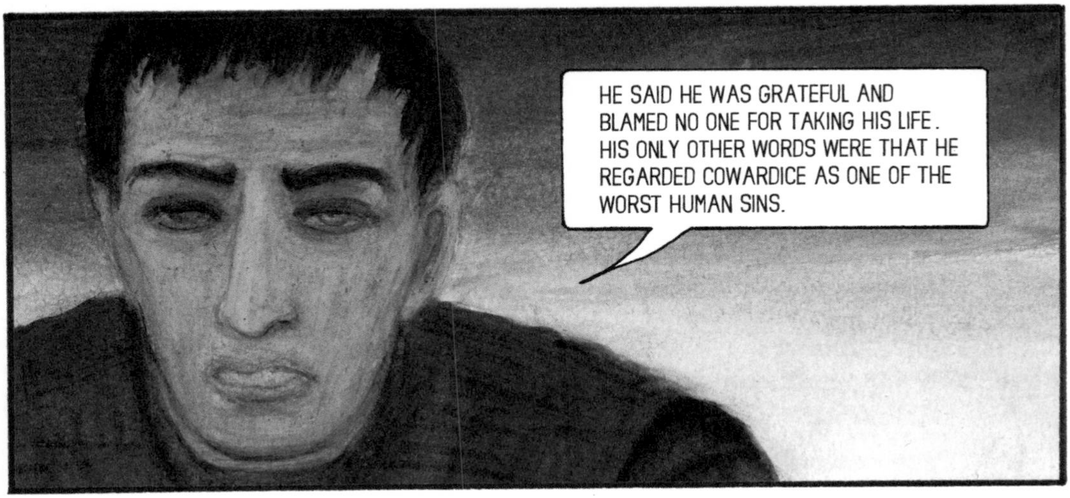
HE SAID HE WAS GRATEFUL AND BLAMED NO ONE FOR TAKING HIS LIFE. HIS ONLY OTHER WORDS WERE THAT HE REGARDED COWARDICE AS ONE OF THE WORST HUMAN SINS.

TO AVOID TROUBLE FROM HA-NOTSRI'S FOLLOWERS, PLEASE REMOVE THE BODIES AND BURY THEM SECRETLY.

VERY WELL.

THIS MAN JUDAS, WAS HE PAID FOR TAKING THE LUNATIC HOME?

HE WILL BE PAID AT CAIAPHAS'S PALACE TODAY.

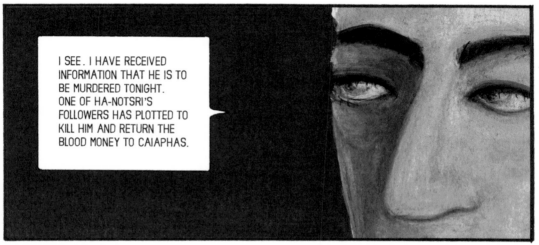

I SEE. I HAVE RECEIVED INFORMATION THAT HE IS TO BE MURDERED TONIGHT. ONE OF HA-NOTSRI'S FOLLOWERS HAS PLOTTED TO KILL HIM AND RETURN THE BLOOD MONEY TO CAIAPHAS.

DO YOU THINK CAIAPHAS WILL BE PLEASED WITH SUCH A GIFT ON PASSOVER?

I THINK IT WILL CREATE A MAJOR SCANDAL.

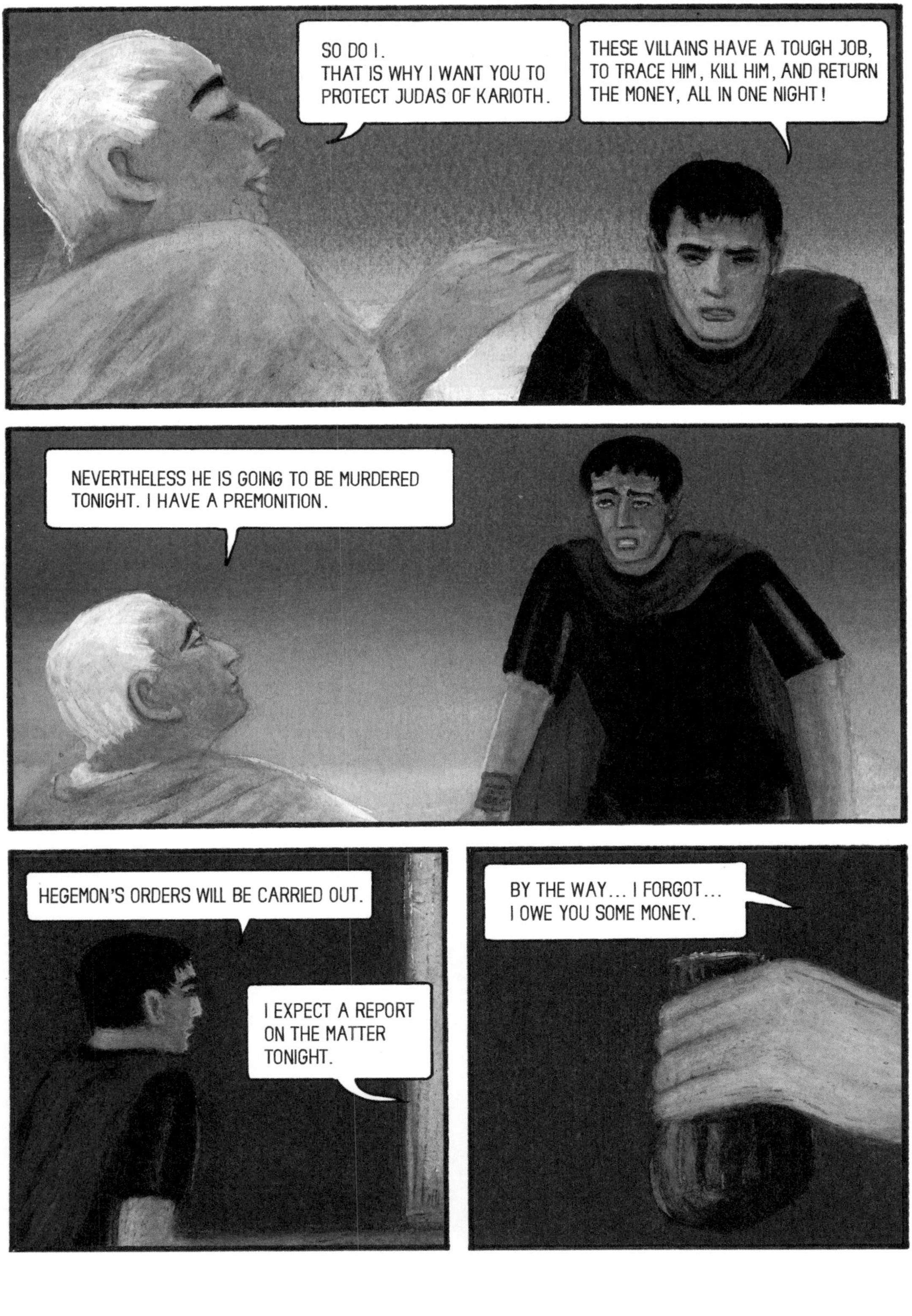
SO DO I.
THAT IS WHY I WANT YOU TO PROTECT JUDAS OF KARIOTH.
THESE VILLAINS HAVE A TOUGH JOB, TO TRACE HIM, KILL HIM, AND RETURN THE MONEY, ALL IN ONE NIGHT!
NEVERTHELESS HE IS GOING TO BE MURDERED TONIGHT. I HAVE A PREMONITION.
HEGEMON'S ORDERS WILL BE CARRIED OUT.
I EXPECT A REPORT ON THE MATTER TONIGHT.
BY THE WAY... I FORGOT... I OWE YOU SOME MONEY.

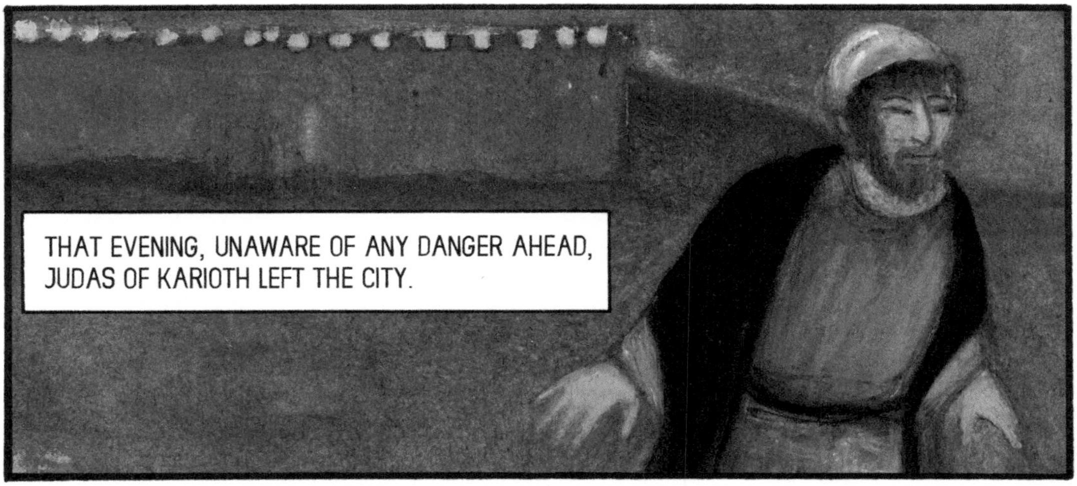
THAT EVENING, UNAWARE OF ANY DANGER AHEAD, JUDAS OF KARIOTH LEFT THE CITY.

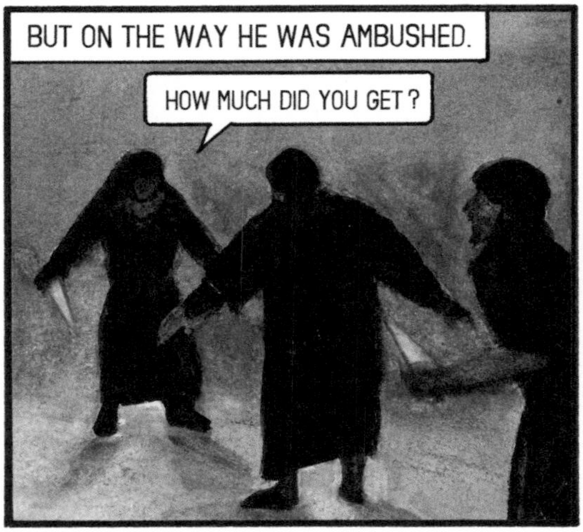
BUT ON THE WAY HE WAS AMBUSHED.
HOW MUCH DID YOU GET?

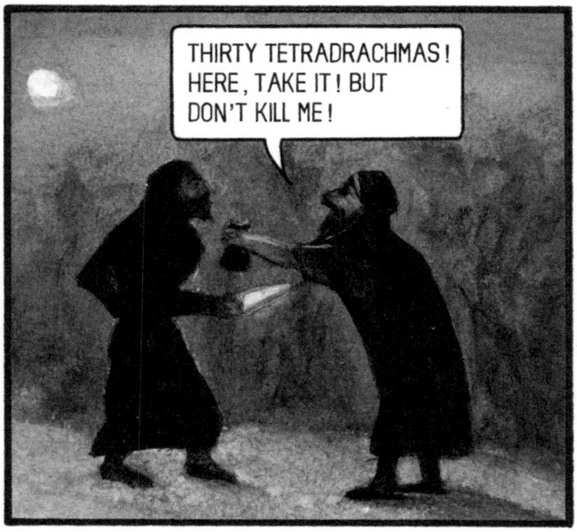
THIRTY TETRADRACHMAS! HERE, TAKE IT! BUT DON'T KILL ME!

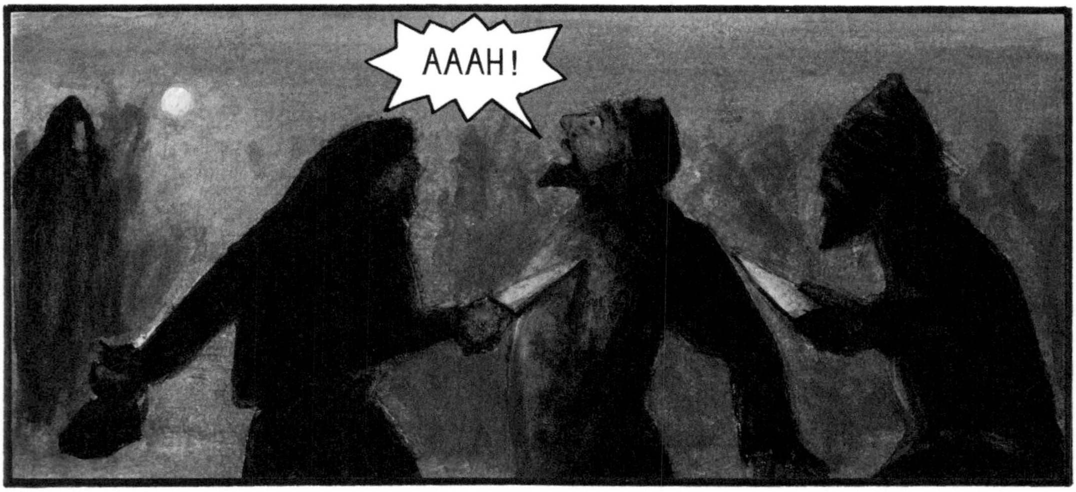
AAAH!

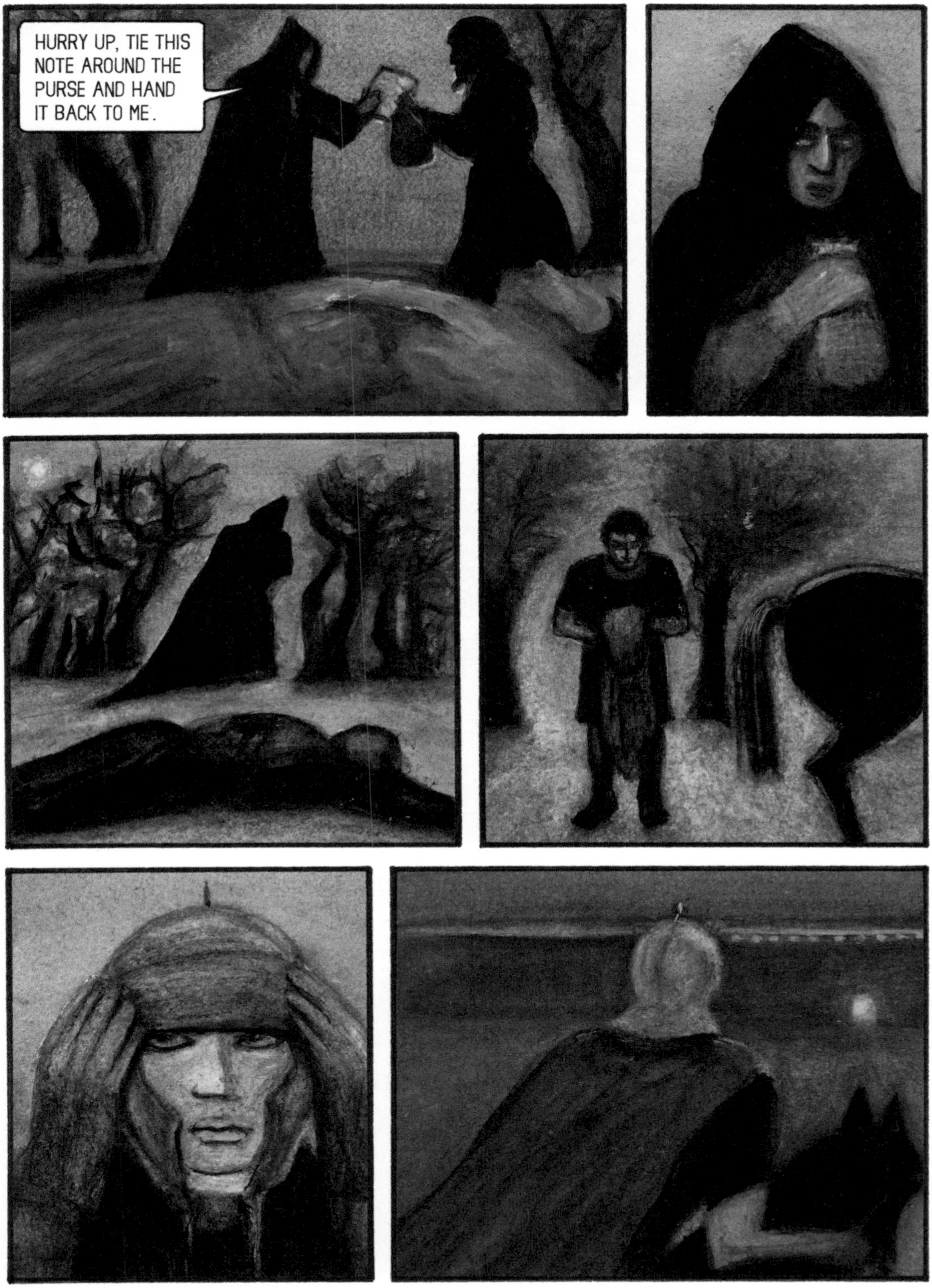
HURRY UP, TIE THIS NOTE AROUND THE PURSE AND HAND IT BACK TO ME.

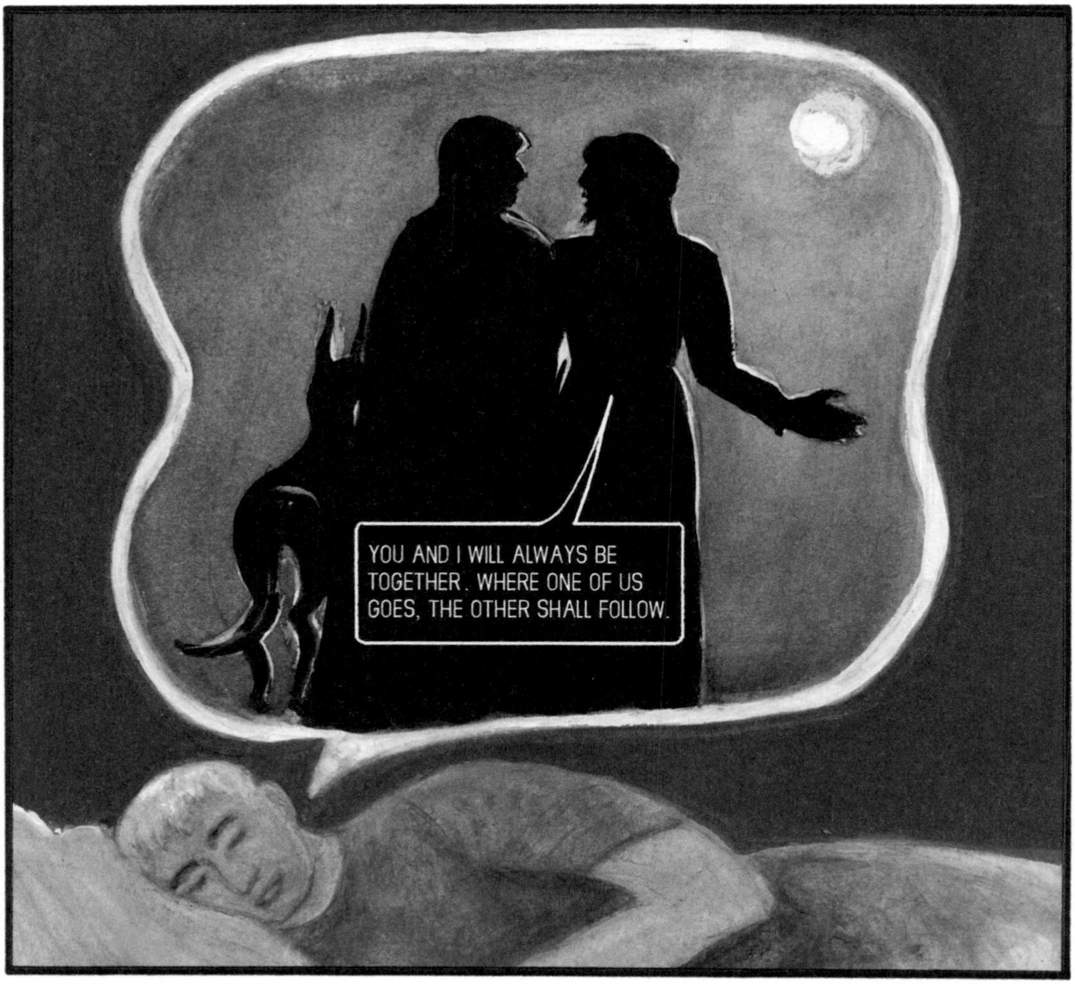
YOU AND I WILL ALWAYS BE TOGETHER. WHERE ONE OF US GOES, THE OTHER SHALL FOLLOW.

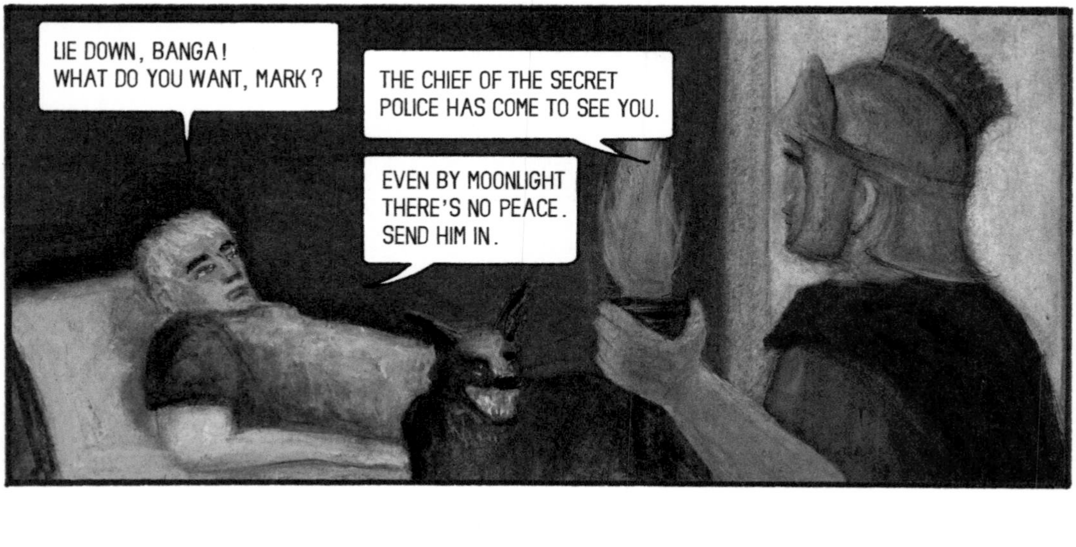
LIE DOWN, BANGA! WHAT DO YOU WANT, MARK?
THE CHIEF OF THE SECRET POLICE HAS COME TO SEE YOU.
EVEN BY MOONLIGHT THERE'S NO PEACE. SEND HIM IN.

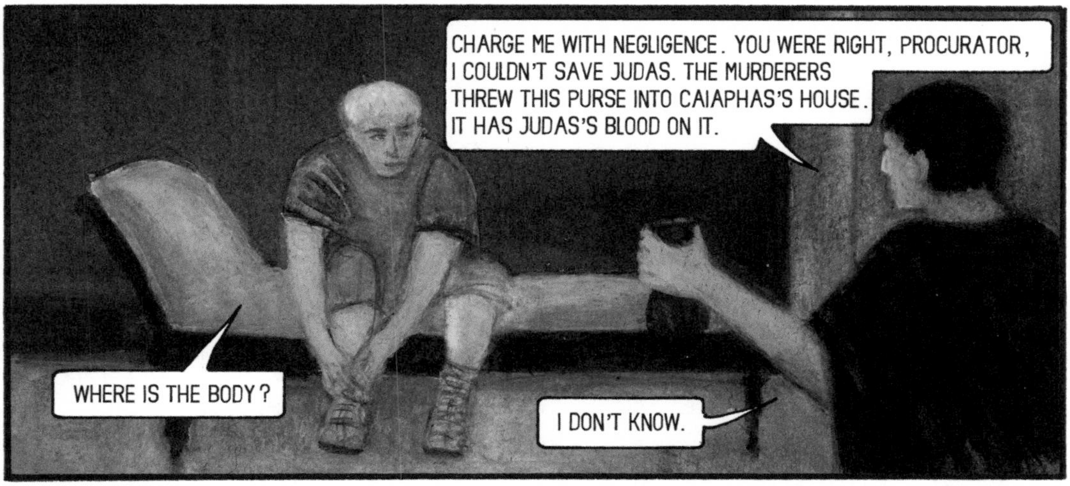
CHARGE ME WITH NEGLIGENCE. YOU WERE RIGHT, PROCURATOR, I COULDN'T SAVE JUDAS. THE MURDERERS THREW THIS PURSE INTO CAIAPHAS'S HOUSE. IT HAS JUDAS'S BLOOD ON IT.
WHERE IS THE BODY?
I DON'T KNOW.

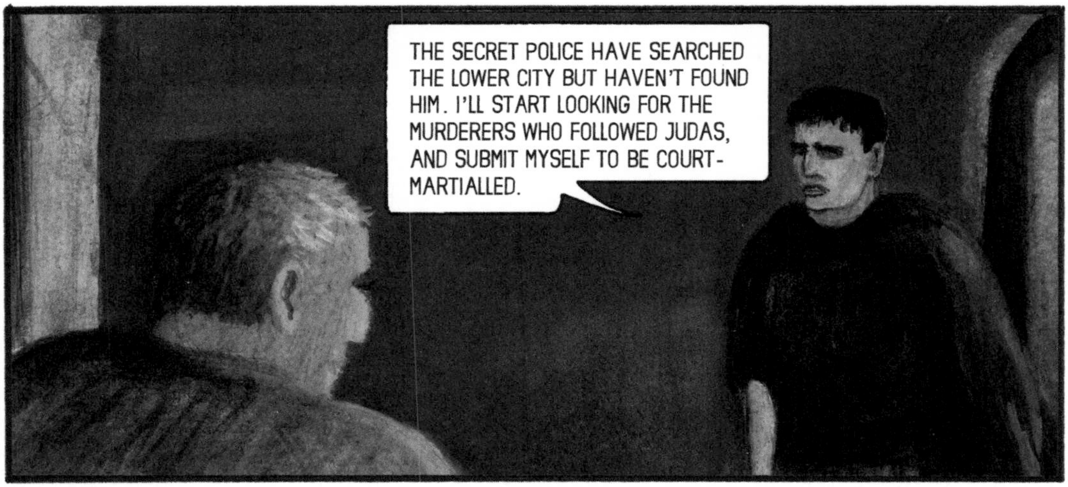
THE SECRET POLICE HAVE SEARCHED THE LOWER CITY BUT HAVEN'T FOUND HIM. I'LL START LOOKING FOR THE MURDERERS WHO FOLLOWED JUDAS, AND SUBMIT MYSELF TO BE COURT-MARTIALLED.

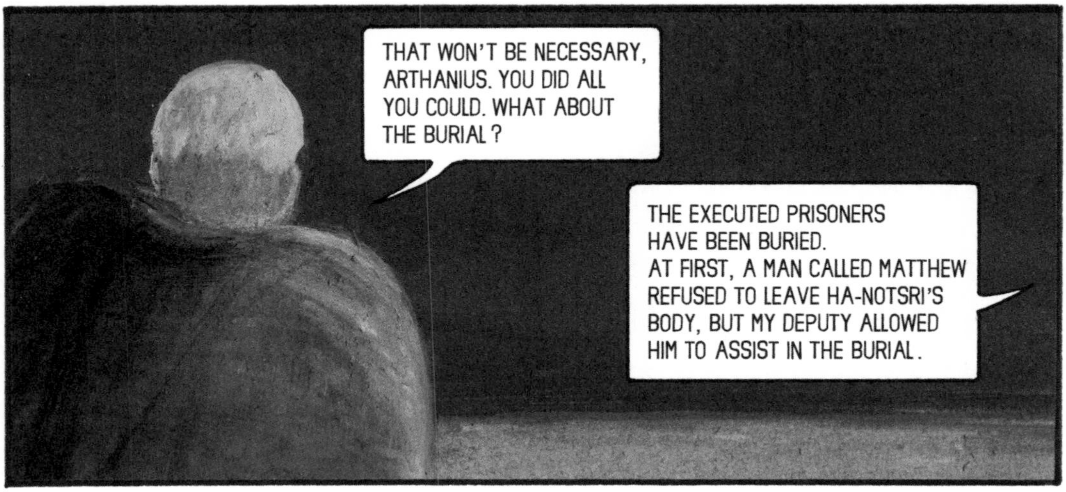
THAT WON'T BE NECESSARY, ARTHANIUS. YOU DID ALL YOU COULD. WHAT ABOUT THE BURIAL?
THE EXECUTED PRISONERS HAVE BEEN BURIED. AT FIRST, A MAN CALLED MATTHEW REFUSED TO LEAVE HA-NOTSRI'S BODY, BUT MY DEPUTY ALLOWED HIM TO ASSIST IN THE BURIAL.

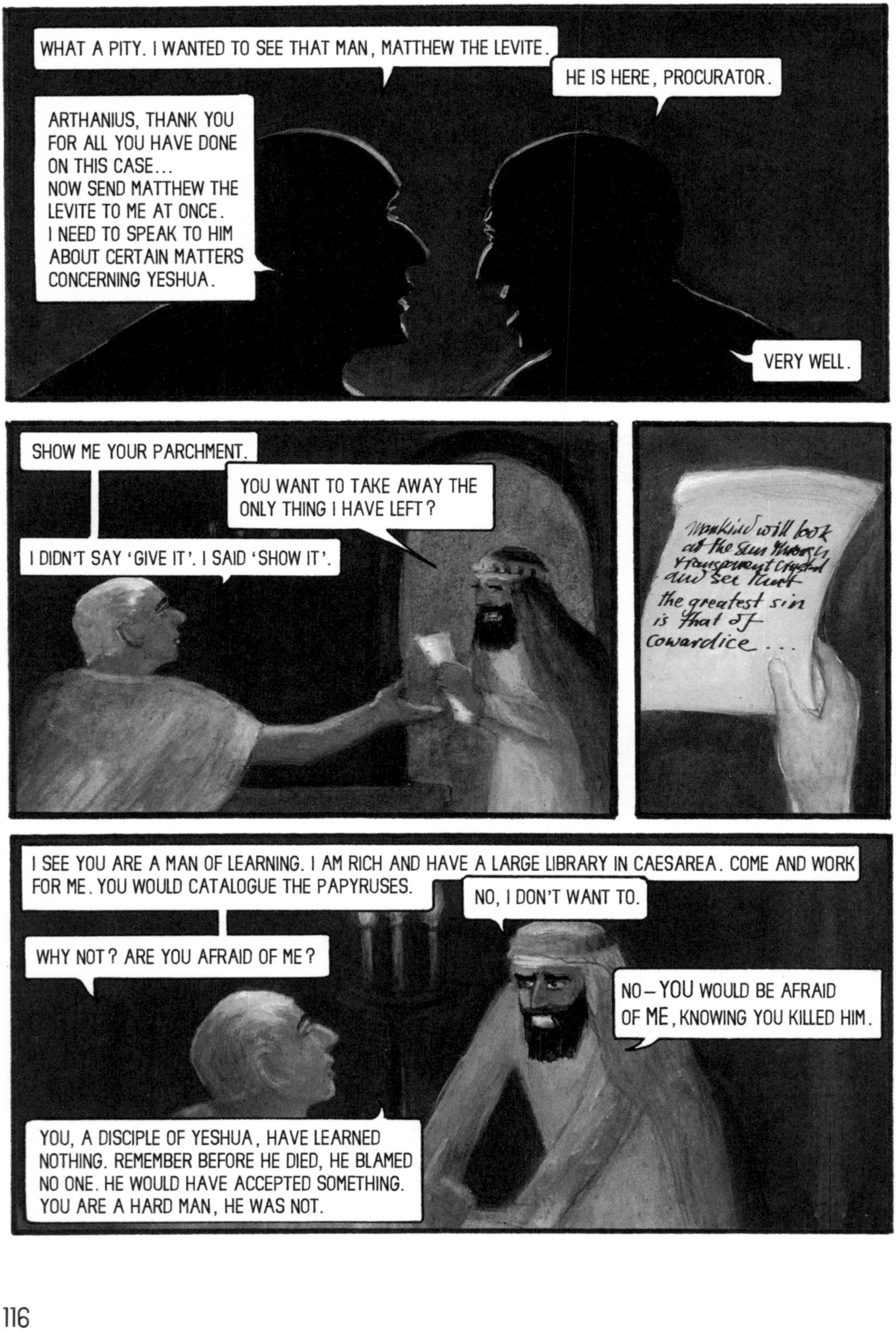
WHAT A PITY. I WANTED TO SEE THAT MAN, MATTHEW THE LEVITE.
HE IS HERE, PROCURATOR.
ARTHANIUS, THANK YOU FOR ALL YOU HAVE DONE ON THIS CASE... NOW SEND MATTHEW THE LEVITE TO ME AT ONCE. I NEED TO SPEAK TO HIM ABOUT CERTAIN MATTERS CONCERNING YESHUA.
VERY WELL.
SHOW ME YOUR PARCHMENT.
YOU WANT TO TAKE AWAY THE ONLY THING I HAVE LEFT?
I DIDN'T SAY 'GIVE IT'. I SAID 'SHOW IT'.
Mankind will look at the sun through transparent crystal and see that the greatest sin is that of cowardice...
I SEE YOU ARE A MAN OF LEARNING. I AM RICH AND HAVE A LARGE LIBRARY IN CAESAREA. COME AND WORK FOR ME. YOU WOULD CATALOGUE THE PAPYRUSES.
NO, I DON'T WANT TO.
WHY NOT? ARE YOU AFRAID OF ME?
NO – YOU WOULD BE AFRAID OF ME, KNOWING YOU KILLED HIM.
YOU, A DISCIPLE OF YESHUA, HAVE LEARNED NOTHING. REMEMBER BEFORE HE DIED, HE BLAMED NO ONE. HE WOULD HAVE ACCEPTED SOMETHING. YOU ARE A HARD MAN, HE WAS NOT.

YOU WANT TO KILL ME, I SUPPOSE?

NO, NOT YOU, BUT I SHALL KILL JUDAS OF KARIOTH, EVEN IF IT TAKES ME THE REST OF MY LIFE.

DON'T TROUBLE YOURSELF. YOU WON'T SUCCEED. JUDAS WAS MURDERED TONIGHT.

WHO DID IT?

I DID IT. DON'T BE JEALOUS, YOU WEREN'T THE ONLY ONE WHO ADMIRED HIM. NOW WILL YOU ACCEPT SOMETHING?

ORDER THEM TO GIVE ME A CLEAN PIECE OF PARCHMENT.

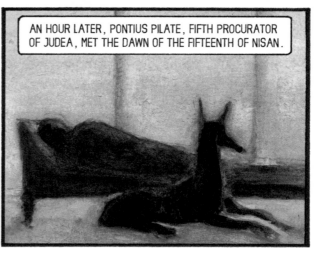

AN HOUR LATER, PONTIUS PILATE, FIFTH PROCURATOR OF JUDEA, MET THE DAWN OF THE FIFTEENTH OF NISAN.

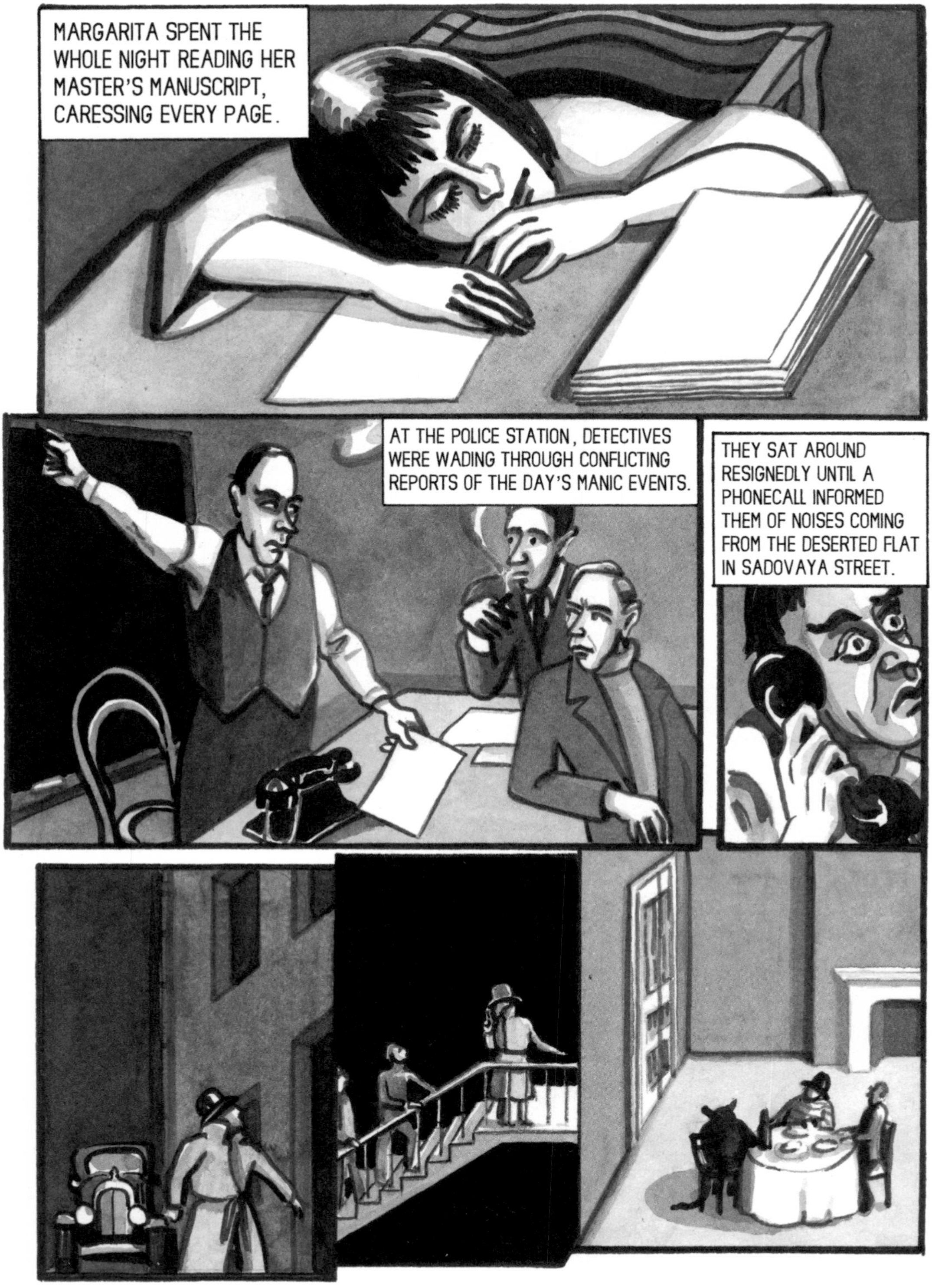
MARGARITA SPENT THE WHOLE NIGHT READING HER MASTER'S MANUSCRIPT, CARESSING EVERY PAGE.
AT THE POLICE STATION, DETECTIVES WERE WADING THROUGH CONFLICTING REPORTS OF THE DAY'S MANIC EVENTS.
THEY SAT AROUND RESIGNEDLY UNTIL A PHONECALL INFORMED THEM OF NOISES COMING FROM THE DESERTED FLAT IN SADOVAYA STREET.

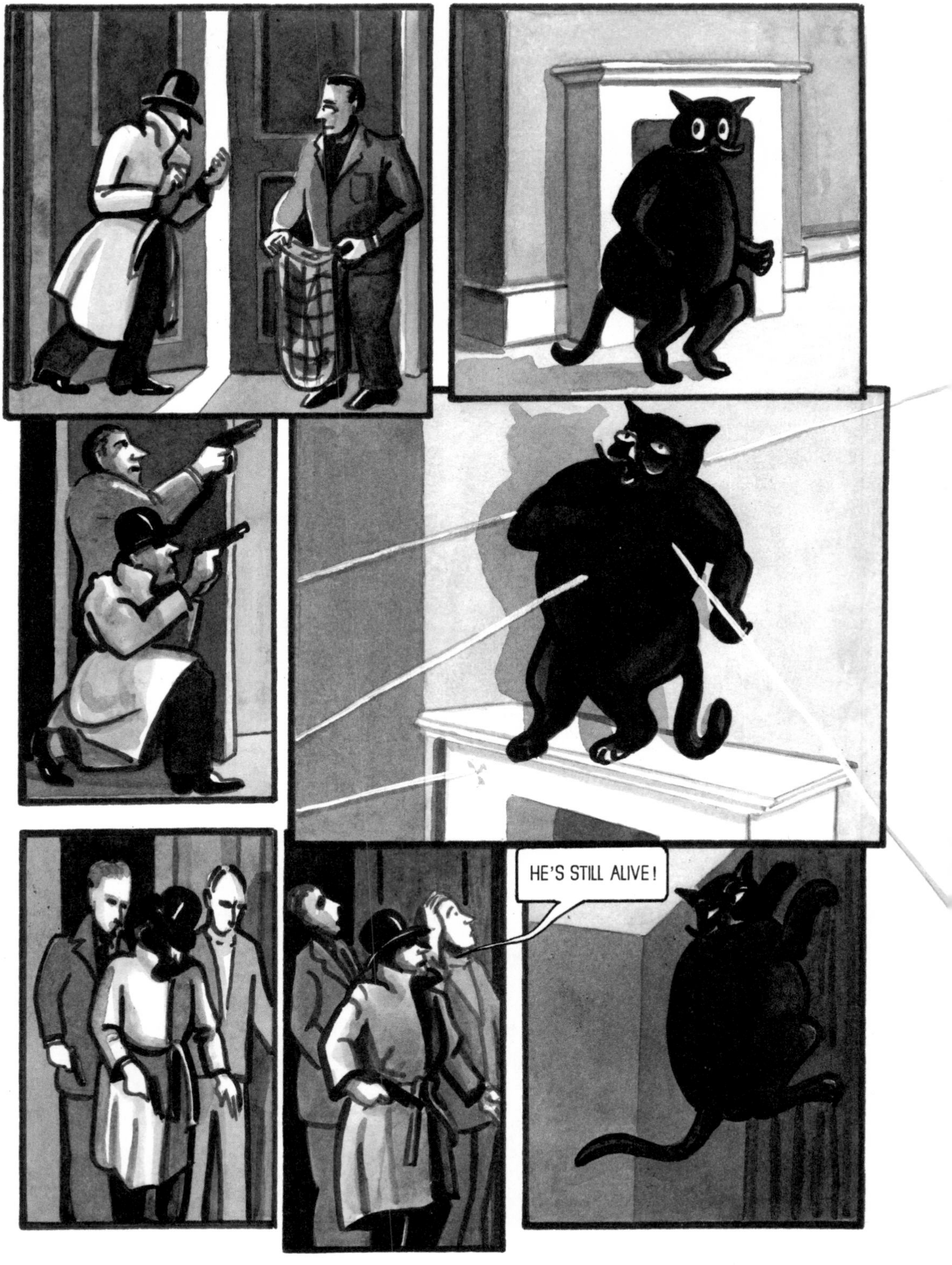
HE'S STILL ALIVE!

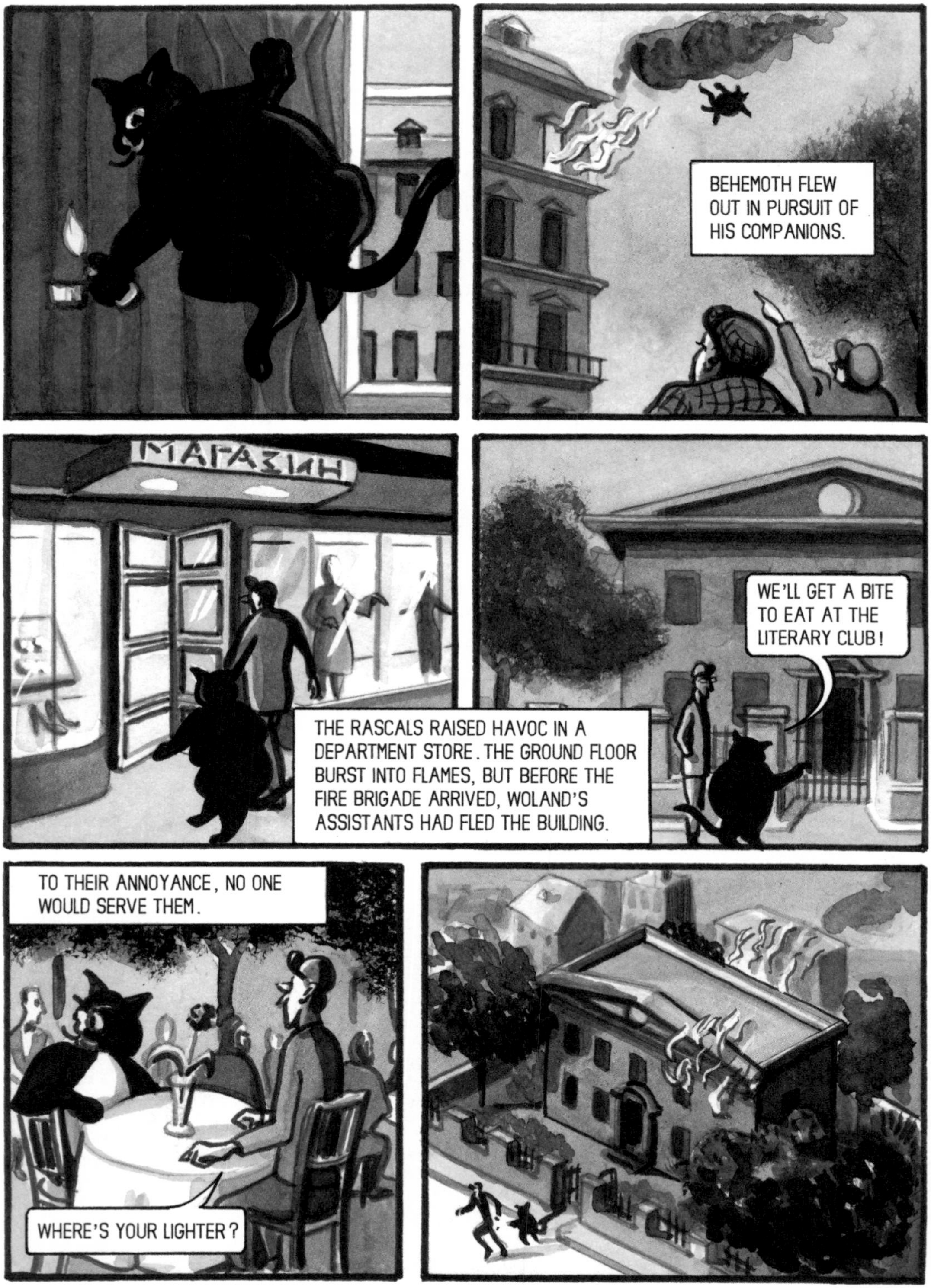
BEHEMOTH FLEW OUT IN PURSUIT OF HIS COMPANIONS.
МАГАЗИН
THE RASCALS RAISED HAVOC IN A DEPARTMENT STORE. THE GROUND FLOOR BURST INTO FLAMES, BUT BEFORE THE FIRE BRIGADE ARRIVED, WOLAND'S ASSISTANTS HAD FLED THE BUILDING.
WE'LL GET A BITE TO EAT AT THE LITERARY CLUB!
TO THEIR ANNOYANCE, NO ONE WOULD SERVE THEM.
WHERE'S YOUR LIGHTER?

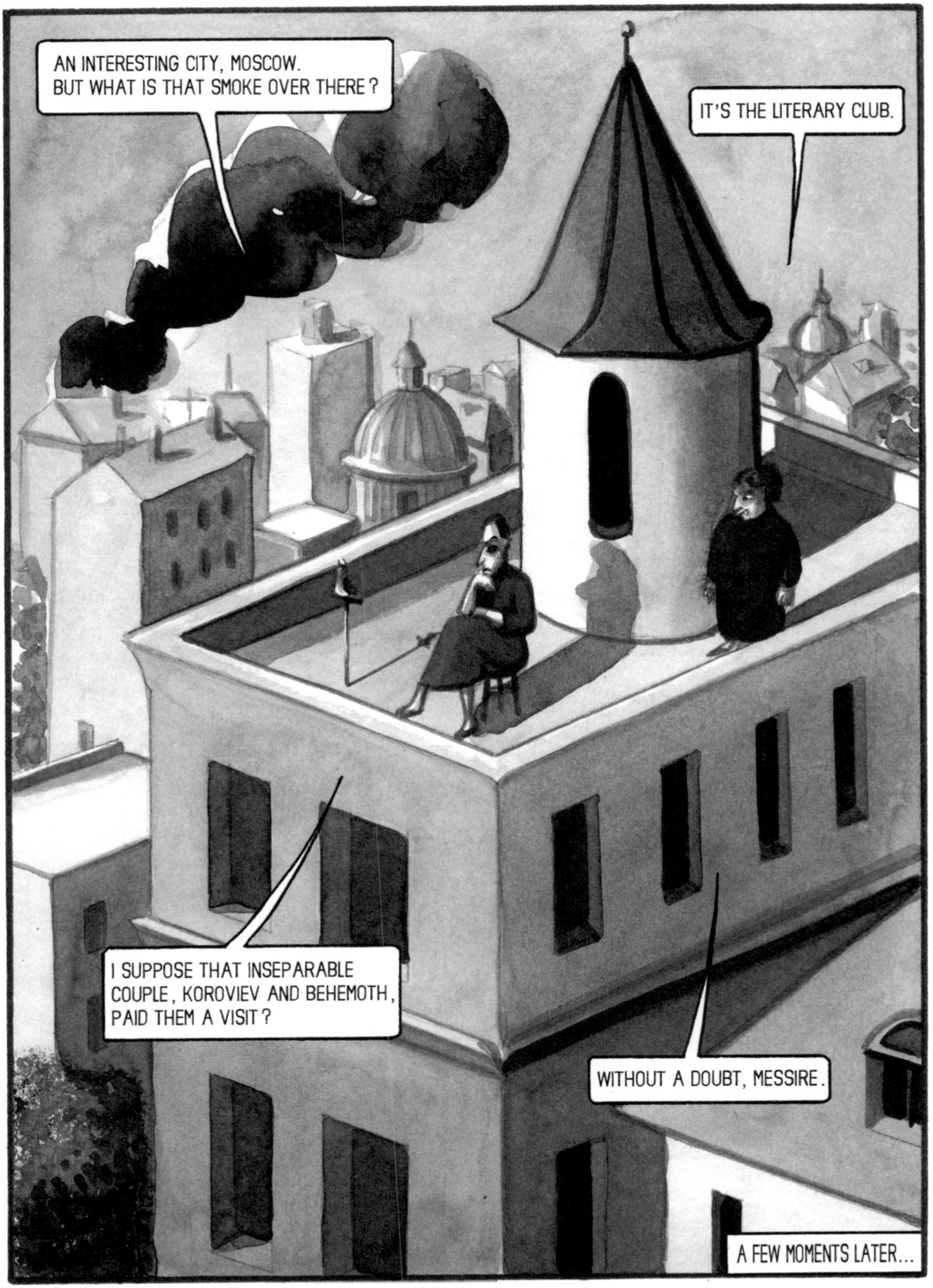
AN INTERESTING CITY, MOSCOW.
BUT WHAT IS THAT SMOKE OVER THERE?
IT'S THE LITERARY CLUB.
I SUPPOSE THAT INSEPARABLE COUPLE, KOROVIEV AND BEHEMOTH, PAID THEM A VISIT?
WITHOUT A DOUBT, MESSIRE.
A FEW MOMENTS LATER...

HE HAS SENT ME.

WHAT MESSAGE DID HE GIVE YOU, SLAVE?

HE HAS READ THE MASTER'S NOVEL AND ASKS YOU TO TAKE HIM WITH YOU, AND REWARD HIM BY GRANTING HIM PEACE.

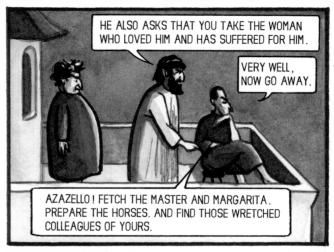

HE ALSO ASKS THAT YOU TAKE THE WOMAN WHO LOVED HIM AND HAS SUFFERED FOR HIM.

VERY WELL, NOW GO AWAY.

AZAZELLO! FETCH THE MASTER AND MARGARITA. PREPARE THE HORSES. AND FIND THOSE WRETCHED COLLEAGUES OF YOURS.

WHO WAS THAT, MESSIRE?

MATTHEW THE LEVITE.

A STORM IS GATHERING; IT IS TIME FOR US TO GO!

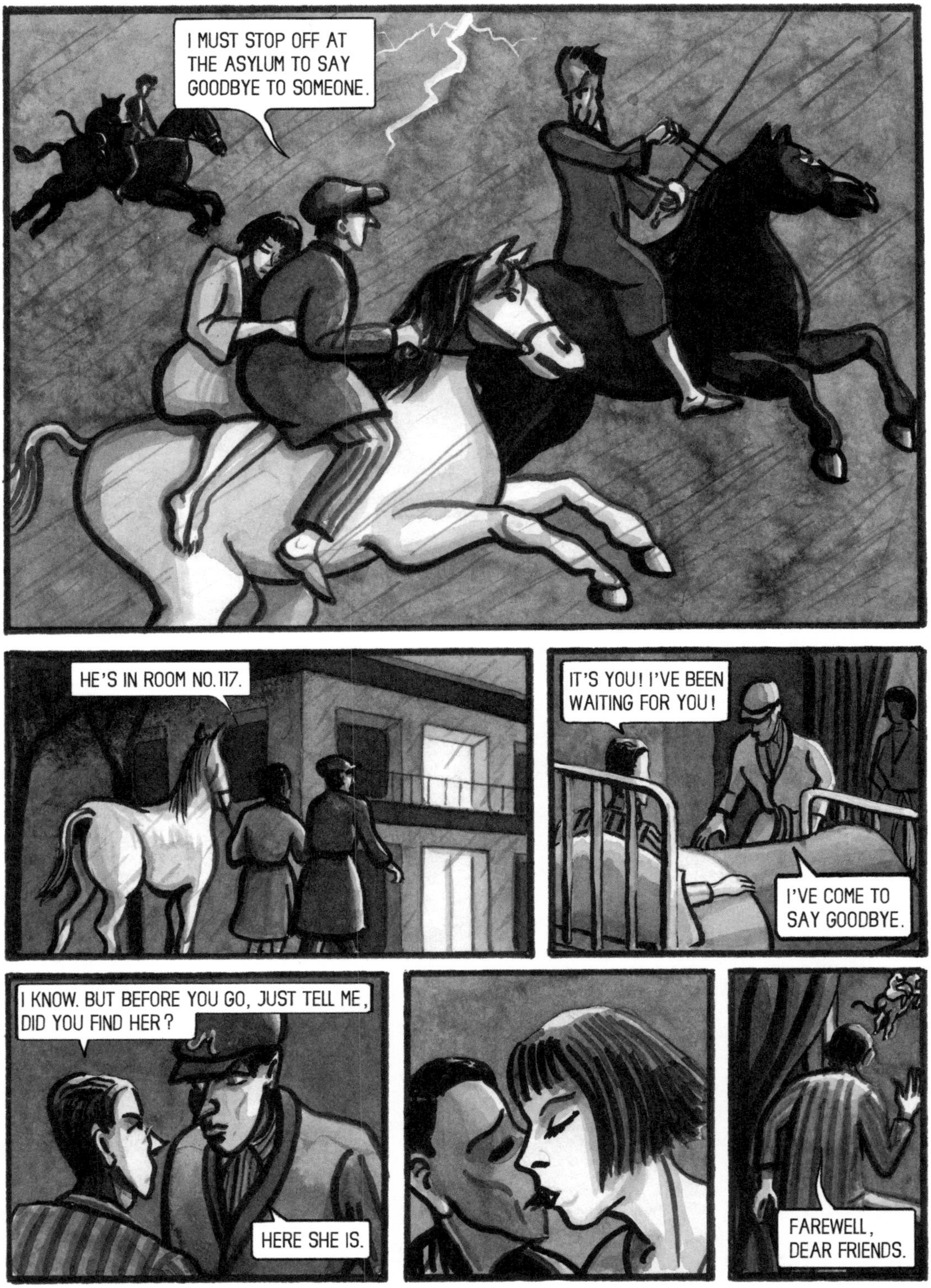
I MUST STOP OFF AT THE ASYLUM TO SAY GOODBYE TO SOMEONE.
HE'S IN ROOM NO.117.
IT'S YOU! I'VE BEEN WAITING FOR YOU!
I'VE COME TO SAY GOODBYE.
I KNOW. BUT BEFORE YOU GO, JUST TELL ME, DID YOU FIND HER?
HERE SHE IS.
FAREWELL, DEAR FRIENDS.

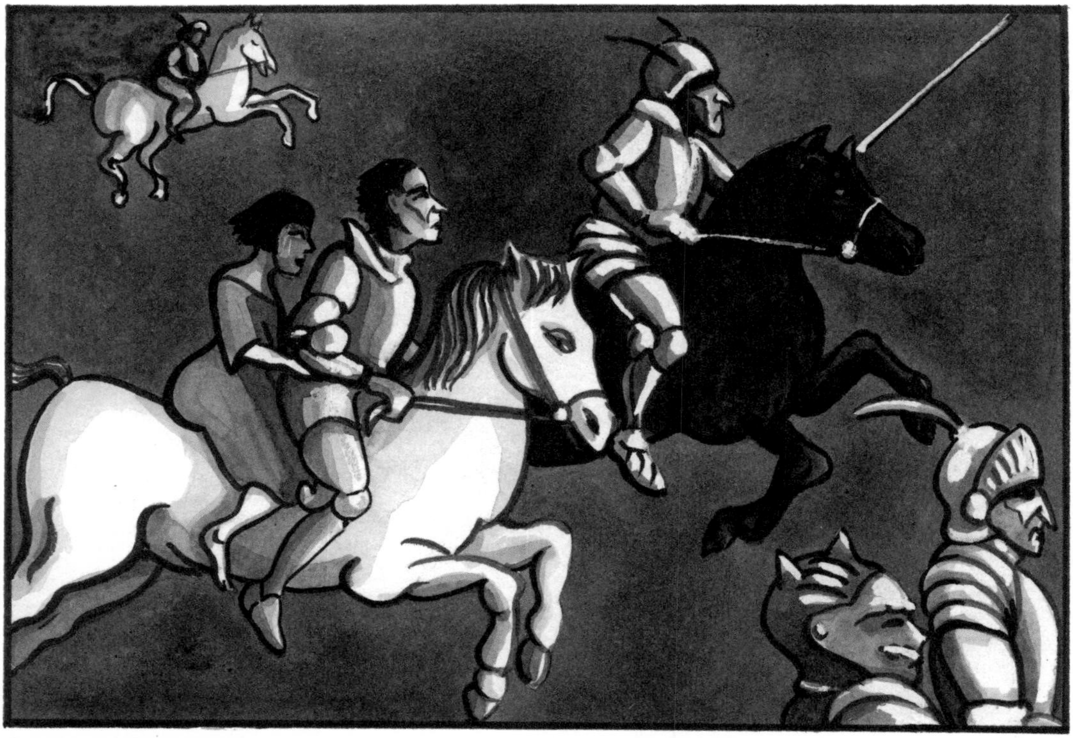

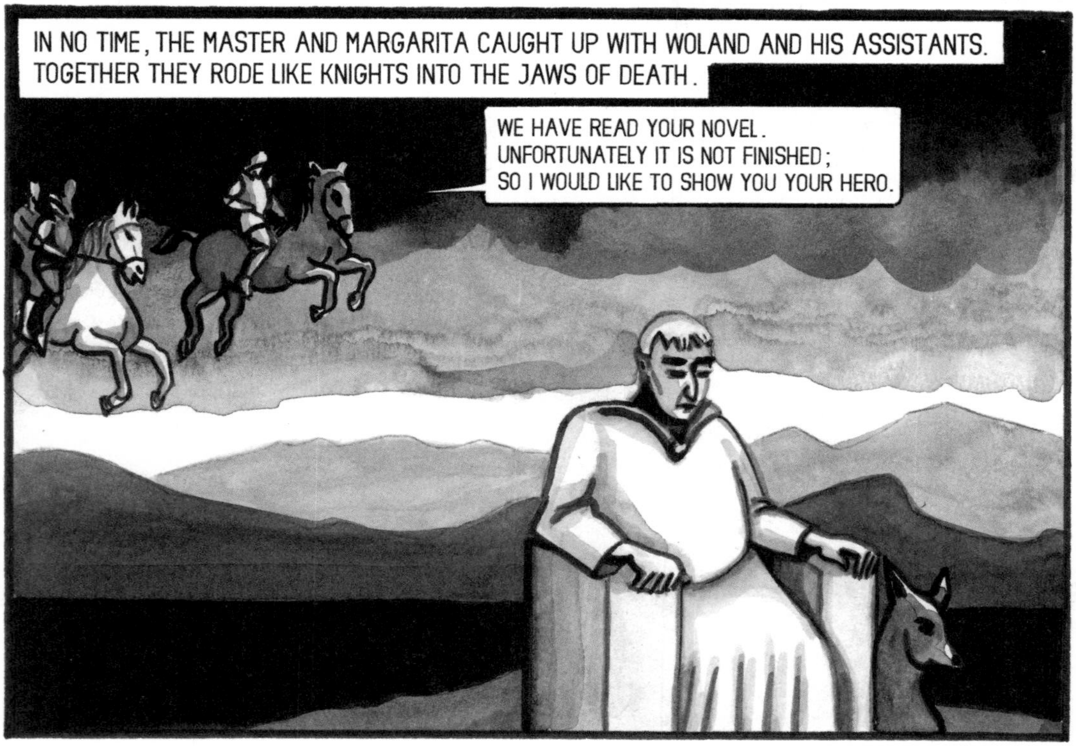
IN NO TIME, THE MASTER AND MARGARITA CAUGHT UP WITH WOLAND AND HIS ASSISTANTS. TOGETHER THEY RODE LIKE KNIGHTS INTO THE JAWS OF DEATH.
WE HAVE READ YOUR NOVEL. UNFORTUNATELY IT IS NOT FINISHED; SO I WOULD LIKE TO SHOW YOU YOUR HERO.

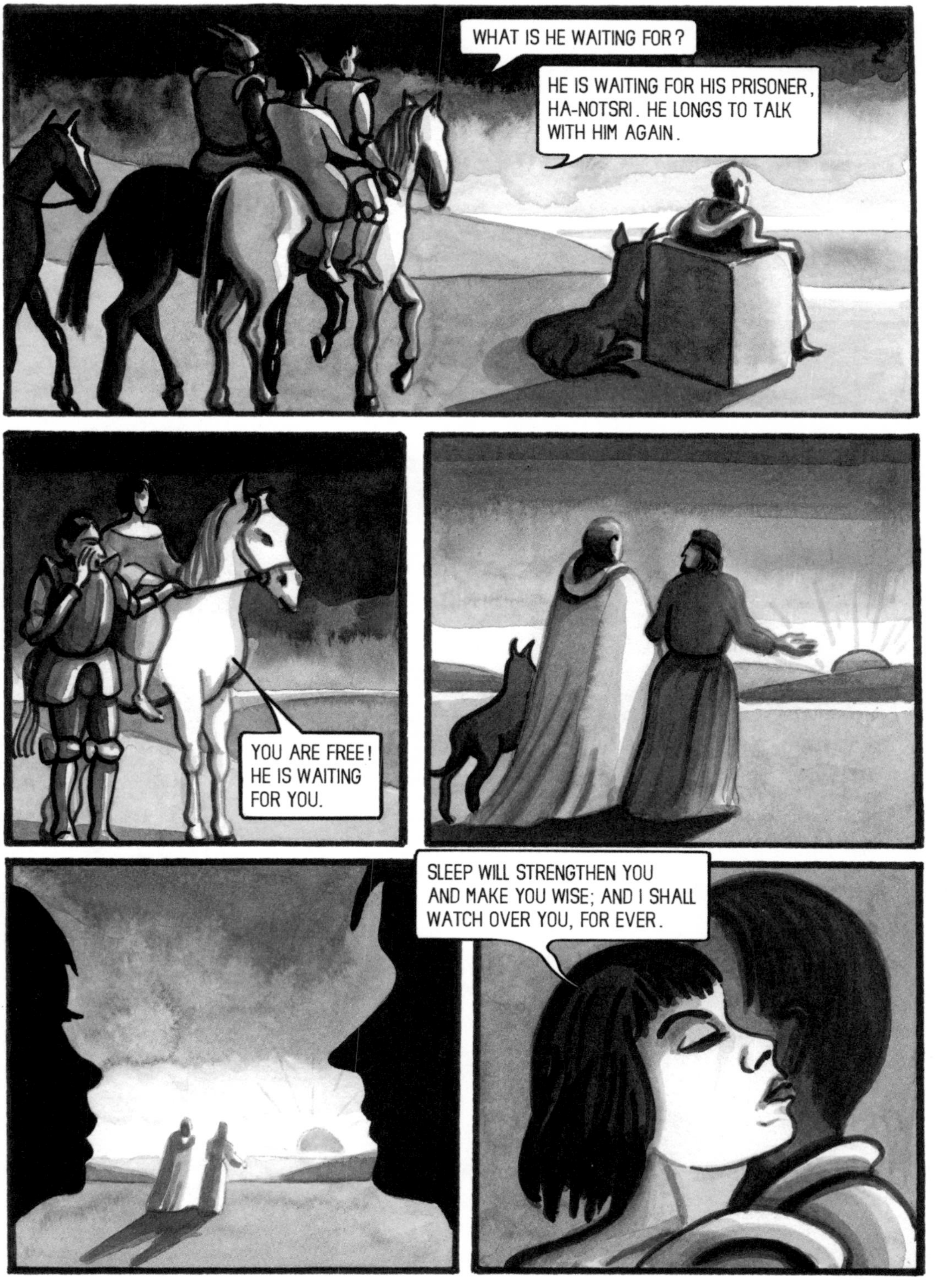
WHAT IS HE WAITING FOR?
HE IS WAITING FOR HIS PRISONER, HA-NOTSRI. HE LONGS TO TALK WITH HIM AGAIN.
YOU ARE FREE! HE IS WAITING FOR YOU.
SLEEP WILL STRENGTHEN YOU AND MAKE YOU WISE; AND I SHALL WATCH OVER YOU, FOR EVER.

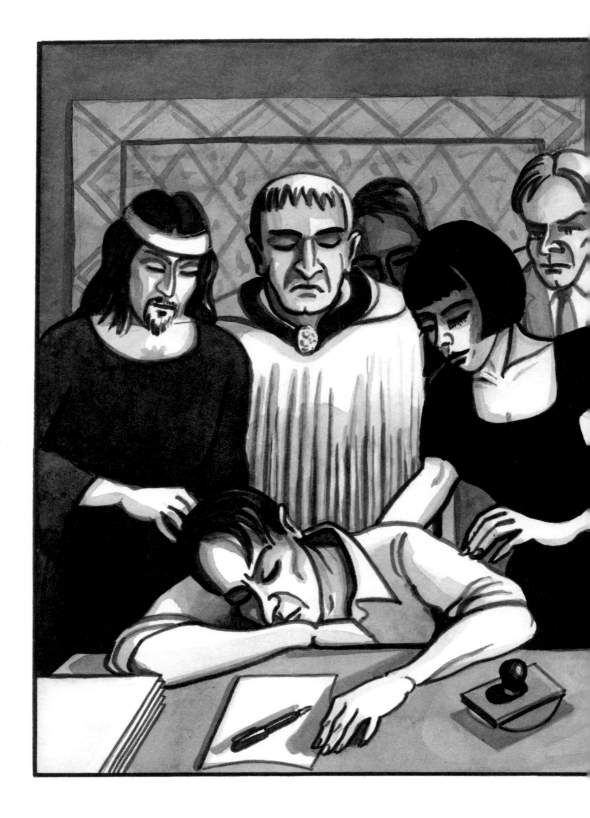

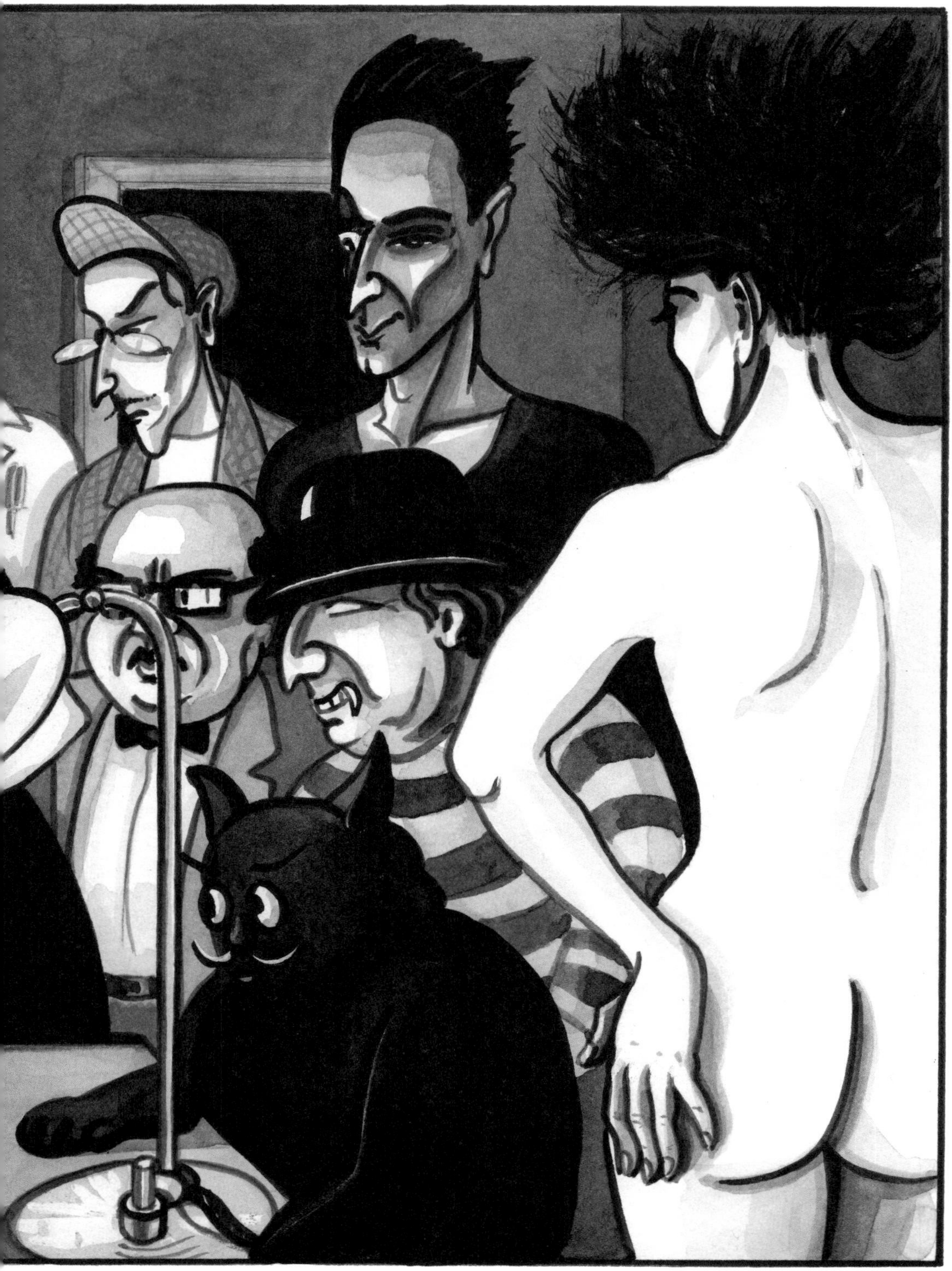

AN HOUR BEFORE THE RIDERS REACHED
THEIR DESTINATION, THE NURSE AT THE
ASYLUM ENTERED BEZDOMNY'S ROOM.
SHE WHISPERED HESITANTLY, 'YOUR
NEIGHBOUR FROM ROOM 118 HAS JUST
DIED.' THE POET WAS NOT AT ALL
SURPRISED. 'I TELL YOU, NURSE, THAT
ANOTHER PERSON HAS JUST DIED IN
MOSCOW. I EVEN KNOW WHO.' HE SMILED
MYSTERIOUSLY. 'IT'S A WOMAN!'